MAGGIE'S HOME

LIFE ON PENNINGTON CREEK

BOOK ONE

GLENDA CLEMENS

Edited by
JAN FORMISANO
Edited by
DAVID CLEMENS

Text copyright © 2024 by Glenda Clemens
Narration copyright © 2024 by David Clemens
Cover art copyright © 2024 by Glenda Clemens
Cover photo, Pennington Creek, Tishomingo, Oklahoma
copyright © 2024 by Glenda Clemens
Family photo © 2024 by the Rains family, including Glenda Clemens
All Rights Reserved
eBook ISBN: 9781958356250
Paperback Book ISBN: 9781958365243
Audiobook ISBN: 9781958365267

 Created with Vellum

This book is dedicated to:

My mother, **Beverly Jean Casey Rains.**
She always loved being in nature,
but especially, she
loved Pennington Creek
and the nearby Blue River.

I also dedicate this book to:
My great-grandmother,
Lucretia Adeline Pennington Rains
My great-grandmother Pennington,
was my inspiration to write about
Pennington Creek,
The Trail of Tears,
and the Chickasaw Nation.

SPECIAL THANKS

SPECIAL THANKS TO MY FRIENDS:

Nelda and **Shirley** were my friends in Tecumseh, Oklahoma, where we attended high school together. Their kindness when I was often afraid and often not a part of the social structures at the time has helped me become who I am.

They were always kind, loving, and helpful to me, even though it would be years before I understood why many shunned them. They were beautiful women of the Native American Tribes in and around Tecumseh, Oklahoma. These two young women were descendants of those who traveled *The Trail of Tears*.

APPRECIATION

Without Beta Readers and Editors,
no book would ever make it to publication.
I appreciate every one of you.
David Clemens, Editor
Jan Formisano, Editor
D. T. Rains, Beta Reader
Cindy Brumley, Beta Reader
John Brumley, Beta Reader
Heather Hall, Beta Reader

AUTHOR'S FORWARD

Agnes Repplier

This story is about Maggie Pennington, her family, and the friends they made in 1898 on Pennington Creek near the town of Tishomingo, Indian Territory. Maggie, her family, and her friends are fictional characters.

Most of the story takes place near Tishomingo, Indian Territory—now part of the State of Oklahoma—in mid-1898. Most of the story is fiction, but some of it is true. The foundational events of the story included *The Trail of Tears* and the formation of *Indian Territory* and *Oklahoma Territory*, which later joined with *No Man's Land* and became the state of Oklahoma.

For example, Pennington Creek is a real place and one of my favorites. The story of how Pennington Creek got its name is real—at least, I think it is. However, remember that this is a work of fiction.

There are no log cabin homes in the areas on the map along the banks of Pennington Creek that I could find, but I wished for them to be there, and there they remain in the story and my mind. Of course, there might have been such homes, but no historical evidence existed where I wanted them to be. In the story, Maggie, Aurora, Silas, and Clay loved living in those homes and raised their children with love and honor on the banks of Pennington Creek.

While the characters in this tale are figments of my imagination, the town they inhabit is not. Some of the events I've woven into the narrative may have occurred, but I can't claim to know the exact details as a storyteller. This is, after all, a work of fiction.

I cannot, in all honesty, say the historical events are accurate. Though it may not always be precisely correct, I've tried to be truthful as much as possible. I've researched every detail I could think of, drawing from the rich annals of Oklahoma history. While future discoveries may shed new light on this era, I've strived to present a faithful and informative depiction of the past. This dedication ensures that readers, particularly history enthusiasts, will find this story enlightening and engaging and can trust the narrative.

One inevitable reality is that life in the late 1800s and early 1900s was rugged and brutal. The human endeavors and their astounding accomplishments, though, are amazing. The making of the town of Tishomingo seems like a miracle. After all, the Chickasaw people trod the horrid Trail of Tears to come to this part of the Indian Nation and fill it with like-minded people. Although, as usual in human behavior, sometimes there were, sadly, not like-minded people. The joining of different people with different ideas, cultures, and ways of living all happened despite their clashes and the rugged existence in which they lived.

To further enrich your understanding of this historical period, I've included a comprehensive list of the resources I used to tell this story in the *Author's Notes* at the end of the book. These resources delve into the rich history of Indian Territory and Oklahoma and will provide hours of enjoyable reading, especially for history buffs.

And now for the story.

MAGGIE'S HOME

*"The power of
finding beauty in the
humblest things make a home
happy and life lovely."*
Louisa May Alcott

CHAPTER ONE

Aristotle

IT WAS the last night Maggie Pennington would have to sleep in the buckboard, Conestoga-style wagon, and the relief of the journey's end couldn't come too soon. Relief would be an understatement in her mind. On long, weary days, she was riding on a wooden bench with nothing to comfort her weary and very pregnant body but a folded blanket.

The trip from Columbia, South Carolina, to Tishomingo, Indian Territory, had been tedious and, at times, challenging. What started out as an adventure moving to a new place had become dreary work, day in and day out. Arriving at their destination couldn't come soon enough for Maggie. She was ready for a home, and the comforts she hoped would be available.

She stood up and said, "Let's get tucked into our beds and close our eyes. The better we sleep, the happier we'll be in the morning."

Her son Ben asked, "Momma, will we be at our new home tomorrow?"

She smiled. "Yes, sweetie."

"Good. I'm tired of the wagon."

Maggie brushed her four-year-old son's hair from his forehead and sighed. "Me too, Ben."

She took the hands of her twins, Bea and Ben, and walked from the campfire for their last night to the covered wagon. Tonight would be the last night she would sleep on the wooden slat beds in the wagon and cook over an open fire on the ground—she hoped.

Bea said, "We'll have a great big house, won't we, Momma."

"Oh, my goodness, darling, I hope so. Regardless, I'm eager to be in our home, no matter how big or small it is. Now, it's time for the two of you to go to sleep. Papa, Noah, and I will join you soon."

She kissed their cheeks and wished them sweet dreams. She watched as they both curled up, back-to-back as usual, and quickly went to sleep. It always amazed her how quickly the twins would settle and go to sleep. She thought *it was being in the open air all day and all night for many weeks. Indeed, the newness of travel was beginning to wear on them. I am weary and ready for my home.*

Once the twins were settled and sleeping, she climbed out of the wagon, went to the fireside, and sat beside her husband, watching the small fire's flames lick at the wood and occasionally send up a golden spark. She mused about the log cabin home she would see tomorrow, just west of Tishomingo. Silas's Uncle Jacob had built it for them but died before they'd decided whether or not to move their family to the wilds of Indian Territory.

She'd yearned for a home of her own for years, and now she would have one. She remembered when she and Silas had first talked about the move.

She had said, "I remember my mother and father standing side-by-side building their home, plowing and planting their land. I don't remember even once hearing them fuss or fret about it. They got busy building the life they wanted. It was hard work, but they made it. I know it will be hard to pack up and move to Indian Territory. But, Si, I've always worked hard."

"Yes, you have, even when you didn't have to."

"That's just it, Si. Working to build a life for ourselves and our children is exactly what I want to do. A little hard work—even a lot of hard work—won't bother me. I know how to do many things I don't bother doing because others have been doing it for me. I'm ready to spread my wings, have an adventure, have a home, and build a life we can both be proud of."

"I know you can do anything you set your mind to, and it's part of why I love you, darlin'."

"Thanks, Si. I believe we can do this. Lest you forget, you and I met when I took a load of watermelons to market—by myself, in a rickety wooden wheelbarrow. I'm a strong woman, and it would be your mistake to think otherwise."

He nodded. "When I saw your auburn hair glistening in the sun, and you were lifting those big watermelons as if they were small biscuits, I was smitten. I'd never seen a woman do what I considered man's work."

She humphed, rolled her eyes, and shook her head. "Mr. Pennington, you try pushing and squeezing something as big as a watermelon out of your body. Then, after hours of working to bring a baby to life and, moments later, feeding that newborn baby—that sort of work is called labor. It is done only by a strong woman. It's a woman's work. No man can ever match the task."

Now, thinking of what they were doing and remembering how eager she'd been, she was determined to make a go of her life even though tonight she was weary. She and her family had lived with Silas's parents for several years. It was a lovely home filled with antiques, servants at her beck and call, and gardens that she missed daily. But it wasn't her home.

She knew everything would be hers to deal with once they arrived in Tishomingo. Everything would be on her shoulders—cleaning, cooking, sewing, dusting, mopping, and slopping. She touched her burgeoning belly and sighed. In a few months, she would be delivering her fourth baby. She wasn't worried about all of this, exactly. But she was anxious about being able to do what needed to be done as quickly as possible and birth a baby.

She'd been eager to make this journey so she, Silas, and their children could have their own home and make their way in the world. Now, she was feeling a little anxious and a lot weary. The monotony of traveling in a covered wagon with no servants to help, cooking over open fires, and digging latrines every evening was wearing thin, as was the adventure of the journey. She was ready to be in a real house but wasn't sure about living in a log cabin.

Maggie was startled when her husband took her hand. He said, "You seemed miles away, darlin'."

She nodded and smiled. "I suppose I was."

Her oldest son, Noah, asked, "How can you be miles away and sitting here with all of us, Momma?"

She chuckled. "I wasn't really miles away, but my mind went wandering a bit."

He nodded and said, "I feel like I'm just playing in the woods, Momma."

"Really?"

"Yep. Every night when we go to sleep in the wagon, I have this strange feeling that when I wake, we'll be back in Columbia at Granny and Pops's house."

Silas said, "Well, son, we aren't close enough to South Carolina to wake up there in the morning. Besides, tomorrow morning, we'll wake up and, in short order, be at Tishomingo."

"I know, Papa. It's just that my body and mind haven't gotten the message we aren't in South Carolina anymore."

Maggie laughed. "I think that's the perfect way to put it, Noah."

Noah said, "At first, when Mr. Marlow was helping us go from Granny and Pops's house to the Mississippi River, it was like an adventure."

"It was son," Silas said. "How does it feel now that we are nearing Tishomingo?"

"Well, Papa, it feels like every day we've been riding in the wagon away from that big river, we've been going deeper and deeper into a story—you know, kind of like it isn't real."

Conrad Davidson, a Chickasaw tracker and guide helping the family get to Tishomingo, nodded. He said, "I agree, Noah. Sometimes, when I pick up a rock and hold it in my hand, I know it is real, but when I throw it as far as I can, I wonder how the rock is doing."

Noah grinned. "Yep. I feel like I'm that old rock still sailing through the air, wondering when I will get back on the ground."

Conrad wore buckskins over his heavy canvas pants, a calico shirt, a canvas coat, leather moccasins, long braided hair, and a giant cowboy hat. The children had become enthralled by Mr. Davidson, who insisted they call him Conrad.

Noah felt Conrad was the most brilliant man he'd ever known. He asked, "Do you know how to get to our new house, Conrad?"

"I do. Your great-uncle Jacob was a friend of mine, and I miss him daily."

Noah nodded. "Papa said great-uncle Jacob was giving us his house and some money and was a good man."

"He was the best white man I ever knew. Because of Jacob, I'd do anything to help you and your Papa."

"What about Momma, Bea, and Ben?"

Conrad smiled. "Them too. I'll look after you all as if you were my family."

Conrad told them stories of his people—the Chickasaw—their journeys and Pennington Creek every evening. He even told the children stories about rocks, creeks, trees, and animals they met along the way. One day, Noah asked, "Are all the stories you tell us true?"

"They are true as I know them."

"Even that coyote we saw yesterday?"

Conrad nodded. "Especially him. He's a good friend and was looking out for us."

"How do you know he is the particular coyote who is your friend?"

"He told me."

Noah nodded, unsure if he believed Conrad. He decided if the coyote was protecting Conrad, it was a coyote he wanted to have around. He kept close to Conrad, who sometimes let him ride on the horse with him.

Ben and Bea thought Conrad was the best guide in the world—not that they'd known many—actually any. Besides, they loved his stories. The whole family was more than a little in awe of the Chickasaw man who was becoming a friend of the family.

Maggie said, "Conrad, I'm in deep need of a story tonight."

"What is your need, Maggie?"

"I'm worried I'm not up to the tasks ahead of me. Most especially, I'm worried about my family's safety."

Conrad nodded, tossed a little tobacco into the fire, closed his eyes, and started humming. Maggie, Silas, and Noah watched the native Chickasaw man. They knew this was his way of settling into the tales of his people.

He opened his eyes and said, "Near Pennington Creek, where your home stands, big, ancient rocks surround Pennington Creek. These rocks had been brought to our lands by giants surrounding the creek many years ago. The giants were friendly and loved the creek, so they dropped their rocks and stayed near the creek. One Giant, Ishto Atumpa, particularly loved the creek more than anyone else of the giants. He loved the creek so much and remained so still that he became one of the biggest rocks. He did this because he wanted to help protect the creek and all the people near the creek. For many years, even before the Chickasaw came to live here, he stood guard over the creek and the people. Ishto Atumpa guards us all even now."

Maggie nodded and smiled. "Thank you, Conrad. I'm sure with Ishto Atumpa watching over us, we will be fine."

"Yes, but it would be a mistake to be foolish. Ishto Atumpa can't keep you from being foolish."

Silas asked, "Can you give us an example, Conrad?"

"Well, if you hear a rattle in the grass, it would be foolish to walk further in the grass. It's best to stand very still and let the rattlesnake mosey on by."

"I'll watch out for rattlesnakes."

"There are others out there. The copperhead loves his skin so much he'll lay in the sun for hours, getting more and more coppery. Step on one of those, and you'll have a nasty bite."

Maggie said, "I don't like the idea of rattlesnakes and copperhead snakes."

"Well, they have their way of being and don't want to hurt people—not really. You're too big to eat."

Maggie laughed, and Conrad grinned. "Of course, you need to learn the difference between a black water snake, which is mostly harmless, and a cottonmouth, which is absolutely not harmless."

"Do we have them in our creek?"

"Yes, but usually, if you leave them alone, they'll leave you alone."

"Because we're too big to eat?"

He chuckled. "Yes. But don't go for a swim in the creek without being sure there isn't a cottonmouth snuggled close along the banks of the creek. They love to lie quiet and are still waiting for a juicy frog to be too eager and foolish. Frogs are known for being eager and occasionally foolish."

Silas nodded and smiled.

Noah asked, "Will Ishto Atumpa protect us from snakes?"

"No. Ishto Atumpa protects us from each other but never interferes with Nature."

"Oh." Noah sighed and shook his head.

Conrad nodded. "Noah, as long as you live with honor in the Nature around you, you'll be fine. But. Carry a hoe just in case."

Maggie asked, "Why a hoe?"

"To chop off the head of an eager snake."

"What if the snake isn't poisonous?"

"Can you tell in a split second which ones are poisonous and which are common garden snakes or corn snakes or bull snakes?"

"No."

"Until you can know them, keep a hoe handy and sharp."

"I will," Maggie said, then yawned. "I think I'm settled enough to sleep. I have my courage back, especially because of your stories, Conrad."

"Good," Conrad said. "While you prepare for sleep, I'll draw a map for Silas on how to get to Tishomingo. It's less than two miles away. I'll be gone to my home before you wake."

Maggie stood up, as did Conrad. She went to him and asked, "May I hug you, Conrad."

"It would be an honor, Mrs. Pennington."

"Please call me Maggie."

He smiled. "It would be an honor, Maggie."

CHAPTER TWO

"Life is either
a daring adventure
or nothing at all."
Helen Keller

MAGGIE AND HER HUSBAND, Silas Pennington, sat on the seat of their buckboard wagon at the edge of the town, looking down on Tishomingo, Indian Territory, at dawn on the first day of May in 1898. The day was already warm, and the mugginess didn't help Maggie feel more comfortable, especially with her fourth child due in a few months. The baby was resting for now, but the night of kicking had left Maggie tired and irritable.

Maggie smiled at the memory of the story of Ishto Atumpa and appreciated how Conrad helped her settle herself on the last night of traveling. She was eager to see her new home but also a little apprehensive. She couldn't stop herself from crossing her fingers, hoping the house wouldn't be a log shack. Conrad's story had helped her sleep last night, even though her baby tumbled and kicked a bit all night long, leaving her with a backache this morning.

Now, in the morning light, she remembered her dreaming of Ishto Atumpa, who sat on a big rock in Pennington Creek looking over their home and land. She waved to him, and he smiled and nodded. She released a sigh of anxiety and decided to trust Ishto Atumpa.

Now, Silas and Maggie sat on the buckboard seat facing west from a small hill above Tishomingo. The sun peeked above the horizon, spreading a golden-pink glow across the land. With a clear blue sky and gentle breezes, she told herself it was a good day to arrive at their destination and new home—at least as long as the breeze continued. She wrapped her long, dark, auburn hair into a loose bun at the base of her neck, tied her hat on her head to help keep the sun off her face, and turned to her husband. She raised her eyebrows, cocked her head, and sighed. "It's not Columbia, South Carolina."

"No, darlin', it is not," her husband agreed with a wide smile. "And I, for one, am glad."

"South Carolina wasn't all bad, Si."

He nodded and looked at his wife, her dark blue eyes and freckles glowing and the sun reflecting on her face. He loved everything about her, including her willingness to speak her mind. "You're right, Maggie. But there was no way forward for me in South Carolina. I peaked at being the editor of the Columbia Dispatch. Uncle Jacob made all of this possible."

"You were a good editor, Si. I was, and still am, proud to be your wife. Don't get me wrong, though. I'm glad to be here and ready to see what we can make of our good fortune. I am eager to see our home." She wanted to see the home Ishto Atumpa watched over, although she didn't tell her husband she fully believed Ishto Atumpa was watching over their house.

He touched her hand, gave it an affectionate squeeze, and said, "Thanks, Maggie, I'm relieved to hear you say so. I knew there wasn't another rung on that ladder to climb at the newspaper. Daddy wanted me to join him at the bank, but I couldn't stomach being inside that building thinking about money day in and day out. Numbers make my head swim."

She chuckled. "You did a lot of good in the community with your essays, stories, and poems in the paper."

"Yes. Those came from my heart but didn't earn much more than a few pennies for my efforts."

"Did that bother you?"

"Yes, and I'm ashamed of that fact. I wanted to—and still do—want to make my way, preferably with my writing or something associated with my writing."

"I do understand, Silas. Although I didn't mind living in your parent's home, I'm relieved we are going to our own home. Your father and mother were always kind to me and our children."

"I know and appreciate your kindness, especially to my mother. She is a fine woman. Without my parent's help, we would have struggled to arrive here safe and sound."

She laughed. "Oh, my love! It was a struggle at times, but we're here. I'm glad we've arrived, and I can finally get off this buckboard. I have faith in us. We will be fine."

He smiled and nodded. "Yes, we will. Still, I want to make my way in the world."

"I do understand, my love. I'm sure you'll find your way forward and make your mark on the world. I'd go to the ends of the earth to help you. However, not yet and not on a buckboard any time soon."

He chuckled and nodded. "I'm right there with you, darlin'."

She turned and looked down at the small town that was barely a settlement to her mind, but then she knew she'd been living in a city all of her life. She expected that living near a town rather than a city would require some accommodation of thoughts on her part.

The road into town was deeply rutted from the spring rains. The red clay was evident all around. There were a few walkways, and only a few buildings had stoops and rails in front of the establishments. Some, but not all, of the buildings had signs. Many were one story, but nearly as many had a second floor.

Beyond the town's main streets were scattered houses of varying sizes, including several two-story homes. Some had fence rails surrounding their homes, and a few had white picket fences gracing their front gardens. She could see the dirt roads in the town, which were spread out further than she'd imagined.

Maggie knew she'd eventually learn who was who and what was what in the town. For now, it was a monumental change in her life. She said, "I wanted an adventure, and so far, it's been an adventure!"

"That it has, darlin.'"

"Now, I'm ready for home. It doesn't look like much yet, Si, but I feel we can become a part of a very nice town here."

Silas said, "I agree. The place doesn't look like much right now, but I fear that's only because we've been living in a city. I hope that we will help the town of Tishomingo to grow."

"Exactly what I think, too."

"I hope to leave some of the War Between the States behind us. When Uncle Jacob died and left his estate here in Indian Territory to me, I wanted to jump at the chance to move away from all the grief and constant unrest. It was such a long time ago, and I feel it should not still be a problem."

"I agree, love. I don't understand all the issues, but I know there will always be differences among folks. My guess is there will be issues here. They may be different than in Columbia, but I strongly feel we can make friends here."

"I agree, darlin', and I hope that we will have a positive effect on our new town."

He sighed, "Well, at least new to us."

Maggie asked, "What's pulling you down, Si."

"Oh, just my silly meandering mind. I am grateful for the estate from Uncle Jacob and your support in moving far from everything you've ever known. My only regret is not coming here before Uncle Jacob died."

She smiled. "After Daddy and later Momma died, too, it was an easy choice for me, Si. I am an only child, and you, my dear heart, and our children are my whole world. I want to be wherever you are. I agree with your yearning to come here, and in many ways, I'm relieved to have loaded up our wagon and headed west. It's simply very different and very wild."

He grinned. "Gotta love the wild and the new."

Maggie kissed his cheek. She was still anxious about everything but wanted to see what she and Silas could make of their good fortune. "I'm looking forward to building our lives to be how we want it to be. Still," she shook her head and looked at the town again, "once we were across the Mississippi River, the wild became ever more wild with each mile we traveled. I did not expect that."

"You're right." Deep in his heart, he had misgivings, too, but to be in a place where white people weren't necessarily the top dogs and he could make something grand for his family's future felt like a dream come true. He hoped there would be a good outcome for his family. He nodded, "There will be a lot of hard work, but this is our chance to make our path in life."

"I asked for an adventure and a home of my own, Si, and so far, every day has been an adventure. Even though it has been hard, I'm glad we have made this journey. Right now, I'm just a bit grumpy and tired. I want to see our home." She placed her right hand on her growing abdomen and said, "As Momma would have said, let's make hay while the sun shines, husband. I want to keep moving. The sooner I can be off this wagon, the happier I'll be. I'm tired of bouncing around in a wagon daily while being kicked from the inside. A folded-up blanket on this buckboard seat doesn't do much to ease the thumping."

He kissed her cheek again and said, "I'll find you a satin pillow if needed, darlin'. We'll keep moving so you can have a proper place to sit, at least for a bit. Thank you for this adventure, darlin'."

She smiled as he patted her abdomen. She knew he loved her and their children, but the adventure was getting tedious and tiresome. She was ready to be at their new home.

Silas loved his wife, who was pregnant with their fourth child. He was amazed she had wanted to make this trip immediately. It was still a wonder to him but also a joy and delight. He was anxious about her, though. Her abdomen seemed more prominent than he'd remembered in her pregnancy with Noah, their eldest son. He grinned and asked, "Are you sure you're not having twins again, Maggie?"

"I'm sure. Only two feet are kicking in there. I can say with certainty there is only one child in there." She crossed her fingers, hoping she was right. She adored the twins, Beatrice and Benjamin, but they were a handful as infants—still were occasionally. One baby at a time suited her just fine.

It had been a long trip, and their three children had slept in the back of their buckboard wagon under a canvas tarpaulin covering the raised framework.

Now Maggie was exhausted. She felt a little anxious at being so tired at this point in her pregnancy. During her previous pregnancies, she'd felt these few months before the last few weeks were a time of feeling energetic and hopeful for the future. She felt none of those things with this pregnancy.

Maggie felt worry creeping up. She must get things settled in their new home before the birth of her fourth child. She tried not to worry about the baby and her bulging abdomen. She sighed and silently prayed: *"Please be all right, my baby."*

She could and would make a home in this wild land and was eager to do so. Even so, at this moment, she was exhausted. *I'm simply tired. A few days' rest will help a lot.* Being nearly seven months pregnant had not made the trip easy for her.

She smiled and shook her head. Easy had never been her path, and she took some pride in that fact. Whatever the future would bring, she would be with Silas, who loved her, honored her, and wanted her by his side.

She pointed to a few buildings and muddy, rutted roads. "I suppose I thought Tishomingo would be more of a city. In that regard, it is a little disappointing. If I consider it a town, I can see the potential blooming around here."

"You're right, darlin'. All towns and cities are like this in the beginning. We're on the edge of what we think of as civilization. For the folks that have been here for many years, it is their town, and I want to honor that. We have land, a house to make a home, a cabin. Remember, my Uncle Jacob has a couple living in the smaller cabin. I'm keeping my fingers crossed they'll stay on for a bit."

Maggie smiled and nodded. "I'd forgotten about Clay and Aurora. If they can stay long enough to help us get things set up, then it seems pretty perfect to me."

"From what I can tell, my Uncle Jacob liked them a lot and hoped they would stay on with us. We'll need their help for sure."

"You have us too, Papa," a voice piped up from the back of their buckboard wagon.

Silas grinned, turned, and looked at his oldest son. "Your Momma and I are proud to have you, Noah, your brother Ben, and sister Bea, too."

Maggie smiled and ruffled her eight nearly nine-year-old son's dark brown hair with highlights of deep red, much like her own auburn hair. She looked at his earnest face with freckles and dark blue eyes. She always felt a flutter of joy seeing his face—her firstborn child who looked more like herself than he did his father. He seemed much older than a nearly nine-year-old boy. "We're going to be fine, Noah. Things are just different, and I'm tuckered out. It's been a long trek riding in this wagon with our few things across the country."

"I know, Momma. I'm tired too and ready to see our house. But I kinda like Tishomingo. It's different, but it feels good."

She nodded. "I think you're right, Noah. It seems like a growing town. We're here to be a part of that growth."

She reminded herself she had been the one to push Silas to come here and make their way forward. The only emotion she had about it all at this moment was fatigue.

As she'd listened to her son, she looked again at the town they were entering. Yes, it was a little rough, but real people were doing real things and trying to make their way into the world.

I want to know a few people today, but mostly, I want to continue the adventures in my new home.

CHAPTER THREE

"*Wherever there is
a human being,
there is an opportunity
for a kindness.*"
Seneca

SILAS CLICKED his tongue and urged the horses forward into the town of Tishomingo. He glanced at his wife and smiled. Seeing her determination on her face helped him know things would work out fine. Maggie would see to it. He thought, *Thank heavens for strong, beautiful women making our lives better.*

Maggie felt her husband's eyes on her and could feel the love. She had no intention of backing down now. The trip had been fine so far, although challenging at times. Still, she would ensure everything worked out in the best ways possible. It had always been her way, and she would continue to make it so.

She asked Silas, "Do you know where we will shop for food and essentials? I wonder if Clay and Aurora will be here in town?"

Silas nodded. "I don't know the answer to either question, darlin'. I guess the feed and seed store is the place to start." He pointed to one of the most significant buildings in the town. It looked less thrown together than a few of the other buildings. There were even glass windows on the front. "We can probably get some chicks and maybe a hen or two. A sign says *Milk Cow for Sale, $25.00.*"

"Sounds good to me, Silas. Don't forget we'll need a rooster, too, so our hens can always have chicks as well as eggs. We'll also need feed for all the animals. I remember your Uncle Jacob saying there was a small barn, a hen house, an outhouse, our large log cabin home, and a smaller cabin for Clay and Aurora."

"I think you're right. I'm ready to see our new home. How about you?"

"I'm not ready. I'm eager."

Silas nodded and chuckled.

Noah piped up, "I'm ready, too, Papa. The twins are still sleeping."

"That's fine," Maggie said. "They'll wake when they hear us rustling around."

Silas smiled, looked at the brilliant blue sky, and said, "The sun's fully up, and folks are milling around. Let's start with the feed and seed store, Noah. Maggie, you keep a lookout for dry goods or mercantile stores. I think a dry goods store will have what you need for our food and home."

Maggie nodded, and as they were nearly at the *Feed and Seed Store,* she pointed across the street to a store with the words *Shirley's Dry Goods* on the window. "You mean like that store, Si?"

He grinned. "Exactly like that store, darlin'.

She smiled and nodded. "You and Noah take care of getting the critters worked out while I take the twins to *Shirley's.* The sooner we get what we need, the sooner we can reach our home. I want things to settle a bit before we go to sleep tonight."

Noah said, "Momma, I'll help."

"I know you will, sweetie. We'll all have to work hard to put things to right."

Noah nodded, knowing his mother would figure it all out and take care of all of them.

Silas pulled their wagon up to the feed and seed store, tied the reins around a hitching post, and said, "Noah, come along with me while your Momma takes care of the twins and gets the household things across the street at the dry goods store."

Noah grinned and jumped from the wagon. "I'm right with you, Papa, but this ain't much of a street."

"*Isn't*, son—use your best words."

"I will, Papa."

Silas chuckled and ruffled his son's hair. "I think this is the main street in the town, so use your very best words and try not to judge harshly in this new place. It hasn't been a town as long as the city we used to live in."

Noah nodded and ran his fingers through his hair, wanting it to be how he liked it best. "I will be kind, Papa. I promise.

Silas smiled. "Good. I'm glad to have you helping me, son."

Maggie loved watching her eldest son walk with his father to the feed and seed store. Noah mimicked every move Silas made, from pulling his hat down a bit and putting his hands in his pants pockets. He even tried to make his stride a determined one like his father's.

She smiled, turned back into the wagon, and woke the twins. For breakfast, she gave them some leftover food from last night's dinner.

Ben said, "I like apple biscuits and ham for breakfast, Momma."

Maggie smiled. "I'm glad since I don't want to cook right now."

Bea nodded. "That's 'cause we're here, right?"

"Yes, we're here. When you finish breakfast and tie your shoes, we'll go to the dry goods store over there." She pointed to the store and said, "We can get what we need, including more food."

"Then can we go see our house?" Ben asked.

"Yes, sir. I'm eager to get to our house, too."

Bea said, "I want to see our creek."

"We will, sweetie. I hear it's a lovely creek."

"Yep, and it is guarded by Ishto Atumpa."

"I'm glad you heard the story."

"I didn't hear it. I dreamed it."

Maggie smiled and nodded. "I understand, and it is a fine thing to have Ishto Atumpa watching over us."

Ben didn't say anything. He, too, had dreamed about the big rock watching over the creek. He didn't understand how dreams happened, but he liked them—mostly.

Once the twins were dressed and ready to see what was going on around Tishomingo, holding their hands, she walked to the dry goods store. The baby in her belly kicked a few times. She smiled and thought, *Settle down in there. We'll take care of you, too.*

The dry goods store owner, Shirley Duncan, watched a tall, lovely woman walk toward the store with two small children holding her hands. She smiled and said, "I hope they're going to stay. We need more good families around here."

Maggie had ten dollars in gold and silver coins and several copper pennies in her purse. She hoped it would be enough for her current needs. She needed to replenish her food stores, including flour, sugar, lard, coffee, and, she hoped, tea. She smiled, thinking of having tea in the wilds of Indian Territory. No matter what else happened today, she wanted a cup of tea, especially with a drop of honey.

She opened the store door, and a little brass bell tinkled above her head. She looked up to see a tall, beautiful woman. She was a little taller than Maggie, maybe about 5'10 inches tall, with long black and silver hair she'd braided. Her face showed her native heritage with brown, bronze skin. The braid flowed down past her hips. Maggie wasn't sure if she was white or native because of her eyes. Shirley's deep blue eyes suggested white, but everything else about her appearance suggested native, probably Chickasaw.

Shirley Duncan smiled and said, "Welcome to Shirley's Dry Goods."

Maggie returned the smile to the woman standing in front of her. "Thank you. As you might have guessed, we're new to the area."

"Good. I was hoping you and your family were joining our community."

"We plan to do exactly that. Although, I don't know how far from town I'll be. I'm sure my husband will figure it out."

"Ah, he must be the tall man with the curly blonde hair I saw walking into the feed and seed store."

Maggie smiled and nodded, but before she could say anything else, Ben said, "That's my Papa."

Shirley nodded. "My guess is he is a fine Papa."

"Yes, he is. This is Bea, my sister. She's shy."

"No, I'm not," she scowled, raising her nose a bit as she'd seen her grandmother do. "I don't like to talk all the time like you do, Ben. That's different than being shy." She tugged Maggie's skirt and said, "Momma, I gotta pee."

Shirley chuckled, immediately liking the little girl. She thought *any little girl with a bit of gumption is a girl I want to know.* She said, "I have an outhouse out back. Will that do?"

"Is that where you pee?"

"Yes, it is. If you follow me, I'll show you where I pee."

Once they were outside and the children took turns relieving their bladders, Maggie told Shirley, "Thanks for this. They're twins and can be a handful."

"I'm sure. My name is Shirley Duncan, and I own this store." She pointed to the store as the children finished using the outhouse.

Bea said, "I like your store."

"I'm glad. Now let's head back inside and see what your Momma needs to buy."

Ben said, "A lot! We came from South Carolina."

"My goodness! You must be tired."

He nodded. "We are. What's your name?"

"I told your Momma, Ben, but I forgot to tell you and Bea. I'm Shirley Duncan."

As they walked back into the store, Ben asked, "Are you Chickasaw?"

"I am. I'm glad you noticed."

Maggie smiled at her son and told Shirley, "I'm Maggie Pennington, and I'm glad to be here."

Shirley cocked her head. "Did you know we have a creek that runs through town called Pennington Creek?"

"I did, and that is where we're headed—a bit north and west of town. My husband's Uncle left him some land and buildings, including a house for us to live in."

Shirley smiled, clapped her hands, and nodded. "Hooray, hooray! I'm glad you're here. Walter at the Council House said you were on your way here. I was hoping to meet you soon. Your husband must be related to Jacob Pennington."

"Yes, he was. Did you know, Jacob?"

"I knew Jacob for years and years. He told me about his nephew, his wife, and their children. He was a great friend of mine, especially after my husband died."

"I'm so sorry."

"Thank you. It was a few years ago. He slipped on a wet rock on Pennington Creek and split his head open. I'm happy he didn't have a lot of pain. Quick is always the better way to go in my mind."

"I'm sure, but still, it must be hard for you."

"Yes, it was and sometimes still is. Keeping men at bay was easier when Jacob was around. You'd be amazed at how many chuckleheads think I can't possibly run my store by myself."

Maggie smiled. "And yet they expect us to keep house, birth and raise children, launder and press their clothes, cook amazing meals, and dress up just for them. And it doesn't hurt a thing if we take care of the kitchen garden, orchards, cows, hens, chicks, and whatever else they come up with they don't want to do themselves."

Shirley laughed and nodded her head. "You have the right of it, Maggie. I like how you think, and I'm glad you're here. I hope we'll be fast friends."

"Me too."

Shirley smiled, liking Maggie Pennington, and wanted to help her settle into her new life. She hoped Maggie would be someone who thought Chickasaw people were actual humans. She said, "Now tell me what you need."

"I've made a list here," Maggie said, pulling out the small notebook she carried in her purse. She opened the book and read, "I need five pounds of sugar, twenty pounds of flour, five pounds of lard plus molasses, and dried fruit if you have them. I feel a need for prunes, raisins, or any other dried fruits."

Shirley smiled as she wrote down the items as Maggie read them to her. She asked, "What about coffee or tea?"

"Yes. Please. I haven't had afternoon tea in all the months of our journey."

"Where did you start?"

"Columbia, South Carolina."

Shirley looked at Maggie's obvious pregnancy and said, "My goodness. You've had a long trip and must be exhausted."

"I'm tired but eager to see my new home."

"I think you'll like your home. Jacob did a fine job when he built it. It is a log home, but most certainly not a simple cabin. It's bigger than most log cabins and many frame houses around here. It's lovely and very nice."

Maggie smiled. "I'm getting excited about seeing the house."

"I'm sure you'll like it."

"I've heard the summers are sweltering around here. Is that true?"

"Well, it can be, but Jacob built his house on a rock foundation, which helps in the summer heat. But, seriously, I love it because it is a lovely home."

"Thanks, Shirley, for telling me about my new home. My idea of a log cabin has always been a small, smelly, and dirty building."

Shirley laughed. "Your home is quite the opposite. It isn't a fancy, elegant mansion but a large, lovely, clean home. It will be perfect for you and your family for years."

Maggie let out a big sigh and chuckled. "What a relief. Now, I'm even more eager to see my new home."

"Good. Let's talk about what else you might need for today. I have everything on your list. My only question is, would you rather pay two pennies more for your flour sacks to be cotton calico or save the money and have plain white cotton sacks?"

"How many yards in a sack?"

"About a yard. Calico sells for ten cents a yard."

"Then, by all means, I want calico sacks."

"Good. I'll be sure both bags are the same pattern and color."

CHAPTER FOUR

THE TWO WOMEN chatted as Shirley gathered all the items on Maggie's list. When she finished, she said, "I have some fine bacon for ten cents a pound and fresh eggs that are twenty cents a dozen. Would you be interested in those?"

"Yes, Please. But first, how much do I owe you?"

"Three dollars and twenty cents."

"Do you have fresh milk?"

"I do. I milked it myself yesterday evening and kept it cool. I don't skim the cream, so it's rich and tasty. I sell it for ten cents for a quart."

"What a treat. Yes, I'd like a pound of bacon, two dozen eggs, and a quart of milk."

"Perfect. After all your miles, you deserve a little milk or cream in your tea or coffee."

Ben tugged his mother's dress. "What about us?"

Before Maggie could answer, Shirley turned to Ben and said, "I have some nice dried apricots. I'd love to give you and Bea one each if your Momma says it is okay."

Ben looked up at his mother, and she nodded.

"Yes, please," Ben said.

Bea grinned, glad Ben had thought of something sweet for them. Ben said, "Our brother Noah likes sweet things, too."

"Then I'll give you one more for him if you promise not to eat it yourself."

Ben became very solemn, nodded, and said, "I promise."

Shirley smiled, handed the children an apricot, and wrapped another in waxed paper for their brother Noah. She told Ben, "You are a good brother, Ben, to remember to think of your brother. I'm pleased to meet you."

Bea nodded and grinned. "Ben's my twin brother."

"My goodness. Now, isn't that something?"

Bea shrugged her shoulders and said, "He's just a boy."

Shirley laughed and said, "You are a lovely and lively girl, Bea."

Bea preened until her mother asked, "What should my children do now?"

Ben turned to Shirley and said, "Thank you, Miss Shirley."

Bea nodded. "Thank you, Miss Shirley. This is the best apricot ever."

"I'm glad you approved, Bea. You are both welcome, and I hope we'll see a lot of each other."

Ben nodded. "If you come to our house, we can see you there, too."

"I'll make sure I do, Ben."

Ben shrugged. "We haven't seen it yet."

"It's a lovely house, Ben. I think you and your family will love your new home."

He nodded and thought, *I hope it is nice.* Then he said, "I'm tired of the wagon."

"I would be too, Ben."

Maggie smiled at the children and then gave Shirley a five-dollar coin, and Shirley returned a dollar coin, several penny coins, half-dimes, and dimes to Maggie.

"Now, I'll gather everything and have it ready in a wooden box for your husband to take to your wagon. I'll also include some damp straw to wrap around the milk to keep it cool. I ask my customers to return the box when they are in town again."

"Sounds like a perfect way to do things. Once we're settled, I'll invite you to afternoon tea."

"I look forward to it, Maggie. Welcome to Tishomingo."

"Thank you, Shirley. I'm glad we are here and delighted to have made a new friend."

"Me too, Maggie."

Shirley watched Maggie walk back to her wagon, glad Maggie was a new friend. Friendship was Shirley's stock and trade.

For Maggie, it was the next step in the adventure of her life in Indian Territory. She smiled, thinking of old stories of adventures and new places to live. *I'll make sure I do a good job of it all.*

The baby in her belly kicked, and she patted her abdomen.

Ben saw his mother patting her abdomen and thought, *That's a brother or sister in there. Momma said Papa put the baby in her belly. I don't understand how Papa got a baby in there, but I believe whatever Momma says.*

Silas and another man and woman loaded the wagon with all the feed, seeds, chickens, and one grumpy rooster. Silas tied a cow to the back of the wagon. He added several other oversized items, including a plow for the horses to draw. There were two surprises for Maggie, but he'd tucked them away first and covered them to surprise her when they arrived at their new home.

Silas looked up and saw Maggie coming toward them and smiled. "How did it go, darlin'?"

"Very well. I see you've done fine, too."

"Yes, I have. Let me introduce you to our new friends." He grinned and turned to them. He took Maggie's hand and said, "Maggie, meet

Aurora and Clay Harrison. They're living in the small cabin as Uncle Jacob wanted."

Clay said, "It's perfect for us. Word came you'd be here in a day or two, so we decided to go into town each morning and be here to welcome you and help however we could.

"I'm glad you did, Clay." Maggie smiled. She turned to Aurora and held out a hand. "I'm delighted to meet you, Aurora. I'm happy you are living near us."

"Yes," Silas said, "And they've agreed to stay on and live in the cabin. They'll work with us in exchange for the house and thirty dollars a month."

Clay said, "I think that's too much money, but Silas wouldn't listen."

"Of course, it's not too much," Silas said. "I'm paying for both your and Aurora's help. You'll both be helping us. If you'd rather, I could pay you fifteen dollars a month, Clay, and I'll also pay Aurora fifteen dollars a month."

Clay grinned and nodded. "Either will be greatly appreciated, Mr. Pennington."

"Please call me Silas. If we're to be friends, I insist you call me Silas and my wife Maggie."

Aurora nodded, turned to Maggie, and smiled. "I see you need my help." She pointed to Maggie's bulging belly. "I've helped many women bring their babies into the world."

"Uncle Jacob wrote about you both. You're a midwife, right?"

Both Aurora and Clay nodded. He said, "She's the best around here for helping babies into the world."

Maggie turned back to Aurora and said, "What a relief. I hadn't thought that far ahead, but I'm delighted you'll be here to help me."

"Yes, ma'am, I will. I'm a hard worker, and so is Clay, that crazy Irishman beside me. Don't let his blue eyes, freckles, wild, curly blonde hair, and tendency to smile all the time make you think he isn't a hard worker."

Maggie laughed and held out a hand to Clay. "It's nice to meet you, Clay, and I'm happy you'll help us with our home and your home, too."

He smiled but had to work hard to hold back tears. "Home sounds mighty fine right now, Mrs. Pennington. We've been living rough for nigh on a year trying to get steady work and a place to live."

"I thought Uncle Jacob had offered the small cabin to you."

"Yes, ma'am, he did, but it felt like a handout. Now, with you and your family here, you need help. Jacob didn't."

She shook her head. "As the good book says, pride goes before a fall, Clay."

"Yes, ma'am, and I promise never to forget it again."

"Good. You've been living there since Jacob's death, right?"

"Yes, ma'am, and we love living there."

"I'm pleased, Clay."

He grinned and nodded.

Silas turned to Maggie, still holding her hand, and said, "When I was in the feed and seed store, the owner related that he'd hired Clay to work for him, but he got so much hate-filled response from some in the community he couldn't keep them on. He said, "I'd keep them both working with me, but I can't afford to lose the business.'"

Maggie's mouth dropped open. "Are you serious?"

Aurora stepped up and said, "Please don't say you don't want me with you because I'm Chickasaw and African. Please. We want to work and have a place to live. We don't expect anything more than a bit to live on and a house."

Maggie pulled her hand from Silas and wrapped her arms around Aurora. She towered over Aurora by several inches. She told the small woman in her arms, "You are welcome to be with me for as long as we own our home and land. Besides, it's what Jacob wanted for you both. I need you, and I think you need me too."

Aurora stood back and looked up at Maggie.

Maggie smiled. "When I look at your beautiful, soft dark skin, dark eyes, and wavy, flowing black hair, I see a lovely woman. I'm pleased to say that when I first saw you, I only saw your beauty and amazing black hair, wavy like a cloak, nearly to the ground."

Silas and Clay both smiled and nodded. Clay said, "My Aurora isn't very tall, but she is lovely and the light of my life."

Aurora smiled, tucked her hair behind her ears, and asked Maggie, "You mean you won't feel tainted with me being around?"

"You? Absolutely not. Now, we might need to talk about the Irishman you have with you. I'm Scottish to the bone."

Silas and Clay laughed. Clay said, "I have more than one Scottish friend, and I'm delighted to add you to my list of friends. Where Aurora goes, I go. I'm not a drinking man, Mrs. Pennington, if that's what you're thinking."

"Good."

He nodded. "Aurora is my life. I'm a hard worker but enjoy my pipe in the evenings."

Noah spoke up. "That sounds exactly like our Papa."

Ben tugged on Aurora's dress and asked, "Do you like little boys and girls."

"Yes, I do. They are among my very favorite people."

"Good." He looked at his father and asked, "When are we going home?"

"In a few minutes, son. Clay and Aurora will lead us to our new home in their buggy."

Ben looked behind their wagon and saw the smaller wagon his father had called a buggy. He asked Clay, "So you have just one horse?"

"It's all I've needed so far."

"Papa has two."

"Well, he has a wife, three children, and now hens, chicks, and a cow. I'd suppose all that requires two horses."

Ben nodded. "Yep."

Aurora smiled and turned back to Ben. "We've put a lot of things in your wagon. It might be a little crowded. Would you and Bea like to ride with Clay and me?"

"Yes!" Bea said. "I love riding in buggies."

Maggie laughed, knowing her daughter had ridden in carriages a few times but never a buggy. "Good. Noah can ride up front with Silas and me. It looks like the wagon is nearly full." She turned to Silas and said, "A box at the dry goods store needs to be carried to the wagon. I've already paid for everything in it."

Clay said, "Let me get that for you, Silas, while you finish tying things down." Clay wanted to check on something special he'd ordered for Aurora. He hoped it would come soon. His wife would need it, and by the looks of things, sooner rather than later.

"I appreciate your help, Clay," Silas said

Bea tugged on Aurora's skirt. "Can we get in the buggy now?"

"We can. You and Ben both can get in the buggy with me."

Silas turned to Maggie and hugged her. "I appreciate you welcoming Clay and Aurora."

"I like them both—a lot. So many people have suffered from the after-effects of the war. I hate that nearly forty years later, prejudice around skin color is still an issue. I'm inclined to welcome anyone of any color so long as they are good people."

"I'm right there with you, darlin'. Clay and Aurora will be a big help for both of us."

She nodded, turned to Aurora and the twins, smiled, and waved.

Clay added the box of groceries into his buggy and then returned to Maggie and Silas. "I'll be happy to lead the way to your home."

"Thanks," Silas answered. "We need a guide."

Maggie nodded. "Yes, we do, Clay."

He smiled and nodded and went to his buggy.

Maggie turned to Silas and said, "Help me up in the wagon one more time—hopefully the last time until the baby arrives. I hope to keep my feet on the ground when we arrive home."

He smiled. "It's my pleasure to help you, darlin'."

Neither Maggie nor Silas noticed a man in a black suit standing across the street. His jacket was open, showing his rotund belly, and the buttons on his vest struggled to stay fastened.

He glared at them and scowled. He shook his head and muttered, "That silly Irishman and half-breed injun wife of his need to leave town in any fashion possible. The more painful, the better in my book."

He stuck his cigar between his lips and puffed, then turned and walked, waddling his way back to his home a few short streets away.

CHAPTER FIVE

John Howard Payne

SILAS, Maggie, and Noah sat on the buckboard seat, following Clay, Aurora, Ben, and Bea to their new home on Pennington Creek. Each clip-clop of the horses' hooves made Silas eager to see their house, the banks of the creek, and all the surrounding land. He was enjoying the beauty of all the trees, wildflowers, and the wide-open blue sky. His heart loved everything around him. It was better than he'd expected—so far.

Maggie pointed to birds flying and swooping. "Aren't they lovely, Si?"

"Yes, they are. Those are the scissortail flycatchers Uncle Jacob talked about."

Maggie nodded and watched the birds swooping and diving with their long double tails. She loved the wildflowers and the smell of the land. It was all different from Columbia, South Carolina, but the land and vegetation were magnificent. She felt herself begin to relax a bit, knowing she would soon be living in a house she could call home. Maggie hoped she didn't have to do a lot of heavy cleaning before they could settle in. She trusted Shirley's evaluation that the home was a lovely home. She crossed her fingers, hoping it was so.

Noah was quiet about what he saw, but he was eager to put his feet on the ground where they would be living. Noah hoped the house wasn't awful being a log cabin and all. He was a little worried that none of the streets in town or the roads they were traveling over were paved.

When they topped a slight rise, Silas smiled, happy to see a large log house at the end of the lane. A rock wall surrounded the yard of the house and the lane leading to their home. A large oak tree stood between the house and the creek. Silas smiled and said, "I'll need to make a swing for the children to swing on that oak tree."

Maggie smiled and nodded. She wasn't sure it was safe to live this far from town, but the house and scene before her were lovely. She thought of Ishto Atumpa and felt herself relax a little seeing the house. She said, "Shirley was right, at least from the outside. It is a big house, and it is lovely."

Silas set the wagon brake, wrapped the reins around the wagon bracing post to keep the horses still, jumped from the buckboard seat, and turned to help his pregnant wife from the wagon.

Noah followed his parents as he jumped down from the seat to the ground. He was relieved at the sight of the house. It was big and didn't look like a shack. Noah grinned and said, "I like it, Papa. Can we swim in the creek?"

"Maybe later, but first, we have a lot of work to do."

Noah nodded. "I like your idea of a swing too."

Silas chuckled and said, "I thought you might."

Margaret and Silas Pennington stood side-by-side holding hands. They looked up at the long grassy hill facing south and a bit east where the large log house stood. The roof covered a deep porch across the entire front of the home. The roof had a high peak, and two large windows were under the eaves. There were two wooden rocking chairs and a small table on the porch.

Elm and oak trees surrounded the house, with a few small cedars mixed in. A massive Mimosa Tree—one of Maggie's favorite trees—was by the sideyard. There were three wide rock steps up to the porch.

"I like it so far," Maggie said.

Pennington Creek was wrapped around the property to the east, north, and south of the cabin. The flow was brisk. The sound of the creek was reassuring to both Silas and Maggie. The smell of the clean, clear water and the surrounding forest was a relief.

Maggie lifted her chin, closed her eyes, inhaled a deep breath, and let the breeze from the creek wash over her. It was a cool, calm, and welcome respite from their weary journey.

The long days of traveling in their wagon had worn them all to a frazzle. The family had little room to rest in the wagon, even with the braces holding up the canvas. Their journey from South Carolina had been challenging for them all. Maggie laid her hand on her burgeoning abdomen. It would be a couple of months before their fourth child would arrive. The child would be the first in the Pennington family to be born in Indian Territory and on Pennington Creek.

Silas removed his hat, slapped it against his leg, and released a lot of the dust from the roads off his hat. He looked at the crystal clear blue sky and watched a few birds flitting and swooping by. He pointed to a pair of birds with long tails swooping back and forth. He said, "There's some more of those scissortail flycatchers that Uncle Jacob talked about."

"They are beautiful, Si, as is that lovely hawk enjoying the day."

"Yep. That's a red-tailed hawk, and he is terrific to watch."

He smiled, wanting to take good care of his family, but, for the moment, he was more excited to have his own place. He asked, "Well, Maggie, darlin', what do you think?"

She shook her head and chuckled. "I love everything about it, dear heart. The house is much bigger than I thought. It is lovely. The surrounding area is as beautiful as your uncle described in his letter. After we get a better look, I'll judge the rest. For now, it feels like coming home to me."

Silas held back tears of joy, took her hand, and kissed the back of it. "Thank you, darlin'."

Noah, their freckle-faced, eight-year-old son, had followed his parents. He still wasn't convinced this was a good idea. He supposed the house was big enough, but everything seemed wild to him—wilder than he'd expected. The house wasn't painted—it was just big logs, and the grass surrounding it was knee-high. There were no flowers in front of the porch and no mailbox on the lane to the house.

He asked, "Is this where we will live?" He was used to living in a two-story white clapboard and red brick house with his grandparents. His grandparent's home was at least three or four times larger than the house they were looking at.

Silas's parent's home, with six bedrooms, two suites—one for him and Maggie, the other for his parents—a piano room, a large dining room, a breakfast room, a family room, and a vast library, was nothing like the home in front of them. Silas knew this would be a significant change for himself and his family. But when Silas had the opportunity to have a house of his own and 360 acres to boot in Indian Territory, he didn't know what to do. He wanted to have his own place, of course, but he worried he'd not be up to the task of living far from the settled places he'd always known.

Now, standing here looking at his new home, he was glad neither he nor Maggie resisted the opportunity—despite his misgivings. Uncle Jacob had blessed Silas and his family with this home. He wanted to make the best of it all, not only for his family but also for his Uncle Jacob. To his mind, such generosity should never be anything other than filled with gratitude and love.

Silas grinned, turned to Noah, and said, "Son, I'm a Pennington, as are your Momma, you, and your brother and sister. I love knowing we are Pennington's, and this home sits beside a creek named Pennington is ours. My Uncle Jacob has given us a great opportunity. It's up to us to make of it what we will. I plan to make the best of it, and I hope you will, too."

"I'll try, Papa. It just feels wild and not what I'm used to."

"I get that. I know you'll work hard and will come to love living here."

"How do you know, Papa?"

Silas shrugged his shoulders and grinned. "It's just a feeling, son."

Clay and Aurora joined them, and Bea and Ben raced to hear what was happening. They didn't like missing out on anything, especially when adults were talking. Oh, the twins knew Noah wasn't an adult—he was their brother, after all. But sometimes, he seemed so much older than them that he was nearly an adult. They didn't want him to hear anything they didn't hear, too.

Silas nodded to them but continued his conversation with Noah. "Now, son, this is where we will live, and I think it will be a fine place. It's bigger and much nicer than I thought it would be."

He watched his son's blue eyes darken with worry. "It don't look like much, Papa."

"Doesn't, son."

"Yes, sir. I forgot."

Aurora smiled at the grammar correction, knowing Noah wasn't the only one who sometimes slipped in his speech.

Silas told his son. "Good, Noah. It's important to speak as well as you know how. Learning isn't worth much if you don't use it. As far as the house goes—it depends on how you look at it."

Noah looked up at his father and then back at the house. He tilted his head one way and another and finally shook his head. "No matter how I look at it, Papa. The grass around the house is so tall that the white fence around the yard is barely visible. The fence gate is half off its hinges. The house isn't even painted. It doesn't look much like a home to me."

Silas bit his lip not to laugh and turned, smiling, to Maggie.

She smiled and nodded to her husband. To Noah, she said, "I think it's going to be a fine home. It does need to be tidied, and you're right about the grass. It needs to be cut down a bit." Maggie took her son's hand and started walking to the log house, which was much bigger and better than she'd expected. There was a stone pathway for them to walk on, and she was glad not to walk through the knee-high grass.

More important to Maggie was her relief to see how big the home was. She told her son, "Think of it as a poorly-wrapped present, Noah. Once we open the windows, air the house out, and brush off the dirt and spiders, it might look better than it looks now. Your Papa's right. It is bigger than I thought it would be. We'll make a grand home of it."

Silas smiled, loving his wife's optimism and sense of adventure. He said, "Ya'll hold on for a bit. Let's all go into our home together. Come on, Ben and Bea. We're home. Clay, you and Aurora, come along and join us."

Clay said, "After Jacob died, we boarded up the windows to keep the glass from being broken by critters or storms. We wanted to be sure it was safe for you when you arrived."

Aurora nodded. "It needs a little cleaning—especially the windows. I've gone in every few days to wipe off the worst of any dust and chased the spiders back outside where they belong. Otherwise, it is a grand home."

The two four-year-old children looked at each other. Ben grinned, and Bea rolled her eyes. He grabbed his sister's hand, and they raced to catch up with their mother and older brother. Ben claimed his mother's other hand to walk with them. He didn't want to miss a thing. Ben thought today felt more like an adventure than all the days and weeks of traveling and camping in the cramped wagon.

Bea released her brother's hand, sat on the walkway, and kicked off her shoes and socks. She stood again, walked into the grass, wiggled her toes, and grinned. The grass felt cool between her toes, and the air felt just right. She picked up her shoes and socks to carry them into their house.

Aurora said, "What a great idea, Bea." She followed suit, removing her shoes to wiggle her toes in the grass.

Bea laughed and took Aurora's hand. Once they were close to the house, Bea stood staring at the log house. She liked the house and especially the big porch. The house was bigger now that she was close to it— she didn't understand why that was so but liked how big it was. She liked the look and sound of the creek running beside and in front of the house, then back to the other side.

She told Aurora, "I hope catfish are in that creek. I like catfish better than anything other than chocolate cake."

"Me too, Bea. We know what's good."

Bea nodded and turned back to look at the house again. A mosquito landed on her hand, and she slapped the back of her hand. The little blood smear didn't bother her—she licked it off. She was used to mosquitos. She'd lived her whole young life in South Carolina, which she'd believed was the place of the origin of the vile little insects. She had hoped they'd left mosquitos behind.

She looked at her father and said, "We brought these nasty old mosquitos with us, Papa."

He laughed. "No, hon. They're all over the place. I'm with you, though. I'd have preferred there not to be mosquitos in Indian Territory. Let's go see inside our new house."

She shook her head. "It isn't new, Papa. It's not white like Grammy's house in South Carolina."

"It's new to us, and we'll turn it into a fine home no matter its color."

"How long will that take?"

"Oh, a fair bit of time, but not as long as you might think."

She rolled her eyes again. "That means years and years. By then, I'll be lots older, maybe even six or seven years old!"

He laughed, picked her up in his arms, and hugged her. He loved the warmth of her hair from the sunshine. She was a sweet girl, but like her Momma, she was smart as a whip and occasionally wilful. He whispered in her ear, "If it helps, I'll always be older than you."

She leaned back, scowled, looked her father in the face, and squinted her eyes. "It doesn't help, Papa."

Aurora and Clay both laughed.

Silas grinned and nodded. "Let's get started and see if we can make this place our own in fine, fast fashion."

"I thought it already was our very own."

"Yes, and you are right. But it will *feel* more like our home when we've cleaned it up. Your great uncle, Jacob Pennington, gave us this house."

"Do I remember him?"

"Probably not. You were just a baby then and not a big girl like now."

Bea sighed. She wasn't sure she would understand as time went on, but she'd wait and see for herself.

CHAPTER SIX

Jane Austen

WITH BEA IN HIS ARMS, Silas walked up to the house where his wife, Maggie, their eldest son, Noah, and Bea's twin brother, Ben, were waiting on the porch. He put Bea on the porch and turned to his wife. "Well, darlin', what do you think?"

"I love the creek and how the house is up on a hill. The redbud trees are lovely, as are all the oaks, elms, mimosas, and cedars. They are all beautiful. I can see us loving to sit here on the porch and enjoying all the nature around us."

"And the house?"

She smiled. "We'll see. I'm hopeful. I'm certain it beats the dickens out of camping in a wagon for days and weeks on end."

Bea asked, "Is dickens a kind of chicken?"

Clay laughed out loud. "Only when they're grumpy, Bea."

She nodded and thought Clay was right.

Maggie grinned and said, "I'm glad the house is larger than I expected. It doesn't seem like a cabin."

Silas smiled. "I agree." He opened the door, walked into the house, and immediately fell in love with the place. It reminded him of his Uncle Jacob, and at the same time, he felt as if he'd always wanted to live in this house. Maggie followed him, stood beside him, and slipped her hand into his. He smiled and asked, "What do you think now, Maggie?"

"It needs a little cleaning but looks much better inside than I expected. I'm pleased the inside walls have been plastered and not left raw logs. From in here, it doesn't seem like a log house. I'm sure Aurora and I can have it looking even better in a few days. It feels cooler in here than I expected."

Silas nodded. "I agree. It's probably because the big logs with plaster on top and the stone foundation keep it cooler. Uncle Jacob expected to live in as good a home as possible without spending too much money. He didn't like fancy things, but he liked his comfort."

He turned to the children and said, "Noah, go to the wagon and get the pry bar. I want to let the sunshine into our home."

Clay said, "I'll help Noah with that and get the boards off the windows while you and the ladies look around."

Silas smiled and nodded. "Thanks, Clay."

Maggie pulled her hand out of Silas's, removed her hat, and walked around the main room. It was pretty roomy, with a large rustic table surrounded by eight chairs perpendicular to the fireplace's far side. There was plenty of room to walk around the table, too. The table and chairs had been oiled and looked beautiful in their rustic way. She was sure they'd shine nicely once dusted and treated with bee wax and lemon oil. She patted the table and then went to the fireplace.

She brushed away a spider web and looked inside the chimney. She was pleased to see that it seemed sound and usable. She estimated that the fireplace was about fifteen feet wide—enormous, taking up half the wall. It was meant to warm the whole house and be a place to cook. Maggie said, "I don't think I've ever seen a fireplace this large, Si."

"Nor I."

Aurora said, "Jacob wanted a big fireplace with plenty of places within the structure to cook on. See these two dome-shaped openings?"

"Yes, I do."

"Well, that's where you can bake bread, pies, or biscuits."

"Amazing," Maggie said. "Have you cooked in such a fireplace?"

"Yes, there is a similar one, but smaller, in the cabin where Clay and I live. There's only one dome oven in ours. You have one on each side of the fireplace. And here," She pointed to shelves inside the fireplace, "You can cook using pans and Dutch ovens."

"It's marvelous. Thanks for showing me how it works. I'll need a little help with cooking at first. I'm used to a wood stove with places on top to cook, plus ovens."

"I'll happily show you how the fireplace works."

Maggie turned back to the huge open room and saw that opposite the table and a bit closer to the door were two sitting chairs with footrests and a small table between them. They were covered with old canvas. She smiled at them, thinking of how she and Silas could sit here in the evenings after the children had gone to bed. She looked forward to adding a few more sitting chairs—there was plenty of room to do so —and curtains. She was eager to see curtains on the windows.

She waited to look further into the house because the only light was from the open door. Then, turning to Silas, Maggie asked, "What do you think?"

"I think it is a very nice, big house. It's not fancy but beautiful and fits with the hills, forests, rocks, and creek."

Aurora nodded in agreement. "I always thought this home was built for a family, and Jacob rattled around in it."

"I agree," Maggie said, pulling out one of the chairs at the table to sit for a few minutes.

Aurora watched her, and Maggie said, "Come sit with me. I want us to be friends and help each other."

Silas said, "I'll head out and see how clearing the windows is coming along."

Maggie smiled and nodded at her husband before turning back to Aurora. "Please, Aurora, sit, and let's chat."

"Yes, ma'am."

"For all that's holy, Aurora, please call me Maggie—ma'am doesn't suit me. Besides, I want us to be friends."

Aurora smiled. "I will. Thank you, Maggie."

The two women chatted, getting to know each other. Soon, Silas, Clay, and the children had the boards pulled off all the windows, sending the glowing light into the home.

Maggie smiled, looking around her home with the light gleaming off the white walls. She smiled and began to think about what would go where in the room. She said, "I want my treadle sewing machine under the right front window by the door where I can sew with the natural light. The sewing machine was my mother's. I want it to have a place of pride in the room."

Aurora smiled and said, "The small alcove beside your sewing machine will be a great place to store fabric, threads, and other personal things. There is a big chest there, too, which will help."

"I hadn't noticed the alcove, Aurora. Have you been in this house before?"

"A few times. At first, Clay and I helped build the house, and later, Clay helped your uncle build the porch and details of some other rooms. The house used to have just a stoop, but he wanted a real porch with a roof to sit outside whether or not it was raining."

"I should get up and start cleaning and see the rest of the house."

"No, Maggie. You look tired, and you're close to term."

Maggie waved her hand in dismissal and said, "Oh, it's several weeks yet. The baby is due in the summer."

"Which is almost here. You stay seated and rest, Maggie. I'll open the windows so the place can get aired out."

"Thanks, Aurora," Maggie said and watched Aurora as she moved from window to window. She was quite a bit shorter than Maggie and a little round but elegant with every movement. She smiled, watching the sway of Aurora's hair. It seemed as elegant as it was beautiful.

She looked around the room at the two double windows on either side of the door. There were two much larger windows on the side opposite the entrance. She couldn't resist seeing the rest of her home and stood and walked through the house. She walked to the larger set of windows and saw two closed doors on either side. One was beside the fireplace, and the other was across from it.

Between the two doors were the large, tall double windows. The space was several feet wide, helping keep the room open. She could see the creek and the back of the yard opposite the creek. An outhouse stood in the far back corner, away from the creek. Beneath the window was a shelf built into the wall and two stools under the shelf. She envisioned flowers and herbs on the shelf and maybe even a candle. *Better yet*, she thought, *remove the shelf and make the two windows into doors to the backyard.*

She opened the door beside the fireplace and saw a huge pantry with many shelves, baskets, and crockery. In the middle stood a rectangular butcher block table with shelves beneath the table. A knife rack was fastened to the far end of the table. She nodded, pleased that some of the things she'd had to leave behind in South Carolina were here, ready for her use. She touched the butter churn and smiled. She loved churning butter, but, more importantly, she loved having freshly churned butter.

Aurora followed her into the pantry and pointed to a small door in the corner of the floor near the churn. "I think that must be a cold well. We have one in the pantry in the small cabin."

Maggie turned to her and asked, "What's a cold well?"

"It's a hole that's been dug down a few feet. It's lined with rocks and then straw dunked in cool water—like the creek. Then, you can store milk, cheese, and cream there for a few days. In the winter, you can store things even longer."

"I'd never heard of a cold well. Aurora, you're going to be a godsend for me. I grew up with servants primarily. My mother insisted I learn the skills of keeping a home, especially cleaning and cooking, sewing, knitting, and embroidery, but I'd never thought of how to store the milk, butter, or cheese. We always had an icebox."

Aurora nodded, went to the spot on the floor, lifted the lid, and nodded. It was bigger than she'd expected and would hold several jugs or bowls. She looked up at Maggie, smiled, and said, "It's lined with what I think is slate, which will help keep things cold for a few days at least. There's a ceramic container here with a wood block covering it." She pulled it out of the cold well, took the lid off the container, and nodded.

"I think you could keep milk cool here. There's room to store a few things like butter and such—even leftover food if eaten within a day or two."

"Terrific. I bought milk, and we should probably store it before it goes bad. It's in the box of things I bought at Shirley's store."

"Let me take care of bringing it for you."

"Thanks, Aurora. I will," Maggie said, looking at the things in the pantry and touching the bowls, pans, platters, and dinnerware.

While Aurora left to ask Clay to bring in the dry goods, food, and especially the milk and eggs, Maggie looked around the room and saw a large faded tin box on the top shelf. She muttered, "I'll have to use a step stool to reach things on the top shelf."

She returned to the main room. She loved everything she saw and could imagine how it would look after everything was clean, with a few photos and paintings on the walls and curtains on the windows.

She walked to the other door across from the pantry. She smiled when she looked inside the room. It was a bedroom and a large one at that. An oak roll-top desk was next to an oak bookcase in one corner, a large oak closet in another. Close to the window was a big brass bed with a double mattress.

There were two small oak tables with a drawer on each side of the bed. The mid-morning light gleamed through the window panes. The mattress was covered with oilcloth to protect the mattress. She hoped it would be useable. She was ready to sleep on something softer than a pile of blankets on the wooden plank bed Silas had built for the buckboard.

She turned around and smiled at Silas standing in the doorway. She said, "Now, we have a place to eat, a place to store more food and utensils, and a bedroom for us." She pointed to the desk, "And a place for you to write."

"I see that, darlin'. Having a desk is a relief, but writing must wait a few days."

Maggie kissed his cheek as Noah pushed his head between his father and the doorjamb before she could say anything more. "What about us? Where are we going to sleep?"

"I'm not sure, son," Silas said. "I saw some hooks and pegs on the front wall by the doorway. We can hang you kids on the wall when it's time to sleep."

Maggie laughed. "Now, Silas, I'll need those pegs and hooks."

He nodded and rubbed his chin, a sure sign he was thinking or teasing. Bea tugged on her father's shirt. "Ben has gone upstairs. I told him not to, but he did anyway."

Silas smiled. "Let's go take a look and see what's upstairs."

The family walked into the main room across from the fireplace. Ben poked his head through the opening in the ceiling. "There's lots of stuff up here. The mice have been eating the books."

Silas shook his head. "I'm on my way upstairs, son. We'll quickly put an end to the rodent's folly."

CHAPTER SEVEN

*"One of the
most beautiful qualities
of true friendship is to understand
and to be understood."*
Seneca

TWO MEN, astride horses, hid behind a willow tree and watched Clay and Aurora unload the wagon while the Pennington family investigated their new home. One of the men was smoking a cigar. The other was chewing tobacco. He spat out some of the juice from the tobacco and said, "That Chickasaw woman, Aurora, whose daddy was born from a slave, is helping them."

"Yes, and I intend to put a stop to it all. Jacob Pennington should have known that they'd keep wanting a handout if he had let Clay and his Chickasaw woman hang around his home doing odd jobs and helping with some of the building. I have it on good authority that Clay and his woman are shacked up in Jacob's small cabin and have been since Jacob died."

"I heard that Clay married Aurora."

"Maybe he did. Who cares? I'm hoping the new fella and his wife will put a stop to it all."

"I don't think so. I saw them talking at the feed store, and Mrs. Pennington actually hugged Aurora. She should know better than to do such a low-class thing."

The man riding next to Lester spit more tobacco juice on the ground. "Only a whore would hug someone like Aurora."

Lester nodded, pulled out his handkerchief, and wiped the sweat dribbling down his round, red face. "Jacob should have known it would come to no good. He'd gotten all soft in the head helping the Chicka-saws, treating them like real human beings."

"What are we going to do?"

"I'm not sure yet, but I won't put up with a man like Clay and his wife becoming an accepted part of the community, even if they are friends of the Penningtons. Injun lovers and, worse yet, leftover slave lovers do not belong around good God-fearing people. I'll give them something to fear. God willing, it will be a blessing for us all. Let's go back into town and see what we can do to stop this grievous behavior."

Aurora lifted a box of children's toys from the wagon. She smiled, knowing the toys would help the children acclimate quickly to their new environment. She told her husband, "I like Maggie and her children a lot, Clay."

Clay grinned. "What about Silas?"

"I like him too, but I'm crossing my fingers that Maggie and I will be good friends."

He nodded and smiled at his wife. Not for the first time, he counted himself blessed to have her in his life. Her short height betrayed her knowledge, brilliance, strength, and determination. More importantly, in his mind, it betrayed the depths of her willingness to be helpful and kind. He said, "I'm certain you and Maggie will be boon companions for many years. Besides, with all your education to go with hers, you two will create ways of being most families haven't even dreamt of."

She smiled and kissed his cheek. "Thank you, Clay. Let's finish the unloading quickly. I want to help Maggie as much as she needs and then go home."

"We are blessed to have a home to call our own, at least for now. I appreciate Silas insisting we live here after his uncle's death, even before he and his family arrived. It was more than I'd expected."

"Yes, but he wanted someone to watch over the place until they could be here."

"I know, Aurora, but now Silas has hired us to keep helping him. I think he's paying us too much, but since he insisted on paying us, I'll not dishonor him by declining the money. On top of that, we get to live in the cabin as long as we're working for him. I love our little cabin."

"I do, too. It's much bigger than most homes I've lived in and the best house I've ever had. For the first time in my life, I have a real home. Fortunately, we have a home that's not a tiny room, loft, barn, shed, or, worse yet, a dugout."

"You're right, and I love our home. Added to the fact that you're smarter than me by a lot, I'm a happy man."

"No, I'm not, Clay," Aurora answered, shook her head, and started carrying another load. She knew she was more educated than many white people. The Chickasaw leaders valued education and wanted their people to be able to live in harmony with the white people. All the children were taught to learn as much as they were able.

She'd gone to boarding school at Bloomfield Academy for a few years to learn to read, write, do arithmetic, and homemaking. However, Aurora's parents brought Aurora home after a few years. Her mother wanted to train her as a midwife and healer, and Aurora was glad her mother did so. She cherished those years with her father and mother but especially cherished her pathway of helping women and families. Without her mother's teaching, she would never have had the skills to do everything she did.

Her mother, Jane, was brilliant and read every book she could get her hands on. She continued to teach Aurora everything she knew about many things, not just reading, writing, and numbers. Her mother, with her father, taught her about the land, nature, and the animals surrounding them. They taught her which plants were helpful and which were deadly. Her mother also taught her how to care for women during pregnancy and birth.

She missed having her mother and father near. Jane and Johnathan, her parents, moved to Tulsa. She knew it was still in Indian Territory but not within the lands of the Chickasaw. Even though her parents were no longer near her, Aurora continued learning as much as possible about everything. She loved reading and kept a daily journal of her life—just as her mother had taught her—including the births she attended and helping others during illness.

When her parents moved, they offered their home to Aurora and Clay, but Clay declined, worried they would think he was marrying Aurora simply because of the house and land. Ultimately, Aurora's mother and father sold their house and land. They used the money to pay for their new home in Tulsa.

When Aurora and Clay carried in the last load of things from the wagon that needed to be carried in, Clay said, "Well, that went much faster than I thought it would."

"Yes, it did. What's next?"

Before Clay could answer, Silas stuck his head down from the attic. "Come on up, you two. See the marvels of our new home."

Aurora laughed. "We'll be there in a few minutes. I want to get the milk cooling, and then we'll be up to see what wonderful things you have found."

Upstairs, the family discovered four bedrooms for the children—each room with a window. Two storage places were on the west and east sides of the second floor. The walls were plastered and painted white, just as the walls downstairs were. Silas laughed. "Now, isn't this amazing? We have a two-story house and not a simple log cabin. Uncle Jacob did not share adequately what a marvelous house this is."

Maggie smiled and nodded, "It feels that everything we need has been given to us."

Silas hugged his wife. "I agree, darlin', but I'd live in a shack to have

Uncle Jacob alive and here with us. It's up to us to make it work, though, which will mean a lot of hard work."

"I agree, and we will make the best of it all," Maggie said as she turned and walked into each bedroom. There were no beds yet, but underneath each window was a chest. Silas watched his wife and followed her into each room. She turned to her husband. "I'm pleased with everything, Silas. I'm sure you and Clay could build beds for the children."

"I agree. What do you kids think?"

Noah grinned. "I think it's a good idea, Papa. Can we sleep up here tonight?"

Silas looked at Maggie, who shook her head. "We must clean your bedrooms before you can sleep here. I don't think we have time to build the beds and clean the bedrooms with all the work we have to do today."

Noah nodded but said, "I know, Momma, but we've been sleeping in the dirt or the cramped-up wagon all the way here. Please let us sleep in our rooms tonight."

She looked at Silas. He raised his eyebrows and shrugged his shoulders. He would not go against his wife unless it was crucial. He thought this was a little thing, but in his mind, she was the ruler of their home.

Noah sighed but stayed quiet. *I want to start making my bedroom my own.* But then he thought, *I can wait even if I don't want to.*

Bea and Ben held hands, hoping she would say yes.

Finally, Maggie said, "IF you get your rooms clean and tidied up a bit, I suppose you're right, Noah. If all the dirt you've been sleeping in for several weeks hasn't bothered you, I suppose you can make it through a night or two on the floor."

Noah grinned, and Clay said, "Aurora and I will help you bring up your sleeping things, Noah. Then we must get busy helping your father settle things with the livestock."

Maggie smiled and patted his shoulder. "Thanks, Clay. Now I want to see what's in the boxes and trunks in the storage spaces."

Bea asked, "Which bedroom do I get?"

Maggie shrugged her shoulders and looked at Silas. He smiled. "Whatever you think, darlin'."

"Well, in that case, you may choose which one you like the best.

Why don't you, Ben, and Noah talk that over and decide while I look at what's in the storage rooms."

The three children quickly started talking about which rooms were best and why. Silas and Maggie went to the storage rooms. Once inside, she shook her head and smiled. "There is so much here, Si, that I feel silly having brought as much as we could cram into the wagon."

"No, darlin', you did just right. Over the years, we'll be glad to have the things we care about near us."

She nodded and smiled, knowing he was right. Bringing a part of their lives in South Carolina to Indian Territory would be a balm in times of need. They opened one of the trunks in the first storage room and smiled. "Come, Si, and see this."

He stood beside her and saw family photos, diaries, books, and linens he was sure Maggie would use. "It'll be fun to go through the albums and see what I remember and what Uncle Jacob has been up to here in the wilds of Indian Territory."

Maggie nodded and looked against one wall, where a few large rugs rolled up were carefully stacked. She turned to her husband and said, "Let's leave most things as they are—for now, at least. We'll take a few rugs down for the floors by the fireplace, the sitting area, and our bedroom. I'm sure we'll have many hours to discover what other surprises our home has for us."

Aurora poked her head into the storage room and said, "I've swept the floors, and the children and Clay wiped down the windows. I think it is satisfactory for tonight at least."

"I'm sure you've done a fine job," Maggie said. "Thanks for helping the children with their rooms."

"Clay and the children are bringing up their bedding and clothes."

"Good," Maggie said and pointed to the rugs. "There are plenty of rugs for you to take home, especially for your sitting area and your bedroom."

Aurora smiled. "Thank you, Maggie. Let's settle yours first, and then Clay and I can show you our home."

"I look forward to seeing where you are living. I hope it is adequate."

Aurora laughed. "It's more than adequate. It's the perfect home for Clay and me."

Once they carried the rugs downstairs, Silas said, "Come on, family, let's see Aurora's and Clay's home."

Clay chuckled and said, "This morning, Aurora and I were talking about how marvelous our home is before you arrived. It isn't as big and grand as this house, but it is perfect for us, and we love living there."

Aurora nodded. She decided to tell the truth about her feelings and trust Silas and Maggie. She said, "I'm hoping it will be my home until the end of my days. I think you will like it, but it is perfect for us. I feel connected to the earth around us in ways I haven't had since leaving my mother's home."

Maggie hugged her. "I'm so glad, Aurora. I know it's only a ten-minute walk, but I'm not up for a hike. Let's take the wagon, Si."

CHAPTER EIGHT

*"What is a
farm but a
mute gospel?"*
Ralph Waldo Emerson

AURORA AND CLAY led the way in their buggy while Silas, Maggie, and their children climbed into the wagon to follow their new friends.

Clay asked Aurora, "Are you excited?"

"More than you can imagine. It's like a dream come true. We have a house of our own and now friends close by. I know Maggie and Silas will like our home."

He patted her knee. "I'm sure they will, Aurora. You've done a lot to make it a pleasant home, and I appreciate all your work."

She laid her head on his shoulder. "Thanks, Clay. I know being married to a Chickasaw woman whose father is part slave creates social burdens for you, though."

"Not a bit. I couldn't take another breath without you in my life. Everyone else can be damned to hell for all I care."

Aurora smiled and thought of how quickly her life had changed and how settled and at peace she felt. Living with a man she loved in a house she'd never thought to have and now with new friends close by created a feeling of peace, contentment, and wonder.

When they crested another slight rise, they could see their cabin. It was closer to the road than the creek, but there was a large natural pond east of the house within sight of the road. Jacob had called it a lake, but Aurora smiled at the thought. It wasn't big enough to be called a lake, but it was bigger than most ponds.

Clay said, "You know, during the war, there was a big battle near here, just a mile or two south of this."

"I didn't know that. I'm glad I was born years and years after the war."

"Me too. Fighting battles to enslave any human being would never be right for me. It's even more important to me now with you in my life. I know I'm on the outside, lookin' in with society, but I'd rather be on the outside than lose the love of my life."

"Thank you, Clay. It's amazing how our lives are changing. I hope it lasts for at least a little while. I worry men like Lester Blunt will turn Silas's and Maggie's attitude about the social order of the white people, and we'll be homeless again."

Clay said, "I'll do my best to see that we have this home for a long time. I trust Silas, for now at least." He thought of a conversation he'd had earlier with Silas.

Silas had said, "We'll get on just fine, Clay. I worry about you two, though. There are many places in this country where your marriage would be illegal."

"I know. We'll keep moving if we have to. My home is with Aurora, no matter where it is or what the shelter is."

"Folks are talking about changing the name of this place from Indian Territory to a state. They would call it Oklahoma."

"I don't care what they call it," Clay said, "so long as my wife and I have a place to live and love and care for those who honor us."

Silas nodded. "We'll do everything we can to make it so."

"I appreciate you and Mrs. Pennington a lot. I want us to be friends and help you with your property."

"Maggie and I feel the same way. I think she and Aurora are already becoming friends."

Clay smiled and stopped his musings when the small road—more of a trail, really—curved, and they could see their home. Although they'd lived there for several weeks—nearly three months—it still felt new to him. He pointed to the cabin and told Aurora, "I love the sight of our home. I have faith Silas and Maggie will help us keep it."

She smiled, loving the look of their home. "How can you know they will help us keep our home, Clay?"

"I trust Silas, Maggie, and Jacob. They've all wanted us to live here, and I don't think they'd ever turn their backs on us."

She nodded but was still worried about it all. Maggie had been kind to her, and Silas had even insisted they move into the cabin months before they arrived. She made a decision and turned to her husband. "First, thank you for all of this, Clay, but second and maybe most importantly, I'm going to follow your lead and believe Maggie and Silas will be our friends and will not forsake us."

"Thank you, my love. Now, let's show our new friends our home."

Silas pulled their wagon to a stop beside Clay's and Aurora's buggy. He helped Maggie down from the buckboard, and they walked hand-in-hand to stand with Clay and Aurora while the children raced to keep up with the adults.

Silas stood beside Clay and looked at the log cabin. He noted that its structure resembled their bigger house. Across the front of the cabin was a broad porch covered by the roof. There were two windows on each side of the door. The foundation was made of native stone, like the bigger house his uncle had given them. The roof was tall, but there were no windows on the upper part of the cabin.

He said, "It's not as big as our home, but I like it—a lot. It is yours for as long as we all get along."

Aurora smiled, nodded, and said, "It's paradise. We've had some sorry places to live. One was a room, one time a dugout, slept on porches or even in the buggy. By comparison, this is a grand mansion."

"Good," Silas said. "I promise we'll work hard to keep you and Clay around for a long, long time. For one thing, Aurora, I need you to help Maggie when her birthing time comes. I'd probably drop the poor mite rather than be of any help."

Clay laughed. "We understand, Silas. We'd seen this cabin before when we helped Jacob a time or two. Jacob even offered the cabin to us while we worked, but neither of us could have borne leaving it once the job was done. We shared our feelings with Jacob, and he offered us this house, and he would live in the big house."

"Why did you turn him down?"

"It felt too much like charity. Neither of us was willing to accept charity."

Maggie shook her head. "Jacob wasn't offering you charity. He was offering you a permanent place to live to help him. That's how we feel now."

Clay blushed a bit but nodded. "You are right, of course."

Silas chuckled. "She often is."

Clay's blush deepened, then said, "It's been a great blessing to have a real home. We love every inch of the cabin. I agree with Aurora. It seems like paradise."

Maggie pointed to the side of the house and said, "You've got a garden already."

Aurora smiled. "Yes, we do. Clay helped me with the digging and carrying compost to work into the soil."

"When did you start the garden?"

"As soon as we got the telegram, you were on your way to Jacob's home."

"I'm so glad," Maggie said. "We'll need gardens too, but yours seems to be growing well."

Clay nodded. "Aurora insisted we make it as big as our backs would hold out on us."

Silas laughed. "I can see you've been working hard. When's the harvest."

"Well, there's another way my wife has the leg up on me. We started with things that would take the longest to grow and the things that would be most useful to your family and ours."

Aurora said, "I've harvested a few turnips but left most to grow a bit longer. The potatoes and yams will be ready in a few weeks. Right now, we have tomatoes, squash, peas, beans, leaf lettuce, green onions, radishes, and spinach. The okra and corn won't be ready for another few months."

Bea asked, "What about cantaloupe?"

Aurora grinned. "They aren't ready yet, but maybe in a few weeks."

"Watermelon, too?"

"Not yet. I ran out of places to plant, but I've got a few trays of starter plants that we can plant over at your house."

"How long do we have to wait?"

"About two to three months."

Clay grinned and said, "She's got trays filled with dirt and seeds that are sprouting, so as soon as we get your plots plowed, we'll have a few weeks' start on everything at your place."

Maggie sighed. "My goodness. I didn't expect you two to have been working so hard on our behalf."

Aurora shook her head. "Not a bit of it. First, it's my pleasure to plant and grow things. I have herbs of all kinds surrounding our cabin, including a few flowers. Second, starters for your planting will help ensure you have food sooner. I have starters of everything I've planted, so Clay and Silas need to get busy and prep your land so we can plant things for your family."

Maggie gently squeezed Aurora's hand. "You've made my life much easier today, Aurora. I wasn't sure how we would get all the food needed. I have a deep need for fresh vegetables and fruit."

"And, with the pregnancy, you need the food we've been growing. I've got some of everything I've harvested to bring to your house."

"Thank you, both. You've done amazing work. Now show us the inside of your home."

CHAPTER NINE

"Every beloved object
is the center point
of a paradise."
Novalis

Maggie said, "After seeing your home, please look in our attic closets to see if we have anything else to make your cabin more of a paradise than it already is. I'm sure it has been a bit like our house was for us today. We didn't know what to expect. It can all be overwhelming."

Clay said, "Aurora has cleaned our home to a fine shine and cleans it daily. It was a great place to live, but she's made it even better. As time passes, we'll add more furniture, rugs, and such."

Maggie nodded, knowing she would give them anything in the attic they didn't need that Aurora and Clay could use. Wasting things because they belonged to her never set easily on Maggie's conscience. Besides, the fewer things she had to dust, the better in her mind.

Everyone walked around the cabin. Silas pointed to the outhouse to the north, the small barn, and the well on the east side of the house.

Aurora said, "Now that you know the lay of the land here, I want to show the inside of our home." Before she stepped onto the porch, she turned to Silas and Maggie and said, "Having a porch with a roof is far more than I ever expected. Thank you for asking us to stay here and tend things. Clay helped Jacob with building this porch and the porch at your home. Now that we have a home with a beautiful porch, I feel blessed daily. Everything else that comes our way will be a blessing, too."

Clay kissed her cheek and whispered, "I love you."

She nodded and whispered back, "I love you, too." She took his hand and invited the Pennington family into their home.

Maggie smiled. Although she knew this house wasn't as grand as the one she and her family would live in, she was relieved they didn't feel they were getting second best. The windows glistened in the sun, and no speck of dust could be found when they walked into the house.

Silas followed them into the house and smiled. "Well, Clay and Aurora, it seems my uncle stuck to one house plan and went no further."

Clay chuckled. "It's smaller than yours by a fair bit but still about the same layout as your place. I like the layout and love living here."

Noah said, "We don't have to take boards off the windows either."

Aurora laughed. "That was done when your Uncle Jacob asked us to be the caretakers and live in this house."

Maggie said, "Everything gleams, Aurora."

Clay pointed to the interior of their home. "She cleans everything every day."

Noah and the twins were tired of listening to the adults talk about their houses. Instead, he asked, "Can we play outside, Momma?"

"Sure, but don't wander around too much—stay close to the house. I'm too tired to chase you down."

He grinned. "Yes, ma'am."

He liked Clay and Aurora, but listening to them talk was boring, and Noah wanted to know every inch of the place where they lived. He liked it a lot even if the houses weren't painted white like the ones in Columbia. The trees weren't as tall as the ones in South Carolina, and the mountains and hills were covered with big rocks, just like Conrad had told them. To his mind, the best part was that the sky was a lot bigger here than in South Carolina.

Bea and Ben followed Noah, and both children watched their brother as he surveyed everything around them. Bea asked, "Do you like it here, Noah?"

"I do. It feels just right to me."

She nodded. "I like our big house better, though."

He grinned. "Me too. But there are five of us, and Clay and Aurora have only the two of them."

Bea nodded. "Soon, there'll be six of us."

"You're right, Bea."

Ben said, "I like it all, especially the creek."

"I like it a lot too. But I love how big the sky is here."

Bea looked up at the sky and asked, "Why is the sky bigger here than in South Carolina?"

"I don't know, but I like it."

Ben gasped and pointed to a large brown bird flying above them. It was big and had a rusty-looking tail. "What kind of bird is that?"

"I don't know," Noah said, "But I think before long, Momma and Papa will have time to tell us about a lot of things around here. Come on, let's go see what's behind the house."

Bea shook her head. "An outhouse is all I saw."

"Then we'll look again."

Noah started walking around the house, and the twins followed him just as he knew they would.

Inside the house, Clay said, "I like your family. How old is Noah?"

"He's eight but always says he's nearly nine, and the twins just turned four a few weeks ago."

"Noah seems older than eight or even ten."

Silas nodded. "Maggie always says he was born a hundred years old."

Clay chuckled. "Seems about right. He's a fine young man."

"For which I am grateful. He's a good son and a great big brother."

Bea said, "I want to go back into Aurora's house."

Ben said, "It's Clay's house too."

"She lets him live there. The house is the woman's. That's how houses work."

Noah smiled and thought, someday Bea would have her own home, and some man would believe her house was his. He shook his head, not understanding much better than Bea, but he knew the mothers were the bosses in the house.

He said, "Let's go see what's inside since Momma won't let us explore much." He walked with the twins back inside the house. Noah looked around the house and said, "The only thing I think is different, other than being a little smaller, is there is no upstairs."

Silas agreed. "I think you're right, son, but it would be nice to put up an attic to help keep the cabin warm in winter and cool in summer."

Clay said, "It sounds like a good idea, but we've got other fish to fry before we build an attic here at our house."

Bea clapped her hands and asked, "Catfish?"

Maggie laughed. "Our daughter is besotted with catfish. She'd eat it every meal if we let her."

Bea nodded, her gold curls bouncing. "Catfish is the best food in the whole world."

Clay laughed. "Well, I think it will take all our time today to get your home ready for the evening."

She nodded. "Yep. You don't have an upstairs."

Aurora smiled and said, "No, but we have a bedroom over in the corner with a bed and tables. I like there's a wall there. I'll want to add a door."

"I like it," Bea said. "You don't have a door, but it looks nice. It has a big bed too. I like the way your house smells."

"Thank you, Bea. How does it smell?"

"Like outside. I like that."

Maggie smiled, watching her family with Clay and Aurora. She was happy the children took to them nearly instantaneously. She sighed and sat on one of the four stools around the small dining table.

Aurora looked at her and said, "You've done enough work for today, Maggie. You should go home and rest. Clay and I can set things right here in no time. There are just a few rugs to put down, and then we'll come and help you get things more settled."

Maggie nodded. "I am feeling a little tired." She patted her belly and said, "It's hotter than I thought it would be."

Bea said, "I'm tired too, Momma. Can we have a nap?"

Silas laughed. "That's the first time I remember Bea asking for a nap." He turned to Clay and said, "I'll take my family home and keep busy getting as much settled in as we are willing to do today."

Aurora said, "You've driven a long way, and though it feels like you should be doing a lot, the excitement of being here will wear off soon." She turned to Maggie and said, "You must go home, lie down, and rest. Everything that needs to be done today has been done. The rest can wait until tomorrow in our own good time."

"You're right. I'm feeling a little weary."

Noah said, "Don't worry, Momma. Ben and I will help Aurora with their things and will come home with them when we finish."

"Thanks, Noah. You're a good son."

He kissed her cheek and said, "Thanks, Momma."

Noah was worried. He hadn't seen his mother ever be tired in the middle of the afternoon. He thought, *I'll ask Papa about it. He'll know if Momma's okay or not.*

He took his brother's hand and said, "Let's go help Clay and Auorora so Momma can go home."

"Why?"

"She needs to rest."

"Is the baby making her tired?"

"I think so."

"When the baby is out of her belly, will she feel better?"

"I hope so. I'm sure Papa will take good care of her."

Ben nodded and said, "Yep," but he was worried, too. His father had cooked dinner once, and although it wasn't awful, it wasn't very good either. He thought *We need Momma to take care of us.* Then he had another thought—a question. *Who takes care of Momma?*

He looked at Noah and asked, "Who will take care of Momma if she gets too tired?"

"We all will, Ben."

"But I'm little."

"Then you'll do little things to help."

Ben nodded but still wasn't sure everything would be right with his mother. He thought *I'll pray tonight to be sure God is taking care of Momma.* He felt certain his mother needed to be cared for no matter who did it.

Silas, Maggie, and Bea Pennington left for their home while Noah and Ben helped spread the rugs. When they were finished, Clay looked around the bedroom and sitting area and said, "I can hardly believe our good fortune."

"I agree. We need nothing more, Clay. We are living in a castle."

Ben wasn't sure what kind of castles were this small, but he liked their house a lot. Noah had seen the homes of some of his friends in Columbia who didn't live in big houses. Some were nice enough, but others were barely livable to his mind. Clay and Aurora's house seemed very nice for two people.

Aurora said, "Jacob left us all his plates, bowls, and furniture. If I had to pick my favorite thing he left us, it would first be the bed and second the dishes."

He laughed. "I agree. I hope to never again eat out of a tin pan. I never knew how much I liked eating off a plate."

She smiled. "I love our bed, too. It's nice and soft. Sleeping on a real mattress and not on the ground has been much more comfortable."

Clay wrapped her in his arms. "I don't know how long our good fortune will last, but I plan to work hard to keep things going in this direction as long as possible."

"My heart feels we'll live here for a long time."

"Fingers crossed," he said.

She smiled. "No need to wish or cross your fingers, Clay. I'm certain we've finally found a place to live, be ourselves, and help others. I feel the house welcomes us home whenever we walk into the house."

He kissed her forehead. "It feels that way to me, too, Aurora. Now, let's go and see what else we can do to help Silas and his family. After we finish, I want to return to our lovely home and have one of your dinners."

She smiled. "I have something special planned."

"I look forward to it. I am yours to command."

"Remember that in the future."

He laughed, took Aurora's hand, and told Noah and Ben, "Let's go see what else we can do to help your Papa and Momma."

As they walked together to Maggie and Silas Pennington's home, Ben felt something very nice had happened that day. He couldn't quite figure out what it was, but he liked it.

CHAPTER TEN

"Everything you look
at can become a fairy tale and
you can get a story from
everything you touch."
Hans Christian Andersen

SILAS AND NOAH worked in the barn and henhouse for the rest of the day to settle things for their first night in their new home. Noah was excited to be working with his father, but he didn't understand all the ins and outs of taking care of the animals. It was a new experience for him—he'd never done any of the work on the farm. In South Carolina, there were hired hands to do this sort of work. He watched his father, amazed at how much he knew about taking care of the animals since he'd not done much of taking care in the barns in South Carolina.

Noah asked, "Papa, how come the cow and horses stay in the barn at night?"

"Well, son, bobcats, cougars, coyotes, foxes, and even a few black bears roam in these hills. At night, when folks don't bother them, they go hunting. We don't want the cow, horses, hens, or chicks to be eaten."

Noah nodded. "Momma said she'll teach me all about milking the cow and caring for the chicks and hens."

"She's a great teacher. Your Momma's good with a lot of farming work. She grew up on a farm and knows much more about it than I do. I might even need some reminding how to do farm things myself."

Noah grinned and shook his head. He was sure his father could do anything he set his mind to. Still, he also knew his father would welcome his mother's advice.

Once they'd fed all the livestock and settled them for the night, Noah asked his father, "When will we get the other things from the wagon?"

"You mean the rocking chair and cradle?"

Noah nodded and grinned. "It's hard to keep that big of a secret, Papa."

"For you and me both, son. How about we do this? You ask your mother where she wants her kitchen garden behind the house. While she shows you where she wants the garden, I can quickly bring the cradle and rocking chair into the house."

"I like it, Papa. She'll be surprised! Can we do it right away?"

"I think that's a grand idea. She'll want to start dinner soon, so we should probably do it now so she can have a sit down in her new rocking chair before dinner."

"I agree, Papa."

"You know what to do?"

"Yes. I'll ask Momma to show me where she wants the kitchen garden."

"Exactly. While you're doing that, I'll bring in the rocking chair and cradle. Then I'll stick my head out the back window when it's ready for her to see our surprise."

Noah grinned and nodded. He liked surprises.

When they walked into the house, Noah said, "Momma, if you show me where you want the kitchen garden to be, I can help you with that tomorrow."

"Oh, just out back behind the house."

"Will you show me?"

"Sure. Hang on a minute, and let me dry my hands."

She walked outside with her son. Silas carried the rocking chair and cradle inside the house when they were out of site. But Silas didn't work fast enough for Noah's needs, so Noah had to think up more questions to ask his mother—'What's a kitchen garden?' 'What do you plant there?' 'Does everyone have a kitchen garden?' He finally said, "I hope we don't have to eat lima beans, Momma."

She laughed. "If you get hungry enough, you might find them tasty."

He shook his head. "I'd have to be starvin' hungry—near to dyin'— to want to eat lima beans."

Maggie laughed and shook her head. Before she could say anything else, Silas looked out the back window and said, "How long does it take to figure out where to put a garden?"

Maggie smiled and told him, "It takes as long as we decide it does. What do you think, Noah? Are we finished talking about the garden?"

He looked as solemn as he could. "I suppose so. I'll let you know if I have any more questions."

She chuckled and ruffled her son's hair. "Good. I've got more work to do inside, and I could use your help."

Noah nodded and smoothed his hair back like he wanted. "Yes, ma'am."

Maggie walked into the house and, at first, didn't notice the rocking chair and cradle. The twins were grinning and pointing at her, but Maggie didn't understand the twins' antics.

Silas smiled and said, "Now, Maggie, why don't you sit down and put your feet up for a bit?"

"That's a good idea, Silas. She walked over to the sitting chairs by the fireplace and removed the canvas covers."

Bea and Ben giggled and pointed at their mother. She smiled, and when she asked, "What's got you two so tickled?" They laughed even louder.

Silas touched her arm and nodded to the front corner of the room. "I thought you might want to use that rocking chair and footrest."

Her mouth dropped open, and she turned to the front corner of the house and clapped her hands. "Silas, it's perfect."

Ben said, "There's a cradle too, Momma."

"I see that. What a great surprise."

Bea giggled. "We helped Papa. It was a secret."

Maggie walked over to the rocking chair, sat down, and put her feet on the footrest. She rocked briefly. She closed her eyes and muttered, "It was lucky Noah had a sudden interest in kitchen gardening."

He blushed. "It's what Papa came up with so we could surprise you, Momma."

"He's quite a thinker, your father."

Silas grinned. "So is Noah."

"Thanks, Papa," Noah said, beaming.

Cooking dinner in the open fireplace was much easier than cooking over a campfire. Maggie's cast iron Dutch ovens, skillets, and pans were perfect for this way of cooking. It wasn't as easy as cooking on a wood-burning stove, but it was no more challenging than she'd learned to cook in a fireplace in her mother's home.

Tonight, she made a beef stew from leftover dried beef and a few vegetables, including potatoes she'd bought or found along the way. Maggie was glad to have the fresh flour and lard she'd bought today. When she made the biscuits for tonight's meal, she added a touch of sugar—her mother's secret. She cooked a few pieces of bacon until it was crispy, then broke it up and added in the spinach Aurora had given her with a few green onions.

Everything was going very well so far—in fact, much better than she'd expected. She was content to keep working, planning, and hoping for an abundant and happy life here on Pennington Creek. The baby had kicked a few times while cooking, and she'd noticed it was a bit easier to breathe and eat over the past few days.

She was worried the baby might come early but equally worried about how big the baby would be. In her previous pregnancies, her abdomen hadn't been as large at the end of the seventh month as it was now. She sighed, patted her belly, and thought, "What will be, will be, and in its own good time."

After a long day of work, their first night on Pennington Creek was one of celebration and a feeling of belonging. Silas sat at one end of the long table, Maggie at the other. The twins sat on one side, and Noah was opposite them.

Noah said, "You were right, Momma. The house does look better, and it feels like home. I like it."

She smiled. "I think any house wants people inside, and the house will always look better if people live in it and we take care of the home."

Silas smiled, watching his children and wife talk about their home. They were taking a risk moving to Indian Territory, but his Uncle Jacob had left him not only the house and the property but ten thousand dollars in the bank in Columbia, South Carolina—a veritable fortune.

Silas was determined not to feel guilty about everything his Uncle left him. The best thing he could do to honor his uncle's legacy was to be the best man he could be with whatever resources came his way. With care, Silas knew the money he earned, added to his uncle's generosity, would last them for many years.

He wanted to get busy writing. He felt an almost itchiness in his fingers to pick up a pen and put his thoughts on paper. More importantly, he feared the stories in his head would leave him if he didn't write them down soon.

Maggie looked up and smiled. She knew her husband was thinking of how to do everything needed and how to have time and a place to write. She had ideas about that and would share those ideas tonight in their bed. For now, she was happy and contented with their home. It felt like she was living a fairy tale, but of course, she wasn't. It was hard work and the work would continue day after day. Still, it was exactly what she wanted—a place of her own—her own home—where she and her family would take care of and create their lives with love and belonging.

They had all worked hard today getting the linens, rugs, books, clothes, and furniture settled. There was much left to do, but they had done what needed to be done for the day. Their home was clean and smelled of sunshine, lavender, lemon, and bee's wax—all smells she'd loved in her mother's and mother-in-law's homes. Now, it was her turn to have a lovely home filled with love.

The baby in her belly kicked up a fuss a few times, but she felt happy with her lot in life. She loved her new home, her husband and children, and her new friends Aurora and Clay. It wasn't the first time today she felt like she had finally come home and the adventure was just beginning.

Maggie smiled at her husband at the other end of the table and said, "Silas, will you pray and give thanks for our good fortune and the food on our table?"

Silas smiled and nodded. He folded his hands and bowed his head, and he was pleased to see his children and wife follow suit. He was a lucky man and a thankful man.

CHAPTER ELEVEN

"Those who tell
the stories
rule society."
Plato

AFTER DINNER, the family cleaned the dishes and cooking pots. Maggie had transported a jug of sourdough starter from South Carolina in the wagon to their new home in Oklahoma. She spooned some starter into a bowl and added more flour, sugar, and a bit of water to make the dough. She kneaded the dough, and when it was just as she wanted it, she placed it in a small cast iron Dutch oven on stones near the fireplace. She wanted it to rise slowly overnight. She would move the Dutch oven into the fireplace in the morning to bake the bread.

When all the work necessary for the day was finished, the family sat around the table after dinner, as they'd always done in South Carolina.

Maggie sat as she darned socks for Silas and the children. It was a never-ending task but one she found relaxing. Before she married Silas, her mother had given Maggie a wooden darning egg in a large basket filled with several things she would need to set up her own home. The basket of gifts from her deceased mother was one of the things she insisted she had to bring with them to Indian Territory. Not only were they functional, but they also represented her mother's love.

Maggie found some fine woolen thread the same color as the sock and began the darning process. She wove the thread with the needle, picking up threads surrounding the hole. She created thread lines across the hole and then turned it to weave more thread through the lines of thread. She turned it once more, threading the wool through the stitches below to be sure the hole was filled, and the sock was sturdy enough for the hard work Silas demanded of himself and his clothing.

Silas watched his wife darn his sock and smiled at her grace in these simple chores—not that he could darn a sock. He loved watching Maggie use the needle and thread to create something useful. Her hands were busy all day until she finally settled for the night.

Maggie saw Silas watching her and said, "Although we've been here just one day, it feels like we have belonged here for a long time. I don't know about you, Silas, but I feel like I'm finally home, and the adventure has just begun."

"I agree, darlin'. We've ridden all those miles and are finally coming home—to our home. For tonight, though, I want no more adventure but rest and sleep."

"You are exactly right." Maggie smiled, picked up another sock, and began the darning process again. She looked at her children and said, "Children, I want to tell you all how proud of you I am."

"Why, Momma?" Bea asked.

"Everyone worked hard today and didn't fuss a bit. You did everything I asked you to do and did it very well."

Bea preened a bit and glowed from her mother's praise.

Maggie nodded to her daughter, smiled, and continued. "We are much further along in creating a home here than I expected we would be."

Silas nodded, watching his wife commend their children. "Your Momma is proud of you, and so am I. We must continue working together to make our home and lives successful."

Noah nodded. "I'll work hard, Papa."

"I know you will, son. We don't have servants caring for things like we did in South Carolina."

"Yep," Bea said. "Pops said we were going to be poor."

Silas laughed and shook his head. "I think your Grandfather—Pops—was worried about us. However, we are certainly not poor. I want all my children to continue to help your Momma whenever you can. She's carrying a baby along with everything else there is to do."

Noah nodded. "I'll help Momma—I promise, Papa." Bea and Ben both agreed they would help, too.

Bea asked, "How heavy is a baby, Momma?"

"Do you remember that big watermelon we had last summer, the kind that was so big you couldn't pick it up?"

Bea nodded.

"Well, the baby in my belly probably weighs about that much."

Bea's eyes and mouth popped wide open. "Wow!" she whispered.

Silas chuckled. "Now you know part of why your Momma is tired. Carrying a baby around is heavy, especially when moving and setting up housekeeping in a new place. That's why we all must help each other, especially your Momma."

Noah paled and nodded. His mother's explanation about how heavy the baby was inside her helped him to understand why she was tired. He was exhausted and hadn't lifted anything nearly as heavy as a watermelon today. He knew he couldn't carry that watermelon very far, even if he could manage to lift it. He asked, "What do we need to do first, Papa?"

"Well, it would be grand to whack down the grass around the house tomorrow. Do you remember how to do that with the scythe?"

"Yes, sir, I do."

Ben grinned. "I can do that, too."

Maggie shook her head, trimmed the threads on the hole she'd finished darning, and said, "No, sir. I want no blood spilled in my front yard. When you're as tall as Noah, then maybe. Besides, I need you and Bea to help me in the house."

She picked up another sock, dropped the darning egg into the sock, and continued to darn another sock.

Ben watched his mother carefully but sighed. "Okay, but I don't want to do girly things."

"Hey, now," Silas said. "The only reason I don't do the cooking and tidying is because we'd starve, and everything in the house would be a mess. My Momma taught me how to sweep and dust when I was younger than you, young man."

Maggie smiled and nodded as she wove the thread through and over the hole. "After Aurora swept the entire second floor, your Papa mopped the floors. He did an excellent job."

Silas nodded. "I don't know if you children noticed, but when we went up to the attic, I was the last one up there. Do you know why?"

The children all shook their heads. "When your Momma is carrying a baby, she is a little off-kilter occasionally. Imagine carrying that watermelon up the ladder to your bedroom without dropping it or falling. I didn't want her to fall climbing that ladder, so I made sure to be behind her to protect her and your new baby sister or brother. I expect you to help your mother when I'm not around. If anything happened to her, we'd have to eat the terrible food I make."

Maggie laughed, shook her head, trimmed the threads on the sock she'd just darned, and then picked up another sock that needed repair.

"Don't worry, Papa," Noah said. "We'll be careful and help Momma."

"Good. Now, what's next?"

"A story, Papa!" Bea said and clapped her hands.

Maggie smiled at her husband and children. Every night, he told the children another story. She was amazed he could pull a story out of thin air, open his mouth, start telling it, and mesmerize them all.

Silas nodded. "A story it is. But first, let's go sit in front of the fireplace so your Momma can put her feet up and sit in her new rocking chair."

Noah said, "I'll bring the rocking chair close to the fireplace for you, Momma."

"Thank you, Noah."

Ben said, "Bea and I can carry the footstool."

"Thank you, Ben and Bea. What fine children I have." She stifled a chuckle but smiled as she watched Ben and Bea carry the footstool and Noah struggle with the rocking chair.

Silas smiled as he watched the children ensure their mother would be comfortable for the storytelling. Soon, Maggie put her feet up, relaxed, and continued darning socks while her husband regaled them with the next new story.

Silas reached into his pocket and withdrew his well-worn pipe, its wooden stem smooth from years of use. He filled the pipe's bowl with tobacco, tamped it down, and lit it. He puffed a few times, winked at his wife, and smiled softly, looking at his children over the puffs of smoke from his pipe. He shook his head and sighed. "I thought you would be too tired for a story."

Maggie smiled, knowing he was teasing.

Noah said, "Papa, don't be mean. We've worked hard and need a story before we go to sleep."

Ben nodded. "Make it a good one, Papa. I'm tired, but I need a good story."

Bea clapped her hands and said, "Yes, please. Make it about a little girl, Papa. Let her be the bestest and smartest little girl in the whole wide world."

The boys groaned. Silas puffed on his pipe, smiled at the boys, and nodded. They understood their father meant to tell a good story, but it wouldn't be only for their sister. Silas sat his pipe on the little tray his wife had given him so his pipe wouldn't mar any surfaces.

He said, "Here's tonight's story."

Once upon a time, a long, long, long time ago, a young girl wanted to be all grown up, bigger than her brothers, and more important to everyone than any young girl had ever been. Her mother and father loved her and decided to help her. They taught her to read even before most children went to school.

When she was nearly four years old, her mother said, "I think you are the smartest girl in the world."

The girl nodded, knowing this was the truth. The girl loved her mother even more because her mother understood her daughter's brilliance.

Days, weeks, months, and years passed—a long time, you understand —at least two or three years. Every moment of every day, the little girl got smarter, wiser, and more important to everyone around her.

Noah and Ben scowled, but Bea preened, knowing her Papa understood her better than anyone else. Both Maggie and Silas smiled, watching their children's reactions. Maggie bit her lip to keep from laughing as Silas continued the story.

One bright sunny day, the most important man—for miles and miles around—came to the little girl's home and said, "My, what a lovely home. I remember when it was beginning to lose its luster and was on the way to falling down."

"Really?" the little girl asked.

The man nodded. "Yes, indeed. Your house has been here for years, and now it is glad to have people inside its walls. Your Momma and Papa and Brothers came to this house and said, 'It needs a little help.'"

The little girl nodded. "That's true, but without my help, it would still be a very sad house. Now, the house loves to show its luster, all because of me."

He raised his eyebrows. "Really?"

"Oh, yes, indeed."

"You did it all by yourself?"

"Well, no, but..."

"So it wasn't all because of you?"

"Well, sort of..."

"Sort of isn't the same as all because."

"I guess not. But I'm the smartest girl around. Everyone knows I am the smartest girl around."

"Can you prove your claim, young lady?"

"I can," she said and nodded her head vigorously.

The man looked down at the little girl and asked, "Is it going to rain tomorrow?"

She looked up at the sky and saw no clouds. She said, "I'm not certain, you understand, but it hasn't rained for many days. It doesn't smell like rain, and there are no clouds in the sky, so no—it isn't going to rain tomorrow."

He nodded. "I have two copper coins in my pocket. If it doesn't rain tomorrow, I'll give them to you."

"What if it rains?"

"Then I'll give the coins to your brothers." He stuck out his hand to the little girl and asked, "Do we have a deal? Shall we shake on it?"

She sighed and thought about it for a few minutes. Then she smiled, shook her head, and said, "No. Please give the coins to my brothers, and don't worry about the rain."

He smiled and gave her three coins: one for herself and one for each of her brothers. As it turned out, she was more intelligent than the man had thought.

The End.

Maggie put down her darning, laughed, and clapped her hands. But the three children sat in stunned silence.

Noah asked, "Is that a true story, Papa?"

"No, son. It is a made-up story."

Bea said, "But it felt true."

"Ah. You are a smart little girl, Bea. Truth can be told in stories, and lies can be told as truth."

She shook her head, not understanding. "I like true stories."

"What about truth told in stories?"

"Do I get a coin?"

"Not yet. It depends on how much work my children do to help their mother tomorrow."

Bea shook her head and sighed. "Fine. I'll work hard. I promise, Papa. I like true stories and not true stories, but I like coins too."

Maggie chuckled, watching her daughter, then said, "Those are wise words, my daughter."

CHAPTER TWELVE

CLAY AND AURORA wanted to put their house back in good order again—not that it was a mess, but things were a bit changed. They worked through the late afternoon and early evening, making their cabin feel like home again. They'd added the rugs and a few other things they'd brought from Maggie and Silas's attic storage rooms.

While Aurora started working on dinner, Clay worked on the outside of the house. He swept the porch, cleared spiders from the eaves, and used a scythe to clear a trail to the outhouse, the pond, the well, the water trough, and the cabin. He thought, *as much as I hate swinging a scythe, I hate more having rattlers come cozin' up to my house.*

It was hot, heavy work, but Spring was busy growing things faster than he could keep up with. However, summer would be here soon, and things would settle a bit with the warm weather and fewer rain showers.

For now, the scything was necessary. The last thing he wanted was a rattlesnake, copperhead, or moccasin sneaking close to their home in the high grass, so he swung the scythe. He wanted to see them coming or, better yet, going.

He muttered, "I need to talk with Silas about the snakes and help trim the grass around his house, trails, and outhouse."

Aurora had planted many herbs and flowers bordering the house, which bothered the snakes and helped keep them away. She had told him snakes didn't like marigolds, lemon grass, onions, garlic, chives, and basil—things Aurora loved to have near her home. She used them for their scent and cooking.

Mostly, the snakes stayed away from people, but they loved lying in the sun, especially when the grass was tall and they could hide. Hiding was essential for the snakes—not because they wanted to bite humans, but because they wanted to catch gophers, moles, rabbits, squirrels, mice, and rats for dinner.

Clay grinned and continued to swing the scythe. "So long as we are careful, the snakes will keep the other burrowing and nesting critters from our house—and that's a good thing." He shook his head, then said, "It's a snake-eat-critters world out there, folks."

He laughed, enjoying his self-made humor. Clay was a man much like Silas. Both liked to work hard and not take much of anything too seriously—other than family and friends.

When he finished cutting down the grass with his scythe, he smiled and looked back at their log cabin. "It's not big or fancy, but it is ours for as long as Maggie and Silas are willing to have us around. Someday, I want to have a home all our own. Fingers crossed, it will be as nice as this one. This house is more than I ever thought I'd have." And that was why he worked hard to keep it clean and polished. He was not inclined to be proud but wanted Silas to see him taking good care of his property.

Clay and Aurora had talked about keeping back every penny they earned, and hopefully, in a year or two, they'd be able to buy their cabin from Silas. Clay felt Mr. Franklin had been right when he said, ' A penny saved is a penny earned.' The old addage fit nicely in Clay's paradigm for life. He intended to be the best caretaker, neighbor, and friend—especially with the Pennington.

He smiled and said, "Whatever we cherish and save brings us all we need in life."

All of that was important to Clay, but more important was to have a place of their own that no one could turn them out of. Both he and Aurora were tired of sleeping pillar to post on someone else's meager handout.

He looked over at the large pond, which was actually a small natural lake. He watched a few fish jump after insects silly enough to get close to the water, especially in the evening when the fish were frisky and hungry. He loved everything he saw. The sun was lowering in the sky, although it would be an hour before sunset. The golden quiet filled his soul, and he rejoiced in his abundant good fortune.

He brushed a tear away and muttered, "I could love living here for the rest of my life." He looked up at the sky and said, "God, if you're anywhere near, would you please bless us and our endeavors here?"

There was no answer, but he decided to wait and see what happened next. He knew whatever happened next wasn't up to God but to himself, his wife, and their new friends.

Maggie and Silas Pennington seemed like good people who wanted and needed the help he and Aurora could provide. But, he'd learned even good people could be susceptible to the pressures of society—like the fellow at the feed and seed store. He hoped he was right in his assessment that Maggie and Silas were more honest and determined than a few others had been in Tishomingo.

"If my wife's skin color were a little lighter, there would be no problem." He shook his head and muttered, "Don't be a fool, Clay. She is glorious the way she is. Her reddish ebony skin glows, and her hair sways in ways that tug at my heart. She is a small woman but determined, and I'm the luckiest man in the world that she chose to love me."

Aurora had walked out to the porch and heard Clay talking to himself. When she listened to his last words, she couldn't hold back. She went to him and wrapped her arms around him from the back. He reached up and touched her arm. He grinned when she kissed the back of his neck. He said, "Now, darlin', we don't want to scare all the critters out here."

"I think they can handle a little cuddle."

He nodded and turned around to her. "You are right." He kissed her and asked, "What's next, darlin'?"

"Dinner and a quiet evening at home."

He smiled. "Those are the sweetest words I could hear."

"Really?" She raised her eyebrows.

"For now."

She smiled, kissed him, took his hand, and walked with him into their home. Although they'd lived there for several weeks watching over the Pennington property, their home felt bright and new today. She looked around their cabin's large, open room and felt deep in her soul this would be their home for as long as they lived. She wasn't sure how, but deep inside, she felt the truth of her feelings.

Although the cabin was smaller than the home of Silas and Maggie Pennington, it was still quite large and sturdy. Clay looked around the room and smiled. "You amaze me, Aurora."

"Why?"

"We've been here for a few months, and every day and every night have always been a blessing. We were in town so much the past few days that our home became dusty. Now, with the curtains, rugs, and a few pieces of pottery from Maggie and Silas, it truly looks like a home. It's better than any place we've lived in."

"You're right about that, Clay. I felt at home already, but with the linens, pottery, and a few rugs Maggie gave us today, it feels welcoming and is exactly where we belong. Somehow, our cabin feels larger than it did even yesterday. Come, let me show what I've done with our bedroom."

He smiled and followed her to the bedroom. It was nearly as large as the dining and sitting areas. He'd always liked the bedroom, but now it felt special. Aurora had curtains on the windows and small rugs on each side of the bed. She'd used a long, soft yellow curtain as a door covering for their room. A narrow, low cedar chest leaned against the long wall. She went to the chest and showed him all their personal belongings.

He nodded and said, "It was a beast to carry in here, so I suppose it'll stay right where it is."

"You suppose correctly."

"It's almost as good as a closet."

"Yes, it is, and I expect you to keep your side of the chest tidy."

He laughed. "I'll try, but you know tidy isn't my best suit."

She smiled, leaned against him, and whispered, "I have faith in you, Clay. But make no mistake. You make a mess of my home, and you'll sleep on the porch."

He laughed and kissed the top of her head. "I'll do my best."

"Or better if needed," Aurora responded. "I'm certain you can learn a few new habits. Now. Go wash up. Dinner will be on the table in a few minutes."

He kissed her cheek and said, "I love you, Aurora."

"Good. You should." She smiled and added, "I love you, Clay, for reasons beyond my ken."

He laughed as he left the bedroom and cabin. Then he went to the trough by the well and poured a bucket of water into the small trough. He washed his hair, face, arms, and hands and dried off with the towel Aurora had given him. He ran his fingers through his hair and let the warm breeze help dry him a bit.

He returned to the cabin as his wife put plates and flatware on the table. She had moved the table and chairs so they could sit looking out the west window. He smiled, loving the colors of the sky. He knew they could watch the evening sky change from gold to orange to red, lavender, and deep blue.

She turned and saw his smile. She said, "Since it's just the two of us, I put the table against the wall to open more space in the living area. Besides, I love watching the sunset."

"I like the changes, Aurora. I can hardly believe we have such a home."

"I know. Me too." She patted her chest with her hand and sighed. "I love everything about our place. I know we've been here several weeks, but I feel I'm finally coming home today."

He nodded, feeling the same but feared saying so—he didn't want to jinx their luck at this moment. He wanted to stay here for as long as possible—years and years.

She held out a hand, smiled, and said, "Come sit beside me, Clay. We can watch the sunset and talk while we eat."

After dinner, Clay and Aurora sat side-by-side on an old settee Jacob Pennington had left behind. Aurora had centered the settee in front of the fireplace. He smiled as he looked at the small table Aurora had created by turning a wooden crate upside down. The table was covered with a piece of calico flour sacking, and a small bowl of flowers in water sat in the middle. Beside the bowl, she'd laid his pipe, tobacco, and an ashtray.

There were two books on the table, too. One was the Bible, and the other was a book of poetry by Henry Wadsworth Longfellow. They were the only books Clay possessed, though he longed for more. His parents had left their books behind when they sailed across the ocean to America. He loved to read and had read every word in the book of poems several times. He read the Bible, but not every word. Instead, he let the begets keep on begetting and read the stories and poetry.

Aurora was knitting a sweater for Clay and hoped she would finish the sweater in a few weeks. She wanted him to have something soft and warm—a loving gift from her—during winter's long, cold days, though winter was a long way off. She said, "Clay, read to me from your poet."

Clay filled his pipe with tobacco, lit it, and picked up the book of poems. He smiled, "I'd be delighted." He turned to the first page and read, "*Pleasant it was, when woods were green, and winds were soft and low, to lie amid some sylvan scene....*"

As Clay read softly, Aurora felt the words flow into her heart. The poem spoke to her about their great good fortune in meeting Maggie and Silas Pennington. When he finished the poem, she put aside her knitting and said, "Come, let's go to our bed, Clay. We need to rejoice in our good fortune."

He smiled, closed the book, tamped the tobacco from his pipe into the tray, laid it on the table, and stood beside her. He held out a hand to his wife. "From your lips come my desire."

She smiled. "You are becoming a poet."

"Only for you."

The lovemaking on this night helped Aurora feel more settled in her home and life. As Clay softly snored beside her, she thought of Maggie and her pending birthing. *I need to verify Maggie's dates. She is much nearer to birthing than she thinks. If her dates are correct, we must discuss more rest and more time between babies. Her fatigue is too apparent for the months she has talked about.*

She sighed quietly and rolled back to back, loving the feeling of her husband beside her. She whispered to remind herself, "I need to ask Clay to go into town and get dried fruit for Maggie. She needs more iron."

As she drifted into dreams, she thought, *I wish I could have my own babies,* but she knew it wasn't possible. The brutal rape by several men when she was still a young girl—not yet a teenager—had ruined all hope of her ever having children. Still, she knew she could help other women give birth to their babies. It was a joyful path, and she welcomed it, though motherhood would never be for her.

CHAPTER THIRTEEN

H.P. Lovecraft

AURORA ASKED, "What shall I do first, Maggie?"

"First, I want you to look in the storage spaces and let me know if you find something I've missed. There may be things that might be useful here in our home or at your cabin. If there's anything you want or could use, let me know that too."

Aurora smiled. "I will, but there isn't much we need or want right now. You've given us more than I ever expected to have. You have helped us make our home feel special."

"I'm glad. Next, I'd like you and Ben to go upstairs with the bee's wax and polish the floors and chests. We also need to wash the windows."

"Good, Ben and I will start the upstairs rooms."

"That will be a relief for me. Silas said he and Clay would build beds for the children today. I want their rooms ready for the beds by the time they are finished."

"I was wondering what the lumber he'd bought was going to be used for," Aurora said. "It makes sense you couldn't haul all the beds across the country in one buckboard and have room for anything else."

"Well, Silas built beds for the children in the wagon and a bed for us, too. That lumber will be repurposed for the children's new beds and other projects."

"Waste not, want not, as the old saying goes."

Maggie nodded. "Exactly."

Aurora turned to Ben and said, "Come on, let's get started upstairs."

Ben scowled. "What about Bea? What's she going to do?"

Maggie tousled his hair and said, "Don't worry, Ben. She'll work with me."

He ran his fingers through his hair to return it as he wanted.

Maggie smiled. "I expect you to work hard with Aurora so you, Bea, and Noah can have a clean, tidy place to sleep tonight."

"I will, Momma."

"Good. I'm counting on you."

Aurora picked up a pail of water she'd brought in and handed several old rags to Ben. She turned to Maggie and said, "Don't work too hard. Give yourself a few times of sitting with your feet up."

"I will. I promise."

"Good," Aurora said and turned to Ben. "Let's get busy, Ben, before it gets too hot. The sooner we get started, the sooner we'll be finished."

He grinned and nodded.

Maggie turned to her only daughter and said, "Now, Bea. Here is a dust cloth. I want you to use that small stool to stand on and wipe all the dust off the windows down here. They aren't too dusty, but we want them to be clean so the sun can shine into our house. Be careful you don't fall."

"I'll be careful, Momma."

"Now, I've already dusted the windows in our bedroom, so just the six windows in the main room need dusting. I'm going to the well and bring in some fresh water."

Bea asked, "Why don't we have water in the house like in South Carolina? Why do we have to pee in a bowl or go to the outhouse? It's creepy."

"I know, and I agree, but Uncle Jacob didn't run any pipes to the house. For now, carrying water, using a chamber pot, and an outhouse will do just fine. I'm certain that Clay and your Papa will figure out how to have indoor plumbing soon."

While Bea sighed and started dusting, she had her own thoughts about running water, bathtubs, flush toilets, outhouses, and chamber pots. She missed having a bathroom and tub, but she especially missed running water and a flush toilet.

"I'll be back with more water in a few minutes. Now let's get to work."

"I'll do a good job, Momma."

"I know you will."

Maggie went to the well and pumped fresh water into two one-gallon galvanized buckets. She smiled as she pumped water from the well, watching the water pour into her buckets. "I'm with Bea and hope Silas can run water lines to the house soon," she chuckled to herself. "It beats boiling river and creek water on an open fire and sleeping in a wagon."

She shook her head, knowing there was much work to do and some of the finer things in life would have to wait. She looked up at the bright blue sky with a few cotton ball clouds floating by. The scissortail flycatchers were putting on a show, flitting around, swooping, and soaring. The babbling creek created a backdrop of music in her mind. She smiled. "I love this place with the running creek, clear skies, and the quiet peace of owning our land and home." She chuckled and shook her head. "Still, Bea is right. Even rudimentary plumbing would be nice."

She covered each pail with a muslin cloth and carried them into the house. She sat the buckets on the hearth, poured a little hot water and soap in a bowl, and added some of the fresh, cool water. She took the bowl and a muslin rag to the pantry.

Maggie shook her head. Although the pantry was lovely and had been well cared for, it needed cleaning. Dust and a few dead spiders and insects had accumulated over the past months since Jacob's death. She moved everything from the pantry out to the dining table. Then, she used the hot, soapy water to wipe down all the shelves in the pantry. She still couldn't reach the top shelf, though.

She returned to the main room and asked Bea, "How are you doing with the windows?"

"I'm finished, Momma."

"Good. They look brilliant, Bea. You've done a great job. Now, bring your stool to me in the pantry. I can't reach the top shelf."

Aurora was coming down the ladder from the attic and heard what Maggie said. She said, "Oh, no, you don't. A pregnant woman on a step stool is begging for trouble. You let me do those sorts of things."

"It's just out of my reach. I want to clean the top shelves and look in the large tin box on the top shelf."

"I understand. Let's see if I can get it down."

Maggie doubted Aurora could climb that high on the small step stool, but she agreed she probably shouldn't be climbing on step stools.

Bea watched and listened to the two women. She wasn't sure how to help, but she followed them into the pantry. She didn't want to miss any excitement—not that cleaning windows had been exciting.

Bea shook her head when Aurora tried to reach the top shelf. She wasn't nearly as tall as her Momma, even with a step stool. No way could Aurora reach the top shelf and the tin box.

Maggie shook her head. "I don't know how to get that box down or clean the top shelves."

Bea smiled, tugged on her mother's skirt, and said, "I know what to do. Remember, Momma, I'm a smart girl."

Maggie smiled and turned to her daughter. "Yes, you are. What is your idea, sweetie?"

Aurora watched Maggie and her daughter, pleased Maggie listened to her daughter's idea.

Bea beamed and said, "Aurora can lift me and help me climb the shelves like a ladder. I can clean the shelf and get the box for you, Momma."

"What a good idea, Bea. You are a smart girl. What do you think, Aurora?"

"I think it's a fine idea. Come on, Bea, let's boost you up to the top shelf."

Bea raced to Aurora and raised her hands. "I'm ready!"

Aurora helped her climb from one shelf to the next. When she came to the top shelf, Aurora said, "I'll have to push you from the hiney. What do you think, Bea?"

"Do it! I'm almost there."

Aurora laughed and gave Bea another long-armed but gentle push, and the little girl was on the top shelf. She grinned and asked, "Do you want the box first?"

"Yes, please," Maggie said.

She pushed the box to the front edge of the shelf, but it was hard to move because it was heavy. She told her mother, "It's really heavy, Momma."

"Hold on a moment." Aurora said, "I'm shorter by a few inches than you, Maggie, standing on the stool, but I think we can handle it. You be sure to hold the stool still while I tip-toe." Maggie nodded and held the stool while Aurora tip-toed, looked up at Bea, and said, "Very slowly and carefully push the box to the edge, Bea. When I can hold it, I'll let you know."

Bea slowly pushed the tin box, her pink tongue peeking out between her lips, moving the box one inch at a time. As the box began to go over the edge of the shelf—one slight push at a time—Bea knew it was almost there. Finally, Aurora said, "I've got it, Bea. Stay right where you are."

"I will. Don't forget to help me down."

Aurora laughed. "I won't. You wait a minute or two." Aurora handed the box to Maggie, who said, "My goodness, it is heavy."

"What's heavy?" Silas asked as he poked his head into the pantry.

Maggie smiled. "You're just in time. Would you please take this box to the table? It is rather heavy."

He shook his head and took the box from his wife. "You shouldn't be handling anything this heavy.

Bea said, "I did most of the work, and Aurora helped me."

Silas looked up to see his daughter kneeling on the top shelf of the pantry. "I hope you were careful, Bea."

"I was, and so were Momma and Aurora. Besides, they needed my help. Without me, they would never have gotten the box down."

Maggie chuckled. "That's mostly true." She looked at Bea and said, "Now, let Aurora help you back down."

"Not yet, Momma. I need to clean this shelf first. It's really dirty with dead spiders, too."

"You're right. I'd forgotten. You stay put, and I'll hand up a dirty rag and then a clean one."

"I'll make it all clean, Momma. I promise."

Maggie smiled. "I know you will." Today's adventure would be a story Bea would tell for years, and over time, the panty shelf would get higher and higher with each telling of the tale.

Silas stood by the big table with the tin box and asked Maggie, "Have you looked in here?"

"No. We were cleaning and putting things in order. That box was the last thing we had to get down. You're the first to open it."

He nodded, and as Aurora entered the room, he smiled at her and said, "I'll take this to our bedroom. I think it belongs in my study area."

When he left the room, Aurora said, "You go talk with your husband. Bea and I will finish the pantry."

Maggie nodded. "Thanks, Aurora."

Maggie followed Silas into their bedroom and saw Silas sitting on the bed with the box beside him. She asked, "What is it, Silas?"

"Money. Lots of money."

"What? Just piled in a box and left in the pantry?"

He nodded. "There's a note here from Uncle Jacob."

"Have you read it?"

"I have, but I'm not sure what to do."

"May I read it?"

"Sure. Uncle Jacob meant it for both of us." Silas handed Maggie the letter, and she read:

"January 4, 1898"

Maggie stopped reading and said, "That's only a few days before Uncle Jacob died.

"You're right. He died on January 14th of this year. Go on, Maggie, and read the rest of it.

She smiled and returned to the letter.

"Dear Silas and Margaret,

If I am dead, I hope one of you, Silas or Maggie, finds this letter and the box's contents. If someone else finds it, you won't be bothered to read about this money. Either way, it's out of my hands.

Inside the box are several hundred dollars in gold and silver coins—it may be as much as a thousand dollars—I never bothered to count the money. I do not know where it came from or why. This box and its contents came to me about twenty years ago.

One morning, when I woke and went out to feed my horse, I found the box on my porch. There was no letter or identifier. I spent a few dollars on this and that around the place—including building your house—but didn't know what else to do with it other than hang on to it. No one has ever come around to inquire about the money. The day this box appeared was April 12, 1876.

My feeling is this money is yours. All property laws in this country accept that when a property is bought, everything in and on the property belongs to the buyer. The same applies to an inheritance.

Regardless, I know you will use the money wisely. My dearest hope is that it does not burden you. However, as I have done for several years, I suggest you keep it hidden in plain sight.

With love and affection to you both,

Jacob Pennington

CHAPTER FOURTEEN

*"One must still
have chaos in oneself
to be able to give birth
to a dancing star."*
Nietzche

MAGGIE READ THE LETTER, shook her head, and sighed. She carefully folded the note and handed it back to Silas. "This is amazing, Si. What are we going to do with all this money?"

"Nothing, for now. Most of our inheritance is in the bank in Columbia, South Carolina. I'd planned to leave the money there, let it grow some interest, and only pull money out when we needed it. I brought five hundred dollars in coins for our use on the trip and to begin our lives. It will be a long time before we need to take money out of the bank, which is good."

"I agree. I remember talking about how much money to bring. This looks like much more than we brought to Indian Territory."

"It is—I'm sure. We should hide it in plain sight, as Uncle Jacob suggested."

"Do you have a place in mind?"

"How about under my desk in the foot well? I can use it as a footrest, too."

She smiled and nodded. Even when her husband was being serious and careful, he couldn't help but let his natural joy come through. "Well, my dear and rich husband, it sounds good. If it's ever stolen, I won't worry about it. For now, you prop your feet on this good fortune."

"I won't worry, but I like the idea of resting my feet on a box filled with money." Silas grinned, scratched his head, and then shook it. "Still, when no one is watching, I think I'll put most of it in bags and hide it in a safer place."

"Just be sure you remember where you've put it. Which makes me wonder—where have you put the rest of the money we brought?"

He nodded and smiled. "I should have told you already, darlin'. You need to know where the money is, at least as much as I do. When I finished tidying up the hen house, I put the extra money under one of the hen boxes after I kept a little out for our daily living." He pointed to the desk and said, "The money for our daily needs is in the upper right-hand corner drawer of Uncle Jacob's desk."

"Good. Does Noah know where the money is?"

"No. I'll show him when he's a bit older. I don't think anyone would think to raise the hen's laying box and look for money there."

She nodded and chuckled. "The chickens have the perfect guard."

He laughed, thinking of their new rooster, who was fearless, bold, and loud. He asked, "Lord Foul Feather Head?"

She nodded and shuddered a little. "He scares me."

Silas held her hand and chuckled. "He is a cantankerous old rooster, but he's doing his job and doing it well. He certainly knows when the sun is near to coming up."

"Oh, yes. His bossy crowing comes across loud and clear."

Silas grinned, nodded, then looked at his wife. "You're working too hard, darlin'. You look pale, and there's a little sweat above your lips."

She lifted her apron and wiped the sweat from her lips. She shook her head. "I'm fine, dear heart. In case you haven't noticed, it's May and already nearly hot enough to fry bacon on the stone walkway. Thank heavens it's cooler in the house."

"Maybe so, but I'm worried."

Aurora knocked on the bedroom doorframe and asked, "May I talk with you two?"

Silas stood with the tin box and pushed it under his desk's kneehole. He pulled the desk chair out and offered it to Aurora. "Sit down, Aurora." Once she was seated, he sat beside Maggie on the bed, held his wife's hand, and asked, "Did you hear what we were talking about?"

"No, sir. Only the last bit about you being worried about Maggie."

He smiled and nodded. "Please call me Silas. Sir isn't a moniker I'm particularly fond of."

"I know, and I'll try to remember."

Silas said, "In my heart and mind, we're friends working together."

"I understand."

"Now," Silas said, "I am worried. Maggie looks pale, and her belly is nearly as big as when the twins were born. They were born about five weeks early."

Aurora nodded and turned to Maggie. "I agree with Silas. It doesn't feel right. Are you sure about your dates, Maggie?"

"I think so. I keep track of my bleeding times in my journal. My mother taught me that my cycles will usually revolve around the moon, which has always been so. My menses usually come during the new moon."

"Your mother taught you well. May I look at your record?"

"Sure." Maggie started to stand up, and Silas said, "You sit right there, darlin'. I'll get it for you."

He went to the small table on Maggie's side of the bed, brought the journal to his wife, and handed it to her.

She smiled at her husband. "Thanks, Si." She lifted her Waterman fountain pen from the cover of the book. It had been a gift to her from her mother on her graduation from college with a general degree. The fountain pen was a luxurious gift for Maggie, and when she touched it, she remembered her mother, wishing not for the first time her mother was alive and with them. She tucked the pen in her apron pocket and said, "Now, let me go back a few months."

She went back to November and shook her head. She found an entry about her nausea abating and said, "This can't be right." She turned to October and read entries about being sick in the mornings. She shook her head, brushed a few tears away, and went back to September. She shook her head and sighed, then read the entry aloud, "The date is September 6, 1897, and I wrote, *I'm one week past my time, and the moon is nearly half full. If I don't start soon, I must accept I'm pregnant. Again.*"

She shook her head, closed the journal, clipped her pen to the cover, and sighed. She looked at Aurora and Silas and asked, "How could I be so wrong about the dates."

Aurora smiled and said, "You've been working hard to get here so your babe would be born in the summer in Indian Territory. You must have forgotten how far along you are."

"I've never been that silly," Maggie said tersely, lifting her chin to keep from crying, her voice a little angry.

Silas held her hand. "You've never been silly a day in your life, darlin'. Oh, perhaps you've been a little outlandish, outspoken, occasionally brash, and maybe even out of line a time or two, but never, ever silly."

Maggie couldn't help herself and chuckled. She punched his shoulder. "I've never been any of those things."

He nodded. "I agree, darlin', but this time, with all the travel, work, and leaving South Carolina, on top of your parents dying a few months earlier, I think your mind settled on summer for the baby."

Aurora nodded. "I agree, Maggie. Will you lie on the bed and let me feel your abdomen a bit?"

"Sure. Lying down sounds pretty good right now."

Silas helped her lie down and said, "I'm taking your shoes off, darlin'. Your ankles are fairly well swollen."

Aurora felt Maggie's ankles and nodded. "Silas is right, Maggie. Now, let me look in your mouth."

Maggie rolled her eyes. "I'm not a horse, you know. Besides, there's no baby in my mouth."

Aurora chuckled. "Of course, you're not a horse, nor is a baby in your mouth. I want to see your gums and tongue."

Maggie opened her mouth, and Aurora nodded. "Now I'm going to feel your abdomen. Have you felt any dropping?"

"Not yet, but the baby has been kicking a lot. Do you think it's twins again?"

"I'm not sure. I'll lift your dress a bit so I can feel skin-to-skin. Will that be all right?"

"Absolutely."

Aurora raised Maggie's dress enough to get her hands on Maggie's abdomen. Then she closed her eyes and felt her friend's abdomen. After a few minutes, she looked up and smiled. "It's just one baby, and the head is down and ready for birthing fairly soon. I'd estimate the baby is at least seven pounds now but could be as much as eight. You're close to your birthing, Maggie." She pulled Maggie's dress down and sat beside her on the bed.

She asked Maggie, "If I remember correctly, the date you wrote you was a week past your usual bleeding time—September 6th. Is that right?"

"Yes. Sadly, that was the date."

Aurora smiled. "No need to feel bad about the mistake of dates. You're here in your new home, and I'm here to help you. Let me think and do a little counting."

Silas and Maggie watched Aurora as she muttered and used her fingers to count. In a few moments, she said, "Yes, I think you're near to term. The top of your womb is near the middle part of your chest."

"So, another month?" Silas asked.

"Maybe, but maybe sooner. Maggie, have you felt pressure up against the bone in the middle of your chest?

She nodded. "It was getting pretty painful, and I was having indigestion. A week or so ago, it eased up a bit. I think the baby is lower than it was a week or two ago. But I'm still fatigued."

Aurora smiled. "Will you look in your records, Maggie, for the first part of August when you'd be bleeding?"

"Sure." She opened the journal again, and on the page labeled August 3rd, she said I wrote, "Lucky me, my bleeding was very light— just spotting—and lasted only a bit over a day."

Aurora said, "I thought that might be the case. I believe you were already pregnant then."

"But I bled."

"Sometimes women have a little spotting when they ordinarily have their usual bleeding time. This most often happens for women who've had more than one pregnancy."

"It's May 5th already, so that means I'm close to birthing?"

"Yes, I think that is what it means."

Maggie blew out a loud sigh and brushed away tears. "Well, isn't that just damned Jim Dandy?"

Silas looked stunned. He'd never known his wife to curse. Before he could say anything, Noah poked his head in the door and asked, "Is Momma all right?"

Silas stood up and said, "Yes, son, she is. I'll be out and talk with you about it all in a few minutes."

Noah looked over at the bed and saw his mother's pale face. She smiled and said, "I promise, Noah. I'm fine, and so is the baby."

He nodded. "I love you, Momma."

"And I love you, Noah. Thank you for checking up on me."

He nodded, turned, and entered what his mother called the dining room, even though it was just a part of the big open room. He sat at the table with Bea and Ben, waiting for their father to come and explain what was happening. He told the twins, "Momma says everything is fine, so I guess we'll wait and see."

Ben nodded but said nothing.

Bea said, "Her belly looks like a big old, ripe watermelon." Since their discussion yesterday about their mother's big belly, watermelon had been on Bea's mind. She wished they had some cold, sweet watermelon right now.

Her brothers chuckled, but Noah was still worried. He thought *I don't know how we'd get anything done without Momma.* In the past several weeks, he'd learned that his mother knew at least as much as his father about life and how to get by without servants bustling around. He sighed, brushed a tear from his face, and determined to be strong for his mother, brother, and sister. He trusted his father to take good care of them all. Still, he was worried.

Ben saw his brother's distress and said, "I trust Momma. She'd tell us if something was wrong."

Bea nodded. "Momma always tells the truth."

Noah smiled at the twins. "You're both right. I get a little worried that something will happen to make all this harder."

"It's hard enough for me," Bea said. "So, it won't get any harder."

"How can you know that?"

"Cause Momma says, 'the Good Lord never gives us more burdens to carry than we can handle.' I can't handle any more burdens."

Noah smiled and patted his sister's hand. He hoped the Good Lord, his sister, and his mother were right. He knew all he could do was wait.

What he knew for sure—right here and right now—was that waiting was hard.

CHAPTER FIFTEEN

"I know you're
tired, but come,
this is the way."
Rumi

SILAS KISSED HIS WIFE. "DARLIN', you are amazing, and I love you."

She smiled. "Thanks, Si. Will you talk with the children while Aurora and I talk? I'm sure they are worried about things with us here and talking away from them. They've gotten used to hearing and knowing everything happening while we traveled from South Carolina to Indian Territory."

He nodded and kissed her again. "You're right. I'll go reassure them."

"Tell them the truth, Si. I never want my children to distrust a word we say."

"I will. I promise." He kissed her cheek and whispered, "I adore you, Maggie."

She smiled and touched his cheek. "And I you, my dear heart."

As he walked past Aurora, he touched her arm. "I can't begin to tell you how glad I am that you are here."

"I'm glad to be here, too, Silas. Now go tend to your children while Maggie and I talk."

He nodded, smiled, and patted her arm. "Yes, Ma'am."

Once he left the bedroom, Aurora said, "If what I think is true, your baby will be born any day now. However, I'm worried you are anemic— low on iron."

"I thought I might be, so I bought some molasses. That was always mother's cure."

"It's a start but not enough. I know you had some spinach for dinner last evening. Do you have any fresh meat?"

"I have dried beef but no fresh meat."

"When did you last take molasses?"

"I forgot to. I haven't unpacked it yet."

"Don't worry about it. I'll take care of the rest of the unpacking. I want you to rest. I'm going to my house and bringing you a tea mixture. It's lemon balm and peppermint and tastes great with a bit of molasses. I love it, and it will be good for you to drink to help get your iron up. The molasses will help, too. I want to see if we can get you some fresh meat. I'll bring more spinach, too. For now, please stay in bed and rest for a bit. I'll be back as soon as I can."

Maggie nodded and brushed away tears. "I can't believe I made such a mistake. Even if I hadn't known about the bleeding some women have when they are pregnant, I made a big mistake."

"I understand your feelings, and I'd feel the same way, Maggie, but I don't blame you. Your mother died a few months before you and Silas decided to move west, which added to your stress. As soon as you knew of Jacob's death, you, Silas, and your children loaded up your wagon and headed west to Indian Territory. Getting here was a long, tiring journey, but you did it. You have three children to care for and a house to settle into. Be kind to yourself, especially for the next few days. I'm here to help you, not just because you and your husband pay me. I'm here to help because I am your friend."

"Thank you, Aurora. I feel the same way. I am tired and would enjoy a rest while the baby isn't kicking so much."

"Good. Try taking off all those clothes and wear only your shift. You will rest better if you are cooler."

"Good idea."

"Please have a nap. Naps will help your body revive itself before the birthing. It takes a lot of work to bring a baby into the world. You could start labor in the next few days."

Maggie chuckled. "Whew! What a whirlwind few days we've had. And you are right. I need to rest and get ready to do the work of birthing the baby. They call it labor for a reason."

Aurora smiled and patted Maggie's hand. "You are right."

While Aurora went to her cabin to bring the tea she wanted Maggie to have, Maggie undressed, pulled on her soft muslin shift, and then returned to the bed. She rolled to her left side and was quickly asleep.

Ben poked his head inside his parents' bedroom. He was worried about his mother and asked his father, "Why is Momma sleeping?"

"She's fatigued—exhausted—and the closer to the baby's birth, the more rest she needs."

"Can I go sleep with her?"

Silas smiled. "Sure, but don't disturb her. Take off your shoes to be as quiet as a mouse before you go in there."

Bea nodded. "Mice don't wear shoes, do they, Papa?"

"They most certainly do not. That's why we can't hear them sneaking around." He turned back to Ben and admonished him. "Your Momma needs to rest before the baby comes, so be quiet and ease onto the bed."

"I'll be careful, Papa."

Noah smiled, then turned to Bea. "Do you want to nap or help me prepare the garden for Momma?"

"I want to help you with the garden!" She clapped her hands. "Momma will be surprised and happy."

"Yes, she will," Noah said, "and it will happen faster if you help me."

Silas smiled at his eldest son and nodded, grateful for his son's understanding. He knew Noah was worried, but his usual calm way of dealing with things was a blessing. He took his role as the 'big brother' very seriously. Bea might slow her brother down, but keeping them busy would help them to settle and not worry about their mother.

Silas muttered, "It's hard to believe sometimes that Noah is only eight years old, but I'm grateful every day for him in our lives."

Ben lay on his mother's bed beside her and snuggled close. She wrapped an arm around him, and he laid his head on her belly. He heard not only his mother's heartbeat but the baby's too. He closed his eyes and dreamed of his new brother, who would arrive soon.

While Maggie and Ben slept, Noah, Bea, and Silas worked on getting the kitchen garden ready to dig. Silas was sure that, with the baby coming sooner than anticipated, it would be a few weeks before Maggie felt up to working in the garden, and by then, a lot of growing time would be lost. Working here with the children would help them settle and not worry too much about their mother.

When Aurora returned to Maggie and Silas's house, she worked to finish cleaning the pantry so everything could be tidy and in its place. Once the room and shelves were clean and dry, she began to put things on the shelves. She worried a bit that Maggie might want things differently, but for now, Maggie's only duty was to rest.

She'd talked with Clay about the need for fresh meat, and he went hunting. He'd seen a few rabbits in the area. Though they weren't beef, they would be better than nothing. He took his snares and told Aurora, "I'll bring you a couple of coneys home for dinner and hope that helps."

She smiled at her husband and his manner. She agreed: "You bring the rabbits—cleaned, of course—and I'll make a hearty stew for us all."

She began to cut onions, sweet potatoes, and a few carrots she had on hand. She boiled a small pot of dried kidney beans to add to the stew. They would add lots of flavor and be filled with iron. Once she finished the prep work for dinner, she went through the box of clean linens and found pretty rose calico curtains. She hung the curtains over all the windows downstairs except for the window in the pantry and Maggie and Silas's bedroom.

She arranged the furniture so that Maggie's rocking chair was close to the fireplace. She moved one of the flat-topped trunks and placed it in the sitting area. She added a pretty red clay bowl on the trunk, poured some water in the bowl, and added a few wildflowers from the yard— Indian Paintbrush, bluebells, and yellow honeysuckle brightened the room and brought with them the luscious smells of Spring.

When she finished, she looked around the large room and smiled. "Maggie's home is starting to come together—just in time to add another child to the family."

She went up the ladder and hung curtains on the windows of the children's bedrooms. She dusted the window sills and trunks. She knew the children were eager to sleep in their rooms in their own beds. Soon, there would be beds for the children. For now, they'd do just as they did last night and sleep on the floor of their very own bedrooms.

Aurora was uneasy about Lester Blunt. He and his few buddies hung around him like children following the candy man. They were not kind people, nor were they willing to accept anyone who was not white or pure native. She shook her head. "He puts up with pure natives because he has no choice. This is Chickasaw land—The Chickasaw Nation—in the heart of Indian Territory. Our Council House in Tishomingo is the seat of government in our nation."

She knew in time—hopefully, a long time—the land she stood on would all belong to the white man. She was sure, regardless of her desires, that the white people would soon take over all the land in Indian Territory and Oklahoma Territory and even the Unclaimed Lands. She knew it wasn't theirs to own, any more than the Chickasaw could own the land. The land belonged only to the Earth, but she could no more stop the land grabbing than she could turn a catfish into a donkey.

She sighed. "For now, I'll be Maggie's friend and hope for the future for all of us. I'll never give up hope."

CHAPTER SIXTEEN

*"Life itself is
the most wonderful
fairy tale."*
Hans Christian Andersen

BEN'S DREAMS deepened as he slept close beside his mother. He saw
the new baby in his mother's belly in his dream. He smiled and asked
the baby, "What's that rope for?"

"It gives me food from Momma."

"That's what Noah said, too. What about all the water you're in?
What's it for?"

"I'm not sure, but I swim around in here and stay nice and warm."

Ben felt the baby kick and asked, "So you have to kick to keep
swimming?"

"I don't know, but I like to kick."

"What do you know?"

"I know I want to be named Teddy."

"Why?"

"Our great-great-grandfather's name was Theodore Benjamin Pennington."

"I was named Benjamin."

"Yep. And I want to be Theodore, but call me Teddy."

"Like a bear?"

"No. Of course not. Like our great-great-grandfather. I want to be Theodore Owen Pennington," the baby answered. He kicked hard and turned his back to Ben, then sighed and snuggled close in his mother's womb for a nap.

With his head close to the opening, he thought he could see a tiny sliver, more like a shadow of light different from what he was used to. He knew soon the opening would widen, and he could meet Ben and Momma in person. He wanted to see everything outside of Momma. For now, he was safe, warm, and happy to be part of his mother.

Aurora came downstairs on the ladder from the second floor of the house. She knew there needed to be a staircase and not just a ladder. She wasn't sure why Jacob hadn't built a staircase in the first place. She planned to talk with Clay about it and that a staircase would be safer for the children. Standing around the large room, she wondered if Jacob had intended to build stairs but didn't get to it before he died. There was an obvious place for them against the wall. Regardless, she was sure it needed to be built.

Clay walked into the house and brought two skinned and cleaned rabbits to Aurora. "We finished building the children's beds, and I've gone on a little hunt. All around a great day, I'd say."

She smiled. "Thanks for doing this, Clay."

He kissed her cheek. "My pleasure. I also told Shirley about the dried fruit. She'll bring out more than she had this morning after the stagecoach comes through. She's hoping to get some things she'd ordered."

"Thanks for talking with her. I've already made a fruit cake with the fruit you brought this morning. Fingers crossed, we can keep Maggie healthy. "

"I know you will do your best. I'll help Silas finish digging the kitchen garden. Then we can bring the beds upstairs for the children."

"Good. I have plenty of clean linens for their beds. I've already hung curtains in their rooms and dusted their chests again. I'll make their beds as soon as we have them upstairs."

Clay wrapped an arm around Aurora and asked, "How are you doing, my love? You seem to be working very hard."

"I'm doing very well and enjoy working. However, I'm a little worried about Maggie. I love helping her, and she ensures she works at least as hard as I am. I want to take as much workload off her as possible."

"I'm glad you two get along well, and I know she appreciates all your efforts."

"I think we are beginning to be friends. I haven't had many close friends."

"You will have more as time goes on—I'm sure. There are at least as many kind folks around here as scoundrels."

She smiled and nodded. "Go get busy doing anything that needs to be done. I have more work to do."

"Yes, ma'am."

Clay kissed her, walked around the back of the house, picked up a shovel, and helped Silas and the children finish digging the kitchen garden. He said, "Silas, I'm assuming you saw the pile of manure mixed with dirty straw and leftover food behind the barn."

"Yeah, I did. It'll be grand for the kitchen and bigger gardens, which we need to prep for, too. I was a little surprised to see there was food there. I'd have thought it would attract critters."

Clay nodded. "My guess is a few dine there now and again, but as time goes on and things rot, they find other things to eat. The critters are part of making good dirt to grow things in."

Noah's mouth dropped open in shock, and he asked, "You mean we're going to put poop in the garden?"

"Yes, son, we are. It's filled with many things that help our food grow."

"If you say so, but I'm not sure I want to eat anything grown in poop."

Clay laughed. "Well, I know your Momma and Papa will ensure everything is clean before they let you eat from the garden."

Bea nodded. "Momma washes and washes and washes. She wants everything to be clean and cleaned again."

Clay laughed, but Silas grinned. "That's a good thing, Bea." He looked up and saw a small buggy coming their way. He waved, and the woman in the buggy waved back.

Clay smiled. "Mrs. Duncan is coming to visit."

Bea grinned. "She gave us an apricot the day we came to town. I hope she has more apricots."

"She's a good woman. She's always been kind to Aurora, and that counts for a lot to me."

Silas smiled and leaned his shovel against the side of the house. Clay followed suit. Bea dropped the rock she was getting ready to carry to the pile of stones by the outhouse and ran to the front of the house. She had no intention of missing out on any fun, especially if Mrs. Duncan brought a treat.

Shirley waved as she stopped her buggy in front of Silas and Maggie's front yard. Clay helped her down from the small buggy and asked, "Did you get it?"

"Yes, I did. Do you still want it to be a surprise for Aurora?"

"For the moment. I'm sure she'll be out here in a few minutes."

Shirley smiled and pointed to the doorway where Aurora stood waving. Shirley picked up a tin box and walked through the fence gate and to Aurora. "I brought you all the figs, prunes, and raisins I had, plus some apricots, too, to add to what Clay brought earlier today."

"Thank you. I'm worried about Maggie and think I'm right to be worried. She is losing iron with this pregnancy. I plan to make her another fruit cake with what you've brought. Will you be staying for dinner?"

"No, thank you, Aurora. Maybe another time, but for now, I'll be heading back to town in a few minutes. I don't like driving the buggy at night, especially alone."

Bea tugged her skirt. "You brought apricots?"

"Yes, I did."

Bea smiled. "I liked them a lot."

"They are good, but Aurora will make another fruit cake. Maybe she'll let you have a few bites."

Bea clapped her hands. "I love fruit cake."

Clay walked up to the women, and Silas followed. Shirley pointed to the sack draped over what he held in his hands. She said, "I see you found it."

"Yes, ma'am, I did, and I even have enough money to pay for it."

"Oh, no, you don't. You aren't paying even one little farthing for it."

Bea tugged on Shirley's skirt and asked, "What's a farthing?"

"A farthing is a very, very small amount of money," Clay said. He shook his head and turned back to Shirley. "Now, Shirley, I asked you to get one here, but I intended to pay for it."

"I know you did, Clay, but this isn't just for Aurora. It's for lots of women around here."

Aurora asked, "What are you two talking about?"

Clay smiled and said, "I know you've wanted one of these for a long time, and with all the birthings you help women with, I knew you could use it."

She smiled. "A birthing stool?"

"Yes, ma'am."

He sat the chair on the ground and removed the cloth from the stool. She came down the steps and threw her arms around her husband's neck. "This is the very best thing you could have bought me."

"I'm glad you like it. I know you'll use it to bring new babies into the world.

Shirley nodded, "Yes, you will." She knew that almost everyone in the area recognized Aurora's skills. When a midwife was needed, she was who they called, even though some folks slighted her the rest of the time.

Aurora grinned and sat on the low stool. It was made of oak and had a very short, scooped back that tilted back slightly. The seat was open on most of the bottom and at the front, leaving a sturdy rim to sit upon.

She pulled her feet close to the legs of the stool and pretended to bear down. Next, she tucked her feet around the front legs of the stool and did the same thing. She smiled and said, "It's perfect, Clay. Thank you."

Bea frowned and scrunched up her face. "Where's the rest of the seat?"

Everyone laughed, and Aurora said, "It's a special stool for when babies come."

Bea shook her head. "Are you sure?"

"I am."

Bea had her doubts. She was certain any baby with even the slightest lick of sense wouldn't sit on that stool. A tiny baby would fall right through. She sighed and decided to wait for the next silly thing adults would do. To her mind, they did a lot of ridiculous things.

She took Shirley's hand. "Come see the garden. Papa, Noah, and Clay helped me dig it for Momma."

Noah stood with his mouth hanging open. Silas patted his head. "Don't worry, son. I appreciate how you helped Clay and me with the garden."

"But, it was my idea to dig the garden."

"Now you have the right of it. Dream up an idea requiring lots of work and get others to sweat it all."

"But, Papa!"

Silas laughed. "I'm just teasin' you, son. Mostly."

Clay shook his head. "Well, when you two get through teasing about the garden I dug, we should follow Shirley and Bea and look at my mighty fine garden."

Silas laughed. Noah did not.

Clay grinned and followed Shirley and Bea to the back of the house.

Aurora picked up her new treasure and set it on the porch by the front door. She wanted to take it home and admire it, but she'd bring it back when Maggie's time came.

She took the two coneys into the house, chopped up the meat, and seared it with bacon grease in one of Maggie's fine cast iron skillets. She deglazed the skillet with broth from the cooking beans when the meat was fully browned. Once that was completed, she poured all the cooking food into one large Dutch oven, covered it, and set it to finish cooking in the fireplace.

She sighed and looked around Maggie's house. "I can't find another thing that needs to be done." She smiled and sat in Maggie's rocking chair, put her feet up on the footrest, and gave herself the pleasure of sitting quietly for a few minutes. The smells of the cooking stew, beeswax, and a clean home lulled her into a sweet, gentle nap.

CHAPTER SEVENTEEN

*"When love and
skill work together,
expect a masterpiece."*
John Ruskin

MAGGIE WOKE to the smell of something marvelous. She sighed and
then saw Ben in bed beside her. She smiled and touched his face. He
opened his eyes and asked, "Are you feeling better, Momma?"

"Yes, I am. How about you?"

"I feel good. I talked to Teddy in my dream."

"Who is Teddy?"

He grinned, pleased to know something his mother didn't know.
"He is the baby in your belly, Momma."

"Good to know. What else do you know?"

"He wants to be named after our great-great-grandfather, Theodore
Benjamin Pennington. That's why I'm Ben, and he wants to be called
Teddy and be named Theodore Owen Pennington. Also, he likes to kick
and is ready to come out and play."

She laughed and said, "Well, as soon as we both are ready, he'll come out for all of us to see."

"And he wants to play. Don't forget!"

"I won't forget. I love for my children to play. Now I smell something good. Why don't you find out what's cooking while I get dressed?"

Maggie walked out of the bedroom into the kitchen and saw Aurora busily preparing dinner. She smiled and said, "I was going to say you didn't have to fix our dinner, but instead, I'm going to insist you and Clay eat dinner with us."

Aurora smiled. "Thanks, Maggie. We'd be happy to join you for dinner. How are you feeling?"

"Much better. Where are the men and children?"

"They're upstairs setting up the beds and linens for the children."

Maggie looked at the ladder going upstairs, and as she turned, but before she could take a step, Aurora touched her arm and said, "Silas said to tell you in a few days you might be able to climb up the ladder, but for now, he hopes you'll leave everything to him, Clay and me."

Maggie smiled and nodded. "That's probably best, but I feel uneasy not seeing the beds where my children will sleep."

"Of course you do. I promise to go upstairs and be sure they have done a good job setting things up for your children."

"Thanks, Aurora. What would I do without you?"

"You'd make do, but you don't have to. I'm here and love helping you."

Maggie hugged her. "I worried and wondered if I would have any friends in this wild place. With you here, I don't worry about having friends. I have you, and for now, that is a monumental blessing. I will give thanks for you in my life every day."

"Thank you. I feel the same. Now, you sit in your rocking chair with your feet up while I finish dinner."

Maggie went to her rocking chair and said, "I like how you've rearranged the furniture, Aurora, and the lovely table, too."

"I'm glad. I thought you'd want to sit close to the fire and have the cradle nearby."

"It's perfect, and something smells marvelous. What are you cooking?"

Aurora smiled. "Clay brought me a couple of coneys, and so tonight, you shall have rabbit stew with sweet potatoes, onions, carrots, corn, and kidney beans."

"Makes my mouth water. I haven't had that combination of food in a stew before, but by the smell, it will be delightful."

Aurora set a slice of fruit cake on a small dish. She then filled a cup with tea and sugar and carried the afternoon treat on a small tray to Maggie. "You taste this and see what you think."

"Dessert before dinner?"

"This is just a sample. I have some thickened sweet cream for the cake after dinner. I've added some herbs to your tea to help the baby and your uterus."

Maggie took a bite and sighed. "That's the best cake I've ever eaten." Next, she sipped the tea and said, "The tea is perfect."

"Good. It's how my mother made fruit cake. I always loved it warm, but sometimes she would cut it into small chunks and dry them so we could have them for many weeks without them going bad."

"Where did you get all the fruit?"

"Clay bought what Shirley had earlier this morning, but then she brought more after Clay talked with her about my anxiety about your health. I thought then and confirmed today you are losing iron. The cake and tea are chocked full of iron, and dinner will also be."

"You are a marvel, Aurora, and I appreciate your care of me and my family."

She smiled and said, "Thank you, Maggie. Wait until you taste the stew." Aurora felt the truth of her new friend's feelings. She hoped there would be no backlash for Maggie and her family. If there were, Aurora would leave and not turn back. She wouldn't allow herself to be the cause of heartache for this family.

When Maggie finished her slice of cake and cup of tea, the children came down the ladder. Clay had created a rope handhold so the children had something to hang on to rather than simply the ladder. Even Ben and Bea climbed down without slipping.

Bea raced to her mother and said, "We have beds, Momma, and stuffed mattresses and pillows too."

"My goodness, that's great."

"Yep. And we have drawers under our beds, too."

"Lucky you."

Bea bobbed her head, her blonde curls bouncing. "Papa and Uncle Clay made them for us."

"They are very nice to build your beds for you. Did you say 'thank you?'"

"Yes, I did. Papa said we have to keep our beds tidy and our clothes in the drawers."

"Well, if Papa says so, I hope you will do as he has told you."

"I will. I promise, Momma."

Silas smiled at his wife, walked over to her, and kissed her cheek. "How are you feelin' darlin'?"

"Much better, and Aurora is intent on taking good care of me."

Clay smiled. "There's no one better to care for you." He looked at his wife and thought she had grown more beautiful by the hour. Being with kind people and helping others was exactly what he wanted for Aurora and himself. She seemed to blossom daily, being with good people.

"I agree with you, Clay. Aurora is a Godsend for me."

Aurora smiled and pointed to the door. "Ya'll go wash your hands and faces. Dinner will be on the table in a few minutes."

The children raced out the door to the well, with Clay and Silas following them. They weren't quick enough to keep the children from splashing water all over each other.

Clay shook his head. "Come winter, they won't be frolicking in the water."

Silas nodded. "For now, I'm delighted they like being here. They were used to running water, bathtubs and sinks, and flush toilets. I'm proud of them for how well they've done."

Clay asked, "Have you thought about installing modern plumbing?"

"Yes, but I've no idea how to get started on such a project."

"Well, there's a fella in town who can help us with getting you set up. He has full running water and a bathroom to boot. He's helped others bring running water into their homes. He has the honey bucket business around here."

Silas laughed, "I'll be forever grateful that isn't my occupation."

"You and me both. Still, he is a good man. One day, when you're in town, check with him. I'm sure he can get you set up."

"I will after we complete all the planting and settling in. I don't want to spend too much money, but I hope to be bringing in money soon."

"Well, you know the crops won't bring in money any time soon, especially the orchards you've thought of planting."

"I do understand. My hope is that the land will meet my family and home needs. However, that's not how I hope to earn money. I'm a writer, you know."

"I didn't know that, Silas. I guess I thought you'd always been a farmer."

Silas nodded and answered, "Oh, I can do a bit of easy farming, like milking the cow, gathering eggs, and tending fruit trees and vegetable gardens. Beyond that, I'm fairly useless except with my pen."

"I don't believe that for a minute. Still, there are things I can do for you and with you that you could not do yourself—at least not easily. It's the big part of why I'm here."

"I appreciate it a lot, Clay. I depend on your services as I gradually get back to writing."

Clay smiled and nodded. "I'm your man." He was glad to have a friend like Silas Pennington, but he appreciated even more that helping his new friend helped himself and his wife.

Dinner was a feast, and Maggie said, "I loved every bite, Aurora."

"I'm glad. The stew was how my mother made it. Sometimes, she used different ingredients, but always with plenty of butter and onions. When edible mushrooms were available, she'd toss those in as well."

"What's a mushroom?" Bea asked.

"It's a small fungus that grows in the forests. Sometimes, you might see them form a fairy ring, but you must be careful. Some of them are very poisonous."

Noah stopped eating and looked at his plate, not at all sure he was willing to eat another bite. "Do you know which ones are safe to eat?"

"I think so. I haven't died yet."

Silas laughed. "Okay, then. Perhaps we won't be eating mushrooms."

Aurora grinned and shook her head. "I would not go that far, Silas. I highly prize mushrooms for eating. However, I only harvest the ones I know for sure are safe. I'll never feed you poison mushrooms. If I'm not certain, I don't harvest."

"Seems like a sound way to go."

"You're right, Silas, but please leave the mushroom harvesting to me for now, and we'll all live long, healthy, and happy lives."

Silas nodded. "Our South Carolina gardener sometimes brought mushrooms for us to eat. No one died, so I suppose he knew what he was doing."

"Did you like them?"

"Yes, I did. Very much."

Aurora smiled. "Good. Then, as time goes on and I find safe mushrooms, I'll teach you and the children about them."

Silas asked, "Do you sometimes make a mistake?"

"About mushrooms—never. But that's mainly because I am a cautious woman about the wild plants around us. Many are safe, but just as many can be lethal."

"What's lethal?" Bea asked.

"Something that steals your life."

Bea's eyes got big, and she paled a little. "I like my life."

"And I like mine and yours, too. So let me help with any wild food."

Bea nodded. "I will. I promise."

Maggie smiled and decided to change the subject. She looked at

Aurora and asked, "Do you know how our creek became known as Pennington Creek?"

Aurora smiled. "I do, and my people are part of the story. In fact, the Chickasaw are integral to the story."

Noah nodded. "Now, that's the story I want to hear. I asked Papa, but he didn't know."

Silas nodded and grinned. "I try to know as much as possible, but I don't know everything. I'd love to hear the story, Aurora."

Aurora said, "Good. Let's clear the table and wash the dishes. When we've finished, I'll tell it to you."

Bea asked, "Can we have more cake while you tell us the story?"

Aurora looked up to Maggie, who smiled, nodded, and said, "I think that's a fine idea, Bea. I'm rather partial to Aurora's fruit cake."

Silas chuckled. "Fruit cake it is, then. For now, my dear wife, I want to see you back in the rocking chair with your feet up. Clay, the children, and I will help Aurora clean things up. Then it's story time."

"And cake time, too, Papa," Bea said.

He grinned. "Absolutely, we'll have cake."

Maggie chuckled, thinking about Marie Antoinette saying, "Let them eat cake," and smiled. She went to sit in her new rocking chair and thought *we would not be losing our heads tonight, but eating cake and listening to a story felt like the perfect ending to a grand day.*

With her feet up, rocking gently in her chair, she touched her abdomen and whispered to Teddy, "I'm ready whenever you are, dear Teddy." She looked up to see Silas watching her, and he smiled. She nodded and smiled back at her husband. She sighed and thought *I love everything in my life at this moment. I'd never imagined sitting rocking and watching Silas and the children help clean up from dinner. I'd never imagined living in a marvelous house like this one. I'd never imagined looking forward to labor, either. I wonder if that is because of Aurora or because I'm beginning to settle into my way of being.*

She smiled and shrugged. *It doesn't matter. It's glorious, and I'm home. I've come home to Pennington Creek and am eager to hear how it became a creek with our name.*

CHAPTER EIGHTEEN

*"Let us accept
the truth, even when
it surprises us and
alters our views."*
George Sand

Aurora said, "Before your creek was called Pennington Creek, and before the town was called Tishomingo, my people settled here. We didn't name the creek right away—the naming came later. We called our settlement Good Spring because of the crystal clear and sweet water that flowed and bubbled, causing the creek to be.

"For now, you want to know how the creek got its name. It is all because of a man the Chickasaw honored, Alonzo Pennington. I'll tell you the story the way I heard it from my mother, and she heard it from her mother before that. It was long before either my mother or myself were born."

When everyone was quiet and settled, she began with a whisper of blowing as a light breeze and a soft hum. The children, as well as the

117

adults, listened closely. She hummed again and then asked them in a whisper:

Did you hear that?

The fiddle?

Did you hear the fiddle?

They all shook their heads. She smiled and continued:

Ah, I can see by your faces you did not hear the fiddle music, but I'm sure your heart wishes you had listened to the fiddle of Alonzo Pennington.

Many, many years ago, everyone around here heard his fiddle, but only for a short time. Even now, sometimes when you are very, very quiet, you can hear his fiddle and his lovely singing. He used to play his fiddle and sing along for our people.

Sometimes, we would teach him our songs and stories, and he would pick up his fiddle and sing them back to us. He was a very kind and generous man with his fiddle and voice. Because he sang our songs as well as his own, we loved him and protected him.

Then, one sad day, when we were listening to his fiddle music and brilliant singing, things changed for us all—for all time.

A Texas Posse—white lawmen, you understand—showed up one day. They came riding in on their great big horses, thundering their hooves and shaking the very ground on which we dwelt.

We were terrified and didn't know what to expect. One of the lawmen slid from his horse to stand proudly in front of us, his chest pushed out and his white hat perched on his head. He asked, "Where is Alonzo Pennington?"

Now, we were and are people who never lied. But then and even now, we wanted to protect our friends. Before any of our people could speak, the lawman said, "Come on, now. We heard his fiddle. We heard his voice singing. We know you harbor this vile man in your house."

One of our elders stepped forward and said, "We know of whom you speak, and for us, he is not vile. He is a man with a big heart, a strong voice, and fingers that dance on his fiddle. We love him as a brother and would not betray him."

The lawman talked to our elders for a bit and finally said, "I understand a lot of folks like him, even back in Kentucky. However, when he was last in Kentucky, Alonzo Pennington killed a man in cold blood. The man's family and the law demand Alonzo face trial for his misdeeds in Kentucky."

The elder nodded. "We do not allow anyone to take another human's life. It is our law as it is yours."

"Good. I see you understand what you must do."

The elder shook his head. "What is it you think we must do?"

"You must give him over to the law so we can take him to Kentucky. He must atone for his misdeeds. A life for a life."

The elder sighed. "I know it must seem so to you, but in our community, we would never take a life unless absolutely needed. This man Alonzo Pennington was supposed to have killed—who was he, and why would anyone kill this man?"

"Well, now, the story is Alonzo, and this man had a deal for Alonzo to take over his farm. They argued, and Alonzo hit the other man on the head with a big stick. The man died on the spot. Alonzo couldn't bring him back to life, so a friend of both men helped Alonzo hide the dead man in a nearby cave. After that, Alonzo Pennington got on his horse and headed west. We believe he is here with you."

The elder nodded. "If what you say is true, will you give him a fair trial?"

"That would be my expectation," the lawman said. "We are here to bring him back to Kentucky and face the law there. He will be tried for murder."

"Can you give your word he will have a fair trial?" insisted our elder again, but before the lawman could answer, Alonzo Pennington stepped out of the council house and said, "I will surrender if you will not harm my friends."

The lawman agreed.

Alonzo was tied to a horse—with his fiddle in his hands—and led away from our people's company. We learned he was found guilty of his misdeeds and was hanged. We also learned that while waiting for his death, he played his fiddle and sang a merry tune.

When the night is fair, and the moon is high, many still hear his fiddle playing and his voice singing joyfully.

Everyone applauded.

Noah said, "I wish he had not killed anyone."

"I do, too," Aurora said. "It is a great sadness. But if he had not and hadn't become famous around here, our creek would have another name. Our creek is named Pennington, so we always remember him, his friendship, his music, and his singing. We also remember that we must never harm another human being."

Silas smiled. "I'm glad we know the story. Is it true?"

"I believe so. It is the story my mother told me and her mother told her."

"When was this?"

"I think about 1845. So it would have been more than fifty years ago."

Maggie smiled and nodded. "What a story. Did Jacob Pennington know the story?"

"Yes, he did. He knew both my mother and grandmother and many of our people. Jacob Pennington was a white man but he was also a kind and generous man. My mother said Jacob was pleased to live on a creek with his name but sad about its beginning."

Silas nodded. "I've heard variations of stories about Alonzo Pennington from the South Carolina family, but I've never known this part of the story. He was said to have sung and fiddled while waiting for his execution, but I never understood all the whys and wherefores."

Maggie smiled. "Well, that's enough of what we need to know now. Besides, the sun is down, and it's time for children to be in bed."

Silas nodded. "I'll take care of tucking in the children, Maggie, until you have less to haul around."

She smiled. "Thanks, love." She stood and hugged Aurora. "Thank you for everything you've done today. The food was marvelous, and I will love eating your cake to help boost my iron needs. It will be my excuse for eating cake for the rest of my life."

Silas laughed, as did Clay.

Bea clapped her hands and said, "I need iron too!"

Aurora smiled. "Yes, you do, Bea. We all need it." She turned back to Maggie and said, "I'll be here early tomorrow morning to fix breakfast unless you need me sooner. Please, let me help as much as possible for these few days. Someday, maybe I'll need your help. It's what friends do."

"Yes, it is, and I am grateful you'll be here to help me."

They waved goodbye, and Silas took the children upstairs to their beds. Maggie sat back in her rocking chair and put her feet up. She rocked slowly until Silas returned from tucking in the children and returned to the main room. Maggie said, "I'm ready for Teddy to be born."

"Teddy?"

"Yes. Ben talked with the baby in his dreams. The baby wants to be named Theodore Owen Pennington but called Teddy."

"Okay. I'll try to believe Ben's dream, but I won't be sure until the child is born. Wasn't Owen your grandfather's name?"

"Yes, it was."

"I like it. I have one more thing to bring into the house."

"What?"

He grinned and shook his head. "It's a surprise for the moment. I'll be right back."

"What is it?"

"Something I've been working on the past couple of days. I think you'll like it."

While he left to bring in another surprise for Maggie, she went to their bedroom, shed her dress and undergarments, and pulled her muslin gown over her head. Just as she was beginning to worry about Silas, he came in carrying a chair with arms. When he set the chair down against the bedroom wall, he turned and said, "I know it is a struggle to squat in the middle of the night over a chamber pot if you need to go. This is an idea Clay and I came up with. I know it's neither unique nor pretty, but I'd never thought of this before Clay came along and suggested it."

He stepped aside, and Maggie laughed, then clapped her hands. "Si, it's perfect. Get the chamber pot from under the bed. I want to try it out."

He grinned, pulled out the clean chamber pot, and handed it to her. She slid the chamber pot under the seat and nodded. "I feel like royalty having my very own commode chair."

"Well, you aren't the only one. I made one for the children, too. We took two old wobbly chairs from the upstairs storage room and fashioned the shelf for the pot. We shortened the one for the children. Clay and I carried it upstairs while you were napping, and I taught the children how to use it. They'll have to have a taller one as they grow, but I didn't like them going outside alone at night."

She kissed him and said, "What a terrific husband and father you are, Silas."

"I aim to please."

"And you succeeded in fine fashion. Now I'm ready to lie down and get some more rest."

"Good. I want you to rest as much as possible until you have to start labor."

"Somehow, I'm not dreading it as I have before. I think it is because of Aurora and her way of being with me."

"I'm glad. I like her a lot and Clay, too. They are everything Uncle Jacob said they would be." He pointed to the bed, "Now to bed, to sleep, perchance to dream."

Maggie chuckled. "Ah, a true bard comes to my bed."

"With love and joy," he responded.

They both slept soundly, but Teddy was beginning to be eager. He hoped he'd be out in his Mother's arms soon. He kept his head close down near her legs, and occasionally, he'd kick and push a little, hoping to come out soon.

Maggie felt a nudge now and again, but not enough to awaken her.

CHAPTER NINETEEN

"*Motherhood: all love
begins and ends there.*"
Robert Browning

MAGGIE WOKE LATER than usual with the sun streaming through
their bedroom window. She smiled, seeing Silas sleeping soundly with a
slight smile on his face. She loved that he almost always smiled when he
slept. Her heart was filled with the love of the man beside her. She
watched for a few more moments, enjoying the blessing of their love.

Then she felt a deep twinge in her pelvis. She sighed and hoped
today would be the day. She was ready for her baby to be born.

She left the bed and walked around it as quietly as possible to avoid
waking Silas. Her back was hurting, and she thought perhaps it was a
sign Teddy would come today. She decided to walk around a bit more to
help ease the pain. She smiled to see the commode chair in the corner of
their bedroom.

She walked over to the commode, gathered her gown hem, and sat
on the chair. It was a tremendous relief to empty her bladder without

squatting. Just as she finished urinating, she felt a deep cramp, and her water broke and overfilled the chamber pot.

She groaned, and Silas woke. Then she cried.

When Silas started toward her, she held up a hand. "Be careful, Si. I've made a terrible mess."

He nodded and smiled. "I can see that, darlin', but it's just a mess. I am grateful that you didn't do this in our bed. Thanks for that."

She nodded and laughed a little. "You're welcome. I need a little help, Si."

"Of course you do, and I'm here to help you. Let me help you to the desk chair. Then I'll clean this up and get Aurora in here."

He laid a small old blanket on the chair and helped her sit in it. Once he had helped her into the chair, he asked, "Are you having any contractions?"

"Just the one that came when my water broke."

"Good. He took his pocket watch from his bedside table and handed it to her. "You can time the contractions while I get this cleaned up and get Aurora."

A knock sounded on their bedroom door. Silas opened the door to see Aurora standing there. He said, "My heavens, but you are a grand sight! You've arrived at exactly the time we needed you."

She looked to the corner, smiled, and said, "Let me take care of Maggie while you clean up the corner."

"Thanks, then I'll wake up the children."

"They're already awake and eating their oatmeal. You two slept a little longer than usual. When I heard your voices, I decided to see if Maggie needed me."

Silas nodded. "I'm sure we needed the rest—especially Maggie did. But, right now, you have the right of things. Maggie needs you. I'll clean up the overflow in the corner while you care for Maggie."

Aurora smiled and went to Maggie. "How are you feeling?"

"Good, but embarrassed by the mess."

"No need to be embarrassed. Besides, it does a man good to clean up a mess now and again, especially when birthing is going on."

Silas chuckled and carried the soaked linens out to the front yard. The children all sat at the table with their mouths hanging open. As he passed them, he said, "Nothing to worry about. Momma made a bit of a mess while on the commode chair."

He dumped the wet linens on the ground by the well. Then he went to the barn, took the large galvanized wash tub from the wall, and carried it to the well. He pumped water into the tub, and once it was full, he deposited the wet linens into the water.

Clay walked over, scratched his head, and asked, "So you're going to do the laundry?"

Silas chuckled and shook his head. "What I know about doing the laundry would barely fill my wife's thimble."

Clay laughed. "Well, I know a bit more than you. I'll happily help you. What's going on?"

"Maggie's water broke while sitting on the commode chair."

"And the chamber pot wasn't up to the task, right?"

"Exactly so."

Noah walked outside to his father and Clay. He said, "Clay, Aurora told me to ask you to bring her birthing bag and the stool." He grinned and looked at his father. "She also said once Momma's settled a bit, she'd tell you how to clean the linens."

Clay nodded. "Thank heavens for Aurora, and thank you, Noah. I'll be back in a jiffy with her midwife bag and birthing stool."

Silas put his arm over Noah's shoulder. "Don't worry, son. Between Aurora, your Momma, and Teddy, things will be fine."

"Teddy?"

"So Ben says. He told your mother the baby was a boy and wanted to be called Teddy."

Noah shrugged his shoulders and then shuddered. He asked, "Is it scary for Momma and Teddy? I want them both to be okay."

Silas bit his lip but couldn't stop the lone tear trickling down his face. "Me too, son. Me too. I think Aurora will make sure they both are safe."

Aurora handed Maggie a cup of tea and said, "This is a mixture of red raspberry leaf, camomille, and lemon balm. It will help your uterus stay strong and make your labor easier."

"Thank you, Aurora. I was given a similar tea with my previous pregnancies."

"Have you had more contractions?"

"No, just the one when my water broke."

"Good. Birthing is a few hours away. How about some fruit cake and bacon?"

"Sounds great. How are the children?"

"They are fine, but I think they'd feel better if they could see you and that you are doing well."

"Then let me come out and sit with them for a few minutes. I feel fine."

Maggie sat at the dining room table, sipping her tea, and said, "I think our baby will come out to greet us today, children."

Bea asked, "Where will the baby come out?"

"There's a special place between my legs where he or she will come out."

Ben shook his head. "No. The baby is a boy, Momma. He wants to be called Teddy."

She smiled and nodded. Ben looked so earnest she couldn't speak of the possibility that the baby might be a girl. Instead, she said, "Thanks for reminding me, Ben. Now, today is a day to celebrate. Aurora says there is more cake."

Noah's mouth dropped open, and he asked, "We get to eat cake for breakfast?"

"You've had your oatmeal and milk, haven't you?"

"Yes, Momma."

"Then I think today is exactly the right time to have cake for dessert after breakfast."

Bea clapped her hands. "We should have a baby every day!"

Maggie grinned and shook her head. "I think not, Bea." Maggie was ready for some relief from birthing, but her job today was to birth her next son.

After Maggie finished her cake and had another cup of tea, she said, "I'm a little tired, children. I want to lie down for a bit."

Ben asked, "When you wake, will the baby be here?"

"I doubt it. He and I have work to do so he can be born."

Noah asked, "Will it hurt you a lot, Momma?"

She touched his cheek and said, "A little, but not a lot. Aurora is going to help me with it all."

"What can I do to help?"

"It would be marvelous if you, Ben, and Bea went outside and worked with your father and Clay. I'm sure there is work needed for the kitchen garden."

He nodded. "We will, Momma. Aurora brought a lot more plants for the garden, and we're digging a garden in front of the porch with more flowers and herbs, too."

"I appreciate all you're doing, Noah. I knew I could count on you." She bit her lip to keep from groaning and upsetting the children.

Aurora said, "Come on, children. Outside you go!"

Noah looked over his shoulder at his mother. She nodded and turned to go to her bedroom—slowly and carefully walking through the labor pain.

Before Aurora could shut the door, Noah said, "Please take good care of our Momma. We need her and love her."

"I'll take very special care of her, Noah. She is my best friend, and I love her too."

He nodded and hugged Aurora around her waist. She returned the hug and then said, "Go on, Noah. Your Momma and I will be fine. You help your father with your brother and sister."

"I will."

CHAPTER TWENTY

*"Long ago, you
were a dream in you
mother's sleep, and then
she awoke to give you birth."*
Kahlil Gibran

Aurora laid a thick oilcloth on the bed to protect the mattress. She then added old soft blankets from the attic storage for Maggie to rest on. She laid another oilcloth under the birthing chair to protect the polished oak floor.

"How are you feeling, Maggie?"

"Tired mostly. How close are the contractions now?"

"About seven minutes apart."

Maggie nodded as another contraction started. She rolled over and pulled her knees close to her abdomen. Aurora reminded Maggie, "Take care not to push."

Maggie nodded.

And so the day went for a few more hours. Gradually, the contractions became closer and closer, and the final work of birthing a baby was coming nearer and nearer.

When another contraction started, Maggie grunted and asked, "Can I push now?"

Aurora lifted her friend's gown and said, "Let me look." She looked and couldn't see the head yet, but the vaginal opening was clearly more prominent. She said, "Don't push yet. I'll check with the next contraction. Do you understand what that means?"

Maggie nodded and sighed. "You check with your fingers to be sure the way is clear."

"Yes. Your contractions are about two minutes apart. Now, have a sip of the tea. We don't want you dehydrated."

Maggie nodded, raised a bit, sipped, handed the cup to Aurora, and said, "Here's another one."

Aurora set the teacup on the bedside table and said, "Lie on your back, Maggie, and let me check."

Maggie did, and Aurora checked the opening. She smiled and said, "Let's get you on the birthing chair, Maggie."

"Yes, please. I'm ready for some real pushing."

"I agree, but it will be easier in the chair."

Aurora helped Maggie out of the bed and onto the birthing chair. She said, "With the next contraction, give us a bit of a push. Not a hard one. Controlled pushing is safer for you and the baby."

Maggie nodded.

Aurora said, "Baby's coming, but not just yet." She felt with her fingers and said, "He's nearly here. Relax, take a deep breath. Slowly let the breath go and think of a flower opening."

Maggie closed her eyes, nodded, and took a deep breath, following Aurora's instructions. By the end of the third breath, she whispered, "Now."

Aurora smiled as Maggie pushed through the contraction. When the contraction finished, she said, "Perfect, Maggie. His head is nearly there. Relax and breathe again. Remember the flower opening."

She reached for the clean towels she would use to deliver the baby. The top of the baby's head was visible when the next contraction started. She murmured, "Easy, Maggie. I'll help you a bit. You can push but steady and easy."

Maggie nodded and did as instructed while Aurora gently massaged the vaginal opening with her fingers helping to stretch the opening without tearing. At the end of the contraction, Aurora said, "Do the breathing again, Maggie. He's almost here. He has curly hair, I know for sure, but not what color yet."

Maggie smiled and worked on breathing, but another contraction started before she'd taken a second breath. She pushed, holding onto the handles on the birthing chair, and braced the heels of her feet as close to her body as possible.

Aurora nodded and said, "Good work, Maggie. His head is out. Gentle now. Breathe and think of the flower. For the next contraction, I'll help his shoulder, so just a gentle push."

Maggie nodded but said nothing. The next contraction came, and she started to push. Aurora reminded her, "Gentle little push for his shoulder, and quickly Aurora was able to release his shoulder as the other shoulder appeared, and suddenly he was in her hands. She smiled and said, "He's lovely, Maggie."

"He's not crying."

"Hang on—he will. I'll clear his mouth." Sweeping the baby's mouth clear with her finger, Aurora cleared the mucous and blood from his mouth, then turned his body face down and rubbed his back. He wiggled and bellowed a lusty cry.

She wrapped him in a dry, soft towel and handed him to Maggie. "It's okay to show him your breast, and let's see if he's hungry yet."

The bedroom door opened, and Silas slipped in. "I can't wait a moment longer."

Maggie smiled, reached a hand to him, and said, "Come, my love, and meet our dear sweet Teddy."

Aurora went about the business of letting the placenta come out. She turned the placenta over to be sure it was intact. When she was confident the placenta was whole, she tied two cotton strings to Teddy's umbilical cord about an inch apart. She said, "Silas, here is a clean knife. Would you like to cut the cord?"

"Will it hurt him?"

"Not if you don't poke him anywhere other than the cord." She shook her head and chuckled.

Silas grinned, nodded, and took the knife.

Aurora said, "Cut here between the knots. I'll hold the cord steady for you."

Silas nodded, cut the cord, returned the knife to Aurora, and wept. Aurora smiled, knowing most fathers didn't get to participate in such an essential step of birthing. Maggie reached out to him and brushed her fingers on his cheek. "Thank you, my love, for everything."

He nodded but couldn't speak.

She smiled and asked, "Would you like to hold Teddy while Aurora and I get me cleaned up and in bed?"

He pulled his desk chair over to sit beside his wife and took his son in his arms for the first time. He brushed away his tears, smiled, and said, "Well, Teddy, aren't you grand? I see you have my curly blonde hair. Now, let's talk about who's in charge around here."

Maggie laughed. "Be sure you tell the truth, Silas."

"Of course, darlin'. You're the head honcho—mostly."

Aurora chuckled as she cleaned the birthing debris and massaged Maggie's abdomen. When she was confident the uterus was firm again, she piled all the clothes, afterbirth, and towels into the tub beside her. She said, "I'm going to get some warm water to finish cleaning you up, Maggie. You two behave and don't drop the baby."

Silas and Maggie laughed, enthralled with their newest child.

When Aurora stepped out of the bedroom, the children eagerly gathered around her. They wanted to see their mother and new brother. She said, "I promise everything is fine, but I need to help your Momma a little bit more. Then I'll invite you in to greet your brother and see that your Momma is doing very well."

Putting her elbows on the table, Bea sighed, put her chin into her cupped hands, rolled her eyes, and moaned, "More waiting."

Aurora smiled. "A tiny bit of waiting, sweetie. I promise."

Noah was pale and asked, "Is Momma okay?"

"Yes, she is. I promise she is doing fine and is fit as a fiddle."

Ben asked, "Alonzo's fiddle?"

She chuckled. "No. I meant your Momma is doing very well."

Ben nodded, and Noah said, "Good. We love her and don't want to eat what Papa cooks."

Aurora couldn't help but laugh loudly. "Well, he probably would do in a pinch. Now that I'm here, I can be sure you are well-fed."

Noah touched her hand and said, "We love you too."

Aurora bit back tears and hugged the little boy. "I love you and Bea and Ben and your Momma and Papa. Now, let me get more warm water, and I'll finish caring for your Momma."

Noah nodded, but what he needed was to see his mother. He knew she was strong but also knew that birthing could be hard. He remembered a time during calving last year at his Papa's barn. The calf was born, and the momma licked him clean, let him suck a bit, and then she laid down and died. Noah would never forget that day. Moreover, he was terrified the same thing would happen to his mother.

Aurora watched Noah's face and thought, *Before we know it, he will be all grown up and helping other people.* She had a flash of him helping sick people and wondered if he would be a physician. Then, another flash of him building beautiful things came into her mind.

She smiled to herself. *There's plenty of time for him to decide his path. Regardless, Clay and I will be there for him and all his family.*

Clay had been standing near the door watching his wife with the children and struggled not to sigh or cry. Both he and Aurora longed for children. But he didn't want a child for only himself. Although he longed to be a father, he dearly wanted a baby for Aurora. She couldn't bear a child, but he knew in his heart she would have made a marvelous mother. He sighed and thought, *If I could give you a baby, Aurora, I would.*

Aurora looked over to her husband, smiled, and nodded. He smiled back, feeling the grace and love of her smile. He nodded, then turned to go back outdoors and to the small barn.

Aurora watched him leave, knowing he was feeling melancholy. He loved children but would never have a child as long as he was married to her. Being present at the birthing of a new baby, and one he would see daily, she felt, made it even more difficult for him. For herself, every baby she helped into the world was a blessing, and she felt every baby was a part of her soul.

Clay walked to the small barn and brushed away tears as he entered. He picked up the hay rake and started raking the hay on the floor, getting it ready for Patches, the cow, to come in for the evening.

He smiled, thinking of the day Silas's children named her. There was quite a debate, and Clay and Silas tossed out several names. The children were insistent, though, because she had a white patch on her brown rump that looked like it had been darned like their mother did their socks—they insisted the cow needed a darned patch name. The names socks, yarn, needle, and thread were thrown out, but no one liked the possibilities.

When Noah said, "How about 'Darned'?"

Silas had said, "There's no way your momma will put up with that name. It's a little too close to cursing or swearing."

Noah frowned and nodded.

Ben had said, "I think we should call her Patches," and quickly, they all agreed. Patches became her name. If she were in a good mood or hungry, she would even respond to her name, mooing and nodding her head.

Clay loved the children and even the cow, not because they were important to him but because they filled corners of his heart that desperately needed filling and healing. He sighed and whispered, "Aurora needs them, too."

Patches came up behind him and shoved him a little with her head. He turned around and hugged her and wept for joy and sorrow. The cow allowed the hug and tears for a few minutes, then shook her head. Clay chuckled and wiped his face with his bandana handkerchief. "You're right, Patches. It's time to quit cryin' and get busy filling your hay basket. We have some nice alfalfa on the menu. You're gonna love it."

She mooed and nodded her head. When Clay had filled her hay basket, she nudged him out of the way and went into her stall to eat the fresh hay. Clay smiled and said, "I'll return shortly to milk you. Thanks for the hugs, Patches."

She looked at him, seeming to scowl, and Clay smiled. "Don't roll your eyes at me, girly. Remember, I'm the one that feeds and milks you more often than not."

She ignored him and went back to her hay.

Clay turned and walked out of the barn and down to the creek. He tossed a few rocks, trying to skip them like his father had. His father could skip a stone four to five times. Clay never got the hang of it, though. Just as he was about to give up, he picked up one small, flattish rock and gave it a toss.

He grinned and yelped. "There now. Two skips. It's not much, but it skipped."

He didn't see the cottonmouth hiding in the grass by the creek several feet away. She wasn't hungry and didn't feel threatened, so she ignored the man. She'd just finished swallowing a small, large-mouthed bass and stayed still until the human walked away from the creek.

Clay was too proud of his rock-skipping skills to bother looking at the ground. Lucky for him, the snake was more sluggish than usual, digesting her dinner. She would birth her babies in a couple of months, and then being near her and her nest would be dangerous for any of the humans.

Birthing is a serious business, whether humans or snakes.

CHAPTER TWENTY-ONE

*"The family is
one of nature's
masterpieces."*
George Santayana

ONCE MAGGIE and the baby were clean and settled, Aurora left Silas and Maggie's bedroom and told the children, "Your Momma and Papa want you to join them and meet Teddy."

Noah smiled and hugged her. "Thank you, Aurora."

She returned the hug from the little boy, who seemed to be years older than eight years old, especially today. "It was my pleasure, Noah." She held the door open for them, and after they were all settled, she walked outside to find Clay. He was in the barn, finishing milking Patches and feeding her and the chickens. He smiled when he saw her coming to him.

"How did it go?"

"Very well."

"Did the chair work the way you thought it would?"

"Absolutely. It was perfect and made the delivery easier for Maggie and me."

"Good. I'm relieved. I know a lot of babies and their Mommas will use the chair."

"Yes, they will. You could never have given me anything that meant more, Clay. Thank you again for getting it here quickly."

He hugged her and said, "It was my pleasure and a sure bet to boot."

She nodded and, with a bit of wistfulness in her voice, said, "Maggie is a terrific mother. She followed my lead through the birthing process, and there was no tearing or problems."

"I'm glad." He kissed her forehead and said, "You are a marvel. I'm in awe of all you do, especially when you help a new baby into the world."

"Thanks, Clay." She laid her head on his chest and whispered, "I wish I could have given you a child. I'm sorry I could not do so."

"Hey, none of that, sweetheart. It will happen if it is meant for us to have a child. Before we were together, I knew you couldn't bear a child. It didn't change how much I loved you then or now."

"I know. Still, when I'm helping a mother and baby join together in this world, it is a blessing but also a reminder of what we will never have."

"Never, say never, dear heart. We don't know what will come of our efforts, but I believe when we do good and are honorable, good things will come to us."

"You're right, and I agree, my love. Here, let me have the bucket. I'll take the milk in, strain it, and store it in the cold well. I want to check on Maggie, be sure there is enough stew for their family, and then I want to go to our home."

"I'd like that. We need a little time together in our own home. I'll finish up here in a few minutes."

When Aurora had the milk strained, and in the cold well, she went to check on Maggie. When she finished checking on Maggie, Silas entered their bedroom and said, "I can't thank you enough, Aurora, for all you've done for our family, especially today. Letting me be a part of Teddy's coming into the World is a blessing I'd never thought to have."

"I'm glad. Not every father wants to be a part of it all, and society always stands in the way."

Maggie smiled. "It was the easiest birth yet, and the chair helped a lot. I love that Silas got to be a part of it all. You are amazing, and we are grateful."

"Good. I'm happy you are all doing well and are pleased with the birthing. You've done so much for me and Clay, I'd lay down my life for you."

"No. Never that, dear friend," Maggie quickly said. "You are a jewel in the crown of womanhood and a marvelous friend. When other women hear about the chair and how easy you made my labor and delivery, they'll all want you to attend them. I'll tell every woman I meet about the marvelous chair and your loving help."

"Thank you, Maggie. I love helping mothers and babies. Now, there is plenty of stew and cake for the evening. The fresh milk is in the cold well. I'll return in the morning to fix breakfast and set up things for you and baby Teddy. I'll skim the cream in the morning, too." She turned to Silas and said, "If she needs me or you're worried, come and get me."

"I will," he said, reached into his pocket, and handed her two gold five-dollar coins.

She shook her head. "This is too much, Silas. Most folks pay me a quarter-dollar." She tried to hand him back the money.

He refused, gently folding her hand around the coins, and said, "After all you've done extra for us, this is small compensation compared to my wife's and children's well-being. I believe a quarter-dollar is far too little—frankly, stingy in my mind. You should ask for at least a dollar or, better yet, two dollars. Now. You'll hurt my tender feelings if you don't take the money you've justly earned."

Maggie laughed and shook her head. "Silas's tender feelings aside, he is right. You are the best midwife I've ever had, and we'll be sure to spread the word around. Think of the extra money as a gift to other women who might not have even a quarter-dollar. Take care of them and their babies, too."

"I will. I promise."

"Good. Now go home and rest."

Aurora bent, kissed Maggie's cheek, and patted the baby. "Send your fella if you need me."

"Of course. Now go home and rest."

"I will. Goodnight to you all."

Clay waited outside for his wife, holding the birthing stool. While he stood, he watched the sky. There were a few soft clouds, and as the sun was lowering, the colors of the clouds and sky took on a variety of hues that were lovely to behold. When Aurora joined him at the steps of Maggie's home, she tucked her arm through his and said, "What a beautiful gift to walk home as the sun sets."

He nodded and smiled. "My thoughts exactly, my love."

Neither Aurora nor Clay noticed Lester Blunt sitting on his horse behind a tree, watching them. He grunted, then said, "I can't abide a man like Clay hooking up with a vile woman like Aurora. She was born from slave seed. Hell, she's barely a human. Both of them should be shot."

A man sitting astride his horse beside Lester said, "I can pick 'em both off anytime you say the word."

"Not yet. I'm of a mind to get a crew to burn them out, root and branch."

The other man nodded and chuckled. "Sounds like a fine old cookout to me, boss."

Lester looked at the man, not liking him very much either, but he was mean enough to do whatever Lester told him. He said, "Let's head back into town and hang out at the saloon. I've got an idea or two."

"What about Sheriff Harvey?"

"What he doesn't know won't hurt me a bit."

The other man spit tobacco juice on the ground, wiped his mouth with the back of his hand, and said, "Me neither. I wouldn't mind a go at the woman first, though."

Lester shook his head. "Not me. I have no intention of soiling my manhood with the likes of her. The sooner she is gone, the better for everyone."

The other man didn't say anything, but to his mind, when there's a woman at hand to diddle, he'd take that any old day of the year and enjoy the hell out of it—if she hollered—even better.

What Lester had told no one was before the rape, he'd tried to have sexual intercourse with Aurora—of course without her permission— she laughed at the size of his penis and asked, "Exactly what do you plan to do with that itty bitty stub, Lester." He was furious and slapped her but couldn't keep his penis hard enough to continue, and all because of her laughter.

Later when he and a bunch of his cronies caught her unawares and raped her, he'd hoped she would die. His hopes were shattered. His penis hadn't worked then nor ever again. He was sure she'd put a witch hex on him.

He planned to be sure she suffered for laughing at his manhood. He would love to hear her screams as she burned to a crisp.

Clay opened the door of their cabin home and said, "Before you go inside, I want you to know that every moment of every day, you are in my heart and soul."

She smiled and said, "I know, my love, but for now, I want to go into our house and have a nice quiet evening."

He opened the door and let her enter the house first. She smiled and clapped her hands. "Oh, Clay, I love the bookcase, desk, and even more rugs."

"I'm glad. I've worked on the desk and bookcase for a few days, keeping it hidden in the barn."

She walked over and ran her hand over the desk. "It's perfect, and I didn't know you could make such fine furniture."

"Neither did I until we made the children's beds, drawers, and commode chairs. I learned a lot while we taught ourselves how to do them."

"Still, that's a lot to teach yourselves."

"It was because of Noah."

"Really?"

"Yep. He found a book about cabinet making up in the attic. He'd been reading it secretly until we started making the beds and commode chairs. When we were stuck about how to do it all, he said, 'I know how to do it,' and we laughed at him."

"My guess is he didn't like that."

"No, he did not. He'd said, 'Just wait, and I'll show you how to do it.' He ran into the house and upstairs, returned to the barn, handed his father the book, and said, 'It's not easy to do, I'm sure, but we can do it.'"

Aurora laughed. "I think Noah is smarter than we give him credit for."

"You're absolutely right about that. Anyway, he showed us the pages about how to make drawers and drawer runners as well as building beds, desks, chairs, tables—any furniture we'll ever need to build."

"Well, I love the desk and bookshelf. Thank you, love."

"You're welcome, sweetheart. I know you want to write about all you can do to help others learn."

"Where did the rest of the books come from?"

"Silas loaned them to us."

"I love it all, and thank you, Clay, for this gift."

"You are the best gift I've ever had, Aurora, and whatever I can do to make your life better, I'm ready, willing, and able to do so—or learn how to, even if I need the help of an 8-year-old boy."

She chuckled. "Let's heat our stew and enjoy the rest of our evening."

"So long as you let me help."

"Okay. Go to the hen house, gather the eggs, and milk our cow."

"I'd forgotten them. I'll be back in soon." He started to open the door, then turned back and said, "The children have named our cow."

"Oh?"

"Yep. She is now known as Snowflake."

"Why?"

"Because of the white snowflake-looking spots all over her black fur.

Bea pointed out that she doesn't have round spots but spots that look like stars and snowflakes."

"So why not call her Star."

"Bea likes Snowflake better."

"Reason enough, I suppose," she said and grinned.

"That's what Silas said, so we voted, and it was unanimous—Snowflake."

"What a lucky cow," Aurora said and laughed.

He nodded and smiled as he went out to milk the cow and gather what eggs he could wrestle from the hens.

CHAPTER TWENTY-TWO

By the time Teddy was a week old, Maggie was out of bed and taking care of some household chores with Aurora. She still needed a nap in the afternoons, but day by day, her energy was coming back, aided, she was sure, by the fruit cake, fresh meat, and greens Aurora gathered.

Teddy was an easy baby. He nursed well and generally slept through most of the night. The other children were amazed at the baby. When the baby held Bea's finger, she whispered, "I love you, Teddy." When the baby grinned at Bea, Maggie's heart melted.

Ben touched Teddy's hair and asked his mother, "Will his hair always be this soft?"

"For a while, but as he gets to be a big boy like you, it won't be so soft."

Ben nodded but secretly wished his hair was soft like Teddy's.

Silas and Clay kept busy farming. They had planted a few fruit trees, but now actual plowing was in order. Silas brought out the new plow he'd bought the first day they arrived in Tishomingo. It was time to make a more extensive garden. His family would need every bit of food they could grow. He hooked one of his horses to the plow to start digging and turning the soil. It would be larger than the kitchen garden for the bigger vegetables, melons, and even more fruit trees. Aurora's starter plants were ready to be planted in the ground as soon as the men could get the soil ready.

The horse didn't like dragging the plow and balked at pulling the plow through the soil. However, after a few tries—with Clay leading her and feeding her with old withered apples—she consented to pull the plow. Once she had the hang of pulling the plow, she settled down, and the plowing was quickly done within a few days.

Noah and Clay were quick with shovels to move larger rocks out of the way of the plow. Then, they carried the stones to a pile at the edge of the marked-out garden. Silas thought that they would find uses for the rocks as time went on. He had an idea that he could build more rock walls to outline their property, at least the property near the road and house. For now, plowing was all he was paying attention to.

Silas said, "I wish I'd thought to plow the kitchen garden this way."

"Maybe," Clay said, "But the kitchen garden is small. I don't think the horse, the plow, and a man guiding the plow could have done much in that small space."

Silas laughed. "Of course, you're right. The width of the kitchen garden isn't as much as the length of the horse and plow."

Noah said, "They'd get all tangled up, and then what would we do?"

"I've no idea, son."

Clay laughed and then said, " Aurora says the starter plants in the kitchen garden are growing nicely and will be ready to harvest in a few weeks."

"I'm glad, Clay. I saw green tomatoes on the vines, and the carrots looked like they were ready to pop out of the earth. I know we've been stretching your garden with our big family. For now, I'll assume we did things exactly as they should be done, bein' the incredibly wise and talented men we are."

Noah shook his head and said, "Even boys know that's just plain ol' silly."

The two men laughed as they took the wheelbarrow and three shovels to the compost pile. Noah was none too happy to help dig up the compost and haul it—load by stinking load—into the garden. He could think of many other things he'd rather do that wouldn't smell as bad, but he supposed if his Papa and Clay were willing to do it, he should pretend to be a man and do it with them.

They spent a couple of hot, smelly days working the compost into the soil with the help of the plow and horse. The horse didn't seem as bothered by the stench as the men. Noah thought, *ain't it just like a horse to like the smell of something like this but hate to step in her droppings?* He decided horses were simply weird but necessary.

Once the larger vegetable garden was plowed and the soil readied, Aurora's starter plants were used to plant several rows of corn, okra, watermelon, pumpkins, green and yellow squashes, peas, beans—including lima beans and kidney beans, potatoes, sweet potatoes, and, of course, cantaloupe. Once they completed the garden, the men sketched a design for the staircase to the children's bedrooms on the second floor.

Clay said, "I'm glad you found that book, Noah. It's going to make our building a lot easier."

Noah smiled and said, "Thanks, Clay."

Clay continued, "We should buy new lumber for the staircase. We want it to be sturdy and last for many years to come. Plus, I want it to look good."

Silas nodded. "You and me both, Clay. Building the bookcases will be easier, and we can use a lot of scrap lumber for them. I plan to paint them regardless. But I want to oil and polish the staircase. I love the look of polished wood on staircases."

"I do, too."

Once the men had a solid plan, Silas and Clay hitched the horses to the big wagon. Silas said, "Noah, you go inside and let your momma know you're coming with us into town."

Noah grinned and nodded. He raced to the house, and in a few minutes, he was back and said, "Momma said for you not to spend it all in one place and no drinking either."

Silas laughed. "I'm ever your mother's servant."

Noah shook his head and said, "I think I should be quiet."

Clay laughed and said, "Well, son, you're smarter than the average fella."

"He most certainly is," Silas said, clicking his tongue against his teeth to get the horses moving. They headed into Tishomingo to get the needed wood and nails. The drive was pleasant and easy. There hadn't been any big rains in a while, so though the road was dusty, there wasn't any difficulty in the drive. The two men talked about their lives and families.

Noah sat in the back of the buckboard wagon, quietly listening to his father and Clay. Now and again, he'd look up at the sky. Its blueness never seemed to be less than amazing. The hawks and scissortail flycatchers were always busy flying across the sky. As he watched the birds he listened to the two men on the bench of the wagon. It was one of the things he had taught himself—a boy can learn a lot by listening and watching adults.

Clay said, "I don't know if you are aware, but Aurora cannot have children."

"I'm sorry to hear that," Silas said. "Seems to me she would be a terrific mother."

"Yes, she would. I won't give you the details," he glanced behind him and saw Noah was dozing—or pretending to do so—and then continued, "A few men beat her and violated her so severely that she will never be able to bear a child."

Silas shook his head and glanced back at Noah, who seemed to be dozing, but of course, he was listening.

Silas said, "To know such evil abounds in the middle of a beautiful place like this is heartbreaking. I don't understand why anyone would do such a thing."

"Nor do I, but it was about her mixed heritage—Slave and Chicka-saw. Her mother married a man whose grandfather was a freed slave. The grandfather married a Chickasaw woman. So Aurora's father is part slave and part Chickasaw. Aurora loved both her parents and knew they loved her as well. Her mother bore only one child, Aurora. Her mother is a good woman and a midwife, too. Her father is a good, honest, and loving man. I'm honored to have them as my in-laws."

Silas shook his head. "Yet, Lester Blunt piles sorrow upon sorrow and for selfish, evil ideas."

Clay nodded. "Exactly. I hope Aurora will have a child and be a mother someday. I know it won't be from her womb, but that doesn't matter to me or her."

"If the fates are in her favor in any way, it will be so," Silas said. He hoped his friends would be given the opportunity to be parents. Any child would be blessed to have Clay and Aurora as parents.

The men rode the rest of the way into Tishomingo in the wagon in quiet contemplation. Neither man could understand how vile prejudice could be a pathway anyone would take.

Noah wasn't sure he understood everything his father and Clay discussed, but he felt sorry for Aurora. He liked her—a lot—and couldn't understand why anyone would be mean to her. He crossed his fingers and hoped somehow—someday—Aurora would have her own baby.

Silas knew the words 'sorrow upon sorrow' was how prejudice works. He also knew evil was always ready to pounce.

What Silas didn't know was that Lester Blunt and his cronies were planning revenge on Silas for harboring a woman of Chickasaw and slave descent. Evil was indeed getting ready to pounce and create as much havoc as possible for Silas, his family, Clay, and Aurora.

CHAPTER TWENTY-THREE

"Mother is the
name for God
in the lips and hearts
of little children."
William Makepeace Thackeray

THE WEEKS PASSED, and both families enjoyed each other and everything around them. The summer was getting warmer every day, but they all enjoyed the days they could have a walk or swim in the creek. Teddy was growing, and the other children were acclimated to their new lives and Pennington Creek.

Aurora wiped down the dining table at Maggie's house and then went to the pantry to bring out the porcelain china and silver cutlery Maggie had brought from South Carolina for the family dinner. Maggie walked in from the garden and saw Aurora setting the table for the Pennington family dinner. She smiled, walked over to Aurora, and hugged her.

Aurora smiled and said, "What's the hug for?"

"Everything marvelous and wonderful about you."

Aurora laughed. "If you were Clay, I'd ask what you're hankerin' for."

Maggie laughed and shook her head. "I'll leave you and Clay to your own devices. But I do have something I want to chat with you about."

Aurora paused while setting the table. "Have I done something wrong?"

Maggie shook her head and felt herself near tears. "Absolutely not, my dear friend—you've done everything right. Come, let's sit down and talk." Maggie pulled out a chair. Aurora followed her friend's lead, and they sat at the table. Maggie touched Aurora's hand. "You've been a life-saver, Aurora. I can't imagine doing all we have done together by myself."

Aurora ducked her head to hide her tears.

Maggie put her hand around Aurora's and felt a teardrop on her hand. She pulled her embroidered handkerchief from her sleeve and handed it to Aurora. She said, "Please don't cry, dear friend. There is nothing wrong. You have worked hard and done more than I had any right to expect. You've made my life much easier than I'd ever thought. However, day by day, I'm feeling better—mostly because you cared for me and my family."

Aurora couldn't look Maggie in the eye but nodded and asked, "Do you want us to leave?"

"Why on earth would you think I would want you to leave?" Maggie lifted her friend's chin with a finger. "The only time I'll accept you leaving my side will be if you were to die before me. Even then, I'd not be happy and count it one of the biggest losses of my life."

Aurora brushed the tears from her cheeks with Maggie's hanky and smiled. "I expected to be tossed out again. I know you are kind and generous, but it's hard for me to trust it as a real friendship."

"I wish it were not so in your life, Aurora. I've lived a life of luxury, but my mother made sure I learned how to work hard. She told me once, 'It's fine to let others do work for you, but you never know when you'll need to do everything yourself. When you have help, be gracious and kind. When you don't have help, you must know how to do every-thing for your life, home, and family.' I want to honor my mother always. What I know for sure about our relationship is you are the queen among us all. I hope you will find a way to trust Silas and me and our loving friendship with you both."

"I'll work hard to trust you, Maggie. Clay says sometimes I expect the worst and am disappointed when things turn out fine."

Maggie laughed. "I can understand those feelings. There are times when I feel I'm inadequate. But with you, this isn't the case. You have done everything right and much, much more. Besides, you have your own home to tend to. I simply want to adjust things a bit."

"I don't understand."

"I want you to be my best friend and I yours. I need you as a friend and helper occasionally. I do not want you to work your fingers to the bone for me. When we left South Carolina, I was relieved that no servants would be around me, tending to things I could easily do. I do not want you to be a servant but a friend."

"What would you expect of me then?"

"That you be my friend and we work together helping each other in our homes. I want you beside me in the gardens, ensuring the children are safe and fed, and maybe help a little with keeping my rowdy bunch as tidy as possible. BUT. And this is very important, Aurora. I do not want you waiting on me and my family hand and foot. I do not want or need a servant, Aurora. I do want and need a friend working together with me."

"I can do that, but you and Silas are paying us to work for you."

"We're not paying you nearly enough. Of course, part of the payment is your cabin. Another part is having Clay help with the heavy work with Silas. Clay knows more about building and farming than Silas, and we both appreciate his help. Along with that, Clay is teaching not only Silas but Noah. That's a big deal in my eyes. The main part of the payment is for you and Clay to work with us, side-by-side, and improve your lives as well as our lives."

"I understand, I think. Does that mean you don't need me to keep doing all I've been doing?"

Maggie chuckled. "Yes, mostly. I'll still need help with some household and garden work, but I'd prefer to work with you."

"I can do that." Aurora smiled.

"Good. I smell another of your marvelous dinners cooking, but after today, I'll return to cooking our meals. You need and deserve to have your ways of being."

Aurora smiled and squeezed Maggie's hand. "If you can handle things from here, I'll go home, work on a few things there, and fix our dinner."

"Exactly what I want you to do. You know Teddy has been sleeping through the night for several days, and I feel more like my old self. It's hard to believe he's already nearly five weeks old. He'll be five weeks old tomorrow. It's hard to believe it is already near the middle of June."

"It doesn't seem possible, but Teddy is a sweet baby."

Maggie smiled and nodded, then patted her friend's hand. "Yes, he is. From this day forward, I'll fix our breakfast and our dinner. During the days, you and I can work together in the gardens and whatever comes up. It will be a few weeks before we have much to harvest, so it will mostly be weeding and settling things."

"That sounds fine, Maggie. I also have a few mothers nearing birthing time, so having extra time at home will be a blessing."

"Good. Now, before anything else comes up that you think you should do around here, go home!"

Aurora smiled as the children raced into the house, and Bea started chattering about their day. Maggie held up a finger and said, "Hold on, Bea. Aurora and I are talking."

"Okay, Momma." Bea stepped back and waited for her mother to talk with her.

Maggie turned to Aurora and asked, "So, are we settled?"

"Yes. I saw that the yellow squash and zucchini are getting nearly big enough to harvest. More tomatoes are starting to ripen, too. So, although harvest is a few weeks away, we will need to tend and water the vegetables."

"I'm ready for the fresh vegetables."

Aurora smiled. "Me too, but we must wait a bit for most of them."

Bea piped up again and said, "I'm ready for canteloupe and watermelon."

Maggie chuckled. "It'll be several more weeks. The cantaloupe and watermelon will come a few weeks after the squash is ready."

Noah said, "I want pickles."

"Me too," Ben chimed in.

"Those will take a while, too, boys. If we take good care of our gardens, we'll have all that and more. Aurora needs to go home, and I need to feed Teddy."

Bea clapped her hands. She loved watching her mother feed the baby, but the boys weren't nearly as enthralled with the process as Bea.

Ben thought the baby should learn to drink from a cup. He was slightly jealous of his mother's constant holding of Teddy close to her.

Noah was a little embarrassed to see his mother's breasts, but he was relieved the baby was here, and his mother was looking more like her usual self.

Aurora picked up her basket and pulled on her hat to shade her face from the hot summer sun. "I'll see you all tomorrow morning after breakfast."

Maggie hugged her friend and said, "Thank you for all you've done."

"It's been my pleasure."

After Aurora left, closing the door behind her, Noah asked, "Can I go to the barn and help Papa with the bookcases? Clay's gone to his house to work on his garden."

"Of course," Maggie said. "Now that the staircase is up and stable, the bookcases are the next big thing."

"Can I go, too," Ben asked, and before Maggie could answer, Bea said, "I get to go too."

Maggie laughed. "Okay. But be sure you are helping and not in the way."

"We will, Momma," Noah said. He nodded to the twins and said, "Come on. Let's go see if Papa will let us help."

The twins followed their big brother, hoping to be allowed to use the saw to cut something or, at the very least, hammer something.

Maggie smiled and went to the baby, who was whimpering as he woke from his nap. She sighed with the happiness of her life, including the rowdy children and the new whimpering baby.

She sat in her rocking chair, feeding her newest child. He was a sweet baby who hardly ever cried. His blonde curly hair and blue eyes reminded her most of Silas. She knew she had a nearly urgent need when she thought about Silas. Both she and Silas were eager to make love, although Aurora suggested they wait about six weeks after Teddy's birth. The thought of making love made her smile and lifted a lightness in her spirits.

However, she wanted to talk with Aurora about how to spread out having the babies. She'd been able to put four years between her babies, but she felt overwhelmed with an adolescent boy, twins just coming out of toddler life, and a newborn baby. Added to the children was taking care of her home and property without servants in the background doing everything for her. Having another baby in two or three years wasn't what she wanted.

She wanted time to enjoy each child rather than prepare for and bear the next child every two to three years or so. At the same time, she also longed to enjoy sharing her body with her husband without the specter of becoming pregnant again—at least so soon. She told her baby, "I know some of the things to do, but I'm sure Aurora will have even more ideas."

She knew that she was reasonably safe from conceiving as long as she nursed the baby, but she still wanted something more certain. She caressed Teddy's head and whispered, "I love you and all my babies— born and yet to come. Let's slow down the pace a bit, shall we?"

Bea walked into the house quietly, bored with boy things in the barn. She picked up her baby doll and sat on one of the chairs. She looked across the room to her mother, who was nursing the baby, and watched her mother's face as she talked to Teddy. She wasn't sure about it all but knew her mother loved her children. Bea loved to watch her mother's face while holding Teddy.

Teddy looked up at his mother's face and smiled a little with milk dribbling from his mouth. To Teddy, she was his whole world. Maggie smiled back at the lovely, innocent baby and felt the joy of motherhood. She held out her hand and reached for Bea to come close. Bea quickly came to her mother's side and hugged her. Her mother kissed her cheek and asked, "Would you like to help burp Teddy, Bea?"

"Yes, Momma."

"Well, sit on the footrest, and I'll help hold Teddy on your lap while you burp him."

Bea suddenly felt like a big girl, and helping Teddy was much more important than trying to hammer a nail into a board.

On the far side of the creek, three men on horseback rode by, taking care to be quiet so as not to be noticed. Silas and the Pennington boys were making enough noise, singing songs, hammering, sawing, and having a high old time that they did not see the men.

One man lifted binoculars to his face and said, "I don't see the Chickasaw-slave woman or her man around here."

The second man said, "Let's go across the bridge and see if they are home."

The last man said, "Not yet. There ain't enough trees on the bridge to hide out. Their cabin is in a wide open space close to the road. I want to come at 'em from behind to kill 'em before they know they're in our sights."

Lester Blunt knew the men with him weren't honorable or brave if it came down to it. He didn't need them to be upstanding citizens, but a little bravery would help his plan. Regardless, his patience was running out. Too many new folks were coming to live in what he thought of as his town. He didn't give a tinker's damn what the law had to say about anything.

He thought, *the Chickasaw Nation, my aching ass! An Indian's an Indian, and the sooner we turn the Indian Nation into a part of the good old US of A, the better for me and mine. To hell with the half-breed Indians! Fire and rope are what I have in mind. And that new building they're finishing buildin' for their Council House ain't right. Besides, it should never have been the seat of government for Tishomingo, much less the Chickasaw Nation. The old one burned down, and I thought it was good riddance to bad rubbish. I'm tired of waiting for the rest of the white folks to pull their heads out of their asses. For all that's holy, those white folks who call the Chickasaw First Americans should be shot!*

The men turned their horses and rode back into town. Lester wasn't sure the men he rode with would be up to his planned task. *It takes gumption and grit to fix situations like this. These fellas like to talk like big men, but I've yet to see them do a goldurn thing about all the messes they whine about. I'll burn the whole town down—even the idiots—to the ground before I'll put up with a half-breed Chickasaw woman struttin' around!* He looked at the two men with him, shook his head, and muttered, "All talk and no lead."

Of course, his own wife was a full-blood Chickasaw woman. He didn't find that nearly as objectionable—her being a full-blood Chickasaw. If Aurora had been white and Chickasaw, he wouldn't have minded so much, but being part slave stuck in his craw something awful.

CHAPTER TWENTY-FOUR

*"Where there is
great love, there are
always miracles."*
Willa Cather

CLAY AND AURORA sat in front of the fireplace after dinner, watching the fire from cooking dinner die down to coals as the evening cooled their log cabin home. Clay was reading Walt Whitman's *Leaves of Grass,* which Silas had loaned him, along with a few other books for his bookshelf. He felt honored to read the first edition of the words of Whitman —one of only 795 first editions published.

Aurora was writing a midwifery book in a blank book Maggie had gifted her. Along with the book, Maggie gave Aurora a mechanical pencil with a few spare graphite sticks for the pencil and a small rubber eraser. She wrote with care so as not to have to erase often as it left smudges on the page. She also didn't want to waste any graphite for the mechanical pencil.

Not only was Aurora amazed to have such fine writing implements, but she was also pleased to have a new friend. Aurora smiled, thinking of her friendship with Maggie. She'd never had a friend like Maggie and felt blessed to have her in her life.

Shirley at the dry goods store had been her only real friend before the Pennington family came to live in Jacob's house. Shirley had told Aurora, "If you give a few folks a chance, you might find there are more friends in your corner than you think." Aurora hoped Shirley was right.

Of late, however, she'd been astonished that many women in the area had no one to help them through birthing simply because there were very few midwives or they felt they couldn't afford even a quarter for the delivery of their babies. She'd assumed white women would have white midwives, but there were none as close to Tishomingo as Aurora.

She hoped she could convince a few like-minded women to take up the mantle of midwifery and thereby help more women. She talked with Shirley about how she might teach each woman who was pregnant the fundamentals of birthing. Shirley had suggested that she would tell pregnant women about Aurora. It was beginning to work, too.

A sudden pounding on the door of their cabin shattered her childbirth musings and Clay's reading. The startled couple lay down their books and halted their musings, readings, and writings. Aurora jumped up, her book and pencil falling to the floor, breaking off a bit of the treasured graphite lead.

Aurora felt her heart pounding, worried about what could be happening.

Clay stood up quickly and called aloud, "Who's there?"

When there was no answer, he pulled his shotgun from the wall, checked it was loaded, and cocked the gun. Silas whispered, "Stay quiet, hon. Don't cry out."

Aurora nodded and held a hand to her mouth to keep from shouting out loud. She watched as Clay went to the door and asked again, "Who's there? I won't ask again. If you don't answer, I'll shoot you dead through the door!"

Again, there was no answer.

Aurora tiptoed to stand beside her husband and whispered, "I hear a horse riding away, Clay."

He nodded. He'd heard it, too, and quietly answered, "I hear it too. Still, I need to see what's up."

"Be careful. There's a passel of people who want us gone from the area."

He nodded, "I know, and some want us dead, too," which he simply didn't understand. He shook his head. "Not happening on my watch." He slowly opened the door of their cabin. He saw something on the porch and opened the door wide.

They walked on the porch together to find an amazing thing. There, on their wooden front porch, was a basket with a large woven handle and a closed woven straw lid, but nothing else they could see.

Aurora pushed past Clay, pointed to the basket, and said, "There's a note on the basket."

Clay bent down and picked up the note. He read it aloud:

"June 10, 1898

"Aurora and Clay, I cannot keep this baby. I am not married but fell in love with a native man. My family says they will disown me if I don't kill the baby, but that is something I cannot do. My father insisted that he would rid the family of my illicit child, but finally, he promised not to kill her if Aurora would take my child. My baby's only hope, Aurora, is for you to be her mother and Clay to be her father. Please take care of her and love her as your own child. Do not try to search for me or my family. If it becomes known, the community will shun our family, and my father will put me out of his home."

Clay stood thunderstruck. He shook his head and said, "There's no signature on this note, darlin'."

"Of course, there isn't," Aurora said as she knelt beside the basket and opened the lid. Inside was a newborn baby, lying on a bloody towel, with blood and the oily cheese that protects infants within their mother's womb. She wasn't crying, her eyes weren't open, and she was a little blue despite the summer evening heat.

Aurora said, "She seems a little young for her age. My guess is her birth was at least one month early. I'm worried she might not live." She picked the infant up from the basket, held her close, and said, "I've got to help her, Clay."

Aurora walked into their home with the baby cuddled close to her. She rubbed the baby's back and talked to her as she carried the baby to the table.

Clay picked up the basket and followed his wife into their cabin.

Aurora lifted the baby to her ear, felt the infant's warm breath, and heard her unsteady heartbeat that was a little too slow to Aurora's mind. She turned to her husband and, in an urgent voice, said, "Clay, fill my big bowl with warm water."

He quickly went to the pantry and pulled out the large wooden bowl his wife used to bathe the babies she delivered. He lifted the kettle from the fireplace and poured the still-hot water into the bowl. With a dipper from the bucket, he added a little cool water. He checked the water temperature with his elbow, adding cool water until he was sure the water was safe yet warm. He said, "It's ready, hon."

Aurora gently lowered the infant into the water, began gently bathing her, and said, "I need a small clean cloth, Clay."

As she bathed the baby, she began to sing her own birth song.

Clay quickly returned to the pantry and brought a small cloth and a few clean, dry towels. Aurora bathed the baby, sang, and cooed to her. In a few seconds, the baby kicked her legs and began crying. Aurora laughed, and with tears flowing down her face, she bathed the baby clean with the warm, clear water as the baby squalled at the indignity of being bathed.

When she finished, Aurora looked up at Clay and smiled. He smiled, nodded, and held out a clean towel. She handed him the crying baby.

He wrapped the towel around the baby and whispered, "Hello, baby girl. Welcome home, sweetie." His tears flowed as he kissed her forehead. She quieted and began rooting around for a breast. He held the baby in his arms while Aurora continued to dry their daughter.

Clay whispered to Aurora, "Thank you."

She laughed. "I've done nothing but be here to welcome Okchuli into our home and hearts. You were the one who was sure we'd have a child, and now we do. We have Okchuli."

"Okchuli?"

"Yes, that will be her name. In the language of the Chickasaw, my language, her name means *awake*. She woke in our arms. I think she is part Chickasaw."

Clay nodded. "That would fit with the note."

The baby began to cry in earnest. Aurora took the baby in her arms, lowered the top of her dress, and presented her breast to the baby. The baby began to suckle.

Clay watched his wife with awe and thought, not for the first time in his life, that he was a lucky man and there was much in this world he didn't know. He asked, "Can you breastfeed a baby without having been pregnant?"

"Yes. I've done it before when a mother had problems feeding her baby or was too weak to do so. I'll take some herbs to help the milk flow. I've got lemon balm tea and milk thistle, which will help. Will you go get Maggie?"

"Sure. Why?"

"Maggie already has mother's milk—lots of it. Also, ask her if she has a few baby clothes to spare—especially the tiny ones. We have none."

He grinned, kissed Aurora's cheek, and whispered, "You are the queen of my life." She smiled and nodded, watching her husband kiss Okchuli's forehead.

"Ah, my darling daughter, I'm glad you are home and awake." He smiled, looked at his wife in amazement, and kissed her again. "I'll be quick, girls."

He grabbed his hat off the peg by the door, turned back to Aurora and the baby, Okchuli, and kissed them both again. Aurora saw the tears on his cheek, touched one tear to her finger, and kissed the tear.

Clay nodded, grabbed a lantern, lit it, and went out the door of their home. He ran as fast as he could safely without dropping the lantern— he was eager to be with his wife and daughter. There was no moon in the sky, but the stars were brighter than he'd ever seen them. He laughed with the joy of this night as he ran to Silas and Maggie's house while the stars watched the new father.

When he knocked on their door, he was surprised to see Maggie open it, standing in the doorway, dressed and ready to leave. He asked, "Are you going somewhere?"

"Yes. Aurora needs me."

Clay smiled, "How did you know?"

"I don't know how—I simply know."

Silas stood behind her and said, "A few minutes ago, Maggie sat up in bed and said, 'Aurora needs me.' She put her clothes back on, insistent she needed to help Aurora. You arrived just in time to walk with her so I don't have to leave the children home alone at night."

"Good. We have a baby—a foundling. Aurora says she needs a mother's milk and any extra baby clothes you can spare—especially small clothes. Aurora says she was born a bit early."

Maggie nodded and laughed. "Of course! Teddy is already growing out of a few of the smaller clothes. Give me a few minutes."

Silas shook his head and stood with his mouth hanging open, unable to understand what was happening in his home. "You found a baby?"

Clay nodded, grinned, then turned to Silas and explained, "Someone banged on the door, then rode off. We opened the door and found Okchuli cold and not breathing very well. She's fine now but needs milk."

Silas asked, "Okchuli?"

Maggie came back with her arms full of clothes for the baby and said, "That's her name, isn't it?"

"Yes, her name means *awake*. Aurora massaged and bathed her to wake her. Come quickly now, Maggie. Aurora and Okchuli need you."

She held up a hand. "I've gathered a few diapers and clothes."

Silas shook his head. "This feels like we're in the middle of a fairy tale. Who would have ever thought such a thing would happen?"

Clay grinned. "I did. I told you how I felt. Deep in my heart and soul, I knew we'd have children. I simply didn't expect it to happen now. I certainly didn't know how our baby would come to us, but she found a way."

Maggie handed Clay an armful of baby clothes and said, "I'm ready,

Clay." She turned to her husband and kissed his cheek. "I'll be back as soon as I have helped Aurora and Okchuli."

"Then you can explain it all to me."

She grinned and kissed his cheek again. "Of course I will, darling." She patted his cheek and smiled at his bemused face. Her heart was filled with love for the man standing in front of her and the other man waiting to take her to her best friend and their new daughter.

As they walked quickly on the trail from their house to the house of Aurora and Clay, Maggie said, "Have you noticed how bright the stars are tonight?"

"Yes, I have, and beyond all reason, I feel they are happy Okchuli has come to us."

Maggie smiled and said, "Of course they are. The Universe has its way of being. We're simply a part of it all."

Clay threw back his head and laughed. Brushing a few more tears from his eyes, filled with wonder, he said, "I love everyone, everything, and every star in the sky tonight."

CHAPTER TWENTY-FIVE

Frank A. Clark

MAGGIE HELD Okchuli close and let the baby nurse her fill. She
touched the baby's curly, reddish-blonde hair and smiled as the baby
settled into sleep. She looked up to Aurora and said, "She is beautiful."

"Yes, she is. We have been given a great blessing."

"I agree. How long will it take for your milk to flow again fully?"

"Usually just a day or two."

"Good," Maggie said, then kissed the sleeping baby, stood, and
handed Okchuli back to her mother.

Aurora held the baby close in her arms and watched her daughter
sleep. She touched the baby's soft, curly hair and whispered, "What a
lovely miracle!"

"Oh, my goodness, yes!" Maggie said. She watched her friend

holding her own baby and realized that regardless of how children come to any family, they are blessed and hopefully loved. Certainly, Okchuli had filled a void in her friend's life. Maggie was certain that love and blessings would fill Okchuli's life for as long as she lived.

"I hope her hair remains curly and reddish-blonde. It would be a miracle if she had blue eyes."

"Why?"

"Because Clay has reddish-blonde curly hair and blue eyes."

"Ahhh. You know, blue eyes are not common among any population other than Nordic areas in Europe and some of the British people. I agree it might make life easier in the short run, but in the long run, anyone who cares about you and Clay will love and accept her as your baby."

Aurora nodded. "I appreciate your words, dear friend. Okchuli is my baby and a gift from the Universe. Can we keep her coming into our lives and how she became our daughter between ourselves?"

"Why?"

"I have a feeling if folks knew she was a foundling, there would be lots of gossip, and she and her mother who bore her might be in danger."

"Of course. When the children ask, I suggest we tell them you didn't know you would have a baby. In point of fact, you didn't know you could have a baby. The baby is very small because she came early and unexpectedly. How does that sound?"

Aurora smiled and nodded. "I think that's best and exactly how I want to move forward. Besides, I'm small and frankly a little round. For us as friends, let it all be a miracle, which it is. If we have to have details, let them come later."

"Good. We can work out the details as needed. I'm happy for you, Okchuli, and Clay. However, I need to get home and check on my family. I'm sure Teddy will be waking in an hour or two."

"Thank you for coming to our aide so quickly, ikana."

"What does 'ikana' mean?"

"Friend."

Maggie bent down and kissed Aurora's head. "Yes, we are both ikana. Now I really must go."

"Thank you again for everything—especially coming to help in the middle of the night."

"I'd come in broad daylight or darkest night if you need me."

Aurora felt tears coming but held them back. She couldn't imagine having such a friend in her life. Yet, here was Maggie to help her when she needed her. She said, "Clay will walk back to your home with you. When Okchuli wakes, I'll come to your house. I'll keep working to get my milk flowing again so you don't have to nurse two babies for long."

"Between us, we'll take care of both babies." Maggie hugged her friend. "She is lovely. Do you have any idea who left the baby?"

"No, and I'm not going to fret over it. In fact, I think it might be safer for the birth mother, Okchuli, Clay, and me to accept the blessing of a child—as our daughter from my womb and never, ever guess about who might be the mother or father. I have the baby I've always longed for. Tonight has been a night of blessings for our family—Clay, me, and Okchuli."

"Indeed," Maggie said and kissed her friend's cheek. "Fingers crossed, she will be your daughter forever."

Aurora nodded. "I am not worried, for I am Okchuli's mother. Clay told me we would have a baby but didn't know how or when. No one needs to know the details of her coming."

"I agree. You will be a wonderful mother, and Okchuli is lucky you and Clay are here for her."

"You're right, and I'm glad of her coming," Clay said. "By the note on the basket, I think if we had not been here, Okchuli would not be alive."

"Whoever would let a child die because of skin color should be horsewhipped," Maggie said, scowling.

Clay nodded, but Aurora smiled and said, "We do not need to worry about it all. I do not need to know who birthed the child. I have every reason to be thankful for everything happening in our lives."

Maggie hugged her. "Be sure you get some rest."

"And you too, my ikana."

When Maggie walked into her home, Silas said, "I'm glad you are home. I am sure you are tired and need to rest, but I want to know what happened."

"Of course you do. It is a remarkable story. I'll give you a short version of the story. Someone left a newborn baby girl—part white, part Chickasaw native—in a basket. She was near death—on Clay and Aurora's porch with a letter from the mother that her father agreed not to kill the baby but rather to leave the baby with Aurora and Clay to be their daughter. The babe's mother asked they take her in as their own daughter rather than let her father kill the child."

"Who could ever be willing to kill a newborn child?"

"I don't know, but he can't be entirely wicked. He brought the baby to Aurora and Clay. They will be a marvelous family."

"Yes, they will. What will we tell the children?"

"We will tell them Okchuli's birth surprised Aurora because she didn't think she could have a baby, but as miracles go, it turned out she could."

"You think that will work?"

"In the short term, at least. For now, I need some rest before Teddy wakes."

Once in their bedroom, Silas laid down beside her on their bed, wrapped his arms around her, and said, "I love you, Maggie."

"And I you, Silas. By the way, you and Clay need to find another rocking chair and cradle. For now, I'm going to sleep."

"Yes, ma'am." Silas smiled, thinking of his improbable life.

He was filled with gratitude for the miracles surrounding him. As he drifted to sleep, he wondered about a weekly serial novel for the Tishomingo newspaper—if there was one. He'd call his musings *Life on Pennington Creek.* He shook his head and muttered, "I'll write those musings whether there is a newspaper or not. Life on Pennington Creek has been a blessing for me and my family. A blessing shared is a blessing indeed."

As Aurora had predicted, within a couple of days, her milk was flowing, and she was able to nurse Okchuli exclusively. The tiny baby was growing, and the children of Silas and Maggie Pennington were enthralled with both Okchuli and Teddy.

Bea asked Aurora, "Why didn't you know Chuli was coming to you?"

Aurora didn't correct Bea's pronunciation of her baby's name. "Well, Bea, I think of her as a miracle. Do you know about miracles?"

Bea cocked her head. "You mean magic?"

"No, but sometimes things come our way when we yearn earnestly for them. So it was with Okchuli. When our babies come to us, sometimes it is a surprise like it was for me. No matter how or when our babies come to us, we take good care of them. We love them, feed them, and help them grow up."

Bea nodded and said, "Can I have a baby like Chuli?"

"Maybe when you are all grown up."

Bea watched baby Okchuli sleeping in her mother's arms. "When will Chuli wake up again?"

"Oh, in an hour or two. For now, she needs to sleep so her body grows. She was born early, so she is very tender and small."

"So when she is older, she'll be big like me?"

"Yes, and she will be your friend too."

Bea smiled. "I want a friend to play with."

Ben said, "You have me."

She nodded but said nothing, confident that boys didn't understand how girls wanted to play with girls. She couldn't imagine her brother wanting to play with dolls and have tea parties. But she wouldn't be mean about it. Ben was her best friend in the world—for now.

Maggie said, "Bea, will you and Ben go outside and play for a bit while I talk with Aurora?"

"Is it a secret talk?"

"No, it's a grown-up woman talk."

Bea rolled her eyes, put her little hands on her hips, glared at her mother, and said, "I'm a woman too, you know."

Maggie smiled, bit her lip, and struggled not to laugh. She said, "I know you are a woman and a fine young woman you are. However, you're not a grown-up woman. When you're older, we'll talk with you about grown-up women things."

"How old?"

"Probably when you're about twelve years old or so."

"That's a long, long time, Momma."

"I know, but you are a strong girl and can wait until then."

Bea smiled and nodded. "I am strong, Momma."

"I'm proud of you, Bea. Now you and Ben go outside and play. Aurora and I will come out in a little bit."

Once the children were out of the house, Maggie said, "I need your help and knowledge."

"Anything I can do to help you, I will do, ikana."

Maggie smiled and felt honored at Aurora's use of the Chickasaw word for friend. "I was sure you would. I love my babies. I know many women have them even closer together than I have, but I'm tired and feel four children are enough. I don't want to be a woman who is pregnant every few years, working hard in the fields—becoming old and dying young long before necessary."

She sighed, and Aurora waited, feeling her friend had more to say.

Maggie shook her head and continued. "I sometimes feel drained emotionally as well as physically. About the time I have my wits and body how I think they should be, I get pregnant again. I love my husband and children but want to be me—a grown, educated woman, taking care of her family."

"Well," Aurora said, "You've had three to four years between your babies. That's quite a long time. How have you managed that?"

"First, I nursed them until they were twenty-four months old or a bit older, which I know helps with spacing the pregnancies out. Second, Silas has been careful to withdraw when I would be most fertile. Yet 1-2 years after I no longer am nursing, I am pregnant again. I want not to have any more babies unless I choose to."

"Ah. Have you spoken with Silas about your feelings?"

"No, and I know I should."

Aurora nodded. "I trust you will share your feelings with him. You are a close and bonded couple."

"So, do you think there might be a way not to have more children?"

"Maybe. You must understand that nothing is certain as long as you have a womb and regular menses. However, there are several ways, including the withdrawal method you say Silas has used in the past, but none of them are perfect. Tracking the moon and drinking a few herbal teas works fairly well for most women. I've heard of various barriers the man can put on, but they are expensive, hard to find, and, to my mind, don't work any better than my more natural methods."

"Tell me about the moon and tea."

"Go get your journal, and we can know when your most fertile times are."

While Maggie went to get her journal, Aurora tied her baby close to her body with a long piece of cloth. She smiled, thinking of how if she'd been pregnant, she'd have spent days and many hours making a cradleboard for her baby with the women of her family. She was happy to have a daughter and liked keeping her close to her body. It felt right and natural—*maybe*, she thought, *it's better than a cradleboard*.

Maggie returned to the room and smiled. "I like how you've used the long piece of calico cloth to have Okchuli close to you."

"Thanks. If I'd had time, I would have made a cradleboard with soft leather and decorated it with beads. I had planned to use the cloth to make a new dress for me. However, this fabric is all I had at hand. I love having Okchuli close to me."

"I think it is lovely. I want to fashion a carrier like yours for Teddy."

"It's easy to do, and I'll happily help you. For now, let's talk about your pregnancies."

The two women sat at the table, going through Maggie's record of bleeding times. Aurora wrote down the dates Maggie's menses started and stopped. After going through a few years, Aurora said, "You are a lucky woman, Maggie. Your periods are very regular and in the phase of the new moon. I've seen no times of skipped bleeding except when you are pregnant. So if you make a note in the middle of time—full moon time—between bleedings and mark your journal, that's when you are most likely to get pregnant. You are more likely to get pregnant within three to four days before and after your mid-cycle."

Maggie nodded. "I can mark those days as the most fertile days. Any other signs?"

"Some women have cramping when the egg releases, but most don't. Also, the vaginal discharge is frequently more like a bit of raw egg white. The mucous facilitates the egg remaining viable until some eager sperm meets and mates with the egg."

Maggie chuckled. "I've noticed the mucous a few times. Now, about the herbal teas. Can you fix them for me?"

"Absolutely. But they aren't perfect, nor is tracking your periods. The only perfect method is no intercourse."

"I understand. I want to have no more babies, but if a baby comes along, regardless of my efforts, I'll take that miracle any day."

Aurora smiled. "Good. We can give you a good chance to, at the very least, widen the years between pregnancies."

"What a relief. I love my children and love being a mother, but enough is enough."

"Please let Silas know your thoughts. He has a right to know your feelings."

"I will. I promise."

Bea poked her head in the door and said, "Are you through talking, Momma?"

"Yes, we are, and thank you for being patient."

"You're welcome. Can we go see if the cantaloupes are ready?"

"Yes, we can, but I think it will take a few more weeks. You are right, though—we don't want to miss a single minute of ripe canteloupe. Give us another few minutes so we can bring Teddy and Okchuli with us."

Aurora showed Maggie how to fashion a long cloth like hers to carry Teddy close to her. It took a few minutes longer than Bea liked, but Aurora and Maggie soon had their babies strapped close to their bodies. Teddy fussed at first but quickly returned to sleep once he was close to his mother's body.

CHAPTER TWENTY-SIX

*"For every minute
you are angry, you
lose sixty seconds
of happiness."*
Ralph Waldo Emerson

DAY AFTER DAY, the women and children worked in the kitchen gardens at both homes as well as the bigger gardens. While the vegetables grew, so did the babies and children. Maggie and Aurora became close friends and talked about their previous lives and what hopes and dreams might come their way.

Bea was excited that some of the food was finally ready to be harvested but, most importantly, to be eaten. The first thing they harvested was what Aurora had ripe in her gardens, and then they returned to Maggie's house to gather there. Once the women had picked several squashes, onions, and even a few ripe tomatoes, they returned indoors to store and preserve the harvested vegetables. Silas had bought a few dozen quart-size jars for them to preserve their gardens' bounty.

Both women hoped that all the jars would be filled by the end of the summer. On each jar lid were written in red wax pencil the contents and the date.

Clay and Silas worked together, plowing several acres, which would be a large orchard they would share. The few fruit trees they'd planted were doing well, so the men decided more fruit trees would bring in more money for them and keep their larders full. The warm climates and plentiful water would allow them to plant apples, apricots, peaches, pears, and plums. They were confident they could make a profit by properly tending the orchards.

Clay told Silas, "I tried planting oranges a few years ago, but it was a no-go."

"I'd have thought with all the sunny days around here, they would be perfect," Silas said.

"Yes, but as soon as winter hits, they die. Any temperature below fifty degrees for more than a few hours is too hard on them. Little more than a few hours of cold can kill the crop."

"I hadn't thought of the temperature, just the sunshine."

"That was my mistake, too. Before I could do much other than harvest a few pieces of fruit, we had a late winter blast, and it was all over. Despite the sun, the weather can be frigid, even without snow or ice, from November to March. Many other fruits are hardier, but citrus depends more on warmth than sunshine."

Silas looked up to see a buggy coming down the road. He took off his hat and watched the dust from the horse and wheels of the buggy fly up around it and the man driving.

Silas asked, "I wonder who that is?"

Clay looked up and shook his head. "One of my least favorite people on Earth."

"Why?"

"He's Lester Blunt, a vile man who calls Aurora names I won't repeat."

"Really?"

"Yes," Clay nodded his head. "He is the foulest and loudest bigot around here."

Silas tied the horse's reins to the plow and said, "Well, let's see if we can't send him on his way."

As the men walked to greet the man in the buggy, the door of Silas's home opened. Noah ran out of the house to his father and said, "Momma wants to know if she should set out tea."

"I think not, son. Please let your mother know this man won't be here long enough for tea."

"Yes, sir," Noah answered and glanced at the man in the buggy as Lester Blunt pulled his horse to a halt a few feet away from the boy and men. Noah wanted to find out as much as possible without disobeying his father. Luckily, Clay walked toward the man and said, "Hello, Lester."

The man named Lester nodded but didn't smile. He said, "Clay," as he climbed out of the buggy.

Noah was sure the man didn't like Clay. He turned and ran back into the house.

Lester Blunt ignored the boy—he was just a child, after all, no more than a piss ant—and walked up to Silas, passing Clay with a dismissive snort and shake of his head. When he was close to Silas, he held out a hand. "I'm Lester Blunt. I've come to welcome you to the neighborhood."

Silas didn't take the man's hand. "We've been here for nearly two full months. I'm surprised you waited so long to welcome me and my family to the community. Others have come and welcomed us. Even the Methodist preacher, Josiah Hartfield, stopped by a few weeks ago. Why your delay, Mr. Blunt?"

"Well, now, Mr. Pennington, I've been fairly busy and finally have the time to come for a visit."

"I wish you'd let us know you were coming to visit. I'm up to my knees in work right now preparing my orchard."

"Surely, you could find some hired hand or another to do that dirty work." He glanced over to Clay and nodded.

Silas shook his head. "Dirty work never hurt me, and I rather like doing things for myself." Silas turned to Clay and said, "Clay, will you give Sally some water, then come on back so we can have a quick chat and get back to our work?"

"Sure thing, Silas."

As Clay walked away, Lester said, "Why don't you make him address you in a more seemly manner?"

"Clay is my friend, and I've no idea what you mean by a 'seemly manner.' You, sir, are not my friend yet and might never be."

"Aw, now. No need to get huffy, Silas."

"Please call me Mr. Pennington."

Lester tightened his lip, nodded, and said, "Well, Mr. Pennington, I just assumed, being a Pennington, you would understand the status you have in the community."

"Oh, no, sir. Never that. I've never murdered anyone, been hung, or played a fiddle, and can barely carry a tune in an empty bucket."

"Well, you know who and what I mean."

"No, actually, I do not."

"One bad apple doesn't have to spoil the whole barrel."

"I agree. Neither my Uncle Jacob nor I could ever be considered a bad apple. But, you, I don't know about yet."

Clay came back and stood beside Silas but said nothing.

Lester said, "Then I'll come to the point. We are a community surrounded by Indians, and they mostly stay out of the way. It doesn't mean good, god-fearing folk like having redskins around, in and out of our businesses, and having a say in what we can and cannot do. But those leftover slave folks are good for nothing. It's a sad thing to my mind that we can no longer make them be in their rightful place as slaves."

"I disagree and count it a blessing that no man or woman in our country will ever be enslaved to anyone, Mr. Blunt. That war is over—many years ago. Now, I've got work to do. Good day." Silas turned around to walk away. Lester grabbed his arm and jerked him to turn around.

Silas said, "If you'd like to be able to walk to your buggy, you will remove your hand from my arm and leave my property. If you do not, you'll struggle to pick up your vile bloody body from the dirt in my yard."

Lester dropped his hand. "I'm sorry to have provoked ire, Silas."

"Mr. Pennington."

"Right. I'm sorry to have provoked you, Mr. Pennington. I'll speak my business, though, before leaving."

"Make it quick. My friend Clay and I have work to do."

"If you want to be welcomed to our community, you'll rid yourself of the vermin this man—" he nodded to Clay, "has brought to your home."

Before Clay could respond, Silas doubled his fist and landed a sharp and painful blow to Lester Blunt's face. As Lester lay on the ground, blood spurting from his nose and lip, Silas said, "Come along, Clay. We've got work to do. I'm sure Mr. Blunt knows how to crawl out of the dirt and into his fine, proper buggy."

None of the men saw or heard Maggie come walking across the yard with the shotgun in her hands. Lester jumped to his feet and was reaching for Silas's shoulder when Maggie cocked the hammer of the shotgun—loudly. All three men stopped and looked at her with their mouths hanging open.

She said, "Mister. I don't know who you are, but I recently gave birth. I'm still a little emotional. Right now, I'm up to my ears with work to do. I'm in no fair mood to deal with your shenanigans. Now. You can get in your buggy and ride away, with or without buckshot in your tail—or maybe it was rock salt. I can't rightly remember what I put in there, but I'll happily put it in your hide. Your choice."

Lester paled while Clay and Silas both smiled a little. Silas said, "Thanks, darlin', for having my back. I'm sure Mr. Blunt just stumbled."

"Good. You and Clay have an orchard to prep, and I'm sure Mr. Blunt would rather go on his way with only a bloody nose."

Lester picked up his hat, dusted it off, and nodded to Maggie. "Thank you, ma'am." He started to walk toward his buggy but instead turned to Silas. "You haven't heard the last of this."

Maggie pulled back the second hammer. The sound echoed around them as she raised the shotgun to her eye. She said in a cold, quiet voice, "I've been known to shoot a squirrel right through the eye—no matter how big the shot. My guess is a big old fella like you standing this close —why, I'm certain I could blow your whole damned head off."

Lester paled, nodded, and said, "I'll leave now, Mrs. Pennington."

"Good. Don't bother coming back. I'm not terribly fond of vermin who speak poorly of my friends."

Lester swallowed, nodded again, hurried to his buggy, climbed into the seat, clicked his tongue to the horse, and drove away.

Maggie grinned and turned to Clay and Silas with the shotgun laid on her shoulder and her left hand on her hip. Silas laughed and said, "My heavens, but you are a grand woman, Maggie!"

"Yes, I am. Thank you for noticing."

Clay asked, "Would you really have shot him, Maggie?"

"No. The shotgun isn't loaded."

Silas laughed and shook his head. "You're the best, darlin'."

Clay laughed and then said, "Seriously, Silas. That man has a lot of pull around here. Maybe Aurora and I should move on."

"And leave us to our own devices?" Maggie asked. "Don't even think about leaving us. We are babes in the woods—in case you hadn't noticed. Without you and Aurora, I'm certain we'd make a fine mess of things rather quickly. Never, ever threaten to leave us, Clay."

Clay smiled, "Yes, ma'am. Can you really shoot a squirrel through the eye?"

"I have no idea. I've never shot anything in my life."

Silas chuckled, "And let's keep it that way, darlin.'"

Clay nodded, then shook his head. "I will teach you how to use the gun. We have snakes, bears, coyotes, bobcats, and even a mountain lion or two still roaming around these parts. You must know how to defend yourself if Silas and I aren't here."

"Thanks, Clay. I'd appreciate the lessons."

Silas hugged her and said, "Thanks for sending old Lester packing."

"You're welcome. Now, you two get busy. We don't want to waste the sunshine."

She turned and walked back to the house, her shoulders back with the shotgun resting on her shoulder. Her stride was purposeful, and she was pleased with the day's events so far.

Noah watched his mother coming back to the house. He was increasingly impressed with her as time went on, but today, she sent a bully running. His mother was something to behold today. He whispered, "I want to grow up to be like my Momma."

Aurora heard him and smiled. "Your mother is a woman who knows her worth. You need to learn your worth, Noah."

He turned to Aurora and asked, "How do I do that?"

"Always tell the truth. Always be kind. Never let anyone bully you, but never, ever throw the first punch. When they're in the dirt bleeding, walk away."

"That's what Papa did."

"Yes, and your mother, too, with a little bluffing and urging."

He nodded and turned to the front door as his mother entered. She said, "Aurora, I need a cup of tea, and a few drops of whiskey wouldn't hurt a thing."

Aurora laughed.

Noah said, "You were so brave, Momma."

"I was standing up for myself and my home."

"Would you have killed that man?"

"No. It wasn't loaded, but he didn't know that. Bullies like him are usually easy to run off."

"What if he hadn't turned and left?"

"I don't know."

Noah nodded. He walked outside and sat on the porch steps. He needed to think about all of this. Seeing his mother lifting that shotgun to threaten the bully was unexpected. At that moment, he thought she was a hero—in fact, he was pretty sure she was a hero no matter what she said. Still, needing a bit of whiskey in her tea meant she was scared, too. He didn't understand how anyone could be afraid and be a hero.

Maggie watched her son, then turned to Aurora and asked, "Did I do the right thing?"

"Yes, you did. It won't stop a man like Lester Blunt for long, but for today and maybe a few days, he'll not have the courage to pester you and Silas again. It was all about me and Clay, I'm sure."

"Doesn't matter to me what he was going on about. What matters to me is that my family, home, and friends are safe. Anyone threatening anything in my life had best be prepared to face my ire."

Aurora smiled and said, "Yes, ma'am."

Maggie grinned, raised an eyebrow, and said, "Don't call me ma'am."

Both women laughed as they sipped their tea, laced with a bit of Kentucky whiskey.

CHAPTER TWENTY-SEVEN

FOR THE REST of the day, all the children, Clay and Silas, couldn't stop talking about Maggie running off Mr. Lester Blunt. She tried to explain to the children that threatening anyone with a shotgun was never a good idea, but they were having none of her lectures. Her actions spoke louder than any of her words, which left her thinking she might need to polish up her words. Causing physical harm would never feel right to her.

Noah said, "I think you were brave, Momma, to go out there and tell that man to go away."

"Thank you, Noah, but the gun wasn't loaded."

"I know, Momma, but he deserved you to send him on his way."

"Yeah," Ben said. "Momma sent him packing!" Then he lifted his little fist in the air and jumped up and down.

Maggie smiled but shook her head. "I think you children have some chores to do."

"Aw, Momma," Bea said. "I hate carrying water from the well to the house."

"Do you hate eating dinner?"

"No! I love eating dinner."

"Then you and your brothers had best get busy carrying water. Don't forget to feed the chickens and Patches."

"We won't," Noah said. "I'll milk Patches, too."

"Good. That will give your father, Clay, Aurora, and me a little more time to finish the work we've started for today."

Once the children were busy in the barn, Maggie sat in her rocking chair, nursing Teddy and chatting with Aurora, who sat beside her, nursing Okchuli.

Maggie said, "I've been thinking about the children and their education. They are learning a lot about life, including life on the frontier, but little about how to read, write, and do their numbers."

"Doesn't Noah know those things?"

"A little. He was getting very good at reading and arithmetic. He loves to read. He'll try to read any book, no matter how much it is above his skill level. However, he needs to keep moving forward with his education. The twins haven't had much education, and it's time they start with the simple things."

"Well," Aurora smiled, "Noah may be getting close to my level of education—I went through the sixth grade. But still, I need and want more education."

Maggie shook her head. "I've learned a lot from you, and I want you to help me educate our children. They all deserve to build as much knowledge as possible—not just from books. I want them to know about herbs and natural remedies as well as reading, writing, arithmetic, and the natural order of things in our World. And, most certainly, not the order of things anyone like Mr. Blunt would dish out. Our children must know history, and your history is something I want them to learn

—from the horse's mouth, as it were. In fact, your history is something I want to learn for myself."

"I agree, but I've no idea how to start. I still say I need educating, at least at deeper levels."

"We all do, but in different ways. For example, I knew little about my body until I met you."

Aurora nodded. "I'm glad you mentioned your learning about your body. I've been working on writing a midwifery book to help others learn how to be a midwife. I fear I'm not capable of writing down things in a way that can help women."

"See! That's exactly what I'm talking about. I want us to work together in all things. I aim to educate ourselves and our children and spread what we know. I'll teach you what I know, and you'll teach me what you know. Together, we'll educate our children. Both are important."

"Where and how do we start?"

"I suggest we use the nook under the staircase where the books are to teach the children. Clay and Silas can build us a small table for the wee ones and a bigger desk for Noah and, later, Ben and Bea as they grow. Let's start as soon as we can."

"Today?"

Maggie shook her head. "Let's start in a few days. We should tell the children our plans and start school on Monday next."

"That's four days from now. Can we be ready by then?"

"I think so. We can at least start rudimentary reading and writing. Once they have a bit of an understanding of reading and writing, we can start with arithmetic—a review for Noah, but we can help him with more complex arithmetic. If you can be prepared to teach them about the herbs in our gardens, that would be great."

Aurora nodded. "I like it. My mother taught me by having me draw herbs and flowers and then keep notes. It helped to keep my mind clear about it all. I'll bring the book I created. I call it my herbology."

"Perfect. I'm eager to see your book, and I'd love for my children to create their own herbal and floral books."

"I wish we had more books," Aurora said.

Maggie smiled. "Oh, we have many books in those boxes in the alcove and more in the attic closets. Most of them will be beyond the children for now, though. In the meantime, I've sent a letter to my mother-in-law about the need for books for the children. I've also asked her to send more pencils and penmanship paper as well as graphite for our mechanical pencils. I know she'll help us."

"That will be terrific. When will they arrive?"

"I'm not sure. I sent the letter a few weeks ago. I told her there were carriages bringing goods to Tishomingo and a post office. I haven't heard back, but expect a reply soon."

Aurora chuckled. "You seem to have thought of everything."

"No. Just following how my mother taught me and my brother."

"I didn't know you have a brother."

"I don't any longer. He died in a horse racing accident." She shook her head and muttered, "What a silly way to die!"

"But he wanted to race, right?" Aurora asked.

"Yes. He loved riding a horse as fast as he could. He also liked the money he won when he raced. The thrill of riding fast and the yearning for money killed my brother. But you're right. He died doing what he loved."

"I'm sorry for your loss, but to die doing what you love is a blessing. I do have a question about learning."

"I'm all ears."

"Can I show you my journal about midwifery for you to read?"

"Of course."

"It's not finished," Aurora said, "but with your help on the writing, I think I could make progress."

"Certainly. We might even get Silas to help. He used to be an editor in South Carolina and also writes stories."

"I did not know he had been an editor and author."

"Yes. It is part of why he wanted you and Clay to be a part of our adventure. He wanted to carve out some time from the day-to-day chores for writing. Soon, he hopes to be writing most of the time again."

"I'm glad Clay and I are here to help, but happier still to have a home and friends who support us. That you and Silas might help me write my book is a real blessing."

"The blessing is in helping each other."

Aurora smiled and nodded. She lifted baby Okchuli to her shoulder and patted her back to help her burp. Maggie followed suit as the two women continued to think and talk about educating each other and the children.

After a few minutes of discussing how to educate their children and each other, Aurora said, "There's another thing I want you to do for me."

"Anything."

Aurora pulled a folded piece of paper from her pocket and said, "Please read the paper, and if you agree, I'm asking you to sign the paper."

Maggie opened the paper and smiled as she read. "You are a clever woman, Aurora. Of course, I'll sign the paper, but where?"

"By signing your name, you will agree you were the midwife for me and my child."

Maggie looked up, smiled, and nodded. She stood, went to her bedroom, and returned with her journal and pen. "First, I'll put an entry about the birth of Okchuli in my journal. How did you come up with the date?"

"When my milk came in. For me, that was when I knew I was fully her mother. Besides having her birth date three days after she appeared in her basket, it makes it less clear a baby was left on my porch. I burned the basket and the note that came with her. Only you, Clay, and Silas know the full story."

Maggie shook her head and sighed. "Bea is very curious about babies, how they come to us, and how we care for them."

"I thought of that after my conversation with Bea. If we speak of Okchuli as having been born to me, she might at least let go of the miracle part of the story."

"I hope she'll accept it as just a surprise."

"She hasn't asked me about the birth since that last conversation."

Maggie nodded and signed the birth certificates—one for the government and one for the mother. She noted Okchuli's birth and the details of the birth certificate given to Okchuli's mother. She handed one of the birth certificates to Aurora. "What do I do with this one?"

"You and I will go to our new Council House. You may have seen the building when you came into town. It is built of native pink granite from the Pennington Creek Quarry. The building is the center of government for the Chickasaw Nation. It's not completely finished on the inside, but the outside is mostly finished. The clerk, Walter Thompson, will help us get our children's birth certificates legally entered with the council."

"I did see the building. It is beautiful, and the rising sun made it look even more elegant in the rose and gold light. I'm worried about you, though."

"Why?"

"Won't they question whether or not you were ever pregnant?"

"I don't think so. Especially the men won't—it would be too embarrassing for them—and they are the ones who run everything. I'm more round than tall, so it won't be a stretch for anyone to think I had been pregnant but didn't say anything about it. Besides, I haven't been around town much lately other than to help with birthing a baby—and not many of them. No one will doubt my claim—as an outcast—part slave and part Chickasaw, people only pay attention to my face and only for the moment it is necessary. As soon as I'm out of their sites, most folks never think of me."

"I hope not all people, Aurora. You are beautiful. I'll spend my whole life protecting you and making certain the moniker of the *outcast* is never spoken in my presence. It may take time, but I'll work to keep you safe."

"Thanks, Maggie. I'm not worried about filing the birth certificates. We must also take Teddy's birth certificate to register his birth. Two women with babes in their arms means no one will ever question the truth of our children's births. If a baby whimpers and we start to nurse, they'll sign everything quicker than a rabbit can find his hole with a hawk chasing his furry tail."

Maggie laughed. "I am certain you are right."

Aurora smiled, knowing it was deception, but she needed to protect her child. Having Maggie with her child will help make it seem more plausible. Once the birth certificates are legal, there will be no doubt about who is the mother of each child. Besides, Okchuli's hair looked more like Clay's hair every day. Her eyes were lightening but brown. Still, she felt no one would dare suggest anything about her birth with Maggie Pennington at her side.

CHAPTER TWENTY-EIGHT

"Our birth is
but a sleep and a forgetting.
Not in entire forgetfulness,
and not in utter nakedness,
but trailing clouds
of glory, do we come."
William Wordsworth

CLAY HITCHED ROSIE, Aurora's horse, to her buggy and said, "I'm a little uneasy about you and Maggie going into town without one of us with you."

Aurora shook her head. "We'll be fine."

Silas smiled and watched his wife's face as she began to speak. She looked at Clay and shook her head. "Do you think we cannot go four miles without a big, strong man to help us?"

"No, ma'am. Never that. I'm a bit concerned about Lester Blunt and his ilk."

Aurora sighed. "Clay, if Shirley Duncan can come and go at will on the same road, then Maggie and I can do so as well."

Clay turned to Silas, hoping to find him siding against the women going into town alone. Silas merely shrugged his shoulders and smiled. He, too, was a bit worried, but he knew his wife and her determination. Once her hat was set, both metaphorically and in reality, nothing would stand in her way.

Clay smiled, nodded to Silas, and turned back to the women. He asked, "May I at least help you up to the seat of the buggy?"

"Yes, Clay, that would be very helpful. I've never climbed up on a buggy with an infant strapped to me."

Maggie smiled and said, "I've done it before but always appreciate a steady hand helping me."

The men helped their wives settle in the buggy. Clay handed his wife the reins and said, "Please take care. You are my life."

She smiled, seeing his anxiety and love for her and their child. She touched his cheek and said, "And you are mine."

Silas said, "I have faith in you two. Maggie, send for help if you need it."

She chuckled and pointed to their children playing in the yard. "It's more likely you two will need help with the children," she said.

He turned and watched the children race around chasing each other in the front yard, sighed, cocked his head, and nodded. "There is that."

The two men and three children, remaining with the men, waved their goodbyes. Noah said, "I wish Momma would have let me go with her."

Silas put his hand on his son's shoulder. "Me too, son. But once your Momma gets an idea, she is determined to follow it through to the end. I've learned it's best to step back and leave her to her own devices."

"I know, Papa, and I think she will be fine, but bad men in Tishomingo want us all gone."

"Well, they can want in one hand and piss in the other. All they'll get is stinky and wet. We're here to stay."

The children laughed, and Ben said, "Papa said piss."

Silas blushed, "Don't tell your Momma."

Clay chuckled and then said, "Okay, now, wranglers. Let's get busy with planting the rest of the orchard."

Bea asked, "Can I help too?"

"Absolutely. Without your help, we might get the work done too quickly. Then all we'd do is worry, worry, worry."

"Yep. Worry, worry, worry. Momma says the same thing."

When Aurora and Maggie arrived in town, a few people looked at the two women, wondering why they were coming to town alone. However, most folks didn't seem to notice them at all.

Shirley Duncan watched the two women drive their buggy into town, quickly turned the sign on her door to *Closed*, pulled the door shut, and followed them to the new Council House. The Chickasaw had built it, and the building would not open officially until November. That didn't change that folks needed the Council House so the business of life would continue.

The exterior building was almost completed and beautiful, gleaming in the sun. The clerk was available despite the hammering, sawing, and interior mess. When Aurora stopped the buggy in front of the Council House, two men came forward and offered to help them from the buggy.

Maggie said, "Thank you. With babies in our arms, we feel a bit off balance."

"Yes, ma'am," one of them answered and started to help Maggie down. Neither man seemed inclined to help Aurora.

She said, "Please help my friend, Aurora, first. She gave birth not long ago. I'm already healed from my birthing. She needs more help than I do."

The two men looked at each other just as Shirley arrived. She said, "You two knuckleheads do as Maggie asked and help my dear friend, Aurora."

They quickly went to help Aurora down from the buggy. When Aurora was on the ground, she said, "Thank you, gentlemen. Your gracious help means a lot since I'm so close to my birthing."

They both nodded but blushed a little. One of the men had the good grace to say, "It's a pleasure to help you, Aurora."

Aurora smiled and nodded.

Shirley hugged Aurora and said, "I'm delighted to see you doing so well from your *very* recent birthing."

Aurora smiled. "It's largely thanks to you, the chair, and, of course, Maggie."

"I'm glad." Shirley asked the two men, "Will you kindly help Mrs. Pennington and not keep standing there gawking."

They both nodded and quickly helped Maggie from the buggy.

Aurora said, "I taught Maggie how to help me through the process. She is going to be an excellent midwife, I'm sure."

Shirley smiled and nodded to Maggie. "I'm so glad you could help Aurora."

"Without her lead, I wouldn't have known what to do," which was true. She turned to Aurora and said, "We should get our business done here, and then we can go to Shirley's store for a short visit."

Shirley smiled. "Good. I have some packages from South Carolina for you as well. The coach from Boggy Depot brought the packages earlier today."

"That's perfect. We'll be along as soon as we finish filing the birth certificates of our babies here at the Council House."

"May I come with you?"

"Certainly," Maggie said and nodded. "We'd appreciate your company."

The two men stood staring at the women, unsure what to do or say. Shirley turned to the men and said, "Would you fellas take their buggy to my store? We'll walk back and chat along the way."

One of the men doffed his hat and said, "Sure thing, Miss Shirley. Happy to be of service."

Maggie smiled and said, "Thanks so much for helping Aurora and me. It was a needed kindness and the Christian thing to do."

Both men nodded and smiled, and one of them even blushed, knowing she was right but that he'd hesitated to touch a woman many thought was not quite human. Just a few days earlier, his wife had said,

"You ever mistreat Aurora, and you'll have had your last meal in my home."

"It's my home too," he had argued.

"You go on believing that if you must, but when I quit feeding your sorry ass, you'll remember who the house belongs to."

He felt shamed whenever he remembered that fuss with his wife. He loved her and knew his life would be miserly without her in it. Now, he felt shame he'd ever hesitated to help Aurora. He decided when he went home, he'd apologize to his wife and tell her how much he loved her.

As the two men drove the buggy to Shirley's store, he told his friend, "I think being around Lester Blunt is making me a man I don't want to be. I think I'll spend more time at home with my wife."

"A fine idea. I've told you before that his money isn't worth your soul."

He nodded and thought his friend was right. There was nothing Lester Blunt had that he wanted. "Maybe I'll stick to my farm and spend more time working at home and less around Lester."

"I'm not certain, but you seem to be learning."

He blushed and nodded.

His friend shook his head and said, "It's high time."

The women stood, watching the two men ride away in Aurora and Clay's buggy.

Shirley said, "Good work, Maggie. Those two aren't the nicest men, but they are certainly not the worst. I must say, I'm amazed you two came into town alone."

"So were our husbands," Aurora said. "I was a little nervous, but Maggie insisted we come alone."

Maggie grinned. "I wanted to be certain of two things. First, I wanted no one to question anything about our relationship. Aurora is my friend and helper, too. Second, I wanted to emulate you, Shirley. There is no reason Aurora and I cannot come into town on our own occasionally."

"I agree, and I'm proud of you both."

Aurora nodded. "It is a blessing that Maggie is my friend and helps me as well."

Shirley smiled and patted Maggie's hand. "I'll say it again—well done, Maggie."

She turned to Aurora and said, "Show me your darling baby."

Aurora pulled back the blanket a little. Shirley smiled and asked, "A girl?"

"Yes, ma'am."

"Please call me Shirley. Ma'am implies a hierarchy that I don't believe in. We women have to stick together." She watched as Aurora pulled back the blanket a little and smiled. "Your daughter is beautiful and looks much like you and Clay. Her native skin shines, and her hair is lovely and light with a bit of red shining through."

"I think she is perfect, and we are grateful."

"Her red-blonde hair and deep brown eyes are lovely. She is a delight."

"Thank you, Shirley, and I feel the same about her. Maybe her dark baby eyes will become at least a little blue. I would love to see Clay in her eyes."

"Well, if it is meant to be, it will be as you wish."

Aurora smiled, tucked the blanket around her daughter, and then turned to Maggie. "We should get inside and take care of the birth certificates."

"May I go with you?" Shirley asked.

"Sure," Maggie said, "The more the merrier."

"More importantly," Shirley said, "There's safety and more understanding of our truth when women stand together."

"You are right." For the first time in many years, Maggie felt an urge for the rights of women. She'd been living a life of luxury before they moved to Pennington Creek. Maggie loved her home on Pennington Creek, her family, and her new friends. She decided at that moment she would never again be the lady of the manor but would be a woman with every right she could muster.

The three women walked into the building and followed the notices stating where they could file the birth certificates with the clerk. The pounding and sawing were evident and loud everywhere they went.

Once they were in the right place, filing the birth certificates was accomplished without fuss.

Walter Thompson, the Chickasaw Nation clerk, did say, "Mrs. Harrison, I wasn't aware you were with child. But I haven't seen you recently either."

"Well, when you are as round as I am, it is easy for others to be unaware of the pregnancy until it is very far along. Still, she came a little early. It's part of why I haven't been in town recently."

He blushed a little and nodded. "Of course, ma'am. I meant no disrespect."

"I know, Mr. Thompson, and I appreciate your kindness."

He looked at Maggie and said, "You were very kind to help Mrs. Harrison."

"Thank you, but helping comes as naturally as taking my next breath when a friend is in need. Besides, she helped me with my birthing. The least I could do was to help her with her birthing. She is a good teacher."

"Yes, ma'am." He blushed again. Walter Thompson was a bit uneasy thinking about birthing. Aurora had attended his own wife's birthing several months ago. He had hated the birthing sounds and had no intention of watching a child being born. He'd seen enough calves, foals, and lambs—even puppies and kittens—to know it was a terrifying experience—for him, at least. He was glad to be a man and admired the stamina of women but would never want to attend the birth of a child.

He handed the two women their stamped, signed, and registered birth certificates for their children.

Maggie smiled and looked at her new son's birth certificate. She loved seeing his name. She said, "Thank you for all your help today, Mr. Thompson."

Aurora said, "Thank you, Walter. Please give my best regards to your dear wife, Ellen.

"It was my pleasure, Aurora. My wife will be pleased you have a lovely baby girl. I appreciate your helping her with her birthing a few months ago."

"It is a blessing to help any woman bring their child into our world."

Walter nodded, and as the three women left the building, he still wondered about Aurora's baby. He shook his head and muttered, "I've signed the certificate, and that's that. She has a baby. The baby is hers, and that's all there is to it."

He turned, filed the two birth certificates in the ledger, and closed the book. He decided to think about anything other than women and their babies—at least for the rest of the day.

The three women left the building without speaking until they were walking back toward Shirley's store. Shirley walked between the two women, tucked her arms in theirs, and said, "My heavens, but I do like women who know their worth and don't let bullies—men or women— push them about."

Aurora laughed. "And I like women who love each other regardless of their skin."

Maggie nodded. "And your skin, Aurora, is beautiful, and you are amazing."

"Hear! Hear!" Shirley said.

Maggie said, "You, Shirley, are a lovely and wonderful woman, and your brown skin glows in the sunlight. I love your black hair and would love to see it unbraided.

"Thanks, Maggie. You are beautiful too, although a little more color in your pale skin wouldn't go amiss."

Maggie chuckled. "I'm working on it with Aurora's potions, your dried fruit, and good cooking."

"Good. I want you to be healthy and enjoy your beautiful home on Pennington Creek. It's what Jacob always wanted. Now. Let's see what South Carolina has sent you. I'll let my hair down, too. I think a cup of tea and some of my lovely oatmeal and raisin cookies are in order. We need to celebrate."

All three women laughed and chattered as they walked to Shirley's store. They did not go unnoticed. Some folks smiled at the joy of the women and their babies and then returned to work. Some folks saw the women, nodded, and thought it was a fine sunny day, and they, too, felt joy within their souls.

A very few folks—vile creatures to the core—ran to Lester Blunt to tell him of the harlots walking down the street, laughing and chattering like magpies with not even one man with them. Lester saw them and broke the cigar he had been smoking in half. He ignored the burn and blister forming on the palm of his left hand. He howled at the sight of the women, especially Aurora.

CHAPTER TWENTY-NINE

Benjamin Franklin

"LET'S see what your mother-in-law sent, Maggie." Shirley motioned for Maggie and Aurora to follow her into her storeroom. "I intended to bring them out to you later this afternoon. I also wanted a visit, but you're here, which is grand."

She pointed to three wooden boxes and said, "These are the boxes that came from South Carolina. I haven't opened them, but I thought you'd rather do the opening yourself."

Maggie smiled and nodded. "Thanks, Shirley. I'm certain this will be what I requested my mother-in-law to send. It should be books for the children and a few educational supplies."

"Are you a teacher?"

"No, but I am educated. My parents scrimped and saved to ensure I had a full liberal studies education. I graduated from Columbia Female

College in South Carolina with a general degree. I'm determined that my children will have an education. I didn't see a school here in town."

Shirley nodded and said, "There isn't one yet except for the Manual Labor Academy and Bloomfield Academy. Both are missionary boarding schools for the Chickasaw people's children. A few white children can attend those schools if they pay tuition, but only in the upper grades."

Maggie looked at Aurora and raised her eyebrows. Aurora said, "The Bloomfield Academy isn't in Tishomingo. It's many miles south and east of here—at least if you're walking, it seems that way. It's a boarding school for girls. Momma let me go there for a few years, but she hated not having me at home. She kept me at home when I turned twelve and taught me everything she knew about reading, writing, arithmetic, midwifery, herbology, and helping people with their illnesses. I am educated but not in any manner such as your education, Maggie."

Maggie nodded. "I understand, dear friend. There may be some things I can share with you that you do not know, but never underestimate your education. You have much to teach me for which I have been and will continue to be grateful." She touched Aurora's hand. "Share anything about your life you are comfortable with sharing. You are a marvelous and knowledgeable woman. I will never think differently of you, no matter what. I was given a formal education. You began your learning at the Academy and then at your mother's knee. What you learned from your mother as a midwife, I have no idea about."

"Thanks, Maggie. Some of our elder women also helped me, especially an old Medicine Woman, Onatah. She was known as an Earth Woman and understood healing through the Earth. She taught me many natural medicines and how to help women bring their babies from their wombs and into the light of the Earth."

Maggie smiled. "You amaze me, Aurora. Now. Let's see what's in these boxes. I'm eager to start educating our children and ourselves."

The three women opened the boxes to find chalk, pencils, paper tablets, textbooks, blank journals, other books children would love to read, and several slates. To Maggie's surprise, there was a new A.B. Dick Planetary Pencil Sharpener which she knew would make all their lives easier. There was even a quart of flat black paint. Her mother-in-law wrote a note and tied it on the can: *You can use this to make a giant blackboard. I'm sure Silas can figure out how to create one. The directions are on the can.*

Maggie smiled and nodded her head. "My mother-in-law is a marvel. There are enough supplies here to teach a lot of children."

Shirley nodded. "When you are ready to teach more than just your children and Aurora's children, let me know, and I'll put the word out."

"Thanks, Shirley. My aim is not to become an educator, though. I hope that a school will be built in Tishomingo before long. Until then, I'll educate my children and Aurora's children with every bit of knowledge Silas and I have. My hands are full with a baby, my three older children, and helping Silas build our futures. Aurora will be a terrific help, but she also has a baby. I can't imagine teaching any other children."

"Well, I have an idea that might help you and Aurora. In the process, you'll be helping someone else. It's not a pretty story, but a child needs help. The quicker, the better. I've done what I can, but it isn't enough."

"I'll always be ready to help a child in need," Maggie said.

"Good. She is a young girl without parents but willing to work to have a place to be safe. She would have already been taken to a good Chickasaw family if she were Chickasaw. But, she is a white girl."

Aurora asked, "Sarah?"

"Yes, indeed. She's been with me for a few days, but I'm not suited to having a child around. I am quite simply not mother material. I like my freedom, and though I like her a lot, I do not wish to raise a child. She needs family, love, working, and learning with other children."

Aurora said, "I thought the Reynolds family had taken her in. They didn't have any children of their own. I thought it was a good match."

"Yes, she was originally placed with the Reynolds, but after several months, Mrs. Reynolds has changed her mind. She dropped Sarah at the Council House, and one of the secretaries brought her here a few days ago with a small bag of her few belongings. The secretary said Mrs. Reynolds told them Sarah couldn't stay with them any longer."

"Do you know why?"

Shirley sighed and nodded. "Mrs. Reynolds says Mr. Reynolds is too tempted by Sarah—which, of course, is a steaming pile of donkey dung."

Maggie smiled a little, but Aurora snorted, shook her head, and said, "He should be whipped. We have a tree just for such a man. Thirty-nine lashes at the whipping tree might settle his longing for little girls. Too bad he is a white man."

Shirley nodded. "I agree. Sadly, white men do not have to abide by Chickasaw laws. If they did, I'm sure the Council would consider the whipping tree."

Aurora nodded and turned to Maggie, who was stunned. "Mrs. Reynolds means that her husband is trying to have his way with Sarah, and Mrs. Reynolds objects. She owns responsibility for this as well."

Shirley agreed. "That's exactly what I think, too. However, no one wants to talk about that side of the man. He is considered a pillar of the community—a God-fearing man. Being white makes it hard for the rest of us to do anything."

"Yes, and Sarah is white, too," Aurora said. "I think Sarah would be better off alone than with them. Still, she is too young to be alone, not because she is white. A Chickasaw girl of her age would be too young to be alone, although she might have a few skills Sarah doesn't have."

Maggie asked, "How old is she?"

"She's eight but tells everyone she is almost nine."

Maggie chuckled. "Our Noah says the same thing. They are close in age. Where is Sarah now?"

Shirley smiled to Maggie. She hoped her thoughts about Maggie and her husband were true. In their home—a proper home—she felt certain Sarah would thrive. Maggie's home would be the perfect place for Sarah. "She's staying with me for the interim, but it is only temporary for me. Sarah is a good girl and would love to be helpful if she is in a safe place. She is upstairs in my lodgings. I had planned to bring her with me this afternoon when I brought the boxes that arrived. I was hoping you would give Sarah a try at your home. Can I bring her down to you, Maggie?"

Maggie sighed. She was overwhelmed already. Adding another— totally unexpected child into the mix was nearly beyond Maggie's comprehension. But, she supposed, her home was filled with children, love, and belonging. Then she thought, *What's one more?*

She took a deep breath and nodded but said, "I can't promise anything, Shirley. I'm nearly overwhelmed as it is."

"I understand, but if you let her be with you and your family even for a few weeks, it might be the girl's salvation. In many ways, she reminds me of your children. She is independent—has had to be, for that matter—and is a little forward in her manner of speaking. She is a good girl, though."

"This is difficult, Shirley. I'd never thought to adopt a child and certainly wouldn't have done so without Silas and I talking and thinking about doing so—for many weeks if not months."

"I understand. I'm not suggesting you adopt Sarah, but let her live with you and help you. If you could educate her and let her live with you and your children, she might have more possibilities in life."

Maggie sighed. "I'd never turn my back on a child in need. Still, it's a monumental thing to do without discussing it with my husband. Let me see her and talk with her, and then we'll decide if she can come home with me."

Shirley nodded and left the room.

Maggie sighed, shook her head, muttered, "So much for having no more children," and turned to her friend. "What can you tell me about Sarah and her life?"

Aurora smiled. "At least with Sarah, you don't have to go through pregnancy and birthing."

Maggie chuckled and shook her head.

Aurora was relieved to hear her friend laughing a bit about the circumstances. She said, "First, if Mrs. Reynolds thinks Sarah is tempting her husband for sexual activity, she is wrong. Period. Mr. Reynolds cannot keep his hands off women—especially the young ones."

"Even you?"

"Yes. He had a bit of trouble walking for a few days after he accosted me. I have strong hands and know how to squeeze." Aurora held up her hands and demonstrated how strong she could squeeze.

Maggie smiled and hugged Aurora lightly. "Good for you. Now, tell me about Sarah. What do you think of her?"

"I don't know her well because she is a white child, but I like her and feel she is a good girl. Her parents didn't like letting Sarah be around me because of my skin color."

Maggie shook her head. "I hate that anyone would shun you, Aurora, especially by hateful people like the Reynolds seemed to be."

"Don't worry about me so much, Maggie. I'm happy and feel blessed. Now, about Sarah. I'll tell you what I know. She is bright and speaks her mind, which can be a societal problem, but she is smart and self-sufficient. She's had to be with the parents their God gave her, although it's a mystery why anyone would let folks like them have children. Regardless, she seems like a biddable child who has had a rough time in her young life. She's been mostly alone for nearly a year since her parents died."

"How did her parents die?"

"That's difficult to be certain."

"What happened? Do you know?"

"What I know is mostly gossip. Her mother was found in their barn, face down in the muck by the pig pen. When Sarah went to look for her mother, she found her just outside the pig pen with her head bashed in."

"Where was her father?"

"What was left of him was in the pig pen."

"You mean the pigs were—what?—eating him?" Maggie shuddered at the thought.

"Yes. That's what I mean. No one knows what happened, but the supposition is that the two were having a fight—which wasn't uncommon for them. They hated each other and fought physically regularly, yet seemed unable to part ways. No one knows who did what, but their daughter found them both dead."

"Is it safe to bring Sarah into our home?"

"I think so, but you should decide for yourself."

"Would you be comfortable having her in your home?"

Aurora nodded. "Certainly," she said, and then she sighed and shrugged. "Before now, I wouldn't have hesitated, but now that I'm a mother, I'm not sure. Although she has white skin, I would never have turned her away because of her skin color—I'm sure you understand why. Still, I'm not sure."

Maggie nodded. "We have to take care of our birthed children no matter what need there is for anyone else, even another child."

"That's it exactly. I believe Sarah is a good girl who has been given a sorry lot in life. She is old enough to be of some help, too. She certainly isn't old enough to be alone, though."

"I'll keep my mind and heart open," Maggie said. No sooner were her words spoken than the back door of the storeroom opened.

Shirley walked through the backdoor with a small girl behind her. The child had strawberry blonde hair—braided with curly ends. A few curls were escaping the braids, creating a halo effect with the light from outside behind her. She had freckles across her nose and bright blue eyes. Maggie felt her heart squeeze a little at the sight of the child. Sarah looked as much like a child of Silas Pennington as possible. She was surprised at how much the child looked like her own children, especially Bea.

Maggie smiled and waited for Shirley to introduce the child to her.

CHAPTER THIRTY

George Bernard Shaw

SHIRLEY SMILED AT MAGGIE, then turned to the child behind her and gently tugged her forward. "Sarah, this is Aurora Harrison, who you already know, and her new friend Maggie Pennington."

Sarah smiled and asked Maggie, "Like the creek?"

Sarah's smile was beautiful, and Maggie felt drawn to the child. Maggie nodded and answered, "Yes, Sarah, exactly like the creek."

The girl nodded, smiled, and looked up at Aurora. "Hi, Aurora. You have a baby now."

"Yes, I do. She was born several days ago."

"Can I see her?"

"Of course, you can." Aurora motioned Sarah closer and pulled back the baby's blanket. Sarah tip-toed up a bit to see the baby swaddled close to Aurora. Sarah smiled, lightly touching the baby's cheek, and said, "Her hair looks like Clay's, and her skin and face look a little like you."

"Yes, she does. Her eyes are deep brown but might get lighter as time passes."

"What's her name?"

"She is Okchuli."

"Will you call her Chulie?"

"I hadn't thought of that, Sarah, but it sounds very nice. Would you like to meet my new friend, Maggie?"

The girl nodded and looked at Maggie. Aurora said, "This is my best friend, Maggie."

Sarah's mouth dropped open, and she turned to Aurora. "You have a best friend, and she is white?"

"Yes, she does," Maggie said. "I love Aurora, and she loves me, my husband, and my children."

Sarah nodded and touched Aurora's hand. "I'm glad you have a friend. I don't have any friends anymore."

"Why not?" Maggie asked.

She turned to Maggie and said, "Everyone thinks I killed my Momma and Papa, but I didn't. No one wants to play with me or live with me. They are afraid of me."

"Do you know what happened?"

"No. Just that they are dead." She sighed and shook her head. "I'll tell you the story but you probably won't believe it is true but it is true. I promise."

"Good," Maggie said. "You tell me the story, and we'll see what we all want to do."

Sarah nodded and began the story she'd told many times, hoping anyone would believe in her innocence. She knew she was innocent, but it seemed folks thought what they wanted to.

She said, "We were outside, and they were screaming and hitting each other, so I ran into the house and pulled my pillow over my head. They quit screaming after a bit, so I waited for them to come into the house and go to their bedroom. That's what usually happens."

Maggie nodded, understanding what would usually happen after Sarah's parents had fought. She asked, "How long was it before you found them?"

"I don't know for sure, but the sun was still up. I was getting hungry, so I went outside to ask if I could have a biscuit. But when I got to the pig pen behind the barn, I saw them and ran and ran and ran."

"Where did you go?"

"To the Council House."

"Did they help you?"

"Yes. Lots of people came back to my house with me, even Sheriff Harvey. The Reynolds took me in but then returned me to the Council House.

"Do you know why?" Maggie asked.

"Yep. Mr. Reynolds liked to put his hands in my panties. I told him to stop, but he didn't, so I bit his nose until he yelled, and then he slapped me."

Maggie nodded and smiled. "You did the right thing, Sarah. I'm proud of you. What happened next?"

"One of the secretaries at the Council House brought me to Shirley. Mr. Thompson said it was okay for me to be with her."

Shirley nodded. "That was a few days ago. Some folks are bickering over her parents' property, and a few even want to move into Sarah's parents' house. I fussed about it. The property belongs to Sarah. The council may have authority to sell the property, but I'll make sure if they do, the money goes to Sarah."

Sarah nodded. "It's okay if they take it. They won't let me have the property because I'm just a little girl and don't know nothin' about nothin'."

Maggie decided not to correct her grammar. The child had enough to deal with and didn't need someone telling her how to speak correctly. That could come later. She asked, "Who told you that?"

"Oh, Momma and Papa used to tell me, 'You don't know nothin' more than a gnat's ass,' and then Mr. Reynolds said, 'You're too little to understand what girls are for.' I understood more than he thinks I do."

Maggie held her temper at Mr. Reynolds and said, "I'm certain you do. How old are you, Sarah?"

"I'm nine—well, really eight, but I say nine because folks think eight-year-old girls are still babies. I'm not a baby."

"Of course, you're not a baby. Do you have other family around here?"

"Yep. My granny lives in Caddo. She is old and doesn't want any kids around."

Maggie frowned, "Are you sure? Most grannies want to see their grandchildren often."

She shook her head and sighed. "Not my granny. She said I was more trouble than I was worth and that my Momma shouldn't have married a ner-do-well bounder like my Papa."

Maggie nodded, holding back the fury of what had happened to Sarah through no fault of her own. "Do you know what a ner-do-well bounder is?"

"Yes, ma'am. It's a no good rotten man who is lazy to boot."

Maggie bit her lip to keep from laughing out loud. She smiled and nodded. When she could speak without laughing, she said, "I think that's a pretty thorough definition, Sarah." Maggie looked up at Shirley. "What do you think?"

"I think Sarah is a good girl who has had a sorry life handed to her. With an education in a good home with good people, brothers, and sisters, she might grow up to be a remarkable woman."

Maggie nodded. "That's entirely possible." She turned to Sarah and said, "I can't promise anything, Sarah, other than you could come visit for a few days. If things work out and my husband and our children agree, you might be able to be a part of our family."

"Do I get to agree if I want to stay or say no if I don't like it there?"

"Absolutely."

"What about your husband?"

"He is a good man and would never, ever hurt any child or woman."

"You're sure?"

"Yes, I am. Would you like to come home with me for now?"

Sarah pointed to the baby in Maggie's arms. "You've already got a baby."

"I'm glad you noticed. His name is Teddy. Would you like to see him?"

She nodded and smiled.

Maggie unwrapped him and stooped down enough so Sarah could see baby Teddy.

Sarah touched his forehead and smiled. "He's beautiful."

"I think so, too."

"He's bigger than Aurora's baby."

"Yes, he's a bit over two months older than Aurora's baby."

With glistening eyes, Sarah looked up at Maggie and asked, "Do you love him?"

"I do. I love all my children. I have a little girl named Bea and a little boy named Ben. They are four-year-old twins. I also have a boy named Noah who is about your age."

Sarah nodded her head and then asked, "Is Noah nice?"

"Yes, he is very nice and kind."

Sarah looked at Shirley and asked, "Can I go live with Maggie and her family?"

"Yes, you can for a try-out. The Council House said if it works well for everyone, you can stay with them."

"Will you be okay without me helping you around here?"

Shirley smiled and nodded. "I've appreciated your helping me, Sarah. However, I think I can handle things here. I want you to be with other children and in a loving family."

Sarah asked, "If they are mean to me, can I come back and live with you?"

"Absolutely."

"Then I suppose I'll go home with Maggie and her children."

Maggie smiled. "That will be fine, but I have some rules."

Sarah scowled a little but said nothing.

Maggie said, "You must always be kind to your brothers and sisters, and they will be kind to you. All children at my house must be kind."

"Will they be nice to me?"

"Yes, they will. I promise my husband, who may become your new Papa, will always be kind to you. If I become your new Momma, I will always be kind to you."

"What other rules are there?"

"We all work together and take care of each other. Do you think you can do all of that?"

Sarah nodded. "I'll try my best. I've never had brothers and sisters, which might take some time getting used to. I can clean house, milk cows, and feed chickens, but I don't like when they peck at me."

"I understand. I don't like that either, but my guess is you'll like having brothers and sisters, especially when it's time to play."

"I don't know much about playing," she shrugged. "I never had any toys and no one to play with. Momma said I should be glad to have a roof over my head and food to eat."

Maggie felt a chill race up her back and held back a shudder. She couldn't imagine a child who didn't know how to play. She thought *Aurora was right. Lashing feels about right where her first parents and Mr. Reynolds were concerned—in fact, 39 lashes would be barely enough.*

Maggie smiled and answered Sarah, "I think you'll like playing. For now, just try it. At my house, we all try to be better today than yesterday. How does that sound?"

"Okay, I guess." Sarah put her hand out and said, "Let's shake on it."

Maggie grinned as she watched Sarah's solemn face. She nodded and put her hand in the little girl's hand. Sarah said, "I agree," and they shook hands.

Shirley smiled. "Now that it's all settled, I'll get your clothes upstairs, Sarah. Then we'll all head back to—hopefully—your new Momma's house."

Sarah asked, "Is it a good house?"

"Yes, it is a good house. I think you'll like it. I was surprised by how much I like it."

"Where will I sleep?"

"In your bedroom."

"I will have a bedroom—all my own?"

"For now, yes. Later, if we have more children, you might have to share."

"I can share. I've never had a bedroom. I don't know what it is like. Does it have a bed?"

"Not yet, but it will very soon. All my children sleep on their own beds."

Sarah was surprised, but she wasn't sure about all of this. She knew she could always sneak out and go back to her own house. There wasn't any food there, and the place was a mess, just like her momma and papa left it. Still, it was hers, and if needs be, she would go her own way, all by herself.

Even without her house, she knew places she could hide if anyone tried to make her stay with mean people. She thought *I'd have to steal a hoe to kill the snakes. Otherwise, I could go wherever I needed to be safe.*

Or, maybe I could go to Aurora and her baby.

CHAPTER THIRTY-ONE

ON THE RIDE to their home, Maggie drove Aurora and Clay's buggy with Sarah sitting beside her. Aurora thought the ride could give Maggie and Sarah a little time to get to know each other. Aurora rode with Shirley in her buggy. And, of course, Okchuli was crying and wanting to nurse, so it was easier for Aurora to feed her without worrying about the horses or buggies.

Once they were on the road leading the way to their home on Pennington Creek, Sarah asked, "Do you like niggers and injuns?"

Maggie nodded, then shook her head and said, "Here's another rule you must obey. We do not use those words in our lives, ever. They are mean-spirited and meant to be mean. We always try to be kind."

"My other momma and papa said they were vermin."

"Do you know what vermin is?"

"It's like rats and disgusting creatures."

"Well I think God made all creatures to be just as they are. Sometimes, rats, mice, and insects get into our food or homes, so we chase them out. I disagree with your other momma and papa. Every human being, whether slave, Chickasaw, Choctaw, or other human beings in Indian Territory and beyond, deserves to be treated as such. Do you like Aurora?"

"Yes. I love her, and she is always good to me."

"Would you call her such a name?"

"No. She's a friend."

"Then do not ever, *ever*, let me hear those words out of your mouth again."

"Will you spank me if I do?"

"No, but I will be very sad and wonder if you are a good girl. I might make you write some words, though. They would be kind words to remember about everyone."

Sarah looked at Maggie and said, "Do you think I'm a good girl?"

"I'm not sure yet. I hope you are a good girl. I know everyone can be better than calling other people bad names."

"Some people in Tishomingo call me poor white trash."

"Shame on them!" Maggie glanced at Sarah and said, "No one is trash. God made us all and made us in love. We must love each other."

"Even when others are mean to us?" Sarah asked.

"Even then. Maybe, most especially then."

Sarah wasn't sure about everything, but she wanted to trust Maggie. She asked, "Momma, will you love me even if I am poor white trash."

Maggie smiled, pleased she called her Momma. "I'll love you no matter what anyone else thinks or says. Even when you do something mean-spirited or wrong, I'll love you then, too."

Maggie was surprised at her words and feelings about the child sitting beside her, but Sarah was more surprised and asked, "Why?"

"Because that's what mommas do. Mommas always love their children even when they do or say bad things."

Sarah nodded and didn't say anything for several minutes. Her other mother and papa hit her often and called her names. She didn't understand most of those names but knew they weren't good names.

After a minute or two of thinking, Sarah scooted closer to Maggie and laid her head on Maggie's lap. Before she had thought much more about everything, she was asleep.

She dreamed about having a momma and papa who loved her, and they made her life better. She dreamed of growing up to be a woman like Maggie or Aurora or, better yet, like Shirley.

She dreamed of sisters and brothers and learning how to play. In her heart, she thought she knew a little about how to play but wasn't sure it was genuinely playing. Sarah dreamed of chasing, swimming, and even swinging. She'd seen some children doing those things, but she'd never done any of those things.

Maggie looked down at the little girl, and her heart ached. She thought *no wonder the world is a mess. When we teach children to be mean and filled with prejudice, we create those same things in adults.* She brushed away tears and sighed. *I'll try to help Sarah become a kind and loving woman. I hope I've met her soon enough in her young life. I hope Silas will love her, too.*

Then she shook her head. *Of course, Silas will love her. He'll be surprised to have me bringing home another child. Silas and I must be vigilant in retraining her to be kind and loving. I hope it will be easy, but it probably won't be. Still, every child deserves at least that much from the adults in their lives.*

When they crossed the bridge over Pennington Creek and drove up the lane to their home, Maggie began to think about what Silas would say about having another child in their house. Then she smiled, shook her head, and muttered. "My guess is he'll say, 'I'd best get busy building another bed.'"

Shirley led the way down the lane to the Pennington house, and Maggie followed her. As they stopped the buggies in front of the fence to the house, Maggie was a little nervous and nudged Sarah. "Sarah honey, we're home."

Sarah sat up and rubbed her eyes. "This is home?"

"Yes, it is."

"It's huge and pretty."

Maggie smiled. "I agree, and I like it."

"Me too."

"Are you ready to meet the man who may become your father? You will also want to meet your future brothers and your sister."

She nodded but seemed a little scared. "Trust me, Sarah. They will like you."

"I hope so. If they don't, can I go to Aurora's house?"

"Sure, but I don't think that will be a problem. Besides, Aurora lives nearby and spends many hours with me and our children daily."

Sarah nodded and hoped her new mother was as lovely as she seemed. Sarah thought, *I'm tired, and I want to play.*

As Maggie tied the reins to the buggy post, Silas approached the buggy and helped her down from the seat. He kissed her cheek lightly and glanced over Maggie's shoulder. "You seem to have picked up another child, darlin.'"

"I'm glad you noticed." She smiled, turned back to Sarah, and said, "Sarah, this is my husband, Silas. He is the man that might become your new Papa."

Silas's mouth dropped open, and tears sprang to Sarah's eyes. She said, "He hates me."

Quickly, Silas smiled and said, "No. That's not it. This is my surprised face, is all. Can I help you down from the buggy?"

She nodded and brushed away a few tears.

He reached out for her and lifted her from the buggy. *She barely weighs more than a minute*, he thought. When he helped her down, he squatted to look at her and asked, "What's your name?"

"Sarah. Are you going to be my new maybe father?"

He looked up at Maggie, who nodded. "I told Sarah we would give it some time, and if we all like each other, we can discuss and decide our relationships. I told her I would try being her mother for a while, and you'd try being her father."

He smiled and said, "Well, since your Momma says I am, I guess I'm your new Papa."

"You're just thinking about it," Sarah said, brushing away her tears.

"Yes, I think that's the deal for us all. What do you think about it?"

She smiled, and in doing so, Silas's heart melted. He stood up, but before he could say or do anything else, Sarah grabbed him about the legs and squeezed with all her might. "I promise to be a good girl, Papa."

He pulled his handkerchief from his back pocket and wiped his face. "I promise to be a good Papa, too."

Maggie released the breath she'd been holding and laid her head on Silas's shoulder. "I wish there had been a way to talk with you about Sarah rather than just popping it on you."

He nodded and kissed her forehead. "It's fine. She'll be a fine daughter, won't you, Sarah?" He looked down at Sarah, who nodded. Then he said, "Let's introduce you to the rest of the family."

"I've already met Teddy. I love him."

"That's a mighty fine start," Silas said. He took Sarah's hand, and Maggie followed with Teddy.

Teddy was wiggling and ready to nurse. As she watched Silas walk with Sarah to introduce her to the rest of the family, she was suddenly overwhelmed by the day's events. She sighed and muttered. "I started the morning not wanting more children. Then, I went into town to get the birth certificates settled and bring home the boxes from my mother-in-law. I did all that and picked up another child along the way." She shook her head and said, "Maggie, you need to pace yourself a bit."

She smiled at herself and knew she'd done at least two good deeds today. She'd helped Aurora be sure Okchuli would be known as her daughter and brought home another daughter for herself. She hoped.

She approached her family and listened as Silas introduced Sarah to the children. Noah and Ben were quiet, but Bea was jumping up and down and clapping her hands. When Maggie was close, Bea ran to Maggie and tugged on her dress. She said, "Thank you, Momma. I prayed and prayed and prayed for a sister."

Maggie bent down and kissed her daughter's head. "I'm delighted you are happy to have Sarah as your sister. But we're just trying it on for a few days now. Do you understand?"

"Yes, but she's my sister already," Bea said, then turned to Sarah and said, "Come on. I'll show you our bedrooms upstairs."

"Hang on a bit, girls," Silas said. "We're not finished talking just yet."

Bea nodded but held onto Sarah's hand.

Ben and Noah were quiet. Maggie said, "Well, boys, what do you think?"

Ben said, "I'm glad Teddy was born." He shrugged, then said, "I don't understand girls."

Noah nodded. "Me neither. Sarah seems nice, and Bea likes her, so it's fine."

"I'm delighted to hear your words, boys. Sarah hasn't had a great life, but I think with your kindness and help, we can make her life and our lives better."

Noah looked up at Silas and watched his father's face. His father seemed surprised but also seemed to be like Sarah. Noah still wasn't sure, but he'd give it a try. He felt as if he didn't have a choice in the matter, though. He asked, "What do you think, Papa?"

"I think you and I best get busy and build another bed."

Maggie laughed and said, "I knew that was what you would say."

He grinned and nodded. He asked Sarah, "Do you know your full name, Sarah?"

"Yes, sir."

"You can call me Papa, Sarah. Sir isn't what a girl calls her father."

She smiled and nodded, knowing Silas wasn't like her first father or Mr. Reynolds. She pointed to Maggie. "That's what Momma said when I called her ma'am."

"Well, she is the boss around here, so we all try to do what she tells us."

"Always?"

"Yep. Always. Now, what's your full name?"

"I was named Sarah Darlene Butler, but now that I don't have my first Momma and Papa, I'm not sure."

Silas nodded and looked at Maggie, and shrugged. She smiled. "For now, we'll continue to call you Sarah, but if you and all of us decide you belong to our family, we'll want to call you Sarah Darlene Pennington. How's that?"

Sarah smiled, her eyes brightened, and she nodded. "I like it fine. I love Pennington Creek."

"Good. So do we. Now, Bea, you show Sarah the bedrooms while the boys, Clay, and Papa help Shirley, Aurora, and me unload the buggies. The one empty bedroom will be Sarah's."

Bea turned to Sarah and said, "I like you, and you'll like our beds. Papa made them."

With Bea leading the way, the two girls ran into the house and upstairs.

Maggie said, "I need to nurse Teddy before he gets too fussy."

"You go on, darlin'," Silas said. "You ladies head into the house while Clay and I unload the buggies."

He watched the women and little girls as they entered the house, feeling bemused.

Clay said, "Maggie sure is something."

Silas chuckled and nodded. "Yes, she is."

Noah went to stand by his father. "Is Sarah going to be our sister?"

"Yes, she is—probably. We'll try it out for a bit before anything formal happens. She needs a family, and we are one."

Noah nodded. "She seems nice."

"I agree, but I'm counting on you and Ben being good brothers to her."

Ben asked, "How long must we be good, Papa?"

"Until you are a hundred and one years old. After that, you can be as cantankerous as you'd like."

Ben nodded. "That's forever."

"You're right, son, it is," Silas answered and grinned.

Clay chuckled. "Let's get busy, boys. There's lots to do today. We've got to get your new sister's bed built."

CHAPTER THIRTY-TWO

*"Prejudice is the
child of ignorance."*
William Hazlett

IN TISHOMINGO, Lester Blunt was at Hank Smithson's blacksmith shop talking about Aurora and the Penningtons. He said, "It's one thing to have a halfbreed Chickasaw help out. It's entirely different to call them friends—especially since the woman is married to a white man."

A few men muttered; some shook their heads, but most said nothing. Lester continued, "I think it's past time we set our foot down and insist that those folks keep to themselves."

The blacksmith, Hank Smithson, shook his head. "I disagree, Lester. First, that was decided by the United States with the awful war more than forty years ago. Secondly, I'm Irish, and I remember when folks wouldn't have anything to do with me because I was Irish. I'm white, of course, but I still believe we should live and let live."

"You married a Chickasaw woman, so you'd think that way," Lester said. "It's not that I don't like your wife—in her place."

"And what would be her place?"

"To do as she's told and not actin' like she was as good as a white woman might be."

"You married a Chickasaw woman, too."

"I did, but she knows her place. I think havin' a part slave, Chickasaw woman struttin' around town is an abomination."

"What you think has nothing to do with me or mine, Lester. Aurora has been a wonderful midwife for many women around here, including my own lovely Chickasaw wife. I've heard enough of your bigoted opinions. You are no longer welcome here."

Lester spluttered. "I'll be wherever I damned well, please! How dare you talk to me in that manner!"

Hank picked up his biggest hammer, dangled it in his hand, gripped it tight, and began to swing it back and forth. He said, "Now Lester, this is my place, and I'll dare as I please, you fat, nasty bigot. Leave my place and never come back. I'll not be shoeing your horses ever again."

"You're the only blacksmith around here. Who will shoe my horses?"

"Not my problem. The problem of who will shoe your horses is of your own making, Lester. Now git before my hammer swings too wide and slips from my hand and onto your fat face." Hank swung the hammer wider and wider as he pointed with his other hand to the street. He shouted, "Get out and darken my door no more, Lester Blunt!"

He waited until Lester left the shop fuming before saying another word. When Lester was gone, Hank stopped swinging the hammer and carefully laid it down. He sighed, nodded, and took a deep breath. He turned to the rest of the men and, with a very calm voice, said, "Now anyone here who wants to start trouble over this awfulness can sure as hell get out of my shop and don't bother to come back."

No one moved or said anything.

"Now, I, for one, plan to visit the Penningtons and let them know they are welcome here in Tishomingo, as are Clay and Aurora. I should have done so already. If we all stick together and welcome them, this might blow over—at least, that is my hope."

Most of the men nodded in agreement, but a few had other thoughts and would undoubtedly tell Lester what Hank had to say. Some were on the fence and wanted to stay there rather than think for themselves. They're always around, whether for evil or good—they simply—and simply is the right word—try not to be bothered.

On Pennington Creek, Saturday continued to be a day of everyone settling in at Maggie and Silas Pennington's home. Bea was delighted with her new sister. She ran into the house and told Maggie, "Momma, the chickens didn't even peck Sarah!"

"Well, that's a good thing. How do you do it, Sarah?"

"I just whisper to them and tell them I love them."

Maggie smiled. "That's terrific. I'll have to give that a try."

"They like it best when you know their name."

"I wasn't aware chickens have names."

Bea grinned and nodded. "They do, Momma. Every creature has a name. Sarah said so."

Maggie smiled and turned to Sarah. She knew Sarah was a smart child but there might well be things she knew intuitively that Maggie didn't. She was open to learning from anyone, even a child. "Tell me their names, Sarah."

"Well, the rooster prefers to be called Cockie. He doesn't like the name Lord Foul Featherhead. He thinks it isn't fancy enough for him."

Maggie chuckled and nodded. "Cockie seems to fit him. I'll try to remember his new name."

"Good, but he still isn't nice, no matter what you call him. But he doesn't lay eggs, so that's good."

Maggie laughed. "What a relief it isn't just me. What about the hens?"

"The first one, closest to the house, is Penny. She's the copper one."

Maggie nodded and smiled. "I like it."

"Next is Polly, then Henrietta, Rosie, Sadie, and finally, the biggest one is Clara. She's the gold one. I like her the best."

"My goodness. How will we remember all their names?"

"Papa said he would put boards in front of their nests and paint their names on the boards."

"Ah. How clever of your Papa."

Sarah nodded. "He's pretty smart." She thought he might be a good father but didn't want to be sure about his goodness too soon. Still, if he was willing to make nameboards for the chickens, it was a good start.

Noah came running into the house, breathless and grinning. "Momma, some men are coming down the road. Papa said to let you know."

"Thank you, Noah. We'll be out in a few minutes."

With Okchuli snuggled close, Aurora walked from her home to Maggie's just as the men entered the space in front of Maggie's fence. She opened the side gate and walked to the house as Maggie walked out with Teddy wrapped close to her body. Bea and Sarah walked beside their mother, each holding one of Maggie's hands. Aurora smiled at the sight and said, "You women look lovely in the sunlight."

Maggie smiled and said, "You do as well. How are you and Okchuli doing this fine day?"

"We're grand. I've finished my morning household chores and nursed Chuli. Now, I'm here to help you with whatever you need."

Both Bea and Sarah were pleased to hear Aurora call her daughter Chuli. They thought it was a prettier name and easier to say than Okchuli.

"I'm glad you're here." Maggie nodded to the men, getting off their horses. "Let's go see what's up."

Aurora said, "I see some fine men. I hope it is a friendly visit."

"I do, too. Let's go see what we can make of them."

When the women approached the six men, one of them turned to Maggie and said, "Mrs. Pennington, I'm ashamed not to have visited you and your husband sooner. My wife has sent some plum preserves and her best blueberry scones."

Maggie smiled and said, "Might I know your name?"

The man blushed. "Of course. I'm Henry Smithson, the local black-smith. Most folks call me Hank."

"Then Hank, please call me Maggie and tell Mrs. Smithson I appreciate the preserves and look forward to her scones. It's been some time since I've had a proper blueberry scone."

He blushed and nodded. He would never tell her how awful his wife's scones were. They were hard and brittle and tasted bitter to boot. The plum preserves helped. He ate them nonetheless because he loved his wife and would never say anything negative about her cooking. He turned and looked at Aurora. "Mary didn't forget about you, Aurora. She sent a blanket she knitted for your baby and, of course, some of her scones."

She smiled, knowing the hens would be the ones eating the scones. "Tell Mary I appreciate the lovely blanket and scones."

"She would be pleased to visit with you two ladies when things are more settled."

Aurora nodded, and Maggie said, "We'd love to have her visit."

Sarah tugged on Maggie's skirt and said, "Miss Mary is a nice woman, Momma."

"Good to know. Thank you for telling me, Sarah."

Hank chuckled and said, "I'm glad you have a good home, Sarah."

"Me too. Tell Miss Mary she and Miss Shirley were right about Aurora and my new Momma."

"I will. She'll be pleased."

More of the men walked to Maggie and Aurora. Every man had parcels of food and pieces of knitting or crochet their wives had sent along. There were jars of honey, various preserves, and sauces as well. By the end of the visit, Hank turned to Clay and Silas. "I hate to mar this lovely visit, but you all must be vigilant. Lester Blunt and his ilk are working hard to get up enough gumption to run Aurora and Clay away from Tishomingo."

Silas shook his head. "They can try, but Aurora and Clay are our dear friends. They have made it possible for us to have a solid footing in our new home and land. Anyone who tries to harm them will have to go through me."

"We all feel the same way. Still, evil men won't give up easily."

"Nor shall we."

Hank nodded. "Please take care and watch out for them, Silas."

Sarah stomped her foot. "I'll bite their noses plum off and spit 'em out on the dirt!"

Everyone laughed, but they, too, felt her ire and would do all they could to protect the Pennington family and friends.

When they were alone again, Maggie said, "I tried one of Mary's scones."

"It was terrible, wasn't it?"

"Yes. I don't know what to do."

"Feed them to the pigs and chickens. They'll eat anything."

Maggie laughed. "Good idea. That's what I'll do and tell her how much I enjoyed her scones."

"Please, no! Do not encourage her. She cannot cook."

"Well, maybe I can help her learn."

"You would not be the first woman to try to teach her to cook. But, if anyone can, you can."

Maggie smiled, hoping her friend wasn't right.

Sarah watched the two women talking and laughing. She'd eaten some of Mary's scones and thought they were bitter and dry. Still, they beat going hungry any day of the week. Her preserves helped, although they were a little tart.

She smiled, listening to her new Momma and Aurora. Her thoughts wandered. *My bed was the best thing to happen today. Papa started building it with Clay and Noah and finished it this morning. I didn't mind sleeping with Bea, but having my own bed and room is lovely. Momma even said I could draw, color, and put my artwork on my bedroom walls. Aurora is teaching me about drawing, too.*

Bea is a sweet little girl. I'm a little uncomfortable having her beaming her sweet smile whenever she sees me. She wanted a sister, and I needed one, too, although I didn't know I needed her. I'll do everything possible to stay with Bea, Momma, and Papa.

Noah is okay for a boy, and Ben seems confused. They're boys, though, so it's okay. I hope Noah is older than me. I always wanted a big brother—especially one who would stand up for me.

I'm praying to Jesus every night—well, last night I started. But I'll pray every night to Jesus to please let me stay here. I surely do hope Jesus is listening.

I'll be a good girl, work hard, and learn everything I can. Momma says we're starting school on Monday. I've never been to school, but Momma says we'll have school at home. That's okay, too. Papa is making a blackboard for us!

She sketched a picture of the inside of the house where she lived now as she listened to her new Momma and Aurora talk as they worked shelling peas. She wanted to grow up to be a good woman like her new Momma and Aurora.

Maggie looked up just as Sarah looked up. Maggie smiled at the girl and nodded. Sarah smiled and nodded back but quickly tucked her head down to sketch so her new Momma wouldn't see her tears of joy. For the first time in her life, she felt like she was coming home, and home was made possible by the two women she sat with—Maggie Pennington and Aurora Harrison.

CHAPTER THIRTY-THREE

*"The wisest mind
has something yet
to learn."*
George Santayana

WHEN MONDAY MORNING CAME, breakfast was a busy affair as the children were planning what they wanted to do for the day. Maggie said, "Before your plans get set in stone, children, I have some plans for you all. Remember what we talked about yesterday?"

Noah looked over at the desks he had helped build in the library alcove, nodded, and then looked back at his mother. "We have to go to school, right?"

"Right. I'm hoping we'll work together and learn together."

Sarah said, "I've never been to school. My old Papa told me there was no need for me to go to school because girls can't think."

"Do you believe that?" Maggie asked.

"No, Momma. I can think a lot. Sometimes my thinking makes sense, and sometimes I don't know."

"Like with the chickens?"

"Oh, no. I didn't think of their names. They told me their names."

"Did they whisper in your ear?"

"Nope. In my head. I did all the whispering."

"Ah. Now I understand. What kind of things did you think this morning?"

"I didn't want to eat oatmeal, but when I tasted your oatmeal, I thought—this is good—so I ate it all!"

Maggie laughed. "Well, let's all work together to get started with school. You children tidy your beds and rooms, and I'll finish cleaning the dishes and prepare for school."

Silas watched the children run up the stairs. "I thought you were crazy or, at the very least, overloading yourself with Sarah. I think I was wrong."

Maggie kissed his cheek. "Good thinking, Si. Now you go on and get busy doing the work you've planned for the day."

"I will, but how long will the class be?"

"I think just two or three hours each day. Today will be a short session."

"Good. When school is finished, I'll work with the children teaching about planting, cleaning the coops, and helping around the farm."

"Sounds perfect. Aurora will be here in a few minutes. She wants to learn with the children."

"I thought she could read and write."

"She can read, write, and also do arithmetic but wants to learn as much as possible. Also, I suggested she should show you her ideas about her midwifery book."

"I'd be happy to help her. Now, I'm heading out to get busy working on the new shed. But, first, I need a kiss to tide me over."

She smiled, took her husband's hands, pulled him close to her, and kissed her husband. She said, "I love you, Silas."

"And I love you, Maggie." He tucked a stray strand of her auburn hair behind her ear and cupped her face with his hand. He kissed her again and whispered, "You are the queen of my life."

She smiled, kissed him quickly, and said, "Off with you! You have work to do, as do I."

He grinned and said, "I'll work hard to return to you as soon as possible."

Maggie smiled and then waved to Silas as he turned to walk away.

Neither Maggie nor Silas saw or heard Sarah at the top of the stairs. Sarah worked hard not to cry. She'd never heard her father or mother say they loved each other, or her for that matter. She thought, *maybe there is such a thing as love. I like my new Momma and Papa more than my old Momma and Papa.* She quickly went to her room, pulled out the journal Aurora had given her, and wrote her feelings about her new home and family. Before leaving her room, she knelt beside her bed and prayed, "Please, Jesus, let me stay forever with Momma, Papa, Bea, Noah, Ben, and Teddy. I love them, and I love you too. Amen"

Bea heard her new sister's prayer and decided she would pray to Jesus to be sure Sarah got to stay with them forever. She raced to her bedroom, knelt beside her bed, and prayed, "Dear baby Jesus, please let Sarah be my forever big sister. I love her, and she loves me. She prayed to you, so hear her prayer, too. Amen." She started to get up, then folded her hands again and said, "Please."

Two hours later, after their school lessons were over, the children were ready to play. Ben especially was feeling cooped up in the house. He wasn't sure about Sarah, but he thought she was probably okay. The only problem was Bea spent more time with Sarah than with him. He wasn't sure he liked that.

Maggie was pleased with the children's progress, but she, too, was tired and ready for a break. All the children, including Ben and Bea, could write their names on their slates and paper tablets. Noah and Sarah were ahead of the two younger children but only by a little—especially Sarah, who'd had no proper education. Noah helped her with words she didn't understand and showed her how to sound out words while Maggie worked with the twins on their ABCs.

Noah understood addition and subtraction, but by the end of the morning, Sarah was nearly as proficient as Noah with numbers. Maggie was pleased that Noah was willing to help Sarah and even give her hints.

Maggie wrote a few more complex numbers for them while working with Bea and Ben on basic numbers.

By the end of the morning's teaching, Maggie was ready to be in her rocking chair with her feet up. She said, "Okay, children. Why don't you go outside and play for a bit? After we rest for a few minutes, Aurora and I will fix lunch for everyone."

Bea asked, "Can we eat outside?"

"That is a great idea. We'll have a picnic close to the creek, but first, I will rest and nurse Teddy."

Sarah looked up at Maggie and asked, "Momma, why do you call it nursing when Teddy sucks on your teat, but the piglets are called sucklings when they suck on their momma's teats?"

Maggie laughed. "You know, I'm not sure. But most people call it nursing when women feed their babies. For now, let's call it nursing when human women do it."

"Okay," Sarah said and raced outside to be with the other children.

Aurora chuckled. "She's a bright girl."

Maggie nodded. "Yes, she is, and I'm glad. However, I'm a tired woman."

"Maybe I should make you a fruit cake or two."

"That would be lovely, Aurora. I feel much better than when I was pregnant with Teddy, but I'm not quite at full force yet."

"Sit down and nurse your suckling."

Maggie laughed and sat down with Teddy at her breast. She thought *I must have better answers soon. Sarah has learned a lot about life but not much about simply being. She'll keep me on my toes.*

Clay and Silas carried a few older blankets to the meadow near the creek. Silas said, "Now, children, no one goes in the creek without me or Clay with you. No one goes closer than the blankets for now. Are you all clear about that?"

Every child nodded but wished they could be in the creek. *It's July, after all—the hottest time of the year,* Noah thought. *Besides, it's nearly time for my birthday.* He was still uncertain about Sarah. She was friendly and hadn't said anything mean or spiteful, but he still didn't trust her. His biggest worry was that she might be older than him. He asked his father, "Do you know when Sarah was born?"

"No, son, I don't. Why do you ask?"

"Well, I was the oldest, and now that Sarah is here, I'm worried she might be older than me."

Silas nodded and held back a smile and instead tried to be solemn. "I can see how you feel, son. I'll talk to your Momma and tell you what she says. How's that?"

"Fine, Papa."

"In the meantime, I expect you to be kind to her. She is your sister, now."

"But is she really, Papa? She just came home with Momma without being birthed or anything."

Silas could not hold back laughter but said with as straight a face as possible, "Well, she was birthed all right, son. It's the only way any of us come into this world. Her Momma and Papa died, so she needs a new Momma and Papa."

"Does it have to be you and Momma?"

"Yes, son, it does."

"Why?"

"Because your Momma said so, for one thing. For another thing, it is the Christian thing to do. Do you remember what Jesus said about the children?"

"Suffer the little children to come unto me. I don't understand the 'suffer' part."

"The word suffer is an old, old way of saying allow. So Jesus said, 'Allow the little children to come unto me.' I think Sarah has had more than enough sorrow in her life. I also think Jesus would be happy we have brought her into our family and home with love and kindness."

Noah nodded but said nothing more.

Silas watched his son's face and said, "I'll ask your Momma and Sarah when she was born. Will it help you to know when she was born?"

"Yes, Papa, it will. I like her but don't want her to be the oldest. She says she's nearly nine, and that's what I say too. I really need to be the oldest, Papa."

"I understand, son. We'll see how things are later. For now, let's get our picnic going." Then Silas turned away from his son so he could smile and laugh softly. Still, he remembered how it felt to know that he would have to make his way in the world as the second son. Silas harbored no ill will toward his older brother, Randolph, but there was still a bit of a sting in some way—a feeling he wasn't good enough for his father.

Noah shook his head. *Papa doesn't understand. Papa was born second, so he doesn't know how it feels to be the first one born.* He sighed and walked back to the house to help his mother carry food for their picnic.

As he carried a basket of bread back to the blankets near the creek, he thought *being nearly nine is good, but if Sarah is more nearly nine, I'm worried I won't be able to be kind to her.*

He shook his head and looked at the creek. He walked a little closer to see what was happening. He thought he saw a baby turtle slip into the water.

He took a few more steps, and suddenly, Sarah grabbed his arm and said, "Come back!"

He pulled his arm from her grasp and said, "Why?"

"I think I saw a big, black snake in the water."

"I ain't afraid of no snake."

Sarah shook her head. "You should be. Besides, Papa told us not to go further than the quilt. We'll both be in trouble if we don't go back to the quilt."

Noah nodded. "You're right. I was thinking how nice swimming in the cold water would be."

"Later, let's ask Papa if we can swim."

He turned and asked her, "Do you know how to swim?"

"Not really. Just doggie paddle. Do you know how to swim?"

He grimaced, shook his head, and said, "Nope. Just doggie paddle." He walked to the quilt and sat down feeling rotten. *She can doggie paddle, too. I hope she isn't older than me. I have to learn how to swim even if a big old black snake is in the creek.*

Silas watched the two older children and smiled when he saw them return from the creek. He was worried, though, at the look on Noah's face. *I'll ask Sarah straight out when her birthday is. Hopefully, it won't be close to Noah's birthday, and he'll settle down.*

The black snake—a water mocassin—was in the water. She saw the children but ignored them for now. They were too big to eat, and she'd seen the baby snapping turtle slip into the water. Now, he wasn't too big to eat. She wasn't the least bit afraid of a baby turtle. She liked turtles nearly as much as she did frogs. A frog jumped up on a soggy log, sticking his tongue out, and grabbed a mosquito flying by. The black snake quietly swam to the log, but the frog saw her glistening back and quickly jumped into the creek and swam away. The jump was good, but the snake could swim faster, and she was ravenous.

The frog had eaten his last mosquito, while the turtle lived to see another day in Pennington Creek.

CHAPTER THIRTY-FOUR

*"Either write something
worth reading or do
something worth writing."*
Benjamin Franklin

SILAS WALKED with Maggie across the yard and down to the creek as they, along with Clay and Aurora, finished bringing out the food for their lunch. The children were already racing ahead, excited to have a picnic. He asked Maggie, "Do you know when Sarah's birthday is?"

"No, I don't. I know she is eight but says she is nine, so folks won't think she is a baby."

Silas chuckled and shook his head. "Just like Noah, who says he is nearly nine rather than saying he is eight."

"Exactly," Maggie said, "Children are always in a hurry to grow up. Why are you asking about Sarah's birthday, Silas?"

"Noah is worried he won't be the oldest child."

"Ah. I wonder why that bothers him?"

"I was thinking about that. Growing up, I remember feeling I wasn't good enough for my father because I was born second."

"How do you feel now?"

He grinned. "I'm happy as a pig in slop. I'm making my way in life —with the help of all Uncle Jacob gave us, and it feels grand. Before we left Columbia, we talked a lot about my brother being older and getting my father's estate. When we decided to move here, I was delighted at the possibilities for me. I'm sure Noah heard us talking about it all. We even used my being secondborn as an excuse to make our leaving easier for my parents. I think he feels being born first is important."

"My guess is you're right, Silas. I'll ask Sarah if she knows her birth-date. For now, let's get busy eating lunch with the children. I hope the age thing doesn't bother Noah too much, though. I've been very relieved they are settling in nicely. I think maybe it's easier for children to adjust than it is for adults."

"I agree, but that doesn't erase their worries."

"You're right, of course. When I brought Sarah home, I was worried that you would not want to keep her with us."

He grinned. "Well, I was shocked when you brought Sarah home, but she seems to be a good girl and eager to please. Besides, she feels like a daughter to me now, and I'm happy she is here."

Maggie sighed. "I worry she's eager to please only to have a stable environment. I hope she will eventually feel she is part of the family."

"Me too, darlin'. I think things are going better than I'd've thought they would. I mean, look at Sarah with Bea. They are as thick as thieves and seem to truly like each other. I'm not sure about Ben, and I'm worried about him. He has seemed a little quiet with it all. He's used to having Bea right at his side."

"I agree. We'll need to watch them all and step in if they feel unhappy with the situation."

Silas nodded but wasn't sure how to approach Ben about having another sister. He wondered if Ben was feeling left out of things. *It had been Bea and Ben as a team until Sarah showed up. Now, Sarah and Bea are enamored with each other. Noah is beginning to work more with Clay and me than with the women. Maybe I'll work on getting Ben to work with us men a little more.*

Once they were all sitting together on the blankets spread on the ground in the shade of the trees near the creek, Maggie said, "Sarah, I've been wondering about you a bit."

Sarah quickly looked up, obviously worried. "I've been a good girl, haven't I?"

"Yes. You have been a very good girl, and I'm proud of you. I just wanted to know when your birthday is. I know you are eight, but you like to say you are nearly nine. I don't know when you were born."

"Do I have to say?"

"No, but why wouldn't you want to say when your birthday is?"

"Because it is an evil day, and I'm not an evil girl even though my first Papa said I was."

Silas shook his head and sighed. He was furious with Sarah's biological father and thought it was a good thing he was already dead. He told Sarah, "Of course, you're not an evil girl. We want to know when your birthday is so we'll know when to bake you a cake and have a party."

"Really?" She looked at Noah and asked, "Are they telling me the truth?"

He nodded. "Momma and Papa don't lie—ever." He crossed his fingers, hoping he would still be the oldest once he knew Sarah's birthday. He couldn't think of an evil date, but maybe her other father knew something he didn't know.

She swallowed and said, "I was born on Halloween at midnight."

Noah grinned and relaxed his fingers. "That's terrific! I love Halloween."

"Really?"

"Yes. We get candy and have a party welcoming in all the saints."

"I didn't know that. I thought it was all spooks, ghosts, and witches."

"Nope. It's not like that. The spooks, ghosts, and witches are just costumes to scare off bad people. We get to eat caramel apples, pumpkin tarts, and chocolate fudge. Halloween is great."

Maggie and Silas laughed, loving how Noah quickly jumped in to help Sarah once he knew he was still the oldest child. Noah said, "Don't worry, Sarah. I'm your big brother, and I'll protect you—always."

"Thanks, Noah." She grinned, delighted that her new family didn't think she was evil or wicked. It was nice that Noah finally liked her, too.

Ben watched and wondered about Sarah. He liked her—at least he didn't hate her—but he wasn't happy Bea had quit playing with him.

Silas looked at Ben and motioned for him to come to sit closer to him and Maggie. Ben walked over to his father, and when Silas opened his arms, Ben quickly settled on his father's lap.

Maggie smiled and nodded to her husband.

Noah looked at his father and said, "Papa, Sarah saw a big black snake in the creek, and she's worried about it."

Silas looked at Clay, who asked, "Sarah, did you see any markings on the snake?"

Sarah shook her head. "I saw a big and fat black snake swimming on top of the water. It was really long, and her head was big and flat on top. I heard a frog jump off a log, and she dove down after the frog. I think she ate the frog for lunch because the frog didn't come back up, but the snake did with her mouth full. She's a big old mean snake."

Silas asked, "Her?"

"Yes, Papa, I think she is a momma snake. Her belly was huge!"

Clay blew out a breath, shook his head, and said, "For now, no one should swim in the creek. I'll go down in a bit and see if she's around. I'll also check off and on for a few days."

"You think it's a cottonmouth, right?" Silas asked.

"Right, and this is the usual time around here when they are pregnant. They aren't nice anytime, but they are extra hungry and vicious and hunt a lot when they are pregnant. She will be even more aggressive once the babies are born. She'll be meaner than a rabid skunk until they are grown enough to be alone."

Silas nodded and said, "Alrighty then, children. No wading or swimming in the creek unless Clay and I are sure everything is safe."

Ben asked, "Could she kill us?"

"Maybe, son, especially a small child like you and Bea. However, no one ever wants to have a snake bite them."

Ben nodded and thought *maybe Sarah would be okay. She's the one who told Noah, Papa, and Clay about the snake.* He leaned back against his father's chest. He liked his father's smell and listening to his father's heartbeat. It reminded him of Teddy's heartbeat in his Momma's belly.

Clay watched the interplay of the children and felt things shift and settle a bit. He smiled, watching the family and the chattering children. When he sighed, hoping that someday he and Aurora would have another child or more, Aurora held his hand and lay her head on his shoulder.

She whispered, "Maybe, in due time, my love."

He kissed the top of her head. "I'm ready for the next miracle."

Aurora nodded and felt a little bit of ease inside her body. She smiled and thought, *don't be silly. You're simply filled with mother love these days.*

And, of course, she was. The only question would be how many miracles one woman would get.

CHAPTER THIRTY-FIVE

*"I do not
wish women to
have power over men,
but over themselves."*
Mary Shelley

AFTER THE PICNIC and all the blankets and food had been brought back into the house, the families sat on the porch for a few minutes. The children played card games in the shade of the porch while the women sat on the two rocking chairs, watching the children as the babies slept close to their mothers on a quilt. The men sat on the top step, discussing their plans for the afternoon's work.

Aurora said, "Silas, I wanted to ask you a favor."

"Sure. Anything within my power I will do for you."

"Maggie said you were an editor and liked to write stories."

"That's true, although I haven't had much time to write since coming here."

"What I want to write can be very important to me and other

women, Silas. I'm writing a treatise on midwifery. I want it to be a book to help other women learn and know what I have been taught. I want some of these women to be able to learn to be a midwife. Most of us are taught by our mothers or wise women, but maybe if we had it all written down, it could help more women."

"I don't know much about midwifery, but I'd happily help with your book. What kind of editing do you want me to do?"

"Well, I'm not sure of my spelling and grammar in all cases, but also, I want to know if what I've written makes sense. Any suggestions you'd give me would be very helpful."

"I'm happy to take a look at it. Do you have it with you?"

"Yes," she stood up, reached into her apron pocket, and handed the book to Silas. "I rewrote all my notes but didn't use any woman's name."

"Good. No woman will want to have her name in a book detailing the birth of their baby."

"I agree. I wouldn't want to read about my baby's birth, so I didn't include details of time, place, or who in my writing."

"Can I have a few days to read what you've written?"

"Of course. I appreciate your help, Silas."

He grinned. "Hey, you keep my wife healthy, and I'll lasso the moon and lay it in your hands."

She laughed and touched Silas's shoulder. "Thank you, Silas, but we should leave our moon where she is to help guide women everywhere. You'll see how she guides us in my journal. But, I do appreciate you and Maggie both helping me."

Clay nodded in agreement with his wife's sentiment. "Absolutely. Neither Aurora nor I had felt a sense of belonging before you and Maggie came along. Some folks like the preacher, Shirley Duncan, and Hank Smithson were kind to us, but we didn't have a feeling of belonging until we joined up with you and your family. Our lives are beginning to blossom in ways we could never have expected."

Maggie said, "We're delighted to have you with us. Now. We've all got work to do. Our lazy picnic is over, and time's a-wastin'."

"You're right," said Silas. "I want to work out some plans with Clay and include Noah in our cogitations. He needs to learn more about keeping our land fertile and adding to what we have."

"Good. Aurora and I will work in the garden after I tutor Sarah in household workings."

Ben asked Bea, "You want to play upstairs while Sarah and Momma work?"

"Yes. What will we play?"

"I don't know. We'll think of something."

"Okay!" Bea said, and the two children raced upstairs to play in their bedrooms.

Maggie smiled and turned to Sarah. "Thanks for telling us about the snake. You have a lot to teach us."

Sarah smiled. "I want to learn how to keep a house like you, Momma."

Both Maggie and Aurora smiled at Sarah's use of the word *Momma*. Maggie said, "The first thing we have to do is get started on a few household chores. If we do it daily, I can show you how to make it fast and easy."

Sarah grinned and nodded. She loved working with Aurora and Maggie. Although she knew she was only eight, working with women, real grown-up women, made her feel a lot older—maybe as much as ten or twelve years old.

That night, as Silas and Maggie were preparing to go to bed, he said, "I need to talk with you, darlin'."

"You sound serious, Silas. Is there something wrong?"

"No. But it is something big, and I might have bitten off more than I can chew." He shook his head and sighed. "But, dang it! I want to do this."

She chuckled. "Maybe you should tell me what it is."

"You're right. Prevaricating isn't a good idea. I've been thinking about it for a few days since Papa sent me a letter and a brochure."

Maggie said, "So long as we don't have to move and nothing is seriously threatening to us, I'm ready to listen with an open mind, my love."

Silas nodded, handed his wife the envelope, and said, "You go ahead and read my father's letter and the brochure, and then we'll talk about it all."

Maggie pulled the letter from the envelope and read her father-in-law's letter with his precise script. When she finished reading the letter, she glanced at Silas and opened the brochure. She read about Mr. Prouty's press but didn't know what to say. Finally, she closed the brochure and tucked both documents in the envelope. "Where would you put this, Silas? I'm putting my foot down about this. There will be no printing presses in my house."

He grinned. "I wouldn't dream of it, darlin'. There are a few empty buildings in town. One that would be perfect is for sale for a hundred dollars. It is two stories tall. I might even rent out the upstairs for another vendor. Hank Smithson looked at the building with me, and he feels it is a good buy."

"So you would be spending more time in town?"

"Yes. Never all day, but every day except Sundays."

"Who would watch after the place when you're here at home?"

"I don't know yet and haven't put my money down, but since my father is willing to buy the printing press for twenty percent of the profits, I think it is a good deal. With a bit of the extra money from Uncle Jacob, I could invest in the building without it becoming a financial burden for us."

"I agree with your assessment. However, this means you'll be an editor again, right?"

"Yes, but more than that, I want to be a publisher of books. Some will be small books of poetry or stories, but some, like Aurora's, will be useful books for many people."

"What about the farm?"

"I have some ideas about that."

She smiled and shook her head. "I'm certain you do. Come to bed while I'm still willing, and we'll dream on it a bit."

"Thanks, darlin'."

Once they were in bed, Maggie said, "I want to see the building before you spend any money, love. I want you to do whatever your heart tells you, but I also want a stable life."

"I do, too, darlin'."

"I can't do all the farming that needs to be done, keep house, and raise and educate our children by myself."

"I agree. I promise to take care of the heavy work around here. Clay or I will do the heavy work. If and when needed, I'll hire another hand."

"When you're making a profit, right?"

"Yes. At first, there won't be a profit, but using some of the extra money Uncle Jacob found should be enough to tide us over for a few years."

She sighed and then touched his cheek. "I'm feeling a bit overloaded, love. I adore my home, you, and our children. However, I'm not ready to have another baby, Si."

He watched her face closely and said, "Does that mean celibacy, darlin'?"

She chuckled softly. "No, it does not. I love being with you in our bed. How many children do you want us to have, Si?"

"I don't rightly know, darlin'. I guess I haven't thought about that."

"I'm wondering if five children is enough."

"We don't have five children," he said, grinning and, using his fingers, named the names of five children. He grinned and said, "Again, you are right, darlin'. We do have five children. I'd forgotten Teddy and Sarah. Here I am, an educated man having to count his children on his fingers!"

"I promise I won't tell them."

He grinned.

Maggie smiled and continued, "Some herbs and teas can help keep me from getting pregnant. At first, I thought about using them to have the next child be born four or five years from now. We'll both be thirty in a year or two. I, for one, do not want to be worn out young from bearing babies. The loss of iron with Teddy felt like a wake-up call to me."

"I understand, darlin'. It was worrisome to me as well."

"I'm glad you understand, Si. When I brought Sarah home, I felt our family was perfect with her added. As I thought about it, the more I thought five children seems about right."

Silas remained quiet and nodded, unsure whether to say anything. He was relieved when Maggie continued.

"I love our home, and I want adventures in my life and not simply more and more work piled on top of my daily existence. I don't want to be a woman who bears children only to create more work for herself. I want to enjoy my children. I want to learn with them and for them. I want a vibrant, healthy life without too many worries and strains. I want to die when I'm old. I don't want to have my body wear out and die young, although my body would be old."

Silas smiled softly, brushed a lock of her shining auburn hair, and tucked it behind her ear. He said, "I don't want that either, darlin'. If you use these herbs and teas daily, will they help you avoid becoming pregnant?"

"Yes, they will. Let me tell you what Aurora has taught me about my body and babies."

They talked quietly about the ins and outs of having babies before making love for the first time since Teddy's birth. Maggie was relieved and hoped she would have many years of a vibrant body and life. Being in Silas's arms and sharing their bodies, she felt, was a sort of consecration, a sacrament of their love.

As they curled together in their bed and began to ease into sleep, Silas said, "I think if we hire help during the seasons of plowing and planting, we might not have to have any other help. For now, I think Clay is settled in to be the one taking charge of things around here as far as the farming goes. What do you think?"

"I think you're right for the near future. Later, we might have to change our plans based on what extra help we need. Now, my dearest love, it's time for sleep."

Silas smiled and said, "Good night, Maggie. I love you."

"And I you."

Silas was relieved and excited about his prospects for the future in Tishomingo, but he, too, wanted his wife to be happy and healthy. Silas sighed as he went to sleep. He wanted to enjoy his children and help them become good people. Five children seemed right, and he dozed off, not wishing for more children.

He was pleased that he and Maggie had reached a grand decision and solution for Aurora and Clay's lives. He wanted to be sure they would be around for a long, long time.

Maggie was relieved to be in accord with her husband. Their plans to help Clay and Aurora have a solid future was, to her mind, a brilliant idea and a blessing for them all. She was relieved to have no more children unless a miracle happened. In that case, she'd love any child in her home. Moving forward was the next adventure of her life.

CHAPTER THIRTY-SIX

*"If one does
not know to which port
one is sailing,
no wind is favorable."*
Seneca

BOTH SILAS and Maggie were kept busy as the days passed on
Pennington Creek.

Maggie, with Aurora's help, was busy with the gardens and children
and preparing the harvest of their efforts to last them throughout the
long winter months.

Silas had to make sure that the homestead and farm were in good
working order before he could set up his printing business in town.
They had discussed taking it slow with his desire to start his own press
company. However, Silas was eager to get busy with writing and printing. He hoped that by the time the building was ready and the press was
up and running, they would have a better understanding of what was
needed in their lives.

Silas's father had bought the press, but it would not arrive in Tishomingo for a few more weeks. In the meantime, Silas was working with Clay to turn most of the farming over to Clay, with Silas being aware of everything on the farm. To that end, he wanted to teach Noah how he could help with the farm and, later, maybe the press operations, too.

His goal was to allow Noah to make his own decisions about his path forward while at the same time learning as much as he could. *In fact*, he thought, *I want all my children to live the lives they chose. I'm grateful my parents encouraged me in my desires for my life and continue to support those desires.*

The day after the picnic, Silas and Clay started indoctrinating Noah into the life of the farm and his responsibilities. Every day began with Noah spending his mornings with his mother and the other children, getting an education. He liked learning to read harder books the best. The arithmetic was easy so far, but it didn't tweak his mind as much as the McGuffy Readers did. He was proud to be already reading the second book. The first chapter reminded him of his mother and the home she had created for the family.

Although he wanted to read the next chapter, his mother had suggested he could help Sarah with the reading of the first book. Besides, as his mother had pointed out, it wouldn't hurt him to re-read the first book. It was a good book, too. He loved that Momma had said, "You'll really know and understand what you learn when you are able to help another person learn what you already know. Not only is it a blessing for Sarah, it becomes a gift you share with her."

Noah wanted to ask his father about how to write a story—but not yet. He wanted Sarah to be able to read any story he might write.

Sarah loved the McGuffy Primer. She took the book up to her room and opened the sketchbook her new mother—Maggie—had given her. She sketched the cat sitting in the garden. With the colored pencils Momma gave her, she added the colors of the yellow and white cat sitting in the middle of all the pretty flowers. She used green, brown, yellow, red, and blue. She cocked her head, looking at the picture in the book and the picture she'd sketched with her pencil and colors. She smiled and murmured, "I like mine best."

After lunch each day, Noah would join Clay and Silas for the afternoon's work on the farm. He didn't like farming as much as reading. He liked it much more when he was allowed to help build things. He especially liked hammering nails into wood. Regardless of the work, he loved being with his father and Clay. Each afternoon, Noah stood with his father and Clay under a redbud tree, talking about what they would do for the rest of the day.

While the men worked on farming and building, the women cared for the younger children, their homes, and the gardens. Both women taught Sarah about cooking, storing food for both short and long-term needs, cleaning, and caring for the younger children. Sarah loved being old enough to help with the household chores and learn how to cook. She especially loved learning about the plants they cared for and was delighted when Aurora gave her a blank book to start making her own notes about each plant and how they could be used or how they must be avoided.

Now, two weeks after the picnic, Noah tucked his hands in his pockets as he watched his father do the same while talking to Clay. Silas saw his son's actions out of the corner of his eye and thought *the lad watches me and emulates me—I must take care what he sees in me is good.*

He ducked his head a bit, sighed, then looked up at Clay. When Silas saw his son do the same, he said, "You know, Clay, I'm a little concerned about having Noah working with us in the afternoons."

Noah said nothing but lifted his head and watched his father. He hoped his father wouldn't make him stay in the house with the other children doing housework or gardening. He wanted to prove he was old enough to be of help doing what he considered to be real man's work.

Clay smiled and said, "Well, some time or another, the lad will have to learn not to spit or piss into the wind."

Noah's mouth dropped open while Silas chuckled, and then he said, "I suppose you're right, Clay. I can remember watching my father and everything he did. I wanted to be like him, but there came a time when I didn't want to be a thing like him."

"Yep. Me too. When I was twelve, maybe thirteen, I was certain my father was a cold-stone idiot and probably wouldn't know to come out of the rain unless someone told him to."

Silas grinned. "Same for me. I suppose we've only a few years—perhaps as many as five years—if we're lucky—to get Noah to learn some sense."

Both men nodded sagely, and Noah shook his head and sighed. He was sure his father and Clay were teasing him, but he'd learned how to tease, too—from watching both his father and mother tease. He decided to embellish a talk he'd had with his mother.

Noah shook his head again and sighed—again. He said, "Maybe Momma's right," and sighed—again.

Silas smiled and looked at his son, then nodded. "She generally is, son. What do you think she's right about?"

"She said, by the time I'm grown and ready to leave home, she figures I'll know just about everything I need to know."

Clay grinned. "Oh, Silas. We may be too late."

Noah nodded. "Maybe. But Momma said within a few years, I'd probably return home and know I'm still wet behind the ears."

Silas nodded but didn't say anything, although he was a little nervous about where his son's train of thought was heading.

Noah looked at his father and said, "Momma said she expects you'll be dry behind the ears any day now."

Both men smiled but held back laughter until Noah said, "And I suppose about the time I'm dry behind the ears, you'll be a downright sage—or so Momma said."

Both men hooted with laughter. Silas shook his head, pulled his handkerchief from his pocket, and wiped his eyes. "Your Momma has the right of it all."

"Good," Noah said. "Although Momma didn't exactly say what I've told you, sure as shootin' I think that's what she meant."

The men kept laughing for several seconds, and then Noah asked, in a very calm, serious voice, "What are we going to do now, Papa?"

Silas grinned at his son and said, "Well, son, I thought I'd best be careful and teach you everything about life and farming. I'm not so sure now."

Noah nodded. "I don't know much, but I think you and Clay can teach me about farming and maybe a bit of life, too. Probably. At least, I hope so. Otherwise, no tellin' how I'll turn out."

Both men laughed even louder for nearly a full minute before Silas said, "Seriously, now, son, I have some thoughts I'm considering implementing. Let's walk to an area I've been thinking about. It's between our place and Clay's place."

"It's all your place, Silas."

"Nope, not anymore."

"Of course it is, Silas."

Silas pulled a folded paper from his pocket and said, "Well, friend, I have this paper in my pocket that says otherwise." He handed the paper to Clay.

Clay stopped walking, took the paper, and read words that stunned him. He shook his head. "You shouldn't have done this, Silas."

"Why not?"

"You've deeded Aurora and me five acres, plus the small lake and the cabin. That's too much, Silas."

"Nope. It's just about right. You and Aurora deserve a place of your own. I can't afford to give you a lot of land or much money, but I can damned well be sure to give you your own home and garden—a place that can be yours for as long as you live and hopefully beyond. Besides, the water is more of a big pond." Silas turned to Noah and said, "Don't tell your momma I cursed."

Noah grinned and said, "Yes, sir."

Silas turned back to Clay. "I've been calling you friend since I met you, and I meant it every time I said it. But it quite simply felt wrong for me to expect you to do for me all my life and do everything I ask for the small salary I've been paying you."

"I can understand how you feel, Silas. But. Still. This is a big deal, Silas." He reread the paper with his hands shaking. Finally, he folded the paper, put it in his back pocket, sighed, and said, "Well, since you're so all fired up, I've no damned course of action but to say thank you."

Silas smiled and nodded.

Clay looked at Noah and said, "Don't tell your momma *or* Aurora I cursed around you."

"Yes, sir." Noah grinned, feeling like he was one of the men—not telling the women about their cursing was a part of it. Even more, he felt accepted as a young man by his father and Clay. He didn't dare try to curse, though. He wasn't sure his father would put up with that! At least, not yet.

"Now," Silas said, "I have a surveyor coming out next week to mark off your land. I paced it off. I wanted to be sure, so with the surveyor's marks, no one can ever say otherwise."

"Thank you, Silas. Give Maggie my thanks as well. This is more than anything I ever expected to happen in my life."

"Good. Now that everything is settled, let's discuss a few things I think we can share that will help both families."

"Sure. I've been thinking of building a smokehouse," Clay said.

"I hadn't thought of that, but it is a fine idea."

Noah asked, "What would be in the smokehouse?"

"Hams, bacon, sausages, maybe even cheese. Anything we can preserve in the smokehouse. How big were you thinking, Clay?"

"Not a very big one, but one to accommodate at least one hog."

Noah said, "We don't have any hogs or pigs, for that matter."

"You're right, son. That brings up another matter—fencing. Once we have hogs and pigs, we'll need shelter for them and a way to keep them penned in."

"Will we buy a hog or pig?"

"I don't think we have to. There are wild hogs and pigs around here. The biggest problem is that they're difficult to deal with. Once an animal is wild, it doesn't like being tamed, especially if we're talking about killing them for our food."

Noah shook his head. "Then how will we get started?"

"We'll try—and *try* is the operative word, son—to find a fat wild sow who is hopefully pregnant. When her piglets are born and weaned, we'll feed and sell some but keep a couple for our tables."

Noah paled, shuddered a bit, and blew out a long breath. He hadn't expected to be a part of killing baby pigs for the food on the family table. He looked at his father and asked, "So we'll have to kill her babies?"

"Yes, son. It's how things work. Killing a pig is necessary if you want bacon, ham, or sausage."

Noah nodded. "I like bacon, ham, and sausage. I'll try, Papa."

"Good. Now, on to another less gruesome idea I have." Silas pointed to the slight rise between his land and Clay's land. "I was thinking we could use this small hill for a dugout. We could store produce like potatoes, carrots, turnips, onions, and such. It would also be a fine place to store canned goods."

Clay nodded. "I agree. It will also be a shelter if a tornado comes ripping through. We don't get them as much as folks northwest of here do, but still, they hop in now and again—I think simply to aggravate us. If we build it right, it can open to your property and ours too."

"Exactly my thoughts. Have you built a dugout before?"

"Yes, I have. They're good enough shelter, but I'm glad I no longer live in one. I like the light shining through the windows of our home."

Silas smiled. "I understand. I feel the same way. Now, I like seeing things drawn out before I start any project. Do you think you and Noah could work on that project—pace it out and draw the construction plan?"

"Sure we can."

"Good. I would also like to see some drawings about fencing, outbuildings, and other such features for both our place and yours."

"We can do that."

Silas nodded. "Good. I'm heading back to the house to finish reading Aurora's book for her. My plan moving forward is that you and Noah take care of the place in the afternoons whenever possible while I'm in town working on my new project."

Clay patted Noah's shoulder and said, "I think Noah and I can come up with some fine ideas, and we'll be happy to take care of things in the afternoons."

Noah smiled and nodded. He was glad his father thought enough of him to be a part of the plans for their land. He felt older than eight years old today. For sure, he felt at least ten, maybe even twelve, years old.

CHAPTER THIRTY-SEVEN

Silas walked into his home to see his wife and Aurora shelling peas for drying. He asked, "Where are Sarah, Ben, and Bea?"

"They are upstairs with their McGuffey readers trying to figure out the stories themselves."

"Great. I'm delighted they want to read."

Aurora said, "Sarah can read a bit better than the twins. It's lovely watching her tutor them on their reading."

Maggie said, "She is such a sweet girl. It's hard to believe she's had so much trauma in her young life."

"Well, darlin', we're all happy to have her here. Maybe a loving family will make a big difference in her life. It certainly won't hurt."

"I agree and hold hope for a loving outcome for us all. Where are Noah and Clay?"

"They're mapping out plans for a cellar and fences. I decided they could handle the task themselves while I finish reading Aurora's book."

Aurora smiled. "I hope it makes sense."

"Yes, it does. When you ladies finish for the day, I'd like to chat with you, Aurora. Just knock on the bedroom door when you're ready."

She smiled. "Thank you, Silas."

He kissed Maggie and said, "The deed is done, dear heart. Chatter it over between yourselves to your heart's content."

"Thank you so much, Si. Now go on to your study and finish reading Aurora's book while we talk and shell more peas."

"Your wish is my command," he answered and grinned.

He went to his writing corner of their bedroom and sat at his desk. He picked up Aurora's book and began to read the rest of her book. He wrote a few notes as he finished reading the book. It was a good book and one he thought could be helpful for all women, not only those who wanted to be midwives.

He laid aside his notes for Aurora and turned to ideas for his printing business.

At the big table, Maggie said, "Aurora, I have a surprise for you. Clay already knows."

Aurora laid down the pea pod she'd started to shell. "Is everything all right, Maggie?"

"Yes, it is, dear friend." Maggie went on to tell Aurora about the land and home they had deeded to Aurora and Clay.

Tears sprang to Aurora's eyes, and she shook her head. "It is too much."

"My best guess is Clay said the same thing and got nowhere voicing his humble thoughts to Silas. You will get no further with me."

"But living in the cabin is part of our payment for service with you and your family."

"Yes, that was the original agreement. However, Silas and I have talked it over for several days. We want the five acres, cabin, and lake to be yours and Clay's—legally. It won't stop hate-filled and prejudiced people from bothering you, but they cannot legally take away your home or land."

"They can burn it down."

"And we can build it again."

"But still, Maggie,"

Before Aurora could say another word, Maggie held up a hand and said, "If you love me, you'll accept the deed. It's already been approved at the Council House. Legally, it belongs equally to you and Clay. We will continue to pay you the money we agreed upon for your work here with Silas and myself."

"It's too much."

"You are wrong there, Aurora. Silas is eager to get writing again and has dreams about the future. You and Clay are integral to what Silas wants to create. He'll spend more time on his dreams and less time working the farm. I'll teach the children, and you'll be helping me with the house and gardens. Today is the first day of our plans."

Aurora nodded and sighed. "It feels like too much, but I promise I'll work hard to help make your dreams come true."

"Good. Remember to make a few dreams for yourself as well."

"I will. Having a home of my own has always been one of my dreams, but I never expected it to happen. Now, added to my dreams, I have a daughter as well. I feel my life and fortunes are tied to not only Clay but you and Silas as well."

"I truly understand about having a home of your own. Until we moved here, we lived with Silas's parents. I have my own home, and now, so do you."

Before Aurora could say anything more, Okchuli wiggled and grunted, then started fussing. Aurora smiled, "I smell a stinky baby."

Maggie smiled. "The stinky parts of babies remind us they are human beings like the rest of us. Go and get her cleaned up while I put the peas on a screen to dry in the pantry. Then you can talk with Silas about your book. You and your book are integral to his plans for all our futures."

Aurora smiled but thought nothing about her book could ever be a part of Silas's future. She hoped, however, it could be something that would help other women.

Maggie pulled out a drying screen for the peas. Her husband had made several for her use. First, he fashioned small boards and mitered them at the corners with nails to form an open two-by-two-foot square. Then, he stretched fine mesh screening onto the wooden frame and fastened it using small nails.

Once the women shelled peas and beans, they spread them on the screened frame and covered them with a light muslin cloth. Maggie checked on the drying food daily and tossed any that had started to mold rather than dry into a slop bucket.

She laughed and muttered, "I never thought I'd be the one drying fruit and vegetables for our meals. I used to live a pampered life, and now I pamper drying food."

Then Teddy let out a cry. She chuckled. "Now, I'll pamper the baby."

She left the pantry, closed the door, and went to Teddy's cradle. He began to cry earnestly, with his little face red and tears on his cheeks. Maggie reached down and picked him up. "You poor little mite. All poopy again."

She chuckled. "Well, my sweet baby, let's get you changed, then we'll sit and rock and let you suckle, you little piggy baby."

Aurora laughed, watching her friend with her baby as she nursed her own baby.

Once Okchuli was fed, she snuggled close to her mother's bosom to sleep again. Aurora knocked on Maggie and Silas's bedroom door. He called for her to come into the room.

He stood up and said, "Come on in and have a seat." He motioned to a chair by his desk.

Once Aurora was settled in the chair, Silas pulled out the writing shelf on his desk and placed his notes and Aurora's book on the shelf. He opened Aurora's book and said, "If you move your chair a little closer, I'll show you my thoughts on your book."

Aurora moved to sit across from Silas. He opened her book and began with corrections of grammar and spelling that were needed. "Most of the writing is very good, and I felt drawn in with the stories and experiences you've had as a midwife. I do have some suggestions, though."

She nodded. "I'm pleased you like my stories. I thought telling some of the stories would help other midwives see my experience and help them with their work."

"It is a good idea, and I like it. Your stories are excellent and meaningful. I'm suggesting, however, that we intersperse the stories with the details of the work and anatomy a midwife needs."

"I'm not sure what you mean, Silas?"

"Well, for example, before Teddy was born, you felt Maggie's abdomen to ascertain if he was in the right position."

She nodded.

"I think a drawing or maybe just a sketch to show how the baby was positioned and how the midwife's hands should be placed to determine how the baby is lying in the mother's womb."

Aurora nodded, smiled, and said, "And you'd want to have an explanation with each sketch."

"Exactly so. The same is true of determining when the woman is in labor, including perhaps, even a watch with a second hand and how to know how far between contractions. The sketches will help the reader's understanding."

"Yes," Aurora nodded. "I can see that as being helpful. When I check a mother, I visualize what's in her belly."

"And that's exactly what I think we should include in the book—the telling *and* showing. Once we have the pages and sketches, we should make an index to make the book most useful. We'll want to be sure to have the sketches on separate pages."

"I don't understand what an index is."

"It's a series of alphabetized headings with page numbers. For example, *Timing Contractions* would be a heading in the *T* and perhaps in the *C* section as well in the index with a page number beside it."

"Ah. Yes, I understand."

"You've also mentioned various herbal remedies, how to tell if the mother is healthy, etc. Much of that could also be in an appendix. An appendix is generally at the back of the book with details of specific things like *iron-rich recipes and foods* or *teas for encouraging contractions.* The medicines, teas, foods, and recipes would be in the appendix."

"I like your ideas, but it will take a long time to write up the book with all the errors fixed, the sketches and explanations, and then the index and appendix. It will take a much bigger book than I have written."

"You are right, of course, but I want to help make it a real book we can sell."

"Really?"

"Yes. Now, let me tell you more about my plans. My father has bought a printing press, and I've bought a building in Tishomingo. I want to write a weekly letter to the community with the comings and goings, stories, and poems. However, I also want to write story books and educational books, including books like yours that are instructional and interlaced with stories and pictures. The printing press will make it easier and faster to publish your book."

"That will cost a lot of money."

Silas nodded. "Once we have the book in its final form, we'll discuss the money and estimate its cost. You will not have to pay upfront, but we'll both receive a part of the income from the book sale."

"For how long?"

"For as long as it sells. We may both make quite a bit of money from the book, but we may also not recoup the cost of printing and selling it."

"So you are going to put down the money for the book whether it sells or not?"

"Yes. It is a gamble, but I think it will pay off. If you decide to let me edit and publish your book, you will sign a contract that the book will be sold through my press only."

"Have you got a name for the press yet?"

"Not yet—at least not until you say yes to the name of the press."

"Why would I tell you what your business should be named?"

He smiled. "You are right, of course, that you should not name my press. That is my responsibility. However, I have an idea for the name, but I need your blessing. I wondered if Okchuli's name could be the name of my publishing business. I want to call my business *Okchuli Press*."

Aurora beamed. "I'd love that, and I love you want to use my daughter's name."

"Thank you, Aurora. I hope that, in time, people will awaken to new ideas, thoughts, and ways of being. Okchuli means awake—isn't that correct?"

"Yes, it is. I like the idea you have behind her name and your company as well, too. What shall I do next?"

"Next, I'll give you paper to rewrite your story with the corrections and drawings. For now, keep the drawings separate from the writing. We'll intersperse them when we do the type setting. Also, the lists of herbs and natural remedies, their uses and formulas, and recipes must be written. Be sure to measure your ingredients so others can replicate precisely how you do things. Lists can be on one or two pages, but we'll want the formulas and recipes on only one page for each. Be sure you do not write on the backs of any pages."

"I can do that."

"Good. When you're finished, I'll re-edit and set up the pages for printing the book. I'll need your help with that, too."

She nodded. "This feels like a dream, Silas."

"You're right. It's a dream come true for me."

"Myself as well," she whispered.

He smiled, happy he was helping her fulfill her dreams while at the same time making his dreams come true.

CHAPTER THIRTY-EIGHT

TWO WEEKS LATER, Maggie pinned on her best hat while Sarah watched her. Sarah thought her new mother was beautiful and smarter than most people she knew, even men. Her mother's dark auburn hair glistened nearly red in the sun, but now inside the house, Sarah thought her mother's hair was magical—first brown, then red, then very few tiny flashes of silver. Sarah hoped her hair would be like her mother's when she grew up, but she knew she was stuck with her bright red hair. She said, "Momma, when I grow up, can I have hair like yours?"

"Probably not, sweetie. I love your beautiful curly hair. Your light red hair color is perfect with your bright blue eyes. Since you've been playing outside a lot, your hair is lighter and looks like spun gold."

Sarah sighed and nodded. "Maybe, but I want to grow up to be beautiful and smart like you, Momma."

"Thank you, Sarah. That's one of the nicest things anyone has ever said to me. I think you are a brilliant girl, and if you work hard on learning as many things as possible, you'll be known to be a brilliant woman."

"I'll work hard, Momma."

"I know you will, sweetie. To me, you are already a brilliant and beautiful young woman." Maggie smiled at Sarah and asked, "Are you sure you don't want to go into town with us, Sarah?"

"Yes, I'm sure. I'm not ready for town yet. I don't want people looking at me with sad faces or thinking I am evil."

"Why would anyone think such vile thoughts?"

"Some folks still think I killed my parents. I promise, Momma, I didn't."

"I know you did not," Maggie said, wrapped her arms around Sarah, and said, "Oh, darling. I'm so sorry you feel those horrible people still think such hideous thoughts. Maybe they do, but if they do, they aren't worth a moment of your time. I hope soon you'll be ready to show all those people what a happy, loving, and beautiful young lady you are."

"I hope so too, Momma. Today, I want to stay and help Aurora with Okchuli and Teddy. Two babies is a lot for one woman to deal with."

Maggie smiled and cocked her head. "Having had twins, I do know how that feels. I'm certain Aurora will appreciate your help. I'm impressed with all the hard work you've been doing."

"Thanks, Momma. Working with you and Aurora is fun." She grinned and said, "Besides, I need someone older than four years old to talk to."

Maggie chuckled. "I understand, and Aurora is the perfect person to talk with."

Once Silas had loaded their wagon and helped the twins settle in the back of the buckboard, he helped Maggie onto the seat beside him. She sighed and looked back at the house, uncertain about leaving her home even for a few hours. Silas patted her knee.

"Don't fret, darlin'. Sarah and Aurora will take care of Teddy and Okchuli just like Clay will work with and look out for Noah."

She nodded and smiled at her husband. "I'm not worried about Noah. He has become Clay's sidekick and is learning a lot and growing like a weed. I know Teddy will be fine, too. The bottle Aurora fashioned for him will help her. I'm not worried. Still, it's my first day without Teddy wrapped close to me. I feel as if a part of my body is missing."

With a flick of the reins, he clicked his tongue to get the horses moving and said, "Well, in some ways, you are right, darlin'. Watching you carry Teddy close has been terrific, but he's old enough to be without you for a few hours. I do appreciate you coming to see the press and what we've accomplished so far."

She tucked her arm around his elbow and said, "I know Teddy, Aurora, and Sarah will handle things at the farm."

"Remember, Clay and Noah are there if they need help. Enough worry for the moment. I want to talk about me and my new business."

She chuckled. "I want to learn about everything you are working on. I am eager to see your building and this marvelous press you own. "

He tried not to be too proud of it all, but he wanted to tell the world about his marvelous Pouty Press and the building he was refurbishing. He felt certain that within a few years, his publishing company would be in the black, publishing books, booklets, and the weekly community letter.

He smiled. "You know I own the building, but the press has to start making money to pay my father for buying it. He won't fuss about it, but it's a matter of honor for me."

"I agree, and I'm sure you'll be able to start making money. Profit is another thing, though."

He laughed and then said, "Yes, it is. I expect it will be a year or two, maybe three before we've paid all the start-up money we've spent."

"You'll make it. Aurora is over the moon about the name of the business. It was very kind of you to use her daughter's name."

"Well, it wasn't until I started reading her book that I realized I wanted to be able to print books. Printing a community newsletter weekly will be a beginning, but I'm hoping the books and stories are the things that will make real money. Besides, using a native name like Okchuli will draw more people to the press."

"I think the name is perfect, especially knowing the meaning."

"I do, too. Awake. The meaning is why I wanted to use it. I'm hoping to bring a little enlightenment to the area."

"To wake folks up?"

He chuckled. "Yes, but in a gentle way. I don't want to beat them over the head with my wonderful mind and deep insights."

Maggie chuckled and let her husband continue. The sound of his voice, sharing his dreams, filled her heart with joy. She'd worried that he would miss the hustle and bustle of life in Columbia, South Carolina, but he seemed to have become more and more himself on Pennington Creek. Maggie felt they were in the right place at the right time and hoped they'd be a part of Tishomingo and Pennington Creek for years to come.

She said, "Tell me more about the weekly letter for the community, Silas."

He continued, "I want the weekly community letter I'll print as a way of getting to know each other, what others are doing, and a story or poem or two. A recipe here and there. Who is getting married, who just had a baby, and who is heading off to other climes? All of it. Eventually, I want to print and sell helpful books and stories that will help keep us all awake to the possibilities of life."

"I hope they sell as well as you think they will."

"I think folks will like having a choice of reading something at the end of their busy days. I know we love reading and re-reading the books we have."

"Yes, that is true. Some of them have been read so often that they are falling apart. I'm keeping my fingers crossed that it works out."

Silas nodded. "Once my father suggested the press, I realized I could write my stories and poems and at the same time be the editor for a small weekly letter to the community. I'm not interested in making a full-fledged newspaper, though. From the thought of a weekly newsletter came the idea that we'd have to use the printing press a lot to pay for it—thus, my concept of booklets and books. It'll never be a big enterprise like the Columbia, South Carolina newspapers or publishers, but it will be a part of everything around us here. I think folks will like having the weekly letter. Some will even buy a book or two once they read the stories in the weekly letter.

Maggie smiled, loving the joy on her husband's face. She knew things at home would be fine with Aurora and Sarah's help around the house. She also knew her husband was an excellent editor, storyteller, and poet. Now, all he had to do was make it work, and she had faith he would do so.

CHAPTER THIRTY-NINE

"*You cannot create*
experience.
You must undergo it."
Albert Camus

NOAH WALKED with Clay to the place where they would start working on the dugout. He woke this morning feeling he'd grown a few inches taller. Not only did his father trust him to work with Clay, but now that he knew Sarah was younger than him, he keenly felt the honor and responsibility of being the big brother to his siblings.

Of course, he wasn't certain what all his responsibilities as a big brother would be, but he was eager to find out. Even Ben and Bea seemed to be looking up to him over the past few days. He was happy they were but was also aware of his need to be the best big brother he could be.

Once Clay and Noah had staked out the planned dugout using small but sturdy sticks they found on the ground. They had even gone deeper into the forest and cut down a few bigger, older trees to use in building the dugout for shelter and storage.

Clay explained to Noah, "When we start digging the dirt will start to cave in the whole structure. What we have to do is build the ceiling of the dugout as we dig the dirt."

"That sounds like a lot of hard work."

"It is, but hard work is how most good things happen.

Noah nodded. "I guess Momma was right when she said hard work never hurt anyone."

"Your Momma is a very smart woman. Now, let's start working on picking out which trees we need."

Noah followed Clay deeper into the woods and watched as he tapped on the trees with his rubber hammer. Now and again, he'd pull out his piece of white chalk and make an X on the tree.

Noah asked, "Why do you tap your rubber hammer on the trees before you decide which ones to cut down?"

"I want to try and be sure not to cut down a healthy, growing tree. All things have a lifetime span. My tapping helps us know which trees might be ready for cutting down with their lives coming to an end or if they aren't healthy trees. With my rubber hammer, we listened for an echo a little like it was hollow. When we hear the echo, we know the tree isn't healthy. For example, we cut down an old loblolly pine that was probably over two hundred and fifty years old."

"Yeah. I remember you said it echoed."

"Do you remember what we found inside the tree?"

Noah nodded. "It was rotted inside but only close to the ground."

"And what did we do?"

"We found where it wasn't rotting and cut there and left the rotted bit in the forest, but I don't know why."

Clay chuckled. "Well, Noah, you know how we put the leftover scraps of food on the manure pile?"

"Yeah, and it stinks!"

Clay laughed. "Yes, it does. But here in the forest, leaving behind that which we aren't going to use for ourselves or our homes is a good thing for the Earth. That old tree will continue to rot and enrich the soil in the forest. Add to that that many critters will get busy making it their homes, too. Someday, another tree might grow up right there using the richness of the dead tree."

Noah nodded but didn't completely understand, so he asked, "How long does it take for a tree to be big, tall enough, and strong enough to be used for building?"

"Many years—maybe as much as a hundred years or more."

"Wow."

"Now you know why I use my hammer. We have to have trees for our homes and cellars, but we should be careful which trees we cut and where we cut."

Noah nodded. He liked that Clay told him the truth about their work. He wanted to understand everything in his life, especially things related to building. His dreams over the past few weeks had been almost entirely about building.

Clay said, "Now, for today, let's start working on the dugout."

First, they trimmed the two trees they'd downed, removing all the limbs and bark. Next, they cut them to the length needed to support the center of the ceiling and posts inside the dugout. Then, they stripped the large limbs to use between the posts. The work was backbreaking and took more effort than Noah had anticipated. It was sticky, hard work.

Clay watched the small boy struggle with the tools, but he never gave up or fussed about the effort required. However, by the end of the day, Noah said, "I thought we'd just be diggin' in the dirt. We haven't dug a single shovel full of dirt."

Clay laughed. "Well, son, if we want to do it right—and I'm sure you agree we want to do it right—we have to make certain the dugout lasts for a good long time. If we do it right, it will last many years and bless all of us."

Noah nodded. "Still, it's much harder than I thought it would be."

"Most good things are. Now. Before we quit, let's get those little branches and use them to double-check our stake out of the footprint of our dugout."

Noah sighed. "At least it won't be peeling bark. I feel sticky enough that if I leaned against any old thing, I'd be stuck there forever."

Clay laughed and nodded. "I'm right there with you, buddy. It will feel better once we get enough dirt on the sticky places. I know I'll feel better when we have checked out our plan on the ground."

They walked around the staked-out area for the dugout several times. First, Clay tied a piece of rope to a stake, and then Noah walked to the next stake. Clay, on his hands and knees, looked down the rope to see if it was straight and even. It took nearly an hour to be sure they both thought the sides of the dugout were true and straight.

Noah said, "I thought all we had to do was dig. We've done a lot more today than I expected, but still no digging."

Clay laughed. "You're right, but my daddy taught me that preparation before starting was the way to make the best project. So far, every time I've followed his advice, things have turned out fine.

"What about when you didn't follow his advice?"

"I generally made a downright mess of things."

Noah nodded, thinking that with Clay and his father, he would learn a lot.

Clay put a hand on Noah's shoulder and said, "You know what the worst part of making a mess is?"

"The clean up?"

"Oh, that's not fun, but it's not the worst part."

"Really?"

"Yes. The worst part is knowing I could have done things better if I'd followed my father's advice. It always left me feeling just downright stupid."

"I hate feeling stupid," Noah said.

"Me too, buddy."

Noah nodded. "What do we do next?"

"Tomorrow, we'll cut a few more trees—not as big as the two we did today. Within another day or two, we'll be finished with the preparation. Then we'll start digging."

"Whew! It feels like all the preparation is a bigger deal than the digging."

Clay laughed. "Just wait until we start digging and see how you feel."

Noah looked at Clay and shook his head. "Anything is better than stripping the bark off trees and getting all that sap all over me."

"You remember that, son, when we're only about halfway through digging through the clay and rocks."

Noah sighed. "Ugh! I forgot about the rocks."

Clay nodded and said, "I try to forget about them too. Come on, and let's get you home so you can wash off a bit of the sap and dirt before dinnertime."

CHAPTER FORTY

"*Never wound a*
snake.
Kill it."
Harriet Tubman

SARAH WATCHED AURORA NURSING OKCHULI. She smiled to see
her friend's face soften as she fed her baby. A few tears dropped from
Sarah's face as she wondered if her first mother had ever let her face be
soft enough to show the world how much she loved her baby.

Sarah quickly brushed away the tears and thought, *whether she did*
or not, I'll love my babies the way Aurora and my real Momma,
Maggie, do.

Aurora had been watching Sarah and could guess what the child was
feeling. Aurora's mother had been kind and loving to her. She knew
although every child should be loved, not every mother or father is
loving to their children.

When Teddy began to fuss, Aurora said, "Sarah, sweetie, can you
bring the bottle from the table and see if it helps Teddy settle down?"

"Sure. Can I take him out of the cradle and hold him?"

"If you're careful, sit on the floor with him. Babies can wiggle and squirm, and we don't want him to get hurt."

"I will be careful, I promise." She went to the cradle, smiled at the baby, and said, "Hi, Teddy. I have some of Momma's milk for you."

He looked up at his sister with bright blue eyes and curly yellow hair. When he smiled, Sarah smiled back, felt her heart squeeze a little, and gently lifted the baby from the cradle. She sat on the floor with him resting in her lap as she'd seen her mother do when outside. Instead of nursing him, though, Sarah held the bottle to his lips.

He licked the drop of milk and then grabbed the bottle with his little hands.

Sarah laughed, looked up at Aurora, and said, "He likes it!"

"Yes, he does," Aurora said and smiled. "Be sure to hold the bottle up and keep the nipple full of milk."

Sarah nodded and ducked her head to watch the baby drink the milk from the bottle. Aurora watched, thinking *this was exactly what Sarah needed—to watch a mother love and feed her baby and then learn to love and feed a baby with her heart.*

Sarah didn't understand how Momma made milk, but she liked holding a bottle of her mother's milk to feed Teddy. She thought, *someday, I'll have my own baby and feed my baby my milk. I'll love my baby and never let anyone be mean to him.* She smiled. *Maybe my baby will be a girl. I'll love her and never let anyone be mean to her.*

She looked at Aurora and said, "Momma said you can draw very well. I want to draw flowers and birds. Will you teach me some more about how to draw?"

"I'd love to, Sarah. It isn't hard, but it does take practice. What brought the idea of drawing to your mind?"

"Momma gave me my journal. She said I could write about my life and draw pictures too. She gave me a few colored pencils too. I drew some of the pictures from the McGuffy Reader, but they don't look as pretty as I want them. I want to draw lots of flowers, birds, and even bugs in my journal."

"That's a fine place to start."

"Maybe someday, Papa will make a book of my flowers and sell it for me."

"I think you have a good mind for something like that, especially if you write about the flowers, too."

Aurora smiled and thought *I'll ask Clay to see where we can buy some watercolors. I want to paint a bit, and Sarah would like it too.*

After Clay and Noah finished their work, they returned to Maggie and Silas's home. Clay told Noah, "Don't forget to tell your Momma about the pecan trees. It'll be a few months before they are ready to pick, but they'll be good eating."

"I will. What about the sand plum and persimmon trees?"

"They'll be ready in another month and are also great for eating. My favorite is fresh plum cake. There's nothing better in my book."

"And they're free since they are on our land."

"That's right, Noah. We want to be sure we don't forget to watch for them and harvest them for our larders."

Aurora and Sarah were sitting on the front porch watching the babies and working on drawing pictures of Indian Paint Brush wildflowers when Noah and Clay reached home.

Clay said, "You're doing fine with your drawing, Sarah."

"Thank you, Clay. Aurora's been teaching me."

Noah asked, "Can I get water heating for a bath, Aurora?"

She smiled and said, "You're the first boy I've known who wants a bath."

"This boy is tired of being sticky from cutting wood all day. If I don't wash the sticky off, I'm not sure I could get out of bed in the morning. I'd just be stuck to the sheets."

She laughed, as did Sarah, who said, "Then everyone would think you are a ghost, Noah."

"Hardy, har, har!" he grinned and shook his head. "At least I'd smell like pine."

Aurora chuckled. "Go on in and set the kettle on the fireplace. Then you and Sarah can go to the barn and carry back the tub."

He nodded and walked into the house. Using the dipper, he filled the kettle with water and placed it on the stone, where his mother and Aurora would heat the water.

Sarah told Aurora, "Drawing the petals is easier than the leaves."

"I agree, but using the side of your pencil to shade in the veins helps."

Sarah tried that and said, "You're right. They aren't as good as yours, but they are better now."

Clay smiled at Aurora and said, "You two will soon be able to draw anything you see."

"I hope so," Sarah said. "I like drawing—a lot!"

Noah came out, started down the steps to the barn, and then screamed, "Snake!"

Before either Aurora or Clay could do anything, Sarah grabbed the hoe standing by the door, flew down the steps, and slammed the sharp hoe down on the snake's head. The head dropped off with his mouth still open, and the rest of the snake wiggled and curled up.

Noah looked at her with his mouth hanging open and said, "Wow. Thank you, Sarah."

She shrugged her shoulders and said, "It ain't nothing to kill a snake, but you need to practice."

Clay nodded and looked at the dead snake. "That was a rattler, son. Sarah did you a great favor."

Noah nodded again but sat down on the top step. He put his head between his legs, which weren't ready to support his body. He wasn't sure whether to cry, vomit, or pass out.

Clay looked at Sarah and said, "You did a fine job killing that varmint, Sarah."

She nodded and said, "My other momma always said it was important to keep a sharp hoe handy for snakes and other creeping things."

Aurora agreed. "It's why I always keep a hoe by the door. You never know when you'll need it."

Noah looked at Sarah. "Will you teach me how to do that?"

"I will, brother."

He smiled. "Thanks, sister."

"Let's sit here for a few minutes while you get more settled. I want to sketch that nasty old snake without a head."

Once she finished the sketch, she quickly dug a small hole under the steps for the snake's head, scooped the head into the hole, covered it with dirt, and then put the hoe back by the doorway when she finished the chore.

Clay said, "You've got a keen eye, Sarah. I'm sure when you finish that drawing, it will look exactly like that old rattler."

Noah blew out a big breath and said, "This is the first time I nearly died, and I'm alive because of my sister."

Sarah smiled. "I'm still counting on you to be a good big brother. But you do need to practice whackin' heads off'n snakes."

Clay chuckled and said, "I'll go to the shed and get the tub for you, Noah. By the time I get back, your head will have cleared, and your legs will work a-might better, too."

"Thanks, Clay."

Aurora smiled and nodded to her husband. She loved how he was with the children and was impressed with Sarah. Not only could she draw, but she was quicker than anyone else she knew about getting rid of the rattlesnake.

Aurora thought *anyone would be lucky to have her in their lives. I'm glad she is here with us and the Penningtons.*

CHAPTER FORTY-ONE

*"I have spread
my dreams
under your feet.
Tread softly because
you tread on my dreams."*
W.B. Yeats

Silas and Maggie pulled up in front of the building he'd bought, and Maggie clapped her hands. "Silas, I love the painted name of your publishing endeavor, *Okchuli Press.* The white letters with black and red outlining are beautiful. Did you do the painting?"

"Yes, I did. I had to start over a couple of times, but finally, I got it mostly straight and even."

"You did a fine job, Silas."

Ben and Bea stood up in the back of the wagon, and Ben said, "Show me, Papa."

Silas pointed to the window of the building. "That's my new store, Ben."

270

Bea asked, "Does it have apricots?"

Maggie chuckled, and Silas said, "No, Bea. It's not that kind of store."

"Someday, I'm going to have a store just like Miss Shirley's with lots and lots of apricots."

"Good idea, Bea. Come on, and let's go inside and see my printing press."

Once inside, the twins ran around the printing press, not particularly interested in the big black machine. While they romped, Silas showed Maggie how the big press worked. She watched as he inked the bed of the press and then carefully laid a large piece of paper on the feeder and made sure it was properly attached to the roller. He grinned and said, "Now watch this, Maggie darlin'." He turned the big wheel of the press, and the paper rolled across the printing bed and printed a page.

"It looks a bit like a big black grasshopper when it's rolling, Silas."

"Yep, and that's what some folks call this press—Grasshopper."

She smiled when he proudly lifted the paper from the press and held the page up for her to see. It was actually four individual pages that needed to be cut. She smiled, nodded, and said, "I like your announcement, Si."

"Thanks, darlin'. I'm pretty proud of it myself. I can have a regular seven-column newspaper setup, too. I won't use it much, but once I get going, this setup is about right for a weekly letter to the folks around here, front and back."

"How are you going to publish books?"

"Well, I've got a lot of learning to do, but this page is the first step in publishing books. I figured out how to make my own plates rather than just the seven-column plate that came with the machine. Hank helped me figure that part out. This one is four pages. I think it is a little big for a book, so Hank and I will keep working on it."

"And how will you put it all together to make a book?"

"Another thing I have to learn."

Maggie chuckled. "Well, so far, you've made a page you can cut and hand out about your press. I'm sure you'll learn all you need to make your publishing dreams a reality."

"I hope so. It will take time, which is why I'll also make small booklets. I'm thinking of poems and short stories in the booklets. I can trim, staple, and sell the booklets very cheaply."

He motioned to her and said, "Follow me back here." She followed him where there were two other big machines—but not huge like the printing press. He pointed to the machines. "I didn't know Papa was sending them. He said Momma insisted on them and told me to consider these machines my birthday presents for the foreseeable future."

Maggie laughed and said, "Your parents are a marvel, and I'm sure once you explain these monster machines to me, I'll understand why they sent them."

He grinned and pointed to the two machines. "Darlin', I'll cut the papers and do the stapling to make booklets and small books with these machines."

"Will you have covers for the booklets?"

"Yes, and I have some colored paper for just that purpose. I wish I could draw and illustrate them, though."

Maggie smiled. "You know both Aurora and I can draw a little."

"That would be outstanding, darlin'."

"Aurora is helping Sarah learn to draw, too."

"Then it will be a grand family affair. I also plan to publish poetry and short stories in the weekly community letter."

"Another good idea. Maybe you could ask Aurora to share her version of the story of Pennington Creek."

"Good idea, darlin'."

She nodded. "Yes, it is. I've missed reading the weekly serial stories in the newspaper. It's a great way to start, Si."

He kissed her cheek and said, "Thanks, Maggie. This whole venture is risky, but I will keep working hard here at *Okchuli Press* and on our farm and home."

"I know you will. I wish Sarah had come with us to see this."

"Me too, darlin'. Maybe as she gets more comfortable being with us, she'll be interested in what's happening here. Besides, I'm sure she was a good help at home today."

Maggie started to respond, but the front door opened, and in walked Lester Blunt. Silas was instantly angry, but he said nothing. Maggie turned and saw who had come into the store, and she, too, was furious but remained calm and cool. Neither Silas nor Maggie said a word.

Ben and Bea stopped running and came to stand by their parents, and like their parents, they said nothing. Ben looked up at his father and saw his stern face. Ben swallowed and thought, *when Papa looks like that, something not fun is going to happen.*

Lester walked around the front of the store, looking at the editor's desk Silas had built and the shelves he'd made. Lester nodded and said, "Other than that big, black pile of iron, I can't see a thing here to sell, Silas."

Silas nodded. "I'm pleased to see your vision is clear, Lester. That pile of iron is a printing press."

"Ah. I'd heard you'd bought the building, but I didn't know why you would bother to do so."

"Yes, I bought the building and have been in the process of refurbishing the place."

Lester put his hands in his pocket, rocked on his heels a little, lifted his chin, and said, "I noticed the sign on the window. I understood the word 'press,' but that other word is new to me."

"I'm happy to help you learn, Lester. No need for you to stand around in ignorance. The other word, *Okchuli*, is a Chickasaw word that means 'awake.'"

"Well, that's a silly-assed word."

In a stern, motherly voice that all children and most men would quake to hear, she said, "Mr. Blunt! Please restrain your vulgar way of speaking. My children are here."

He blushed, took off his hat, and nodded. "Yes, ma'am. I'm sorry I spoke so vilely." He turned back to Silas and asked, "So what kind of press is this going to be, Silas?"

"Well, there will be a weekly community letter with updates on the goings-on around here, plus a few serial stories and poems for folks to enjoy reading in the evenings."

"And you expect folks to pay for the privilege of reading this newspaper—ah, I mean community letter?"

"Not for the first few weeks. At first, it will be free as a gift from me to the community. After that, I'll sell the letter for a penny. Old editions of each pamphlet that are left over anyone can get for free, here in the store."

Lester laughed and shook his head. "Well, Silas, I've got to hand it to you. You'll get a penny here and a penny there, and soon you'll have a dollar."

Silas didn't take the bait of Lester's slur and said, "That's how it works, Lester. I'm delighted not only can you read, you understand the rudiments of finance."

In her chilling voice, Maggie took the children's hands and said, "If you, gentlemen, and I use the term loosely in case you're wondering, the children and I have shopping to do at Shirley's store."

She walked briskly from the store with the children practically running to keep up with their mother. When they got to Shirley's store, Shirley looked up and saw Maggie's face. She said, "Oh, my. I think it's apricot and tea time."

Bea grinned, delighted, but Ben didn't understand why they left his father's store in a hurry just when things were getting exciting.

Maggie huffed out a breath and said, "Thank you, Shirley. Tea would be grand."

"And so would apricots," Bea said. Her mother looked down at her, and Bea said, "Please, Miss Shirley."

Shirley smiled. "Since you asked so sweetly, of course, you may have an apricot."

When Shirley and Maggie had a cup of tea, and the children each had a dried apricot, Maggie was calmer. "I loath the very sight of that man—Lester Blunt. When he opens his mouth, I want to slap it shut. He makes me want to learn how to box!"

Shirley nodded and grinned. "My feelings exactly, too. He's a bully, but unfortunately, he and his friends can cause a lot of pain and trouble."

"The worst part is he interrupted Silas, showing me his new endeavor."

"Well, Maggie, I, for one, am ready for a paper—he calls it a letter, I think—every week, especially since there will be serial stories. I love the name of his press business, but I'm certain Lester is not enamored of the name."

"Yes, and Lester made sure how silly he thought the name was. I wouldn't have Silas change it for anything. I think it is a perfect name for his ideas, dreams, and aims."

At that moment, Silas walked into Shirley's store, and Maggie gasped and stood up, appalled at the sight of him. There was blood on his shirt, and two buttons were missing. All she could do was shake her head and mutter, with a bit of cold chiding, "Oh, Silas!"

On the other hand, Shirley stood, grinned, clapped her hands, and said, "Bravo, Silas. I hope you left him with more than a split lip."

"Yes, ma'am, I did, but sadly, I think a black eye and bloody nose will not improve our relationship."

Both women laughed while Ben and Bea stood wide-eyed, looking at their father.

When the laughter died down, Maggie felt a chill as she thought of what could have happened and might yet happen. Men like Lester Blunt never give up. They are evil to the bone. She remembered all the talk, for years and years, after the War Between The States. Not nearly enough of it had settled down.

CHAPTER FORTY-TWO

*"It is a man's
own mind, not
his enemy or foe, that
lures him to evil ways."*
Buddha

After Shirley and Maggie took care of Silas's bruises, and Maggie had sewn the buttons back on his shirt, he said, "I fear we have not heard the last of him yet."

"I'm certain that is true," Shirley said. "Still, one must rejoice in their victories no matter how small or deserved."

Silas smiled and moaned a little with his bruised lip. "I'm worried he'll do something to destroy what I've started with *Okchuli Press*."

"I doubt it. He owns the buildings on either side of yours, so he won't do anything that might harm his investments. However, you should keep a sharp lookout."

"I will."

"And go talk to Hank. He and his family live next to the stable and blacksmith shop. Their home is directly across the street from your press. Hank and men like him will stand up for you."

"That's a fine idea, Shirley. I'll do that as soon as I get Maggie and the children home."

"Good. I'll put a whisper in his ear, too."

Maggie asked, "Isn't there a sheriff here?"

"Yes, there is. He's Sheriff Harvey. He's a good man and will help if needed. Mostly, we take care of ourselves unless something awful happens. Then he's the man to go to."

Silas said, "I'll take Maggie and the children home, then I'll ride back and talk with Hank and maybe see what I can find out with the sheriff."

"I'll see if the sheriff is available right now. I'll share what has happened today and what has been happening related to Clay and Aurora."

"Good. I'll check back with you after I take my family home."

About an hour later, Shirley talked with the sheriff, Sam Harvey. At the end of their conversation, Sam said, "Thanks, Shirley, for the heads up. I'll go check in with Hank. Lester has gone too far for anyone's safety."

He went immediately to talk with Hank. While he was there, Silas came back in and spoke with the men. They discussed the possibilities of improving the situation but didn't have any great ideas that seemed likely to work.

The sheriff said, "I'll walk the main street here a few times more than usual each day. I'll also have a man-to-man chat with Lester and see if I can't get him to settle down."

"I appreciate it, sheriff. I want my family to be safe. I also want my new printing endeavor to work and bring a little more brightness to our neighbors here with our weekly community letter."

"Of course you do, Mr. Pennington."

"Please, call me Silas, Sheriff Harvey."

"I will. Now, if you fellas will excuse me, I'll go see if I can talk some sense into our local bigot and bully."

Silas talked with Hank for a bit longer, then said, "I need to get back home. Seems my daughter, Sarah, killed a rattlesnake, possibly saving my son, Noah's life."

Hank laughed. "She is a firecracker. I know I speak for most folks here in town—you and your wife taking her in to be with your family and away from the gossip around here is a real blessing for her."

"She's a good girl and fits in very well with our family. Our youngest daughter, Bea, is smitten with her. She's been longing for a sister, and it seems her prayers have been answered. The boys are getting more in tune with having another sister. Right now, Noah thinks she's the best thing since anyone put butter on a biscuit."

Hank laughed and nodded. "I would, too, if she'd saved me the pain and suffering of a rattlesnake bite. I want to be sure we can do everything possible to keep our community safe. We need good families helping each other."

The men shook hands, and Silas returned home to be sure the children knew what to do with vipers. He nodded and thought, *I'm unsure what to do with a viper like Lester Blunt. I don't want to have to cut his head off, no matter how well it works on snakes.*

A few days later, Maggie sat on the front porch of her home with Aurora. The hot summer day was slowly cooling, and sitting outside with the breeze wafting from the creek cooled them while the children played in the front yard. Teddy was on a blanket beside her. He was beginning to try to move about on his own and reached for the small, soft toys Maggie and Aurora had fashioned for him and Okchuli.

Maggie said, "I swear the more peas we shell, the more there are to shell."

Aurora nodded. "Just wait until the purple hull peas are ready to shell."

"I'm not going to think about them yet. Have you seen the work Clay and Noah are doing?"

"Oh, yes," Aurora said. "Clay comes home every night with more sap and dirt than I'd have thought possible. He says Noah works hard and doesn't slack up at all, even when he's tired and grumpy with the work."

"Good," Maggie said, "I'm glad he is doing a good job. Do you know a woman named Adella Rittenhouse?"

"Yes. She is a nice woman. Her husband died a few years ago. She sold her land and home and has been living in town with a friend. However, I think she isn't happy living in someone else's home. Whenever I see her, she talks about regretting having sold her home and land, although she couldn't take care of it by herself and didn't want to remarry."

"Well, she came into Silas's business and asked if he needed help at his store."

"She would be good. When they lived up near Muskogee, she was also a school teacher."

Maggie nodded. "Yes, that's what Silas said."

"He should hire her. She will be a big help with the weekly community letter, editing, and everything Silas is talking about doing."

"He did hire her. She is asking about living upstairs above the printing business."

"Is it safe and clean up there?"

"It is safe, but it is not clean. There are a few storage rooms and a bigger room at the front of the store. It has four windows across the front and four across the back."

Aurora nodded. "Maybe we could all pitch in and make it livable."

"I was thinking the same thing. Silas thinks it could work. Adella has asked to have the space upstairs be part of her wages. She has put most of her money from selling her house and property into a bank back east. She wants to leave an inheritance to her sister's three daughters back in New York."

"I know she is a good woman and would be perfect to help Silas. It would also give his business time to grow."

"I agree, and I'm glad you know her. Silas hired her at six dollars a week plus the living space upstairs."

"I think that's very fair, and I know many of the people in the community would be happy to help her refurbish the living space."

"Good. Now, how many more peas must we shell today?"

Aurora laughed. "Many more than you want, but every single one will be needed come winter."

They'd shelled another few cups of peas when Teddy began to cry. "Ah, the dulcite tones of my baby's crying. I'm released from pea duty for a bit."

Aurora laughed, and Okchuli started to cry as well.

Sarah ran to the porch and asked, "Can I help with the babies?"

"Of course, you can. You can take Teddy into the house and change his diaper while I round up Bea and Ben to come inside."

By evening, the children were ready for sleep. There was nothing like a day playing in the sun to help them sleep well at night. The moon was new on this night, and the daytime heat had dissipated to a cool night breeze. By midnight, everyone was sleeping. Sarah slept in the bedroom closest to the front of the house. The sound of horses and the front gate opening awakened her. She jumped out of her bed and looked outside. There were men with torches, and Lester Blunt was leading them.

She ran down the stairs, pounded on her parent's bedroom door, and ran in shouting, "Momma, Papa, there are men with torches coming to burn us to death!"

Silas jumped out of bed, pulled on his pants and boots, and went to the front door. He said, "Sarah, run upstairs and be with the other children."

"Okay, Papa."

Once upstairs, Sarah woke Noah and told him what was happening.

He jumped out of bed, pulled on his pants and shirt, and said, "Sarah, you stay here with Ben and Bea. I'm going downstairs to help Papa." He pulled on his boots and went downstairs. Just as he started down the stairs, he saw his father open the door and step outside to stand on the porch.

Lester Blunt was standing several feet away with a few men behind him. They all had torches, and a few had shotguns.

Silas said, "Lester, it's rather late to come callin.'"

"I've warned you, Silas, I'll not put up with slaves nor Chickasaws bein' around us as if they were regular folks."

"Well, I'm really disappointed you feel that way, Lester. It's a cryin' shame your soul is in such a sad, sorry state."

Lester shook his head. "You think your fancy way of talkin' will save your ass. Well, it won't! You'd best think again and be talkin' to your maker because tonight you and yours are dyin'. Then we'll give Clay and his slut the same firey treatment."

Noah walked out on the porch, lifted his father's hunting shotgun, and cocked the gun. He pointed the gun at Lester and said, "My Momma is teaching me how to hunt, and I'm gettin' pretty good at it. Your choice is to leave us and Clay and Aurora alone, or I'll shoot ya right where you stand, you ugly old man."

Silas's mouth dropped open as he looked at his son in amazement. His quiet son was standing up to a bully many years older than him. He didn't know what to say but simply watched his son.

Lester laughed at Noah and shook his head. "You're a kid right outta your Momma's belly, the way you talk, that's for sure. I'm certain she is doing a fine job of teaching you to shoot, but you're wet behind the ears and not about to kill me."

Noah pointed the gun at Lester's foot and pulled the trigger. The blast was loud and shocked everyone, including Silas and Lester, but especially Noah.

Noah swallowed back his shock and fear, shook his head, and said, "I'm sorry, Lester. I meant to shoot over your head. I'll give it another try." He cocked the shotgun again and then aimed at Lester's head. He asked, "Are you ready to leave with your friends, or shall I try again?"

Silas said softly. "Take care, son."

Noah said in a firm and loud voice, "I am taking care, Papa. I'm taking care of my own. I'm happy to send this vermin to hell if he doesn't leave us alone."

At that moment, Hank and some friends, including the sheriff, rode up behind the men bent on causing murder and mayhem. They quickly turned, and Lester said, "Hey, Sheriff, I was just chatting with Silas when his boy Noah here took to shootin' at me."

The sheriff said, "Well, Lester, I saw and heard what happened. I suggest you and your friends leave Silas's and Clay's property." He pointed to Noah. "By the way, I'd do it quickly. Young Noah, there still has a bead on you. Your head's a pretty big target even for a young fella just learnin' how to shoot."

Lester looked over his shoulder and then started walking back to his horse. The sheriff said, "All of you yahoos with torches, douse them out in Pennington Creek and leave them on the road. I see you again doin' mischief—even a little, bitty mischief—you'll all go to jail—every last one of you! Except for you, Lester."

"Thank you, sheriff."

"You misunderstand me, Lester. Deputy, we'll be taking Lester to jail tonight."

"You can't do that!"

"I can and I will. We're trying to do good things here in Tishomingo, and you're making it a raggedy old chore to do anything to build up our town. Come along, Lester."

Silas took the shotgun from Noah's hand and said, "Son, that was a brave thing to do, but never, ever point a loaded gun at a man unless you plan to kill him. Killing should be done without malice. Could you have done that?"

"No, sir. That's why there was only one shell in the shotgun. I knew I could shoot close to his foot and scare him. After that, I was hoping you'd take over."

Silas laughed and shook his head. "Good work, Noah. We'll revisit how to shoot a gun for real. Most of the time, we only shoot to put food on the table while hunting."

Noah nodded. "Thanks, Papa."

"Now, back to bed, son."

"Yes, sir." Noah went into the house, his steps none too steady as his nerves gave way.

Maggie stood behind Silas and watched Noah go upstairs and into his bedroom. Silas asked, "Have you been teaching him how to shoot, Maggie?"

"No. I have no idea how to do it. All he learned from me was how to spoof."

"Well, I suppose I'd best teach him the right way to shoot, including the when, how, and why of it all. If he's going to shoot to kill, I want it to be food for the table. That's gruesome enough, perhaps, to keep him from considering killing humans."

She smiled, nodded, and kissed him on the cheek. "I'd appreciate you doing so, Silas."

He grinned and nodded. "He was brave to do what he did."

"Yes, he was. I'm relieved we're all still among the living, though. You should go on down and talk to the sheriff. I'll meet you in the bedroom."

He grinned and said, "I won't be long, darlin'."

CHAPTER FORTY-THREE

UPSTAIRS, Noah went quickly to the little room where the chamber pot was. He needed to pee in the worst way. When he came out of the room, Sarah said, "You scared me silly, Noah. Never do that again."

He grinned. "How silly and scared were you?"

She rolled her eyes, went to her room, and drew the curtain closed, wishing she had a door to slam.

Noah laughed and went to his room and drew his curtain, too. He lay in bed, cupped his hands behind his head, and looked up at the ceiling. He didn't know why he'd done what he did, but he felt about a hundred years old. Tears came, and he let them roll down without sobbing, simply allowing himself to let his fear subside.

At least, he thought the tears were because he'd been scared. His father's words stayed with him, especially about not killing a man in malice. He wasn't sure what it meant, but he had an idea that killing anyone just because they make you angry probably isn't right.

He rolled over, wrapped his arms around his pillow, and wept. When he had no more tears, he decided on one thing he could do. He quietly got out of bed, knelt beside the bed, and said, "God, I meant to be doing a good thing tonight, and maybe I helped save my Papa, but I think killing without need is wrong. I promise to do better. I hope you can forgive my wilful ways and help me grow into a good man. Amen."

He climbed back in bed, turned his pillow to a dryer side, and closed his eyes for a few moments. Then he looked out his bedroom window and saw a star streak across the sky. He smiled and whispered, "Thank you."

Sarah sat on the small stool in her bedroom and looked out the window at the stars glittering in the sky. As she watched a falling star streak across the sky, she made a wish—"I hope I get to be with my new family forever and ever."

She knelt by her bed and prayed. "Dear Jesus, you may not remember me because I haven't prayed in a long, long time. I'm asking for just one thing. Please help me be the best daughter ever so I can stay with Momma, Papa, Noah, Ben, Bea, and Teddy my whole life. I like Bea a lot but love Teddy the most. So, if you can help me be a really good daughter and sister, I'd appreciate it. Amen"

After a few minutes, she went to bed and curled up to sleep. She dreamed of a life where her family—the real ones she belonged to now—were safe and happy. She dreamed she learned to cook and clean and help her Momma. She dreamed Momma and Papa were proud of her.

In their bedroom, Silas and Maggie made sweet, tender love, lay together as the day's weariness took over, and slept. Just as Maggie was settling into sleep, she looked out the bedroom window and saw a shooting star race across the night sky. It was new moon time, and she was grateful her menses would begin in a day or two. She smiled and dreamed of her family but felt certain there would be no more babies from her womb.

Just as she was going to sleep, she thought, *thank you, God, for everything in my life*. She dreamed but didn't remember her dreams, which was fine, too.

Across the fields of their home and beyond the new cellar being built, Aurora woke to nurse Okchuli. Once she'd fed the baby and made sure her clothes were dry, Aurora returned to the bed. Clay reached for her, and she snuggled close. Clay asked, "Is everything as it should be?"

She smiled. "At this moment in time, everything is perfect."

The stars agreed.

The following day was Sunday. Maggie told the children and Silas, "We've been here long enough that I think it is time—probably past time—we joined the community of the church. The Reverend Hartfield was kind enough to visit us and invite us to his church. We should honor his kindness and go to church. We've plenty of time to get ready and be there before Revered Hartfield starts his sermon."

Silas smiled and said, "I agree, darlin'. We have much to be thankful for."

Sarah asked, "Will Clay and Aurora come with us?"

"I'll get dressed and then go and invite them," Silas said. "You children help your mother tidy things up, then go upstairs and put on clean clothes. Don't forget to wash your faces and brush your hair."

Ben groaned, but Noah said, "Come on, Ben, I'll help you."

Within about an hour, Clay, Aurora, and their baby were in their buggy, waiting for Silas and his family to follow into town together. Once Silas and his family were ready, he smiled at Clay and said, "Lead on, kind sir."

Bea giggled, and soon everyone was laughing.

When they arrived at the Methodist Church, they saw many people there. The church itself, a wood-frame building, was built of sturdy trees from the surrounding area and painted bright white. There was a bell tower on the top peak, but the congregation hadn't been able to purchase a bell yet.

Some people were standing under shade trees talking, but more people were entering the church with hand fans clutched close for the warm day. The minister stood at the door, greeting everyone who entered the church as he always did, not wanting to leave anyone out of the services. A piano, not quite in tune, was being played with well-known hymns.

Clay and Aurora got out of their buggy with their baby Okchuli wrapped close to her. While Clay tied the horse and buggy to the rail, Silas did the same with his wagon and horses.

When the friends were ready, they walked to the church, greeting folks along the way and showing off their babies.

Aurora was a little nervous, but no one said anything but kind and loving words. She knew she couldn't trust all those words, but for that day, she decided to accept the kindness and hold the words close in her heart.

Reverend Josiah Hartfield met them at the door and said, "Come in, dear friends. Welcome to our congregation." He turned to Clay and Aurora, "It is truly a blessing to see you two and your lovely baby in church."

Aurora nodded and said, "Thank you, Reverend Hartfield."

Clay smiled and nodded.

The two families, friends to the core, walked in and sat in two pews near the front, which they needed with all their children. Aurora and Maggie sat at the end of their pews so they could quietly leave with their babies if needed.

All the windows were open, letting the breeze keep everyone as cool as possible in the church. Up front, there was an old, out-of-tune piano, but the pianist did a fine job of playing the hymns as they sang—most folks sang about as in tune as the piano, so it all worked out very well.

When the singing part was over, the minister stood and said, "We welcome all to our church." He lifted his hands and said, "Please stand." When everyone was standing, he said, "May the peace and love of God be with you all."

The congregation responded, "And with you."

"Greet your neighbors with the words 'May the peace and love of God be with you.'"

The congregation did so, although Bea, Ben, and Noah were a little nervous about what to do or say. They followed their parent's leads but were relieved when the preacher returned to the pulpit and said, "You may be seated."

Everyone sat and quieted. When the congregation was quiet, the minister said, "I have prayed about this sermon for many days. I came to realize it was my lack of faith and, in point of fact, my fear holding me back. I knew this sermon must be heard despite my lack of faith and my fears. Our community has great need of this sermon."

He opened his Bible and said, "Today I read the scripture from Matthew 19:14." He looked up and smiled. "Yes, one short verse, but by no means nothing less than the best Jesus had to offer each of us. Matthew 19:14 says, 'But Jesus said, Suffer the little children, and forbid them not, to come unto me: for of such is the kingdom of heaven.'"

He closed the Bible, sighed, and began to speak. "Of late, in this community, there have been those who felt Jesus only meant white children would be the ones allowed among us or even into Jesus's holiness. However, in his own words, Jesus did not make such distinctions. If Jesus invited all the children, then so shall I. I expect every faithful Christian to behave exactly as Jesus would have us behave.

"Some have tried to make the word 'suffer' into something that judges which children he spoke of. However, if we think about the ancient ways of speaking, the word 'suffer' meant 'to allow.' So, speaking as we speak now, Jesus said, 'Allow the children to come to me.'

"As a Christian, I try to follow in the footsteps of Jesus. I know I will fall short many times in my life, but I promise you that I will always welcome every human being regardless of the color of their skin—including men, women, and children—as I believe Jesus would. If our Lord Jesus Christ would invite them to be with him, how can we, in good conscience, do less?"

He closed his Bible, turned to the pianist, and said, "Let's stand and sing together, *Jesus Loves The Little Children.* I implore you to do so with love for each other as Christ loves us."

Everyone stood, and their voices rang loud and clear.

Clay held Aurora's hand as they sang and knew there was a chance—maybe only a small one—that everything would be all right. She nodded to him and squeezed his hand.

Maggie was delighted to see her children sing loud, the song they'd learned in Sunday School in South Carolina. She wasn't surprised when Silas sang as loud as the children and certainly not singing a key anyone else was singing.

A few pews behind the Pennington and Harrison families, a young woman stood with her mother and father. As they sang the song, she wept. Her mother squeezed her hand and whispered, "It will all be okay, Candace. She has a loving mother and father, and you have no stain on your soul."

Candace nodded and whispered, "Yes, Momma," but in her heart, grief threatened to overwhelm her. Her daughter was being held in another woman's arms. She knew the other woman was a kind and honorable woman. She was certain she would always love her daughter and take her as her own daughter from her own body.

Still, through her tears and heartache, she couldn't sing the song with everyone else. She could hear the joy and love emanating from the congregation, and she gave thanks to her daughter. She thought, *What can I do with my life now? I'd always thought love would find a way forward for myself and my lover. His reddish-brown skin was beautiful to her, but as a white woman, the community wouldn't welcome her with him.*

She shook her head, brushed away the tears, and let her heart rejoice that her daughter was alive and well. She longed to be Chickasaw but sadly was born white.

THE END

Jesus loves the little children.
All the children in the world.
Red and yellow
Black and white
They are precious in his sight.
George Frederick Root
Clare Herbert Woolston
The End

AUTHOR'S NOTES

"To learn to
read is the light a fire;
Every syllable that is
spelled out is a spark."
Victor Hugo

From Dick and Jane, priests, villains, murders, sleuth, romance, fantasy, and any other fiction you might dream up, I've read hundreds—probably more like thousands—of books in my lifetime. Each and every book, whether serious or playful, is filled with the glory of understanding myself a bit better with each word.

The fire of reading has sparked much of my way of life and the possibilities of what might be learned or known as I write. This book started when I learned my great-grandmother, Lucretia Adeline Pennington, was born 97 years before me and on the same day as my birthday: October 16th. I never knew her, and my parents seldom talked about her. Something in the family background kept everyone quiet about her.

Below is a photograph of her, her husband Thomas, and their daughter Mellie. Lucretia Adeline Pennington Rains died on January 16, 1929, in Platter, Oklahoma. This photo was taken in Platter, Indian Territory, just before the turn of the century. From Tishomingo, Oklahoma, go south and east a bit for 36 miles, and there you'll find Platter, Oklahoma. About 160 folks live there, and they even have a zip code!

As I look back at my birth family and how things were couched, I know that she might well have been a marvelous woman, but the bigotry in which I was raised might have painted an unkind and, probably, false image of her. So, I've done some research over the years about her and found that, indeed, she seemed to be a good woman. I wish I knew more about her. Because of her and Pennington Creek in Tishomingo, Oklahoma, I wanted to write this story.

Pennington Creek is the sole source of clean water for Tishomingo, Oklahoma even to this day. The whole area of what was Indian Territory is riddled with small, medium, and large creeks and even several rivers, all fed by deep springs. Between the mountains of Southeast

Oklahoma and the rivers, creeks, streams, and springs, it is a beautiful and bountiful part of the state.

You can forget about deserts when you're in Southeast Oklahoma and even much of Northeast Oklahoma. It's our little-known secret that although parts of the state are arid and dry, much of the state is a garden not unlike the famed Eden. My mother used to say, "We don't let folks know how pretty our land is in Oklahoma. They might come to visit and stay too long." She was a funny woman.

Here are some thoughts/facts about the story I've written. *The Columbia Dispatch* is NOT a real newspaper. I purposefully didn't call out a particular newspaper because the story wasn't about newspapers but about Margaret 'Maggie' Elizabeth Campbell Pennington, wife of Silas Oscar Pennington. Her desire for adventure, a home of her own, and a place of belonging with friends in her home set the stage for the story.

The home where Maggie and her family lived, near Tishomingo, Indian Territory, is made up. There are no homes at the place on the map I've chosen. But—there could have been and might have been. My husband and I found a log cabin home (boarded up, of course) near the creek. The cabin helped me focus on the house that would be Maggie's domain.

The Boggy Depot trail of the late 1890s runs very close to Silas and Maggie's home and has had a small bridge over Pennington Creek since at least 1892. All of the bridges were talked about as being 'rickety' and that it was safer for humans to walk waist-deep across the creek (unless there was a recent rain storm or a water mocassin) than to walk across the bridge. Horses, on the other hand, seldom crossed any place except the bridge because of the plethora of granite rocks, making the creek bed a slippery issue for horses.

The Pennington family in this story is fiction, but many Pennington folks live in the area even now and are real people. Maggie, Silas, and their children are figments of my rampant imagination, as are Clay, Aurora, Okchuli, and all of the other folks in the story.

As part of my research, I want to honor the real people we met in Tishomingo and their help with the story. I don't remember their names, but at the Chickasaw Council House and its museums, I was given a lot of help and resources. Even the fellas at the local RV place—a marvelous quiet spot deep in the forest off the highway—gave me lots of stories and ideas.

I love listening to stories and telling them, too. When I finally found a great story about how Pennington Creek got its name, I was set to start Maggie on her big adventure to find a home of her own and make new friends. Now, I cannot attest with firm certainty that the story of Alonzo Pennington and his wild and unfortunate past as a murderer, outlaw, and regular cheater is in any way true. But, it is a good story, and there is a link in the list below about the story. Regardless, I think Aurora did a fine job telling the story.

I am grateful to the First Americans we met in Tishomingo and their ancestors, as without them, my story would never have been written. I had always wanted to write historical fiction. The men and women who helped me left me feeling humbled. On reflection, I wonder why the First American Tribes did not simply wipe out the European settlers from their lands. Their decision not to do so says much more about their character than the European settlers who came to take the land already occupied by the native people.

In Wikipedia there is this estimate of the Native American populations:

Population figures for the Indigenous peoples of the Americas before European colonization have been difficult to establish. Estimates have varied widely from as low as 8 million to as many as 100 million, though many scholars gravitated toward an estimate of around 50 million by the end of the 20th century

https://en.wikipedia.org/wiki/Population_history_of_the_Indigenous_peoples_of_the_Americas

Regardless, I truly enjoyed writing this book, but, more importantly, I became more aware of how I can be a better person. The color of skin, the ideas around religion, the haves, and the have-nots—these are institutions of all society from the beginning of humans gathering together. Striving to be a better human being is top of my list.

Here is a list of resources I used in telling the story. Some are background, and some are to get the times and details correct.

LINKS used for research: (in no particular order)

Building:

https://onlinebooks.library.upenn.edu/webbin/serial?id=builder

Pronunciation of Ishto Atumpa

(https://www.achickasawdictionary.com/search?q=giant). The story is one the author created, not one that is in any list of stories of the Chickasaw Natives.

Reagan, Oklahoma (Johnston County)

https://en.wikipedia.org/wiki/Reagan,_Oklahoma

https://www.google.com/maps/place/Reagan,+OK+73460/@34.3489815,-96.7216715,15z/data=!3m1!4b1!4m6!3m5!1s0x87b34ae99dd18541:0x36a35ee03421e1f!8m2!3d34.348982!4d-96.7216715!16s%2Fm%2F04bh_dz

Indian Territory

https://www.okhistory.org/publications/enc/entry?entryname=INDIAN%20TERRITORY

Settlement Patterns

https://www.okhistory.org/publications/enc/entry?entryname=SETTLEMENT%20PATTERN

https://www.okhistory.org/publications/enc/entry.php?entry=LA014#:~:text=By%20setting%20the%20stage%20for,Union%2C%20Oklahoma%2C%20in%201907

Devil's Den

https://en.wikipedia.org/wiki/Devil's_Den

Tishomingo

https://www.okhistory.org/publications/enc/entry?entry=TI008#:~:text=Prior%20to%20the%20founding%20of,Fort%20Washita%20to%20Fort%20Arbuckle

Trail of Tears

https://ualrexhibits.org/tribalwriters/artifacts/Family-Stories-Trail-of-Tears.html

Cities/Towns in Oklahoma

https://www.onlyinyourstate.com/oklahoma/oldest-towns-ok/?utm_source=pinterest&utm_medium=social

https://www.onlyinyourstate.com/oklahoma/small-town-tishomingo-ok/

https://www.hmdb.org/m.asp?m=184270

Pennington Creek Marker

https://s3.amazonaws.com/gs-waymarking-images/59270176-7be7-4cfb-ae74-258dc02e9c1e.jpg

Good Springs Marker

https://gateway.okhistory.org/ark:/67531/metadc962711/

Pennington Creek and Tishomingo Map 1892

https://www.loc.gov/resource/g4021e.ct000224/?r=0.487,0.511,0.106,0.053,0

PENNINGTON CREEK: Alonzo Pennington (hanged 05.01.1846 in Kentucky after being arrested at what is now known to be Pennington Creek just north of Tishomingo, Oklahoma)

https://www.madillrecord.net/news/pennington-creek-important-location-chickasaw-nation

https://www.oklahomahistory.net/ttphotos8a/LonzPennington.pdf

Belle Starr

https://en.wikipedia.org/wiki/Belle_Starr

American Civil War

https://en.wikipedia.org/wiki/American_Civil_War

https://www.frontieramericanillustratednews.com/post/money-in-the-old-west-coins-of-america-s-dramatic-1840s-1870s

Jesus Loves The Little Children

https://en.wikipedia.org/wiki/George_Frederick_Root#:~:text=North%20Reading%2C%20Massachusetts.-,Legacy,the%20later%20God%20Save%20Ireland

The first Methodist Church began in 1843 in Tishomingo, Indian Territory, and later in Oklahoma. By 1844, there began to be buildings and a seminary.

https://www.facebook.com/tishfumc/

Poets

https://en.wikipedia.org/wiki/Category:18th-century_American_poets

Bedding

https://www.saatva.com/blog/history-of-mattresses/
https://www.thespruce.com/the-history-of-the-bed-4062296
Window Screens
https://en.wikipedia.org/wiki/Window_screen#:~:text=In%
201861%20Gilbert%2C%20Bennett%20and,product%20became%
20an%20immediate%20success
Mushrooms
https://www.wildfooduk.com/articles/how-to-tell-the-difference-
between-poisonous-and-edible-mushrooms/
Columbia, South Carolina
https://en.wikipedia.org/wiki/Columbia,_South_Carolina
Chickasaw Tribal History
https://www.chickasaw.net/our-nation/history.aspx
Cherokee Freedmen named Pennington
https://en.wikipedia.org/wiki/Cherokee_freedmen_controversy
https://www.okhistory.org/research/dawesresults.php?cardnum=
1034&tribe=Cherokee&type=Freedmen
Chickasaw Dictionary with vocalization of words
https://www.achickasawdictionary.com
Chickasaw life
https://www.bigorrin.org/chickasaw_kids.htm#:~:text=Chicka
saw%20mothers%2C%20like%20many%20Native,war%20to%20pro
tect%20their%20families
Chickasaw names
https://www.behindthename.com/submit/names/usage/chickasaw
Vernacular language
https://www.alphadictionary.com/slang/?term=&beginEra=
1880&endEra=1890&clean=true&
Birthing
https://thereader.mitpress.mit.edu/birthing-furniture-an-illus
trated-history/
Herbs and Midwife
https://www.holisticbirthingservices.com/midwife-blog/tag/Herbs
https://www.holisticbirthingservices.com/
https://www.wishgardenherbs.com/blogs/wishgarden/midwifery-
roots-and-folk-herbalism

https://www.paullettgolden.com/post/midwifery-herbs

https://warwick.ac.uk/fac/arts/history/students/retrospectives/issues/8.pdf

Uterine and Cervical scarring

https://www.whria.com.au/for-patients/fertility/ashermans-syndrome/#:~:text=If%20the%20scarring%20involves%20the,this%20is%20not%20as%20common

https://boards.straightdope.com/t/a-morbid-question-about-gang-rape/583865/6

Birth Control and Women's Issues:

https://www.civilwarmed.org/birth-control/

https://www.healthline.com/health/birth-control/history-of-birth-control

https://www.tempdrop.com/blogs/blog/a-brief-history-of-basal-body-thermometers-fam

https://en.wikipedia.org/wiki/Julius_Schmid_(manufacturer) (he made condoms first with sausage casings and later rubber. He founded the Schimd contraceptive company with the products Fourex, Ramses, and Sheik. During the World Wars, he was the official supplier of condoms for the US Military.

https://www.womenhistoryblog.com/2014/06/19th-century-midwives.html

Travel Time in Wagon 1896

https://www.fhwa.dot.gov/infrastructure/back0307.cfm#:~:text=The%20covered%20wagon%20made%208,longer%20to%20reach%20their%20destination

It is 1,032.7 miles from Columbia, SC to Tishomingo, Oklahoma, so at a pace of 8-20 miles per day would take about 2-3 months to complete the journey.

Prouty Press and printing

https://www.printmuseum.org/1890-prouty-press

Dugouts

https://www.awhc.org/dugout/

https://www.okhistory.org/publications/enc/entry?entry=DU003

https://www.motherearthnews.com/homesteading-and-livestock/frontier-homes-dugout-zmaz70sozgoe/

https://www.okhistory.org/publications/enc/entry?entry=DU003
https://www.motherearthnews.com/homesteading-and-livestock/
frontier-homes-dugout-zmaz70sozgoe/

Sounding a tree before cutting
https://chrisluleyphd.com/wp-content/uploads/2022/02/7.-
Sounding-Part-II.pdf

A Few Tree Facts:
Elm trees live 100-300 years.
Blackjack oak up to 200 years
Post oak trees live up to 300 years
Bur oak trees live over 300 years and have a big span of their limbs
Pin oak trees live 100-150 years but are tall and straight
Lob Lolly Pines live as long as 275 years

THANK YOU DEAR READER

Thank you for reading our book. We hope you enjoyed reading or listening to our story as much as we enjoyed writing and recording it. If you enjoyed this book, please leave an honest review on Amazon, or Goodreads. As independently published authors, the only way we become known to other readers is through your reviews and sharing our stories.

All of our books, whether written together or Glenda alone, are stories of women who keep their power close to themselves to create the best lives for themselves, their children, family, and friends.

Glenda and David have written seven novels in The Paradigm Books series. In this series, they wrote about women and their lives of love, belonging, and becoming—creating new paradigms for themselves and their families. The books are also available on Amazon and Audible.

The Paradigm Books are:
1. *The Gloriana Paradigm*
2. *The Mother Paradigm*

3. *The Belle Paradigm*
4. *The Father Paradigm*
5. *The Cora Paradigm*
6. *The Dakota Paradigm*
7. *The Adoption Paradigm*

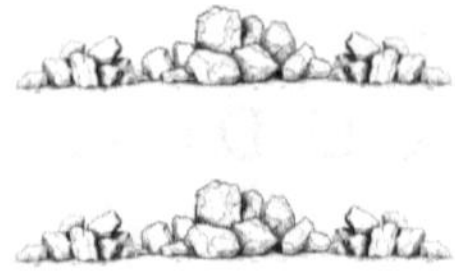

We have also written **The Shaman Chronicles** series. Although Glenda uses Core Shamanism in a lot of her books, in this series, not only do many of the characters practice Core Shamanism, but the mystic side of life becomes an important element. These books are also available on Amazon and Audible.

1. *Buffalo Dreams*
2. *Salmon Dreams*
3. *Bobcat Dreams*
4. *Sparrow Dreams*
5. *Crawdad Dreams*
6. *Elk Dreams*

The **Ouachita Mountain Tales** series is written by Glenda and focuses on women and children finding themselves and their place in the semi-rural southeastern Oklahoma area where Glenda grew up.

The **Ouachita Mountain Tales** Series includes:

1. *The Mountain Beckons*
2. *Ring Around the Moon*
3. *The Water Flows*
4. *Sounds of the Night*
5. *Beaver Moon Rising*

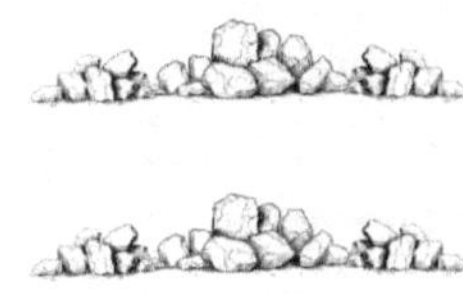

Glenda and our granddaughter Marti have written *Nobody's Home,* a children's book about spending spring break at Grandma and Grand-dad's house during the COVID times.

The Redbud Stories, written by Glenda, are books close to Glenda's heart. The first book is mostly autobiographical, with many changes in the locals and people's names, although much of it is true. The other two books amalgamate some of the life in central Oklahoma while letting powerful women live their lives as they wish to.

1. *The Good and Holy Witch*
   2. *The Keeper of All Things*
   3. *The Creators of New Beginnings*

Glenda is pleased to inform you about the release of our newest collection, *The Minerva Mysteries.* These enchanting tales are over-flowing with romance, sorcery, and courageous women who utilize their talents for the greater good. Glenda isn't sure if there will be more

Minerva Mysteries but some folks have asked that there be more.
We'll see.

The Minerva Mysteries
  1. *Minerva and The Runaway Train*
  2. *Minerva and The Old Wood Stove*
  3. *Minerva and The Upstairs Ghost*
  4. *Minerva and The Rocking Chair*

The upcoming series, *Life on Pennington Creek,* will be available in late
2024 or early 2025. These are historical novels located in the town of
Tishomingo, Indian Territory, during the last 4-5 years of the 1890s
before Oklahoma was a state. The working titles so far are:

1. *Maggie's Home*
  2. *Aurora Rising*
  3. *Eva's Choice*

The people who read my books before publishing (Beta Readers) think
there should be many more than three books about Pennington Creek.
We'll see.

Glenda has written another book, *Calista*, about a few witches and even
druids who live in Pink, Oklahoma. Pink is a real town. The characters

are not! The book will come out in late 2024 or early 2025, depending on how the editing goes. Fingers crossed, there's a little magic involved.

All our books are available on Amazon as e-books, Kindle, or paperback books. They are also available as audible books on Audible and Amazon.

You can follow Glenda and David Clemens on Facebook, Amazon, or Goodreads.